There *May* Be Angels
The Transformation

There was a child went forth:

There was a child went forth every day. And the first object he looked upon, that object he became. And that object became part of him for the day or a certain part of the day, or for many years; or stretching cycles of years ...

~Walter Whitman, "Transformation"

There *May* Be Angels
The Transformation

Charles H. Woods

ISBN 978-1-947656-36-9

ISBN10: 1947656368

Butterfly Typeface Publishing
PO Box 56193
Little Rock, AR 72215

www.butterflytypeface.com

Dedication

To the late William S. Smith,
for his inspiration and benign encouragement.

"Why we fear the *Unknown* is because we know so little of ourselves; for man's greatest fear is of man. Because of the sanctity of the mind, no one can read thoughts."

Charles Woods

"Conscious of the mind"

Table of Contents

Foreword

The first time I met Mr. Woods, he came into my office with this 'huge' manuscript and I was curious about what exactly he had written.

As I listened to him tell me what his story was about, I found myself on the edge of my seat ...

Charles H. Woods is a masterful storyteller and that gift translates well into his writing ability.

The story he tells is one that will not only create excitement, but also a love for the characters.

"There May Be Angels" is a wonderfully told story that you will enjoy taking the time to read. It is not a book to be merely read but to be savored.

Congratulations Mr. Woods on a story well written!

Iris M. Williams

Acknowledgments

To my children,
Ashley and Dominic,
and my grandson, Kyonte...
Thank you for your enthusiastic encouragement and support.

Preface

A frigid rain nailed the dead of night to the city in late December. Arctic wind-gusts hurled a torrent of cold rain in a rataplan rhythm like the chanting of a lost language throughout the complexity of a grand midwestern city. The unforgiving deluge made travel nearly impossible; glinting wet, black, secondary roadways held a dangerous glaze of black ice, which was difficult to determine by an unsuspecting motorist, even if obeying the speed limit of thirty-five MPH. Though motorists were scarce to near non-existence.

The vacant roadway, for the most part, left a clear path for Sheriff Randall Hollister and a skeleton crew of deputies in a precarious but relentless pursuit of lights in the sky, which had seemingly originated from out of nowhere just a short-ways back. A deputy on patrol had radioed-in the bizarre sighting, as the lights had mysteriously appeared high above the water tower of the small hamlet the County Sheriff Department was located.

The sheriff, in the lead vehicle of four other cruisers, noticed the light has separated again into three units; they were of a pale blue hue, somewhat translucent against the perse gloom, and were on a specific course to the north. And they had a consistency to occasionally bond together, becoming a single mass of an obtuse ball of a soft blue light amid the freezing drizzle and blackness of night.

In each cruiser was an experienced "keep of justice," sworn to perform his duty as a lawman to serve and to protect. But this was an engrossed challenge, along with a growing, creeping fear of the unknown. After nearly twenty-seven years on the force, Sheriff Hollister had never seen the like; he'd only known of unproven, ridiculous rumors from fanatic sky-watchers that such phenomena

Charles H. Woods

existed. Now he was faced with whether to accept this looming truth before them as an alternate reality or to sensibly assumed that the government was involved in some sort of project that had somehow escaped their top-secret confinement.

The lights continued ahead, just slightly above three-top level; and strangely enough, they maintained a directional trek feasible enough for the sheriff and his men to follow without risk, other than the mirror-slick black surface of the gleaming wet roadway they traveled. It was ingratiating that the mysterious, seemingly specter followed the path along the two-lane blacktop as a courtesy to the chase.

And they tended to be aligned with an intelligent guidance system, as, so far, they never once veered off course...

Chapter 1

"Sheriff are those things alive?" One of his deputies' patience had finally worn thin, prompted by his increase of alarm.

He was thickly built, single, in his mid-thirties, and only a high school graduate, going on his third year as a deputy sheriff. UFO's wasn't his forte, and neither was strange lights with tendencies to have minds of their own.

That was deputy Jeff Cooper. The sheriff recognized his voice, the moment he chimed in.

"You guys sit tight," Hollister said, no reservation in his voice, which was comforting to his men.

All his deputies had confidence in their leader. He had a calming disposition, despite the severity of any situation they were faced with.

"To be a lawman, you must lay it on the line always, no matter what. Otherwise, you're in the wrong profession," was Hollister's stern, unswerving belief since joining the force; and he'd instilled that philosophy into the heart and mind of each deputy on his staff.

As the lethargic pursuit continued, now closing in on a massive lake just over the next ridge, road conditions worsened. A sufficient layer of thin ice mixed with a goodly amount of snow covered the roadway. The slightest mishandling of either one of the slow-moving cruisers could result in an accident, with an undetermined amount of damage, which could be fatal.

The blue lights, still moving separately, headed straight out over the lake. In the murky dead of night, the lake, normally a bountiful, shimmering body of ocean blue water, was now a pervasive layer of black, cold waves, harboring a more sinister, ominous appearance under the cloak of darkness.

"Sheriff, how far we gon' follow these ... *things*?"

That was T.C. Johnson, a black deputy on edge. Up until now, he thought, in joining the force, he'd follow Sheriff Hollister to the end of the world. But that was before they'd encountered these... Aliens. He was never prepared for this type of adventure; it had never entered his mundane mind. He was a robust man, over six-feet, thirtysomething, had a girlfriend and was unafraid of anything God had allowed to be born. But aliens were *impossible*, and therefore, had never entered the equation. He was drawing close to becoming petrified.

"Another mile or so, we'll be in the lake."

He suppressed nervousness in his voice, for him to be such a behemoth-of-a-man. His fellow officer-friends responded over the radio with mild chuckles.

"Fellows," the sheriff said with reassurance in his voice because he'd determined that his first hunch about these so-called aliens was correct: They were a government experiment on the lam.

He continued, "We're not going into the lake. We'll hold up there..." he looked around, gathering his thoughts.

"Why?" a deputy asked.

That was Lyle "Slim" Mitchell, his aka "Slim" is the label he'd worn since high-school because of his wiry frame: tall and slender. He was also always a jokester, never seemed to allow any serious matters to get to him. But there was a situation unprecedented in the normal flow of natural life situations. This was suddenly an entirely different reality thrust upon them in the guise of a living nightmare... something out of Rod Serling's 'Twilight Zone.'

Radio silence ensued for a long moment. The lake was dead ahead, the vastness of the cold, black water undetermined under the dense cover of the frigid, late at night.

"It's a feeling I have. Just go with it," the sheriff finally replied. That time a vague hint of uncertainty in his voice.

"Sheriff, can we call it a night, after this? I ... don't think those strange lights would really mind. Besides, my mom gets worried if I'm not home by midnight."

That was sarcasm, but it didn't quite take in the humor it was meant from Deputy Lawrence Baily, nearing forty, medium height, good physical shape.

"What about when you have to work the late shift?" the fourth deputy smarted-off.

There was a momentary space of silence.

Finally, from deputy Baily, "Shut up, Russell."

The cruisers made their final approach to the lakeshore without incident, with their emergency lights in a rhythmic twirling of intense blue flares against the dark mire of night. This was, by farthest, the biggest challenge ever faced by a handful of law-enforcers of such a placid, sleepy little villa some twenty-miles outside their neighboring "Big-Brother-City" just north of here.

Upon their final approach, each man remained inside his vehicle – including Sheriff Hollister – with the seriousness in a gulf of silence. The mysterious lights, now glowing with an increased blue radiance, vaguely pulsated far out across, and above the black lake, settled under a dense layer of a frozen mist. Ominous wasn't the word; they looked downright frightfully threatening, like something out of a B-rated science-fiction movie, waiting to pounce at any moment.

However, those impossible, now soft blue lights did nothing in the way of any threat. Finally, they simply just vanished into thin air and the bleak, wet night.

The sheriff was first to get out of his cruiser, leaving the engine idling, with heat going, to maintain its toasty climate inside. Once outside in the frosty, wet night, after closing the driver-side door, he immediately donned his weather gear, having brought along his issued, short-barrel shotgun and service revolver. There was no need of a flashlight; the cruisers' blaring headlights were sufficient for night-vision within the limitation of the men's purpose for being there.

Each deputy followed the sheriff's lead, and they got out of their cruisers in the proper weather gear and appropriately armed. They came together precariously, and extremely watchful, not knowing what to expect – even though the lights, and perhaps a potential threat were no longer a physical presence.

Peering quizzically at one another then up into the dismal, night sky and arctic mist, they mustered close to their cruisers, awaiting further orders from the sheriff, which never came. He was just as lost and bemused as his deputies.

"What now, sheriff?" Deputy Ein Russell asked while the frost-bitten atmosphere continued to be a great discomfort to all of them, as they stood around in the constant, miserable drizzle. The cold, wet, late-night tended to strop a razor's edge along each skein of falling, light rain.

T.C. Johnson piped, "You ever decide what you gon' do about that feeling you spoke about earlier, sheriff?"

That was an anxious plea that they should abandon the area, and the search for whatever those weird lights were, and what they were about. Not that he was a little afraid; he was near horrified.

But the sudden reappearance of the trio of lights abruptly altered any hope he may have had of getting out of this blistering cold, wet night, not only with his life but also his sanity. The ghostly blue lights loomed over the darkened lake in a phantom-quietness, hovering with a much more precise stillness than any helicopter. They were like still, blue statues fixed against the pitch blackness.

As the men gaped in rapt curiosity; they were also apprehensive, engulfed in sheer awe. Neither deputy uttered a word, the sheriff temporarily at a loss. Not from fear, nor bravery ... just a loss for words. He had no clue how to approach these strange light-forms. And the longer the wait, the quiet, the stillness became immensely eerie. Amid the bright flashing and twirling of the cruisers' emergency lights, the pale blue lights, suspended in midair just slightly over the lake, maintained that air of malicious intent.

Then, suddenly, at the blink of an eye, the trio of dismal blue lights swooped out of the black, cold, wet night sky, feather-landing several yards away from where the sheriff and his men stood collectively together near their cruisers; the sheriff suppressing an admission of tentative fear before his deputies.

Nevertheless, two of his deputies – Jeff Cooper and Ein Russell – reacted suddenly, shrieking like two frightened, elderly ladies, grabbing hold, and slamming into each other for a moment at a rush of fear. They received disconcerted-looks from everyone, which quickly passed because of the already pressing concern at hand.

Finally, within the biting cold of the misty night, something was happening. The mysterious, eerie pale blue lights began to merge toward the sheriff and his deputies. This course of action stimulated the men's curiosity other than so much fear, as they looked to one another with that innate interest to learn, along with that red-flag that warns us to be a skeptic.

The illegible forms of lights continued their approach in a wary fashion. Like the sheriff and his men, the trio of soft, sort of transparent blue lights tended to vaguely emit an intelligent show of curiosity of their own. And the closer they slowly gravitated to the men, it became apparent to the sheriff and his deputies that within those what appeared as some sort of alien protoplasmic blue shield were some very strange type of life forms.

As the three light forms made their final approach; up close now, the sheriff and his men could clearly see that the lights were alive! And, for all intents and purposes, the gender of whatever species they came from was female. Although they were not human, the translucent protoplasmic-like shield made it impossible to determine the entire make-up of whatever they were. The vague images of their features, however, were more legible than anything else about their physical makeup – they were clearly feminine.

Their faces looked like carefully constructed, little female China dolls, with hair that appeared plastered to their heads. But the eyes were what was so weird about this whole scenario; they were large, and shaped like the eyes of a cat, complete with that thin, dark, oval pupil dead center, which held more of a demonic effect.

One other discrepancy the lawmen observed about the odd beings, beyond that coat of a thin, pale encasement, they were *blue*. Not to mention they weren't all there in complete form. But they were very much a life form ... a living, breathing organism; and, apparently, with intelligence, along with the capability to fly.

The sheriff and deputies remained as still as stone statues while the strange images moved in even closer. Of the three, the one center the other two came forth, directly approaching the sheriff. Whether it or she bore it or her face to his and uttered, "Motatu."

That sounded like a young teenaged girl, the language very pronounced.

The sheriff has no clue how to respond. He just stood there, totally confused.

A gulf of silence set in momentarily. The remaining two images moved in, taking up positions before two selected deputies, which was Russell and Cooper, just by chance. The blue complexion of the images could very well have been a reflection caused by the translucent shields that shrouded them like an outer garment, which concealed the remains of their true forms, was a thought.

The two softly glowing images, shapeless, other than an uncertain outline of their almost animal-like features, maintained their poise before the two deputies, looking them over like curious little ... *girls?*

Russell and Cooper chanced to shift timid glances to one another, not daring to utter a word, while under such scrutiny by these ... otherworldly creatures. It was safe to assume that these ...*living* blue lights were aliens, right?

That question was certainly pliable in the complexity of this improbable situation, which was intensely shared by both Russell and Cooper, who remained completely still, with the utmost respect for these child-like images – wherever they came from.

The one poised before Sheriff Hollister insisted on driving home her point. "Motatu!" That time the voice was raised, but still small and not hostile.

It got quiet. Neither of the men knew what to expect.

The hissing of falling, pelting ice, mixed with a constant drizzle of rain filled the bleak, sodden night, only to enhance the misery the men suffered, along with an eerie feeling from this type of waiting.

"Motatu!" That was a bit stronger, but this time, the blue image bore her comely features closer in the sheriff's manly face; and he found her rather ... cute? For an alien, if indeed it was an alien. Had he been wrong about his stern hunch that they were government property? That certainly would've made things easier to deal with if they were.

In this quietude, the images settled into just staring eye-to-eye with the subject they'd chosen. The rest of the deputies waited with bated breaths, their department-issued light orange rain gears a bright glistening raiment under the repetitive assault of the dismal weather.

Deputy T.C., desperately wanting out of this cold, miserable, soggy night, stood next to the sheriff. As the image was still beaming directly in the sheriff's face, waiting for some gratifying reply, T.C. braved the chance to get a word to this superior in the most secretive manner possible.

He leaned over cautiously, turning his head aside, away from face-to-face with the sheriff and muttered under his breath, "Do you still have that same feeling about these...whatever they are?"

Apparently, the Motatu-image didn't notice that brief, secret deliverance from T.C., as it maintained its posture, staring Hollister precise.

The other two images conducted themselves in the same manner as did the Motatu-image by holding the two chosen deputies in their wide, unblinking cat-like eyes.

Deputy Cooper, nearly on the edge of panic, leaned closer to Russell, to slip him the message: "Why do they keep staring at us like that? That's creepy."

At that moment, an even more astounding event took place; the images began a shape-shifting method, morphing into a mimicking phase. The Motatu-image transformed its facial features to look exactly like the sheriff's features, strong tattered with age and proven experience at forty-five, with dark hair, dark eyes, though the eyes a bit stormy. Only, the Motatu's complexion of him was a light greenish-hue.

Maybe he should've been impressed, but instead, for some reason he couldn't put his finger on, it was more disturbing than anything else.

Deputies Russell and Cooper were awed beyond comprehension; they were not afraid, to a degree, but reserved the right to haul ass, screaming while tearing through the cold, wet night in sheer panic – if the need should arrive.

Cooper had common features, almost baby-soft white skin, with a weak chin, and a heavy mustache that hid his top lip entirely. One might lightheartedly compare him to a walrus, with baby-blue eyes.

When the ghostly, pale blue image mimicked his facial mask, complete with the mustache, it lifted his spirit a little as he chuckled in hilarity, "Ha! You guys see that? She made herself look exactly like me. How did she do that?"

In savoring that moment of humor, deputy Cooper was suddenly brought back to this new, enigmatic reality shivering on the edge of winter. And the images had returned to their original forms. Then they went on a mission of urgency, like three spoiled brats who couldn't have it their way.

The other two images went about very intently, the one having chosen office Cooper drawing closer in the deputy's face, shouting, "Jor!" It was a strange language, like no other on Earth.

"Motatu!"

"Jor!"

"Koh!"

Finally, they ceased the ranting and chanting and sank into silence then ultimately withdrawing into a calmness.

That eased the tension among the men some, as they began to gain a bit of relaxation, which was good for them. That gave them time to collect themselves. And for the first time, a settling feeling came over them. For some strange reason, the mysterious images began to impress upon them a benign warmth; that they were no longer a threat, not only to them but to society. Wherever they were from... Why couldn't aliens be friendly?

During these moments of silence, in the cold wet night, out in the middle of nowhere, the sheriff took the time to carefully evaluate this...somewhat preternatural situation, at least until he was certain of one way or another. The images remained close; and during this close encounter, the sheriff and his deputies were drawn uninhibitedly into an amiable influence that tended to radiate from the images.

At a much closer range now, the eyes didn't appear so much as demonic; they held a kind of warmth, innocence. Something personifying a blameless child.

The persistent images had not abandoned their effort to achieve, perhaps, a method of communication, as their second approach was pretty much the same as before. They got into the face of the men, repeating the mimicking, and the chanting, once again. Then they ceased, backing away.

However, this time during their pause – the sheriff and deputies again dumbfounded – the luminescent beings assumed an action that was surprisingly familiar. The Motatu-image went about drawing very closely in the faces of deputies, randomly chosen, mimicking their features with her shape-changing ability; then she would withdraw, shaking her head rejectingly, uttering the sound very distinctively clear: "Uh-uh ... Uh-uh ... Uh-uh ..."

As the Motatu-image was going through the rank with her enigmatic inspection, although the deputies had no clue, the sheriff was extremely curious and decided to act on it.

"Ah...excuse me," he said, his first time speaking that meant something since the images first arrived up close.

He advanced the image that had assumed command among the other two, in somewhat of an urgency to be heard.

"Ah...excuse me. Ah...miss."

The two images suddenly turned to the sheriff as though they were abruptly startled; Motatu froze in place, quickly turning her attention to the sheriff. No one, including the sheriff, had the faintest idea what he'd done. The first thing that came to mind as he may have breached some sort of alien-ritual.

But then, the most astounding reaction came from the images, which gave the sheriff and his men such jovial relief, for the images burst out laughing, giggling like giddy little schoolgirls, about boys.

The images kept laughing in their approach to the sheriff, which he no longer felt the slightest amount of any threat from the strange visitors, who were beginning to sound more like humans. His original idea that this whole mysterious ploy had returned. There were no UFO's; this was a gimmick. These were government machines, maybe on some test run, he was thinking. And the more he thought about it, realizing how secretive the government can be; he became thoroughly convinced that his theory was correct.

"Just any minute now…" he uttered under his breath, tacitly looking toward the dismal, dark sky.

The images didn't just stroll over to the sheriff, like normal people; they simply glided across the short way, which suddenly reminded everyone that the *blue aliens* could indeed fly.
But even that bewildering display by those strange … machines, yes, 'Machines!' The sheriff must remember that. He wasn't rattled. He took it as a challenger now.

The sky was empty, except for the blackness, the cold and dense gray, frozen mist. The deputies waited quizzically in a becalm but anxious anticipation as the believed-aliens made their congenial approach over to the sheriff. He couldn't exactly make out their mood by any facial expression, as he couldn't see them clearly beyond their thin blue shields; however, he sensed their smiles. The aura they projected was as pure as the innocence of a child…But wait. Machines don't have feelings…

In semi-surrounding the sheriff, after their affable approach, their ebbing chuckling trailing off, he said to them curiously, "What's wrong? You're laughing. Was it something I said?"

The Motatu-image, for the first time, spoke in a clear sentence, "Miss? You say to me: Miss? Ha! Ha!" She laughed, "No, not Miss … Motatu!"

"Oh, I see." The sheriff finally understood. In the back of his mind, he felt an increasing alarm, though not to worry; he became suddenly dubious about his previous assumption that the aliens were simply machines – and a government leak! Now admittedly so, his mind began grasping at entirely different thoughts. He wasn't sure what to believe.

But he did use the integrity to reply, "Oh, so Matatu is your name?"

"Motatu!" the image replied jubilantly.

"Well, ah … Please to meet you, Motatu." The sheriff cleared his throat then continued with the only proper response he could come up with, "I'm Randall Hollister. I'm the sheriff."

The images paused, looking to one another as if they were soaking in what they'd just heard from the sheriff. A hush settled over everyone for a moment.
Then suddenly, Motatu said in delight, "Randall Hollister – I'm the sheriff. How are You? I am Motatu."

In absorbing this overwhelming, sudden language barrier breach by seemingly magic, T.C.'s rise of suspicion wouldn't allow his silence to persevere any further. He leaned over to the sheriff and whispered, "How is it, suddenly, they can speak our language so clearly – like they were born and raised here? Sheriff, what do you think is going on here?"

"Right now, T.C., I have no idea," was Hollister's earnest reply.

The images had overheard enough so that Motatu replied to everyone's amazement, "We learn many languages through the elements of your environments. We absorb it ... like fresh air."

Since an act of candidness was now in order – feeling like a calming, happy cloud of bliss – Deputy Lyle "Slim" Mitchel piped, "Are you female?"

Motatu quickly replied, "I am Motatu."

Then the others responded, "I am Jor."

"And I am Koh."

Slim tried to explain. "No, no. I meant, are you male or female. You know...like boy or girl?"

The images looked at one another, confused.

The sheriff tried to be more specific. "What may deputy's trying to ask is, what is your gender? For all it's worth, you certainly sound female...The woman, Lady. You know ... girl."

They were still confused.

Once again Motatu stressed, "I am Motatu."

Then insisted the others, "I am Jor."

"And I am Koh!"

T.C. wisely interrupted them most assuredly, "They're female!"

"How do you know?" the sheriff asked.

T.C. quipped, "You ever known a woman to make sense?"

"I've been married for twenty-six years," the sheriff spoke on behalf of his wife, as he was also thankful for their two kids, Katie, and Jeffrey – both in college. "We've never had any miscommunications problems."

"Your wife doesn't talk much, does she?" T.C.'s mask was stern.

"Where're you from?" Cooper asked the images, disregarding T.C. and the sheriff.

The image Jor smarted-off sharply, "You can't get there from here."

There was chuckling among the men.

"It looks like we have three alien comedians on our hands," Russell said not very amused. "Did you come by ship, or did you just ... fly here all on your own?"

Motatu said, which was very puzzling, "We come to live here. But we can't live with you."

"That's a relief," deputy Slim Mitchell said under his breath; but *a take*, he was relieved of the thought that these aliens might try to settle among them.

The sheriff didn't quite understand at first. Then it came to him. Sure, that was it: Motatu was signaling to the others, Jor and Koh, when she kept shaking her head, saying, "Uh-uh." For whatever reason, she probably disapproved of the lifestyle, the atmosphere, or just simply settling here, on Earth; if they were, indeed, breathing, alien organisms and not machines.

"So, where are you going to live?" asked the sheriff.

The images grouped together momentarily, seemingly to come up with an answer. Then, in breaking the huddle, Motatu said, "We must find where we are to live."

"That makes sense." T.C. wasn't the least satisfied with that unclear answer; it sounded evasive.

The images then flashed to the black sky, high-up, and out of sight within seconds. The sheriff and his men were left gawking at the darkened sky, trying to piece together this enigma: Was this real, or was it something else?

Chapter 2

Early Spring ... Four Months Later

Lily Field Foster Home was located along the countryside, just outside the city limit, east of the magnificent Grand City. It was nestled in a scattered wooded area, almost in complete solitude from other sparse neighboring communities in the vicinity. Some very few rural dwellings were widely scattered about; hardly quite enough to include into the main flow of the ordinary jaded city dwellers.

Twelve-year-old Monique Davenport, a black-American, was orphaned soon after birth, left in a bassinet on the doorsteps of the orphanage mentioned, in an infamous manner, by an unknown person. The hospital ID tag with her name on it was taped around her tiny ankle.

By the age of five Elise Newton, Caucasian, was added, along with Wendy Gale, part native-American, now sixteen. She became orphaned at nine. The three of them were left under the care of their guardian Agnes Greene who neared sixty.

They were abandoned, first, by parents. Then, seemingly, a cold, uncaring society. Elise was the only child of a single mom who left her on the porch of an abandoned house for a passing State Trooper to discover later that day. Wendy was from a dysfunctional family, with her parents having no job-skills, and two younger siblings - Amanda, six, and a brother, Chico, at four-years-old. The parents made the despicable choice to leave the oldest, 9-year-old, Wendy, behind due to her budding maturity, to relieve some of the pressure off their responsibilities.

Among the three orphans, Elise stood the chance of becoming adopted into a home with a loving family, the Pinkertons, with one son and only child, a toddler at the age of two-and-a-half. Her case was still pending.

The three children had rather unique cases, with each child—at a very young age—having been put through severe abandonment, which could have resulted in irreparable mental damage, and trauma. But they suffered no ill-effects from their crude displacement.

Monique, orphaned since infancy, only understood she had many brothers and sisters, with a loving mom, in a big house. Even now, with finally, the awareness that she has a parent, or parents, somewhere whom she'd never met, was never a serious issue with her.

Elise and Wendy, on the other hand, in time, came to accept foster care gracefully doing their earlier readjustments. The older Elise became the more her once painful memories became, but Wendy's...a little different.

The crude, bitter memories intensified, the older she got. Yet she'd never shown any rebellious attitude from some unresolved hostility in her past life towards anyone. The three of them became closely knitted little girls, growing to accept what life gave them, to this point. They became united as sisters.

Elise and Monique attended middle school in their district, only a few miles from the foster home. They were bright students, loved school, and they loved to learn. Wendy went on-line schooling, via laptop, since turning sixteen. She was also talented as a seamstress on her Singer Electric Sewing Machine, provided by their guardian, Miss. Agnes Greene. She also earned extra cash with her special talent, from outside customers needing occasional alterations on clothing.

School had let out that afternoon. Kids poured out of the building in droves. The campus buzzed with the horse playing students scrambling to buses, on skateboards and bicycles. It seemed endless on a beautiful afternoon, with a calm, very soft breeze, as spring was in the air, sauntering gently from distant foothills and mountain ranges, bringing about the sweet smells of nature; daffodils, wild roses, and honeysuckles in the mix. The sun dispensed a tantalizing warmth, with hardly a cloud in the sky. It was the perfect day for a leisure stroll, on such a serene afternoon.

The bus-ride from school to the foster home was somewhere between two miles. On such occasions, with this type of weather, the girls, Elise and Monique would often choose to walk along with classmates who walked home, even those of a higher grade. It was fun, laughing, chatting, sharing pleasantries.

But there was a grim side. The girls' arch enemies, Brittany Stewart and her posse-of-one, Natalie Ferguson. Brittany was a gangly, adolescent, with stringy, blond hair; and Natalie, not quite as gangly, but taller, and thin, with cropped, dark hair.

It was like their life-long ambitions were to taunt and berate the two orphans, battering them with snide remarks and insults. And the reason wasn't that they were foster children; it was just because Brittany and Natalie were bigger and worse. No one gave them any heat. And they had nothing better to do with their wasted time than to bother others, preferably those without the will nor the courage to stand-up to them.

That fear, however, never dissuaded Monique and Elise. It depended on their moods; which, most of the time, they exercised their intellectual choices not to stoop to the bullies' level. There were enough incompetent fools, and idiots, around to fill that void. Elise and Monique elected to show intelligence and restraint. Although, there were times restraint just didn't quite work, as Brittany approached Elise, lightly grabbing some of her hair from behind.

Charles H. Woods
35

Elise and Monique looked around, Elise disturbed by Brittany's callous touch of her silky, blond hair.

"Get away, Brittany," Elise said, a quick toss of her head to free Brittany's annoying fingers entangling strands of her lovely hair.

"This one, I think..." Brittany suddenly had a memory lapse. "Hey, what's your name again?"

"Finally, she's lost her memory," Elise quipped. That got some snickering from the other kids, including Monique.

Natalie was indifferent; she was docile. Anything Brittany did or said was fine with her. Brittany didn't like embarrassments; they infuriated her.

She came as brutally as she could, "It's Elise—little, Miss Prissy—I'm-better-than-you Snow White. You, two girls, make me sick!"

Elise, quickly rebounding, "Watch out, she's gonna vomit...she's sick!"

More kids laughing, with Monique adding, "Good one."

Brittany turned her wrath on Monique, "Just what are *you* laughing at, Aunt Jemama?"

It got seriously quiet, everyone there feeling the sting from Brittany's cruel, racial slur.

Monique, a shrewd, smug-look in her bonny features as she calmly retaliated, "Sorry, kiddo...I ain't jo' mama."

That was in-your-face hilarious! The roar of laughter from the kids was so resounding and gratifying that even Brittany, and Natalie—especially Brittany—were forced to laugh.

To keep from being embarrassed, Brittany, surprisingly, grabbed a smaller Monique in a brief, respectful embrace, laughingly confessing, "I love her! She's crazy, hilarious!"

"Does this mean we're friends?" Monique was being facetious.

Brittany's laugh continuing, "No way! I still hate you!"

Monique wasn't finished. "Oh, thank you. I was gonna throw-up on you, if you'd said yes," she replied, pushing away from Brittany, with mild contempt.

"Fascinating."

Elise had the last word of those insulting comments, as everyone began on their separate ways; Brittany and Natalie departing also. This time, Brittany without hesitation to deliver the final, insolent blow.

They reached the grove sometime later, after the last of the small group of students, who lived in areas nearby, had gone their separate ways. The footpath through the groveled to the foster home, a vintage, two-story structure, made of hardwood and stone from the old days. Mullioned windows, from front to back, complete with shutters, enhanced its antiquated, Old English personality. Some years back, the place was converted into a home for orphans. At the time, Agnes Greene, and her husband, Clarence, became the caretakers—until his passing away several years ago. The name, Lily Field, was given to it by Agnes. Lily Field was her grandmother's name.

"You really got her good," Elise laughed.

"Yes, we both did," Monique returned.

"You'd think that, by now, she'd learned her lesson about picking on us."

"Not a chance," Elise disagreed. "Humility is *not* her forte."

"Oh, big word," Monique was alerted.

They laughed, bumped, and giggled through the grove, where they passed underneath a tunnel of freshly budding foliage. The foster home was just up ahead, beyond a patch of sage grass before reaching the huge lawn out front. Once they were in full view of the vintage building, Monique noticed something slightly different about the large, wooden porch; it was vacant, except for a porch-swing, and several empty, metal chairs.

"Where is she?" Monique asked. "She's usually outside, waiting for us."

"We walked home, remember?" Elise reminded her.

"Oh, yes," Monique sighed. "That's our Wendy."

They continued through the shady grove, bumping and giggling along the way, like devoted, loving, young siblings, with pretty Wendy being the oldest. She got great satisfaction out of looking after the two youngest. They were never too much of a load on her every-day learning of the rules of responsibility, simply because she'd grown to adore and endear them as sisters. Already, she was great at housekeeping and was becoming a decent cook.

Miss Agnes had been instrumental in showing her what one should expect out of every-day life, and Wendy was a brilliant student at learning the ways of wisdom. She simply refused to be idly adrift from the knowledge that was to be gained.

At a sudden soft gust of wind, the girls quickly took notice, and covered their heads with their backpacks, until the mild, swift breeze had passed, the sudden rustling of foliage tunneling around them now settling.

"What was that?" Elise readjusted her backpack on her back, as did Monique.

But Monique paused suddenly, pointing straight ahead at something she thought was a freak of nature. "Maybe...*that* has something to do with it?"

Elise hadn't noticed, but when she turned to look ahead, she discerned a soft, very thin blue haze surrounded them. It held a slightly silvery sheen, like looking at nature through a vaguely blue tint.

"This is sort of weird," she skittishly observed, the two of them timidly inching nervously alongside each other, while scanning the strange, blue haze. Finally, more curious than afraid—although with concern—they carefully did a complete circle, gaping in awe, trying to evaluate this minute phenomenon.

"Ghosts?" Monique could think of nothing else that would apply, as a small, creepy feeling came over her.

"Don't start with the ghost-thing," Elise stressed, "Think of something else."

They were yet too far from the building to go racing through the dense grove, expecting to outrun some ghosts.

"Then what else could it be?" There was an increase of fear in Monique's voice, as something glowing in the blue haze that looked like eyes peering at them.

Cat eyes.

Soon, desperation set in, as Elise concluded then shouted, *"Run!"*

It was not necessary that she repeat the idea; they lit out in a panic!

"Where is Wendy, when we need her?" Monique shouted with fright in her voice, she, and Elise in a dead heat, racing across the huge lawn.

"She couldn't do us any good, now!" Elise shouted as they rambled frantically toward the porch.

Under sheer fright, Monique ran, shouting, "If Wendy was here and we out-ran her, the ghosts would get *her*; not *us!*"

"That's rude!" Elise managed under desperation.

"Who cares?" Monique screamed, keeping close beside Elise as they ran.

They never looked back, finally scampering up on to the porch and, with very little effort, bounding up the many wooden steps. They both clasped hands on the heavy brass door handle swung open the wide, weighted wooden door and rushed inside.

In closing the door in a rush, hurling their small bodies against it, for security; they took in deep breaths, winded from their terrifying ordeal. No one was downstairs; the spacious area was quiet and vacant, with a display of Goodwill furniture spread over on an age-worn carpet. The staircase was solid with wide, wooden steps and banisters with a hard, gleaming mahogany finish. A few potted plants were neatly placed about; and pictures hung on the walls, some in large, skillfully designed frames, remnants from days of old. Now, in less of a panicked-voice, the two of them, tentatively, became more relaxed in leaving the door.

Elise dared to call out, "Wendy?"

No answer.

They looked at one another, hesitant to venture farther into the lobby-size living room.

Monique looked about, then called out precariously, using half the volume she typically spoke at, "Wendee?"

Still no answer.

A faint aroma came from the kitchen. Pot roast. It smelled delicious, one of Agnes' famous meals. She was a great cook.

Elise decided to have a quick peek out the window beside the door, on the left. Monique sheepishly followed. She gave a little assist to Elise in peeling back the heavy, dark drapes then looked outside, and around. Nothing was out there. Acres of landscape went to points of infinity, stretching far out across the way, tattered with undergrowths in a widely-spread, scattered forest, along with fields of grass, during the early spring. Nothing other than that was a comfort to them. They withdrew, facing each other, taking in breaths to ease the tension.

Elise, with boldness in her voice, decided, "I'll bet there were no ghosts out there. It was probably just something in the air...some dust particles from somewhere. Stranger things have happened that we don't know about."

"OK, I'll agree," Monique said. "Let's go find Wendy." They went upstairs.

The door to Wendy's room was closed. But from the inside, the girls could hear a soft, quiet whirring noise, so faint that it was hardly audible. However, they recognized the sound, just the same; it was her sewing machine.

"She's sewing again," Monique was certain.

"I should've known," said Elise.

Charles H. Woods
41

Monique knocked softly, but it was only a mute courtesy; Wendy never heard the knock, and the girls just quietly came in.

She looked up at them from behind the sewing machine and paused.

"Well, look what the wind blew in," she said, shutting off the machine. Quite a bit of loose pieces of fabric was strewn across her bed, which was neatly made since earlier that morning.

"Where were you two? I waited outside for you since school let out, but you never showed up. Don't tell me...you walked again, didn't you? You guys need your own cell phones. That way, you could, at least, call, to keep me from worrying about where you are."

Elise cozied over to her, beaming at her pretty face with the high cheekbones and such lovely, long, dark, silky hair.

"Were you worried?" Elise asked, with hardly any worthwhile sentiment in her voice.

Monique never gave Wendy time to respond to the question before she blurted out of turn, "Wendy, how fast can you run?"

Wendy, at a loss over the outright random question, "*What?*"

Elise laughed, "She was debating on whether we should throw you under the bus if you couldn't run fast." Wendy was dumbfounded.

"What, on earth, are you girls talking about? Under the bus... *why?*"

"Never mind, now," Monique was calm about it.

"Not actually do that," Elise made clear. "We were afraid of ghosts."

Wendy asked, without a clue, "Ghosts? What ghosts?"

Monique interrupted, springing off Wendy's bed with a fright, and stood next to it as stiff as a bard. "Like those!"

It became graphically noticeable that the entire room was suddenly enveloped in a thin, blue haze, just like in the grove. It didn't look like ultra-violet sun rays like Elise had suggested; this misty blue...*thing* had followed them home!

"It followed us here!" Monique was convinced, on the verge of another panic attack.

"Ohhh... my god," Elise murmured, gaping in fear of the intruding blue tint.

Then she and Monique went on a frantic scramble, aimlessly scurrying about the room, in a blind attempt to escape. Wendy was baffled but tried to remain poised. In leaving her sewing machine, she warily kept her gaze toward the ceiling, as that was where the strange, blue tint was mainly concentrated.

"Guys calm down," she said, moving to the center of the room, engaging more caution.

"There's got to be a logical explanation about this, I'm sure."

"Where's Miss Agnes?" Monique shouted, attempting to scamper under Wendy's bed.

Elise was on a dead run, rushing for the door, which was ajar. Not paying attention in her frantic haste, she ran into the door from a bad angle, causing it to violently slam shut; and she ran smack into it, careening backward a few feet. Quickly gathering herself, and, in finding the door closed, she hurried about the room, within the thin frame of the blue, invasive light, and commenced bouncing off walls like a ping-pong ball. Wendy persisted to try and calm the girls down but was getting nowhere with her civil intent.

"Girls! GIRLS!" she yelled. "Monique, come out from under my bed!"

"No!" Monique yelled back. "Where's Miss Agnes?"

Flashing tentative stares at the blue, soft glare on the ceiling, which covered the entire ceiling then began cascading down the wall in a gradual fashion, near the door; Wendy attempted to explain, "She's not here!"

"Where is she?" Monique yelled at the top of her voice, still wrestling with trying to hide her entire, small body underneath the bed.

Wendy, frustrated, striving to hold it together, in hopes to make viable sense to this mass confusion, answered, "She went to an appointment at the Human Service department and the Federal Building. Now *come out from under there!*"

Suddenly, the room was back in order, like nothing had ever gone awry. A calming sensation finally settled over them. After a moment or two, Monique skittishly poked her head out from underneath Wendy's bed. Elise was beginning to settle, brushing away the minor pain she'd engrossed in her vain panic attacks. Monique finally crawled out from underneath the bed, noticing that Wendy stood center the room, glaring at the two of them, uncertain what to make of this debacle; Elise took a seat on the end of the bed, still, a bit unnerved. But, once again, the scary appearance of that...unholy...*light* was gone. How long it would stay away was anyone's guess.

"Now, you guys wanna tell me what this is all about?" Wendy stood there with arms folded, holding them in her intent stare. But she must admit, it was unusual, and it did merit concern. However, whatever it was, or came from, it never seemed to pose any threat.

"What time will Miss Agnes come back?"

This time, Elise was curious to know. Monique added, "We smelled her pot roast cooking when we came in. We thought she was home."

Wendy was suddenly jolted to attention excitedly, "My roast!"

Abandoning her interest to listen to the girls' explanation, for the time being, she bolted out the room, tearing downstairs. That blue-light thing can wait, she was thinking. Her roast—her dinner was at stake. She'd worked half the morning preparing it, having followed all the directions Miss Agnes had given her. It was supposed to turn out perfectly. She should've checked it an hour ago! Darn that stupid, distracting light.

In reserving their anticipatory fear for, maybe later, the girls went after Wendy. For one very important reason, they flat-out refused to remain in her room—or any room, as far as that matters—alone. The girls padded down the stairs at a rapid pace, chasing Wendy.

"She's cooking?" Monique was astounded.

"She doesn't cook! We'll be poisoned!"

"Don't worry," Elise was little bit consoling.

"If she's messed up, Miss Agnes will fix it. She should be back at any time now."

"I sure hope you're right," Monique was pessimistic.

Chapter 3

Agnes returned an hour later after everything had pretty much settled down. She bought doing something in another part of the home that took up quite a bit of time. The silver-haired, middle-aged lady with care-worn features had the experience and kindness of a loving grandmother. She wasn't the person for long speeches or conversation; she was soft-spoken and to the point, a hard-worker and dedicated to her job. She never had children of her own; but you wouldn't know that because of her gifted, caring nature.

Wendy and the girls were having supper. Her pot roast was surprisingly delicious. Monique had promised never to criticize her cooking again. But, in making that promise, she held her fingers crossed, just as a safety measure.

The assumed, ghostly appearances were beginning to ebb as a fading memory of some unexplainable freak of nature in the back of their minds. But it made for a rather learning conversation, especially for the two youngest, Elise and Monique. They were kids; docile, impressionable minds, which was more adaptable for them to accept the first illogical thing to come to mind when under such fear and laden duress.

"So, you say the first time you saw these...ghosts, you were coming through the grove?" Wendy sat across from them at the dining table, an antique, a very skillful piece of woodwork, with a highly polished walnut finish.

"Exactly," Elise said.

Since there was still plenty of sunlight left in the afternoon, a natural light pervaded throughout the interior, casting soft, *friendly* shadows, Monique and Elise felt much less threatened by such ghostly-images. In fact, the whole experience, in hindsight, seemed more ridiculous. And, now that Agnes and Wendy both were home, the girls were much better at ease.

"Okay," Wendy said. "Let's keep it real. There are no such things as ghosts; apparitions or specters. Or witches. It's all a part of superstition that began back during ancient times. What you guys..."

She paused to include herself, "Ah...we all experienced was something like.... Well, did you know that lightning can strike on a clear day, without a cloud in the sky, or rain?"

The girls looked at her in disbelief. They'd never heard the like before. They shook their heads, captivated.

"Are you serious?" Elise was flabbergasted.

"As ham and eggs on a breakfast plate," Wendy smiled smugly.

"Where'd that come from?" Elise asked, unamused.

"Nowhere," Wendy said mirthfully, "I just made that up. Clever, huh?"

"No," Monique was brutally frank. She and Elise were seated next to each other, at the table, opposite Wendy.

"About this lightning striking on a clear day," Elise wasn't convinced, "Are you sure you didn't just make that up too?"

"Go look it up online," Wendy told her.

At a sudden rush of excitement, Monique bounded to her feet, pushed away from the table—at Elise's and Wendy's nonexpectations—hurried out of the dining area, through the living room, and up the stairs.

Wendy yelled up at her, "Monique, are you going to my room, to use my laptop?"

"Yes!" she called back. "Don't disturb any of the patterns I've laid out on my bed. Those are what I'm working on!" Wendy yelled at her.

"Okay," Monique assured her, her small voice growing faint as she finally disappeared beyond the soft gray shadows at the top of the stairs.

After Wendy and Elise had finished their meals—Monique having not quite finished because she wanted to check out Wendy's story about lightning on a clear day—Elise was ready to leave the table.

"Oh, no you don't," Wendy halted her. "Someone's gotta help me clear the table and do the dishes."

"Sorry, I got homework," Elise said, motioning to leave the dining room.

"Liar," Wendy scoffed.

"I'm sure you don't have that much homework. You're using that as an excuse, to get out of your share of chores."

"What about Monique?" Elise said. "She doesn't have an assignment about lightning on a clear day."

"Oh, she's not getting out of her chores," Wendy made clear, "The trash needs taking out."

Reluctantly, Elise remained to help with the dishes. Later that afternoon, the girls—including Wendy—had settled in their rooms. Monique and Elise shared the same room, with twin beds. Having completed their homework, they were relaxing on their respective beds. Elise was lying face down, with her head slightly hanging over the edge, thumbing through the magazine, SEVENTEEN, lying on the floor before her. Monique, having borrowed Wendy's laptop, was still checking for other phenomenal events. She was lying on her bed, with her knees raised to better support the laptop on her blue-jeans thighs.

"Was Wendy telling the truth about the lightning?" Elise asked, looking over at her just slightly across the way.

"Yes, she was," Monique said. "It appears that there were two incidents, which occurred in Florida. It was reported that a lightning bolt, out of a clear sky, struck this one person as he was walking along the beach."

Elise was suddenly sympathetic, bringing herself to an attentive position on the bed. "Did he die?"

Before Monique had the chance to respond, there was a knock at their door.

Elise was first to spring off her bed to answer it, although the door wasn't locked. Monique remained in place, being careful with Wendy's laptop. She was just being lazy; holding on to the computer was just an excuse not to trouble herself with lying it aside.

Elise padded across the plush carpet in her sock-feet, to the door, convinced it was Wendy in a courteous mood. She opened the door—It was Miss Agnes. She stood there in a casual, lavender dress, with her usual, vague, cordial smile—so caring.

"Miss Agnes..." Elise was pleasantly surprised.

"Come on in." She held open the door, moving aside. Agnes moved in just beyond the open door; she wasn't for any lengthy chit-chatting. There was neither a show of calamity nor the slightest hint of bad news in her soft gaze. To the girls, her voice, and expression always held a soothing warmth, despite whatever she had to tell them—good, or bad news.

"Elise, your social worker was by here today," Agnes began, her voice soft, warm.

But just that bit of information was bad news to Monique. A feeling of gut-wrenching disappointment erupted in the very pit of her stomach. As near as she could tell, that meant Elise would soon be leaving them. It'd been nearly five months since the subject of her adoption was last discussed. Before any further mention of the social worker Monique quickly sprang off the bed, safely placed the laptop down, then rushed out the door, brushing by both Miss Agnes and Elise. At a glimpse, it was so obvious she was very upset by the collective moisture in her eyes as she rushed past.

"Monique!"

Miss Agnes called to her, but Monique was…. Gone. She'd disappeared to somewhere in the early evening. Wendy, having heard the soft commotion outside her room, appeared in her doorway.

"What's wrong?" she asked, a quizzical look on her face.

Agnes went on to explain, "Monique's run off; and I know why. She thinks Elise is about to leave us, but she didn't stick around long enough to hear the whole story. There was a flaw in the Pinkertons' application…"

"We'll talk later," Wendy said, in a bit of a rush to get going. "I'd better go and find her. It's getting late."

She went up to Elise, as she and Agnes waited just outside the girls' room. "Elise, stay here in case she returns before I get back."

"But Miss Agnes will be here," Elise pointed out.

"Wendy's right, honey," Agnes said in agreement with Wendy.

"If she should come back and find the two of you gone it won't help much."

"Well...," Elise paused briefly to think it over, then agreed, "Maybe you're right."

Wendy left them alone, as Elise was saying to Agnes, "May I use the desktop computer downstairs, to finish-up my homework?"

"Sure, honey," Agnes said kindly as they started downstairs together.

"What was wrong with their application," Elise wanted to know.

"Not good, I'm afraid," Agnes said. Then, at a thought, she added, "Was living with the Pinkertons something you were looking forward to?"

Elise shrugged her shoulders.

She wasn't certain, one way or the other. The idea of becoming a member of a family, other than the one she already had with Monique and Wendy, and Miss Agnes, had been something of interest; but she never could accept the idea of having to give up one family for the other.

"I've thought about it; and it seemed interesting, at first. But if it meant leaving Monique and Wendy," she shook her head decisively, "I wouldn't like that."

Agnes' smile was filled with warmth and understanding. Then she said to Elise, as they continued downstairs, "I thought so, which makes it easy for me to explain to you what happened."

"What happened?"

Not that it was so important that she knew in full details; it was only a casual interest. The evening was bathed in a light more amber than golden. Deep purple clouds, trimmed in a fiery gold, hung oppressively low over the western, to the northern hemisphere. Long, dense shadows stretched endlessly across vast landscapes, as approaching twilight teetered on the edge of early nightfall.

Wendy had not a single clue where to begin her search for Monique. The vastness of empty spaces expanded endlessly. *Where, on earth, could Monique have gone?* There was no sign of her in any direction. Wendy had to choose which way to begin. She started easterly. Monique had not gone far.

She'd held up among a grove of trees, where a soft, gentle wind mildly rustled the leaves in the trees and dense undergrowth all around her. It was remotely quiet, a lonely place. Normally, it would have been a little spooky, that far out from nowhere. But Monique was deeply depressed, teary-eyed, broken-hearted. She ambled about aimlessly, uncaring, grossly saddened, a feeling of dark hopelessness. She couldn't fathom life without Elise; they'd been together all their lives. It would be impossible to cope in her absence.

Little woodland creatures scampered in the grass and nearby shrubberies, thick bushes; even in the trees around her. High in the top of a birch tree, a blue- jay flashed. Other small birds fluttered about, without a care in the world. Didn't these happy, little creatures know the world was near to end? Normally, she loved little creatures, such as domestic animals; but this wasn't the time to even think rationally. She had a heart-ache as big as all this open space, and she wasn't sure how long it would persist. And she didn't care—If ever—when she'd return home.

Strolling along absentmindedly, she came upon a spongy-feeling under her feet, where a spread of scattered, fallen leaves—a hold-over from last fall and winter—had grown stale. And they were wet because they'd been under a patch of trees, with constant shade, all this time, never getting the chance to dry out and blow away. In her somber, languishing strides, she wasn't paying attention to the gradual ebbing of something she stepped on with the inconsistency of rotting boards.

Finally, at a cracking noise under her feet giving way to her weight, she abruptly disappeared from the surface. Her squeal filled the evening air, instantly growing faint as she plunged deeper into a dark pit of an undetermined depth.

Wendy had entered the wooded area behind the foster home, calling out to Monique ever so often, but never receiving a reply. Her journey was painstaking, as she had no idea where, or how far she should venture into this area. Bad thoughts started entering her head, and she began picturing Monique's face ending-up appearing on milk cartons. Or worse.

"Monique?"

She wasn't about to give up now, even if it took all night. She was determined not to return without her. It was still early; she hadn't been gone long. And she shouldn't have gone far. It was just a matter of which direction she'd gone, so Wendy had three more directions to follow.

"Monique, where are you?"

No answer. The soft, occasional stirring of the spring breeze was like the call of lost souls, mocking her vain effort to find a lost child, who may never…. She stopped thinking. It was ridiculous to think the worst, at this point. She trudged through patches of tall grass, across an empty field, until she came to yet another hindering wooded area. Soon, she could lose track of how far she'd go if she didn't change directions.

Deep in a hole in the ground, Monique, after gingerly rising to her feet, shook away the haziness in her head, after the tremendous jolt she got from the fall. She then immediately realized she was some ten-feet below the ground. The hole was dark and dank. From what she could make of her dilemma, she had fallen into an old, dry well, with the circular wall lined with wet stones. Dirt and moss padded the cracks the stone. -mason had left between the stones; and their slickness from age-wear, dampness, was too slippery to try and climb out. The fear inside her began to rapidly increase. She looked around vainly for a way out.

This area of pure solitude gave her no hope of ever returning home. High above the darkness in the deep hole, it tended to reach up to gather even more darkness to completely seal her in this permanent hole in the ground. It was desperation time.

She yelled up into the emptiness and the approaching night, "Somebody, help me!"

Nothing for that frightful, desperate cry. Nothing at all. Her heart raced. Fear began to crowd her brain. The more she began to face reality, the more frightened she became. *There was no way out!* Her stance began to weaken at each passing, horrible thoughts of never getting out of this *alive!*

"Someone, please! Get me out of here!" She was beyond desperation.

A small gust of wind—just like in the grove—hurled a few scattered wet leaves into the dark hole, some of them sprinkling over Monique's head and shoulders. If only she could float like those leaves, her problem would be solved.

As she began to try uselessly to climb out of the grim, dark hole—finding her effort impossible to achieve, due to the highly slippery stones—the now half-light above became a bluish-gray hue, settling slightly above the dry well Monique was trapped.

It was odd.

Very strange, as the dim, transparent blue light began to vaguely take on a more identifying form.

Not human, or animal; but…something out of the ordinary, some alien form. Monique stood frozen, past the stage of fright. She was petrified as the light slithered into the well, opposite to where she stood, entranced in a state of horror. Surely this was the end….

"Hello?"

That voice came out of nowhere, and it surrounded the wet, stone walls, like a surround-sound system; and was it female? Such a charming little-girl voice, maybe her age.

"Who said that?" Monique's voice held a tremor of fear and dread. Uncertain what was happening, it very well could've been she was losing her sanity, due to the weight of fear she was being put through.

"Don't be afraid," the little-girl voice came again, directly from the thin curtain of soft blue light before Monique, who stood, gaping apprehensively. Then, right before her gawking stare, the shape-shifting blue light began to gradually take on the form of a…*person?*

As the form continued its completion, it gradually, finally began taking on the shape of a...*human!* And, of all things, it took on the identical appearance of Monique—in her school clothes, and sneakers. The only striking difference was that the shape-shifter was of a blue tint. Its entire countenance bore the image of a walking, live statue. Everything about it was hazed in that mysterious, blue sheen.

"Who are you?" Extremely nervous and frightfully excited, Monique pressed her back against the wet, stone wall, trying to brace for...well, whatever the impact, if there was to be one.

"Can I live with you?" That was blunt, boldly to the point from this *thing*.

Monique was stymied by fear, with a mixture of a rise of curiosity. The *thing* wasn't making any sense, not that making sense was an important issue, at this point. But with the blue image mimicking her, and that profound friendly-nature *it* projected so convincingly, Monique was near to the conclusion that this was one of those realistic nightmares.

"What...live with me?" That jolting, outlandish request left her at a loss for words.

The blue image of Monique vaguely moved in closer, exposing those warm, innocent cat-eyes; though, strangely enough, that wasn't such a shock to Monique. What she'd gone through over the past few minutes seemed like a horrific eternity. As weird as it may appear, those cat eyes were more charming than frightful on this, apparently, affable, half-human, young creature. And Monique was vastly becoming more susceptible in drawing closer to them... the *thing*, modeled in an entire blue tint, out of a continuous rise in curiosity.

"If I can live with you," the blue creature-that-looked-almost-human continued in that little-girl, friendly voice, "you will be stronger, faster...better."

Monique found her scary situation dissipating rapidly, as if this, God-only-knew what, had placed her under some sort of spell. Maybe the *thing's* amiable disposition was designed to do just that, for some ungodly purpose. But Monique found herself drawing unsuspectingly closer to this persuasive, little strange creature. Whatever it was planning for Monique, so far, it was working. Not only was it so strangely charming, with a child-voice that would melt a heart of stone; it had an aura that suggested purity and trust.

"Wait... You mean just by living with me, I would become...faster, and? ... Oh, forget it. What you said."

Monique got tripped-up in her words and recollection of what was said.

"Faster, stronger, better," the image repeated with no problem, a mirthful smile in her voice.

"Who are you, and where are you from?"

Monique hadn't realized it, but she'd nearly completely dismissed her fear of ghosts; that thing in the grove was now alongside her, and she wasn't afraid. And the *thing* had magically appeared in the hole with her, undoubtedly on purpose. Did that mean she had a way out, with the help of her friend, the blue image?

"I'm Jor," the image of Monique said, "Where I come from is not important. I am female. Are your females? We look alike."

"Yes, thanks to that little trick you just pulled. How did you do that?" Monique wasn't exactly herself. Having dismissed all fears and concerns—for *now, at least—she was deeply intrigued.*

"Are you a ghost? Are there more of you?"

"Yes, there are?" Jor was straight-up honest. "There is Koh and Motatu."

"Who?"

Why did she ask?

"You mean there's more of you?"

"Yes," Jor reassured her.

"I told you. There are Koh and Motatu. Do you live in this hole?"

Finally, something directed toward the immediate problem.

"No," Monique was happy to say.

The curious little blue image of Monique looked her over carefully as if deciding something, which Monique didn't have the faintest idea what.

Then, the image blurred. "Do you want to get out of this hole?"

Finally! What a relief!

"Please...can you help me?" That was a desperate plea from Monique.

At this point, she'd gladly accept any help—even from a ghost if that's what the image was.

Jor answered, "I can help. Jump." As if it was nothing in the way of a problem, in the least.

Monique was baffled. She didn't understand, "What?"

"Jump!" That was Jor's strongest command.

As the old cliché goes, *as calm as a cucumber,* was what Monique had begun to feel. The blue image—*blue?* —and in her exact likeness? *This wasn't real*, she convinced herself. She'd fallen into an empty well, knocked herself unconscious... and this was the results. She was dreaming. And this was a follow-up after what had happened in the grove and in Wendy's room.

"Jump?" Monique asked with more confidence building that this was a state of unconsciousness; so, she decided to just go with it. "OK, if you say so."

"Wait," Monique's image caused her to pause. Then it went on to ask, "Can I live with you, once we're out?"

In a dream, such as this, perhaps you could have a special compassion like Monique had for this benign, blue image.

"Yes, sure," she said.

Chapter 4

Wendy had just about exhausted herself, trying to cover all directions in a single search, on a single, late afternoon, which was ridiculously impossible. You'd have to be a super-person to achieve that task. She arrived at a clump of trees, where she decided to take a short break before continuing.

She wasn't giving up. No, sir; she was in it for the duration. It was Monique she was looking for.

She and Elise were like her baby sisters. She wasn't going to return empty-handed. It was as simple as that. The hour had grown late. Elise had become extremely concerned. After muddling through her homework, which was unfinished, she took a seat in one of the metal chairs on the porch, where she rocked back and forth continually. Her thoughts were cluttered with bad news, all concerning Monique.

Out across the way, the gray evening at twilight looked barren, void of anything fun to do.

Normally, by now, she and Monique would have walked to the nearest store and back—which was a corner market about a mile north of here—for an after-dinner treat, provided by Wendy's hard-earned cash she'd made from her sewing. Wendy was very generous in sharing with them.

The concern for Monique was no different with Agnes. Through the corner of her eye, Elise caught a glimpse of Miss Agnes standing in the window, by the front door. She was looking out across the way, through dark-rimmed, prescription glasses; and Elise could discern the obviously worried-look etched in her face.

Continuing through scores of underbrush, and in coming to a brief clearing up ahead, where waning sunlight was nearly hampered by scattered forest, a faint sound from a distance was a slight distraction to Wendy. She held up, listening. Far away there was laughter. A child's laughter. But she couldn't tell whether it was male or female. Just a little way farther was a footpath, leading to a small suburb, just outside the city. The closer she came to the clearing, the laughter, and some faint clanking noise became more distinct.

Along the footpath, in areas, there were skimpy patches of overlapping vegetation. As the sound grew nearer, Wendy was positive the occasional laughter, and that soft, now-and-then, clanking noise, were headed her way. A sign of life this far out? Was it possible Monique had come this far; met some friends?

Wendy entered the clearing; the sound closer, reassuring. She looked along the path, to the left. Someone was coming.

A spark of hope—

It was only two young boys on bicycles, racing to get home before dark. The soft clanking was when the spokes on the wheels brushed against overlapping twigs and branches on bushes, near the footpath.

A great disappointment, painful anguish, and the feeling of hopelessness came over her. How much longer? How much farther?

Where was she?!

All the empty spaces surrounding her tended to mock her vain effort.

"Moneeek!" That was a sheer fearful shout-out in desperation. Wendy didn't expect a reply, she just kept on ahead, aimlessly taking chances, looking in selective areas, and coming up empty.

It was time for another break. Wendy sat down in the grass, at a tree trunk of the base of a huge oak tree. She was exhausted. While sitting there, she carefully planned the entire area. Not the smallest detail of any minute movement escaped her. Anything that shook a bush, a branch, or scurried through the grass, she paid strict attention to identify it. When she stood up to stretch before continuing her grueling plight, at a glance, she happened to spot something of a casual interest.

Through some hedges just ahead, as there was a clear opening in some of their dense, leafy branches, she could've sworn she saw a flash of movement. It wasn't an animal, although it could've been. Then again, maybe it was nothing, her eyes playing tricks on her; a good analysis right about now.

But still, her curiosity got the best of her.

She had to have a look-see but didn't expect to find anything worth the effort.

Once she stepped through the hedges, an overwhelming wash of emotion came over her. Almost instantaneously, her worried state of mind broke into instant jubilation.

"Monique!" she shouted in triumphant relief.

Monique was sitting on the log of a long-ago fallen tree, not far away from the deep, dry well, where she'd fallen into. She was somber, paying little attention to Wendy as she excitedly rushed over to her then held up with recognition.

"What's the matter?" Monique didn't share Wendy's blithe celebration. Her stare was vacant with a far-away look. For the moment, Wendy sat beside her to try and get a handle on what was going on with her.

"I thought you got lost. We were all worried about you."

"I wasn't lost," Monique said in a hushed, unenthusiastic fashion, as she seemed content to just sit there stoically.

"Well..." Wendy thought a moment, then decided to go out on a limb, for the sake of Monique's drab emotional state that Elise might be leaving them.

"I don't think you have to worry about Elise leaving."

That aroused Monique's attention some, but not to the point of exceeding joy, as Wendy may have expected. She merely stared at Wendy, sitting beside her, and it was a distant stare as if she looked right past her.

"She's not leaving? That's great," Monique said, and she meant it. Only her usual enthusiasm was at its lowest level. Something grim was bugging her, Wendy could tell, because this sullen person, for all intents and purposes, wasn't herself? It was anybody's guess as to what may have happened to her, out there all alone. Wendy caringly puts an arm around Monique. They would be heading back soon, as it was starting to get dark.

"Are you?" Wendy looked her intently in the eye, finding that everything about her appeared normal, except her attitude.

"Come on..." Wendy coaxed her to stand. "It's time we head back."

"Watch it," Monique cautioned her, making sure they avoided the deep hole in the ground, a few paces in front of them.

"Be careful of that hole."

"Oh, my goodness!" Wendy grabbed hold of Monique's shoulders, gently restraining their slightest venture toward the dangerous pit.

"I didn't see that a while ago."

"Neither did I," Monique said.

"That's how I accidentally fell in."

There was nothing in her voice that suggested any post-fear, nor anxiety over the accident, which left Wendy to seriously consider whether to believe her nonchalant claim.

"You what?" Wendy stared at her in total disbelief, as she inched over to the hole to check to see how deep it was. In looking down, she saw darkness and depth; incredible depth for anyone to have survived that fall.

She withdrew and stared at Monique, with a complexity of thoughts, which neither gave her the slightest credibility to her wild story. Wendy then proceeded to thoroughly examine the girl's physical condition. There wasn't a scratch on her anywhere! But as ludicrous as it was, Wendy gave her the benefit of the doubt, simply because she loved her.

"Okay, tell me, how'd you get yourself out—and without a scratch? Did someone happen by?" Monique shook her head in denial, which deepened Wendy's disbelief.

"No?" she said, "Monique, there's no way in... "

"No way in hell is what you want to say?" Monique said with dry humor in her collected voice.

"But I did get out," she insisted.

"Okay, then how?" Wendy stood there, staring at her with arms folded.

"I jumped," Monique murmured.

"That's it?" Wendy surrendered, throwing up both hands.

"Monique"— she started to speak but groped at a loss.

"You wanna know what else I can do?" Monique said, filled with confidence.

Wendy was beginning to fear that whatever may have happened to Monique while she was alone out here had something to do with her psyche.

In disbelief, Wendy took hold of Monique's hand and started leading her away. But Monique pulled away, and stood clear of Wendy a few feet, holding her in a serious stare.

"Okay, fine!" Wendy griped, with hands on hips, "Let's see what *else* can you do!"

Without hesitation, Monique took a leap, and, in a single bound, bolted high into the air, landing softly on a leafy limb high atop a tree nearby. Instantly, Wendy felt faint, which she nearly did, but struggled enormously to maintain her poise. She gaped up at Monique, as her bedazzling, unreal feat left Wendy groping for her sanity.

She was breathless, speechless, her mind reeling in confusion, at the speed of an intense whirlwind. Wendy then barely gathered herself to say to Monique in a shaky, unstable voice, "Monique, please come down now."

And she did...floated down, feather-landed.

Unreal!

The ensuing walk home was quiet; Wendy was dazed and confused, depending on Monique, now and then, to keep her walk stabilized. However, eventually, she was good to move under her own power while still struggling with her severely damaged civility.

After they, finally, reached the orphanage, Monique had explained to Wendy, in detail, what had taken place while she was alone in the woods.

Wendy, still trying to grasp any part of Monique's incredulous ordeal as a remote possibility that any of it held the smallest grain of truth, asked for reclarification.

"So, these things you and Elise came across in the grove, and which appeared in my room, are actually ghosts?"

"Not ghosts," Monique made clear. "Jor told me, entities."

"Entities? That's pretty much the same as ghosts," Wendy said, as she still found it extremely difficult to accept, even after what she'd seen with her own eyes. But such truth without any further analysis was what she was beginning, perhaps, to have to readjust to.

"They're not ghosts," Monique insisted. "I don't think ghosts can do what they can."

"Oh? ... What all did it do that ghosts can't do?" Wendy was beginning to feel more relaxed, after their rather extensive trip back home. But this *new reality* would be stuck in the back of her mind—forever!

"Well, her name's Jor; and they're girls—like us—and that some sheriff named Hollister said they're female. Anyway, she changed herself to look exactly like me. Ghosts can't do that, can they?"

"Guess not," Wendy said, preoccupied with other bizarre thoughts about her horrific experience with Monique.

"But you said, *'They'*. You mean they're more of them?"

Monique nodded, "Motatu and Koh."

She was very calm and, apparently, acceptant of this unearthly intrusion on her person.

"And they want to live with us," she added.

That was shocking, as Wendy was alarmed.

"What?" She held up in her walk, turned to stare at Monique, glaring.

"Live with us? They're not real!" Outraged, and befuddled, Wendy realized she was grabbing for words, to make sense.

"That's ridiculous!" Then it came to her... Monique's ultra-fantastic physical realignment.

"What did you tell them?" Wendy demanded to know.

"I thought I was dreaming, at the time," Monique said in her defense.

Wendy responded almost unforgivingly, "What did you tell them?" So much dread in her voice.

"WHAT DID YOU TELL THEM?!" Monique just stared at her, afraid to answer.

In gathering herself under extreme circumstances, Wendy said as calmly as she could, "You were saying something about becoming faster, and... better-something. What did that mean?"

"Faster, stronger, better," Monique easily recited those exact words from Jor. Wendy just stared at her incomprehensively as they started up the steps.

Wendy paused, holding Monique up at the front door.

"Not a word of this to anyone," she said in a quiet voice, under near overwhelming anxiety. Monique replied, fearing what she hadn't let on to Wendy all she knew about these mystical entities.

But she did finally let out a hint, "Eventually, I don't think it's going to matter."

"Okay," Wendy said, looking Monique ardently in the eye.

"No more surprises. Just don't breathe a word of this to Elise, and especially to Miss Agnes. At her old age, she'll freak-out...like I'm about to."

Wendy then opened the door, and they went inside.

Almost immediately, once they came in the front entrance, Elise appeared at the top of the stairs and abruptly flew into elation.

"You found her!" She squealed in jubilation, then flew down the stairs in a flare of anxious excitement. During this thrilling moment of bliss, Monique dismissed her laden concerns as she and Elise locked arms around each other.

"Is it true you're not leaving me?" Monique sobbed quietly, the two of them tightly embraced.

"It's true," Elise was thrilled to say. "You shouldn't have run off. But I'll explain later. Come on, let's go upstairs. I should finish my homework, and so should you; you never got started on yours, remember?" her voice trailing off as they neared the top of the stairs. Agnes appeared in the foyer to the kitchen, her warmth prevalent as always.

"I see you found her all right," she said.

"Oh!" That mildly startled Wendy...all that stress she was under. She wasn't paying attention to Agnes coming in.

"Yes, she's fine," Wendy replied, considering.

The Pinkerton couple has a drinking problem was the explanation Elise had shared with Monique later that night at bedtime, which had brought about the denial of their application, according to Agnes. But Monique's depleted exaltation, even with the joyful resolve, concerned Elise. The two of them lay quietly in bed, within the dim, silvery-soft night-light, casting gentle, velvety-gray shadows about the room. It was quiet within the span of nearly a minute.

Then came, "We love you." It floated over to Elise in a soft, caring warmth of an innocent child.

Monique quickly sat up in bed *knowingly*; Elise blushed a little but was honored. She remained in bed calmly. "I love you guys too."

She was referring to Monique and Wendy. Monique, hesitantly trying to decide how to respond to such a delicate matter, finally replied, "Elise, I never said anything."

Elise didn't believe her, as she replied affably, "Maybe you didn't intend for me to hear you, but I did, plain and simple. So, don't play coy with me."

"Elise, I swear...." Monique was sincere. Elise chuckled softly.

"Okay, I get it. If you don't want to admit saying it aloud, that's fine with me. Goodnight."

As Elise tucked herself snugly in the blanket, and the comfort of her caring, makeshift family, to slip away into a peaceful night's slumber; Monique lay awake, pondering over what may become of them, which loomed, perhaps, soon in the future.

In the still of the night, something rather disturbing caught her eye as she lay there, trying to fall asleep. Over at Elise's bed, hovering just barely above it was a soft blue shadow. Then it settled over her, and within a moment, it became her, then quickly vanished from its ghostly form into nothing.

"Elise!" Monique sprang out of bed, rushed over to awake Elise. "Elise, wake up!" She shook her more vigorously than gentle with a nervous excitement. Elise finally awoke, groggy.

"What is it?" she dragged the words out of her mouth, barely awake. Monique went silent, looking Elise over thoroughly, worriedly.

"Finally," she stammered, trying to maintain the promise she gave Wendy about what had happened to her out there in the woods, "Are you all right? I thought I saw something over by your bed."

"Did the ghosts come back?" Elise was instantly alert.

"I'm not sure," Monique said, unsure what to say. She didn't want Elise to suffer the same fate she had. But, at the same time, she didn't want to go back on her word to Wendy. What a mess. To make matters worse, a short squeal came from Wendy's room. Elise quickly got out of bed, both her and Monique in their PJ's, and rushed out of their room, into Wendy's.

She was stunned, standing there nearly petrified, hugging her upper arms nervously before the mirror.

"What's wrong?" Elise asked excitedly. "What happened?"

Monique had little doubt of what didn't happen, but she had a good idea what *did* happen. Her and Wendy locked eyes in recognition.

Then Wendy moved away idly, toward her bed, still, a bit disturbed over what had just happened. She took a breath, settling down on the end of her bed in her nightgown.

Agnes appeared in the doorway. "Did somebody just scream?" Her concern stare looking the girls over.

Wendy gave her a tight-lip smile out of guilt.

"False alarm," she said, her shy gaze shifting away.

"Bad dream," Monique gave as an excuse.

"Well, all right," Agnes said believingly then left them alone.

Once she was gone, Elise and Monique went over and sat beside Wendy, on each side.

"Now, what did happen?" Monique asked, staring Wendy in the eye for the truth, as this was a critical time.

Elise was puzzled, only with a vague idea that the blue ghostly thing may have reappeared. Maybe it was a phenomenon they'd eventually have to live with, like the lightning strike on a clear day. Only the ghostly appearances didn't seem harmful, like the lightning bolts.

"They were here," Wendy finally admitted, "Only I didn't see but one. It or she was in the mirror."

Elise got to her feet, bewildered.

"How's that possible? Mirrors only show reflections."

"Yes, but this one was *in* the mirror, and *I* wasn't! Where I was standing before the mirror, just for a second, it took my place. And it looked exactly like me!" Wendy stressed, "Then it was gone. It just... disappeared."

"Wait for a second," Elise said with a thought, "That thing you just saw in our room..."

"It was probably one of them," Monique regretfully informed them. Elise was beginning to feel left out, that the two of them were keeping something from her, which she took it as unfair.

"You guys... is there something I should know? I thought we didn't keep any secrets." Wendy sighed a little with relief, and sorrow, but with a huge amount of concern.

"You may as well tell her everything, as you remember it."

Elise was too curious to be angry. She reserved that for later, if necessary. The three of them sat down on Wendy's bed, as Monique took a breath then began to explain.

Elise interrupted Monique for clarification, "Hold on a sec, So, that voice we heard in the room, really wasn't you?"

Monique shook her head condescendingly. A little chill from a small fright coursed through Elise.

"You're kidding, right?" Again, Monique shook her head.

A sinking feeling came over Elise.

"Stop doing that!" she insisted.

"Do you mean to tell me it was the ghost…from the ones we met in the grove?"

"They're not ghosts," Monique reiterated.

"The way I figure it, they're aliens of some kind. And their names are Jor, Koh, and Motatu. They don't seem mean, or dangerous," Monique sort of chuckled, even after all she'd gone through. But she was beginning to feel a bit more at ease, under the circumstances.

"They seem more like… well, I don't know… like, little kids. And she told me they needed a home—a place to live."

"And you're okay with that?" Elise was bemused.

"I didn't know, at first," Monique made clear.

"So, I told her… well," she cringed a little.

Elise was shocked, gaping wide-eyed and mouth open, "You told them they could?"

"Only Jor!" Monique yelled then quickly calmed down, looking away with regret.

"Oh, that's a big difference," Elise miffed sarcastically.

"When it happened, I thought it was a dream—that it didn't matter," Monique explained.

"How could you think it was a dream?" Elise didn't understand.

"I fell in this deep hole, which is an old well, no longer in use," Monique tried to explain. Elise, now enlightened, suddenly succumbed to a warmth of sympathy for Monique, as she reached out to her, hugging her apologetically.

"Oh, I'm so sorry. I didn't know."

"That's okay," Monique said. "I know you didn't."

"Are you okay?" Elise felt terribly ashamed for being upset with her, after learning what had happened. She could've been seriously injured, or worse, God forbid.

"How'd you get out? Was Wendy there?"

"Not when she got out of the hole," Wendy said. Elise was confused.

"Then how *did* you get out?"

"She jumped," Wendy said to Elise's stunning amazement. "Jumped?"

Elise wasn't clear on the answer. She stared at the two of them incomprehensively.

"Well, it must not have been very deep."

"Monique, just tell her what happened," Wendy suggested.

"Please," Elise begged them.

Monique went on to explain, mindful not to leave out anything that she was aware of. But it just so happened that she left out the most important thing, one she wasn't aware of.

Chapter 5

Ground Saucer Watch, was a secret government facility, located in an undisclosed place far away from the civilizations in mainstream society. Its purpose was to keep track of outer space activities, such as dangerous asteroids, cosmic interference, or anything threatening to the continuous existence of Earth, including UFOs. Anything presenting such a threat in the smallest fashion was not to be ignored.

A staff of three top officials was assigned to the case at hand: Edward Milburn, 59, head of operations, married, with a couple of grandkids from one son. He had two assistants:

Susan Rooker; middle-thirties, never married.

Jillian Connelly, thirtysomething, five-years divorced, with no kids, was the supervisor of top-secret, hundreds of investigations files. She has made concerning alien-abductions, UFO-sightings, and the like. But not one investigation was worthy of the time spent on the matter. Those involved were persons who were homeless, some displaced, dysfunctional, or simply UFO-buffs.

But this assignment had merit. Sheriff Randall Hollister and his deputies had verified the life-forms, which had appeared in the giant lens of the sophisticated telescope at GSW. Since the brief encounter several months ago, frequent visits to where the sighting occurred, was paid to the sheriff and his deputies. The team was grateful to the lawmen for making their reports of the incident unavailable to the public. The sheriff had told them he feared public ridicule, if they had, claiming that their law-enforcement personnel were incompetent visionaries. Since then, GSW took over in a relentless hunt for these mysterious beings. The resolve was to try and capture and dispose of them, unless, otherwise, they would leave Earth and never return. They put together a science team of experts, specializing in paranormal activities, and locating aliens.

They used state-of-the-art equipment, such as infrared cameras, the EMF-device, and highly-technical, and lethal disruptor weapons. Their search-and-destroy mission expanded throughout the Mid-West, leaving no highly-ranking suspicion to chance.

They set up Headquarters in a forlorn warehouse—still in excellent condition for use—along with an abandoned industrial district, west of the city. It was secluded, a perfect setting for such a critical, secret mission. Its cover was labeled as "Vegetational Development *for Government Use Only.*"

Safeguarding the area was done with restriction signs planted all over the place, to keep away nonessential civilians. The only people, other than government personnel, with a clearance for this project only, was news teams—the media. The idea for this deception was suggested by the head supervisor, Ed Milburn, though only his close friends referred to him as Ed. His reason for this allowance was very clever: To give to the populous his intended misguiding via the media.

Though Ed didn't expect to catch the eye of Chelsea Freeman a prestigious news anchor. At twenty-six, she had received several awards during her continuous, commendable achievements in her work. She'd become interested in television as a senior in high school. She got her start as a mail-room clerk's assistant at a local, popular TV station, WCGN, Channel 5. She wanted her own TV show, like Oprah, and a few other successful hosts. But her best talent was in journalism—a course she took in high school and college. After her start in television as a mailroom clerk's assistant; from there, with hard work, she started to climb the corporate ladder to become her own boss as a news anchor person, where she became a popular TV-figure, a favorite among her competition because she grew a knack for presenting the most entertaining and informative news stories to the public.

On a whim, as she and her favorite camcorder operator, and helicopter pilot, Jim Placket, were on their lunch break, downtown; she happened to notice, at a glance, a dark SUV rolled passed with a government license plate. She got this crazy notion.

"Jim," she said from behind the wheel, paying attention to the SUV as it went passed. She'd also noticed the lettering on the vehicle: *Vegetational Development, U.S. Government Use Only.*

"Did you see that van just drive by here?"

They had pulled in to a convenient parking space out front of the diner they'd chosen—The High Chaparral Restaurant, a short drive downtown from the TV station.

"I wasn't paying attention," he said from over on the passenger side of her classy Lexus.

To his mild surprise, she put the car in reverse and started backing out of the parking space.

Jim was puzzled, "Where are we going? We only have an hour for lunch. I was kind of looking forward to their lunch special. Veal Cutlets."

"I bought a chicken sandwich for lunch, just in case," she said, carefully entering back into the moderate flow of the lunch-traffic.

"You can have it if we're running late. I want to follow the van...see where it's going."

"Why?" Jim was puzzled.

Chelsea stared over at him thinking that sometimes his passive attitude can be annoying.

"This shouldn't take long," she murmured.

Jim waited until they were moving along in the stop-and-go traffic, then finally decided to utter under his breath, I don't like chicken."

Chelsea followed the SUV to a gravel-road cut-off. She remained beside the road, looking ahead, sizing up the place the van had pulled into. The age-worn structures of the few buildings were drab, old-fashioned.

The dark van finally parked alongside several sedans and more SUV's. The fact that the decrepit site was so outdated, alone, aroused Chelsea's suspicion. Jim remained indifferent, while they sat there, Chelsea mulling over in her mind what to conclude about this dreary place. She wasn't about to accept the idea that it was just to grow stupid plants. Something was amiss, as she could smell a rat burning for miles away. She didn't get where she's at now, being languid and docile.

"Well, there you have it," Jim was convinced that, for what it was worth, they'd reached a dead end, "They're plant-developers. Satisfied?"

"You give up too easily," she criticized.

He replied thoughtfully, "But, of course, if you apply the fact that the government once set out to destroy massive vegetation; they missed it by that much." He demonstrated by holding his index finger and thumb about half an inch apart, being facetious, "But they did, however, managed to destroy some of our troops with their careless use of the chemical Agent Orange, in the Viet Nam war."

In maintaining her focus on the government installation down the way, Chelsea put the car in gear and started forward decisively, slowly heading straight for the government building.

"What are you doing?" Jim warned her, "We can't go in there. Don't you see all those restriction signs? We could get arrested for trespassing.

"Trust me," Chelsea said with self-confidence, "We won't get arrested. If coming to the rescue of Mother Nature is that critical, and secretive, they'll turn us around at the gate." There was a metal gate on a wire fence ahead, with two military guards standing watch.

As Chelsea drove slowly to the gate, one of the uniform-guards held up his hand for her to halt, his uniform neatly fitting, with a white helmet and a sidearm. She rolled down her window, peering out at him. He was a solid physical specimen, strong features, with an unreadable-look in his hazel eyes, unencumbered by the weight of his responsibility as a military person.

"Yes ma'am, how can I help you?" His hazel eyes flashed over to Jim just for an instant.

"Is this really a classified area?" Chelsea asked, putting on an air of innocent curiosity, and faking to sound a bit naïve.

"Only to nonessentials, like ordinary citizens, who may come around, just out of curiosity," he explained.

"If you're connected to an organized special-interest group, involving the natural order of things, like wildlife... that sort of stuff. Or, if you're with the media—"

"The media?" her voice raised in delight.

"Oh, thank you so much," She whipped out her credentials from her purse, on her seat, snuggled next to her, and showed it to the guard, verifying the fact that she was a television newscaster.

"Oh, I see." He handed back her ID, with a noticeable change in his stoical disposition to a blander attitude, as he then added in recognition, "Yes, I do remember seeing you on TV. You're the news-lady. Go on in. Is that your friend?" He was referring to Jim.

"My cameraman and pilot," Chelsea vouched for him. She was an attractive young lady, with cropped, medium-dark hair, well-kept, comely features; and she maintained her high-school physique in perfect shape. And her smile was radiant, a perfect spread of healthy white teeth. The average man—like the sergeant at the gate, the typical, ordinary type, with nothing to offer such an attractive lady— wouldn't dare make a pitch for her, even in his wildest dreams. She casually noticed the nametag, Milton, on the sergeant's uniform-shirt, over the left pocket as he kindly let her through, moving aside.

"Go right on through, ma'am," he said, giving a welcoming salute.

"Well, whadda you know. This was easier than I thought," Jim made the comment, pleasantly surprised as they moved forward.

"You're right," Chelsea agreed, which during their casual friendship, she seldom did.

"It's almost too easy," she noted.

Chelsea was further amazed and baffled after they came inside. A large assortment of plants filled a huge bay area. Garden tools—some power-operated, while others were manual devices, like hedge clippers, rakes, and shovels—were lying around, along with metal and plastic containers of liquid plant-treatment solutions. People in white parkers, with their plastic picture-ID cards pinned on the front, busily shuffled in and out of a couple of portable labs that had been set-up.

Legitimate? Chelsea thought so, but with reservation; Jim was convinced without question. They soon met with the man in charge of operations, Edward Milburn—a rather tall, distinguished gentleman, to be in his profession. He and his team took their guests to a small area behind a make-shift petition, to be away from the distractions of busy workers. After proper introductions, with brief handshakes, Chelsea having presented her professional credentials; they took their seats in metal, folding chairs at a substituted conference table, in that private, little space.

"I've watched you on television lots of times."

Ed was first to compliment her on her success as news anchorperson.

"I think you've become the favorite of the populace, especially in this area," He chuckled, sitting back in his chair, calm, collected.

"Are you interested in getting footages on what we're doing here?" Susan asked her.

"You never know." Chelsea gave her a tight-lip smile, which was common to her when she was dubious about something she didn't completely agree with.

"It seems interesting enough."

"Maybe you could use it as an exclusive," Jillian Connelly suggested.

"It might just make everyone aware how important our forests—and plant-life, in general—is. If we continue to take nature for granted, it could very well, eventually, affect the entire ecological system."

After more smoke and mirror-talk, Chelsea had heard enough and was ready to take her to leave. She got to her feet to make her departure, and so did Jim.

"Well, this has certainly been interesting," she said politely.

"I'll give the matter of a brief filming on what you're doing a lot of thought. Thanks for the tour."

While on the way out, as Jim walked on ahead a few paces, Chelsea took advantage of a moment along. She paused momentarily, with no one paying attention, and planted a tiny device, which she took out of her purse while no one was watching. She hid it in a secluded place, near the entrance. It was a small shelf right beside the entrance door, nailed to the doorframe. She placed the tiny item underneath the shelf, where it wouldn't be noticed, then caught up with Jim.

It was a state-of-the-art video cam—the only one of its kind—a special design at the request of Chelsea Freeman. It was small enough to be worn on the collar, with a sophisticated system equipped with a roving lens capable of fifty-degree angles in any direction, and with sound.

"Do you think we put on a good show for our media-friends," Susan said to Ed and Jillian, as they proceeded to continue the *real* mission at hand. They were about to load-up in an SUV for a short trip in areas suspected of alien activities for over the past several months.

"I'm not so certain about anchor-lady, Chelsea Freeman," Jillian said, "She does her homework very thoroughly. She's good and is not easily fooled."

"Do you think she's onto something?" Susan was a little concern.

"Oh, I think we have all the angles covered," Ed didn't appear worried.

"There's nothing here to arouse any suspicion, not even hers. But if she'd like to continue a frivolous investigation, she's welcome to do so," Then he made a joke, "The best she would get out of it is the use of a garden tool, to rake leaves after a freshly-cut lawn if she has a mind to."

They laughed while getting into the vehicle.

"Well, that was a wasted lunch hour," Jim spouted, not so pleased with Chelsea's greed for newsworthy stuff.

Chelsea didn't reply; she just drove, looking ahead. But Jim knew her mind was racing at a hundred-mile-an-hour. But, for the life of him, he didn't have a clue why.

"So, are you planning on getting some footage of a government greenhouse?" That was straight-out sarcasm, and he wanted it to sound as harsh as could be. He was starving!

"You know something, Jim; sometimes I believe if your shoes should catch fire, the cuffs on your pants wouldn't know a thing about it." Jim didn't get it, so he went silent.

Chapter 6

"So, you think they're gone now?" Elise was nearly desperate. It was another school-day. She and Monique were hiking it through the grove, headed for their bus stop. Although the weather was just fine, with a few puffs of soft pillows of clouds lazily adrift, they didn't want to risk walking the distance to school. That would take too long, being exposed out in the open. It would give those little, mimicking, alien-ghosts creatures a chance to catch up to them. Whether they were friendly and charming or not; they were creepy.

"I wouldn't say they're gone," Monique said, "We've agreed they could live with us—"

Elise interrupted brashly, *"You* agreed!"

Monique argued, "I told you... It was a mistake! How'd I know I spoke for the three of us? I thought it was a dream, remember? You can do or say anything in a dream. But when you wake up, it doesn't matter."

Elise decided that arguing wouldn't settle the matter; she was just tentatively thankful those "charming," little ghosts were gone. However, other weird things, concerning the ghostly images, were the magical power Monique had briefly acquired in getting out of that dangerous, dry well she'd fallen into.

"Can you still jump really high?" she asked Monique as they continued, now having cleared the previously haunted grove.

"I haven't tried, after getting out of that hole. It was too freaky and scary," Monique admitted, shuddering a bit to even think of it.

"Why don't you try it?" Elise dared her. They were passing through a clearing, still close enough to the orphanage, where no one else was in sight from anywhere. That way, they wouldn't be taking any risk someone might see them.

"No!" Monique scoffed, dead serious. She then walked on ahead, miffed.

"Okay, forget it!" Elise called out to her, picking up her pace to catch up.

"Elise, I've been thinking." Monique had settled down to a building concern.

"Since I told them they could live with us, I wonder what happened to them. The last time we saw them, they were in our rooms."

"I know," Elise agreed, just as puzzled. "Maybe they changed their minds. It would seem to me that, if they are ghosts, they should be able to live anywhere they want."

"And what about all those ghost-tales, and haunted mansions, where the ghost take up residence without anyone's permission?" Monique pointed out.

"Good point," Elise said. "Well, let's just hope they did change their minds."

In the hushed breeze, soft, quiet chuckling came from the girls, which left them staring at one another accusingly.

"What's so funny?" Elise asked, a quizzical smile on her lips.

"Oh, my god," Monique murmured, thinking, not again. She hesitated to reply. It was happening all over again... the-voice-in-the-room-thing.

"What?" Elise anxiously waited for an answer, "I wanna laugh too," she added cheerfully.

"Elise... "Monique cringed a bit to admit, "It wasn't me."

"Darn it!" Elise shouted, a wash of anxiety cascading over her. She looked around, groping, frustrated, trying to find the source that laugh came from.

"It's them. I know it's them!" She and Monique, unafraid, after having become more familiar with the friendly, alien-ghosts, scoured some nearby bushes and shrubberies in an earnest effort to locate the little imps.

Monique said, feeling antagonized and flustered, "Okay, you can come out now. We know it's you and we're not afraid."

Elise tried her influence. "You got our permission to live with us. What'd you do? Change your mind?"

More snickering. That time, it sounded clear like there were two of them, very distinct.

Monique gave it her best serious tone of voice, "Okay... now I clearly heard two of you. Where's the other one? Which one of you is missing? Jor, are you here?"

"Yes," the little voice laughingly replied, with the jest of a playful child. Although she couldn't be seen, she sounded extremely close, like she was standing right next to Monique so close that her voice seems to resonate with *Monique.* That was baffling to an extreme. Suddenly, Monique was no longer certain she wasn't the least bit afraid. That was so close.

"Okay, who's next? Just which one are you?" Elise tested her bravery.

"I am Koh. You should know that by now?"

Elise was almost offended. As being an intricate part of the infamous *unknown,* these little alien-haunts sure had familiar, smart mouths, just like little, smart-aleck brats. And, in a sense, it made dealing with them more acceptable, which regressed the element of fear to a bare minimum.

Elise went on to say, "So, we have Koh and Jor here with us. Then where's... what's the third one's name?"

"Motatu," Monique spoke right up.

"Man," Elise said with recognition.

"You don't forget easily, do you?"

Koh interrupted her, "She lives with Wendy."

"Wendy, our sister?" Elise was surprised to learn. Jor gave no one a chance to speak, as she blasted excitedly, "Yay, sisters!"

But then an immediate take, "What are sisters?"

Monique and Elise laughed.

"Don't you know?" Monique said, then continued. "You know everything else,"

Jor replied with her invisible...wherever, "Is it a good thing? It sounds like a good thing. If it's a good thing, we're in."

"Jor...," Monique grew weary of the little imps carrying on.

"Yes?" Jor replied.

Monique, sighing from word-exhaustion, "Just...shut-up."

It got quiet, kind of seriously quiet. Then a timely distraction.

"Hey, our bus is here," Elise noticed. She and Monique had to speed up their pace while other kids were already loading on the bus.

After everyone was on board, Elise and Monique bringing up the rear; the bus started away gradually, the driver—a portly, elderly man in drab clothing—using the outside mirror to make sure the road was clear.

As the girls moved along the aisle in search of a seat, Monique chanced a soft whisper to Jor, feeling bad for having been so abrasive to her, "Jor, are you there?"

Monique looked about in the most inconspicuous and subtle fashion possible to keep from drawing attention to her.

But there was no reply from Jor, which concerned Monique. Despite the mischievous, little alien-specters becoming annoying, other than scary; both Monique and Elise were beginning to develop an obscured fondness for them.

After they were finally seated at about middle ways the bus, Monique—in the window-seat—quietly called out to Jor again, careful not to arouse curiosities from other students close around her and Elise.

"Jor?"

Still nothing from Jor. Monique and Elise looked at one another, mystified; but Monique felt almost guilty that she had severely offended her little ghost-friend. Alien ghost-friend, that is.

"Jor— "

Her last attempt at contacting Jor was abruptly cut short when the little imp suddenly yelled emphatically to the top of her small voice, "You told me to shut up!"

Heads turned immediately attentive to Monique and Elise, at that sudden outburst.

At the direct stare from a blond-haired girl in their class, Monique could do nothing but to give the girl an embarrassed grin, flashing those pearly-whites of hers.

While on their way to class, Monique and Elise purposely lagged, discussing their oppressing predicament privately.

"I think it was thoughtful of them to remain invisible while we're in the presence of others," Monique pointed out.

"It would be sort of freaky and weird to have ghostly images of ourselves walking alongside us, in public," Elise also pointed out.

The girls hadn't noticed, but Brittany and Natalie had caught up to them and were right on their heels, trying to gather some form of information from their hushed conversation to, perhaps, use against them later.

But, during the entire trip along the corridor, Brittany and Natalie had to finally separate from the girls and get to their own class. They got nothing valid to use against them, after all that trouble listening-in.

Sometime around two p.m., Monique was freshening up in the girls' restroom alone. She was standing over a sink, before the mirror, finger-brushing her thick, dark hair, which was nearly shoulder-length.

At the barely noticeably sound of the restroom-door opening, she looked around and wouldn't you know it, Brittany Stewart walked in, alone. One-on-one. Just the two of them, and it didn't look good for Monique.

"Well, who do we have here?" Brittany sashayed over to her, holding Monique in a tacit stare -something bad impending.

"Whadda you want, Brittany?" Monique moved away from the mirror and sink, not letting her guard down. She wasn't poised to physically fight; she was just carefully watchful.

"I get the feeling she doesn't like us," Jor said as respectfully quiet as she could.

Brittany jumped back with a mild start. She thought she'd heard Monique speak but never saw her mouth move.

"Who just said that?" Brittany stood before Monique, a little tense, her hazel-green eyes roving over Monique suspiciously but couldn't find anything to accuse her of.

"What?" Monique urged the girl, growing intensely annoyed.

Brittany started to leave in refusal to admit the surge of a rise of fear inside her being alone with this suddenly unpredictable orphan. But right before she reached the door, she whirled around, perturbed by her own lack of courage to continue, even her verbal assault.

In convincing herself to make a stand, she strutted back over to Monique, getting aggressively in her face, noticing her flawless, dark features up close was, undeniably, precociously charming. That angered Brittany even more; Monique was better-looking in all phases of her physical make-up than she was.

"This is not the last you'll see of me!" Brittany was fuming, her nose nearly touching Monique's.

Then, out of thin air surrounding them, Jor struck again, "Ew, girl, you got a stinky breath!"

That was both insulting and startling as Brittany jumped back. And, again, she never saw the mouth move.

Maintain a straight face- hiding a snicker in her throat. Jor was turning out to become the type of friend Monique would like to have around. And her invisibility made it that much more conveniently accessible. And fun!

Brittany's anger persisted. She wasn't about to let up, moving in aggressively.

"Oh, now I've figured out what you're doing. So, you've been practicing ventriloquism. Well, you only made matters worse, for you and your Snow White-friend…"

At that instant, the bathroom door was suddenly ripped off the hinges and hit the floor with a loud boom! Such a surprise, disturbing noise startled both Brittany and Monique, not to mention the door was no longer in place. Before either girl could catch a breath, Elise moved in, stunned, and at a complete loss.

"I didn't do anything," she stammered very nervously, looking back at the damages in awe and disbelief.

"I just opened the stupid door, and it came apart." Another denied voice came out of nowhere.

"We must be careful."

Brittany had had enough, as she hurriedly pushed passed Monique, between her and Elise, in a rush to resume normality far away from these weird girls.

"You guys are evil!" she decided, disappearing at a fast pace down the hallway. It wasn't long before the freak-incident with the girls' restroom-door brought students and teachers to the scene, thanks to Brittany's dutiful, word-of-mouth. But no one believed her outlandish accusation that the two girls, Monique, and Elise, were responsible for the horrific damage. The matter was promptly turned over into the hands of the maintenance crew.

So, life's good.

Brittany was sorely disappointed that no one believed her. She'd left the scene in anger, with everyone gathering around, baffled, trying to figure how, even remotely possible that such a weakling, little, twelve-year-old—and a girl, at that—could demonstrate such a disastrous feat. Soon, adult supervision disbursed the students. Mr. Horace Flannigan, a math teacher, deemed it a default in installation.

"You wanna walk home, and talk things over?" Monique caringly suggested.

"No, I think it's best we take the bus," Elise said, "It's faster."

Monique chuckled with a thought that came to her.
"What's so funny?" Elise was poised with a vague smile on her face.

They were about to board the bus, as a short line of students were in front of them. It was a sunny afternoon; the air was soft, gently rustling the leaves in trees bathed in the spring atmosphere.

"Faster," Monique said, "That was one of them... How do I say it; *gifts,* they promised, if we let them live with us?"

"Don't remind me," Elise said lightheartedly, "But you're the only one that was promised those things."

Then it hit Elise like a ton of bricks. "Wait. I remember you saying something like...stronger. Yes!" she shouted with recollection, "You said, faster, *stronger*, and then... What was that last one? It was three things."

"Faster, stronger, better. Get it right!" Koh came from out of nowhere, her small, child-voice surrounding them.

"Thanks, Koh," Elise said in a restrained voice.

"Wherever you are," She tenuously looked about, not drawing attention to herself, but didn't find Koh's ghostly blue form anywhere visibly. Then she refocused her private conversation with Monique, as they slowly advanced behind the line of students boarding the bus. Brittany, and her posse of one, Natalie, lived within walking distance from the school and was nowhere around.

"As I was saying," Elise continued, her voice just barely above a whisper. Other students were gradually closing-in behind them, so she and Monique had to be very careful not to disclose any part of their little secret.

She lifted her gentian-blue eyes in thought, quietly uttering, "Stronger... stronger."

Finally, she brought her gaze peering with enlightenment at her sister, Monique, and whispered, "I don't think the accident with the bathroom-door was the door's fault. Stronger, remember?"

"Oh, my goodness," Monique agreed, as they now were a bit skittish, inching along with the slowly advancing line. "Do you really think that being stronger meant being...*that strong?!*"

"Evidently," Elise regretted to admit.

A kid standing behind them interrupted impatiently, "Hey, you guys going our way, or you just decided to hold-up traffic, yapping?"

Elise stomped her foot, preoccupied with the seriousness of the problem she and Monique were discussing and became a little agitated as they gave ground enough to let him through; and as he rudely started to pass them, Elise, frustrated, yelled, giving him a light shove in the back, "Get on the bus, Bradly!"

He stumbled a little awkwardly on the bottom step, looking around, surprised at her show of strength, for a girl her age. But it wasn't that harsh, only surprising, so he dismissed it.

"Oops," Elise cautioned herself with recognition, a hand to her mouth, "I almost forgot."

"You'd better not do that," Monique felt relieved.

"Let's *not* forget."

After having gotten on the bus, they moved along the aisle, with slow, tedious steps, to avoid painful brushes with ankles, heels, and toes of others.

Monique was ahead of Elise, pressing along slowly, but then she suddenly stopped then turned, with hands over her eyes in sheer panic.

"Oh, my god. Oh, my god!" she shouted, desperately pressing through the congestion of the slow-moving students getting on. Her panic-mode received considerable attention as she frantically pushed and squeezed by kids giving way to her rush back to the door, to exit the bus. Elise was directly behind her, with great concern; Monique, with her eyes, closed tightly, felt her way through, grabbling like a blind person, only at a quicker pace.

"Monique, wait!" Elise, anxious to catch-up with her, managed to do so, once they'd gotten off the bus, "What's wrong? Why won't you open your eyes?" She didn't understand.

"I have to walk home!" Monique said, nearly in tears from fear, "You go on ahead, take the bus."

"No!" Elise wouldn't hear of it.

She placed an arm around Monique's shoulders caringly, leaned her head over, to look Monique in the face. Her closed eyelids were wet with tears, as she simply refused to open her eyes, making Elise more anxious.

"Monique, why won't you open your eyes?".

Other kids passing along, quizzically giving a brief notice of the two girls standing there clutched together, with great concern.

"Something's wrong with my eyes," Monique whimpered, "Nobody has on any clothes."

"What?" That was shocking to Elise.

"Everybody has clothes on, I swear it," she assured Monique, "Come on, it's okay. Open your eyes."

"No, I'm scared," Monique fearfully refused to comply.

"It's fine, Monique," the invisible Jor was encouraging.

"It'll go away. We're bonding. You're only going through a period of readjustment. It's all right. Trust me."

"You mean, it's your fault that I see naked people?" Monique believed her.

"Tee-hee-hee," both Jor and Koh laughed quietly from their invisible hide-away. Then Jor went on to say, "We're becoming a single unit. Once the bonding is complete, you'll no longer have these...surprising metamorphoses."

"Hey, you two. You coming with us, or not?" the bus driver yelled out the open door, to the girls.

Monique and Elise looked at one another, first, indecisively. But after Monique shook her head decisively, Elise spoke for the two of them, "It's Okay. We'll walk, thanks."

The bus driver then closed the door and drove away, leaving behind a faint whiff of that awful diesel fumes, to eventually dissipate in the soft, spring breeze, on such a gorgeous afternoon.

Among the widely-scattered group of kids on skateboards, bicycles and on foot, the girls, Elise, and Monique enjoyed the lengthy stroll in the brisk, gentle spring environment.

Through patches of sparsely wooded areas, they shared a few pleasantries with other kids, until they arrived in the area where they took the footpath that led them to the grove where the foster home was just ahead. That was when the girls felt free to expound on the immediate problem at hand.

As they drew near the grove, Elise said to Monique, "I think it's a good thing we didn't run into that Brittany."

"Or that dumb friend of hers, Natalie," Monique added.

"Oh, she's a softy, compared to Brittany," Elise differed.

In noticing that Monique seemed normal again, her eyes fully open as she and Elise continued through the thinly spread of woods, just before the grove, Elise asked, "How's your eyesight, seeing normal again?"

Monique nodded gratefully, realizing Jor was telling the truth; she felt wonderful.

"I'm just fine." Then she said with a happy thought.

"Okay, you guys, you can become visible again. There are no other people around to freak-out over your ghostly appearances, and Elise and I are no longer afraid."

"She is *so* right," Elise was happy to agree.

"So, come out, come out wherever you are."

A lithe, spirited look on her cute face as she turned aimlessly about in a gesture to lure the friendly ghosts. But nothing happened. Silent moments past without a sound, except leaves, quietly rustling in surrounding foliage.

"Koh?" Elise called out, puzzled. So was Monique.

"Jor?"

Nothing from either.

"That's funny," said Elise, "Why won't they, at least, answer?"

"Jor, where are you guys?" Monique looked about all around them, "I didn't yell at you to shut up, this time."

"Oh, Koh...c'mon! At least say something," Elise insisted.

Finally, "We can't."

That was a tone of regret from Jor. Koh made no comment. That was strange, though Elise, and Monique.

"Why?" That was as emphatic as a confused Elise could muster.

"Yes, *why?*" Monique was in strong accordance with Elise. This was beginning to get weird. If this was indeed real; whoever heard of ghosts, especially from outer space, that couldn't materialize at will? They did it before.

"Because..." Jor hesitated, sounding like a child who may admit to something that may prove disappointing to a friend.

Elise said as a gesture to get them to come forth, "You did it before. Why not now?"

Monique began to say before she was interrupted, "Is there any reason you won't show yourselves? "

"Yes," Koh dolefully replied, then went on to add grimly, "We would...die."

Chapter 7

A light squadron of black helicopters flew over the foster home, just as the girls were passing through the grove. The rataplan sounds from the blades on top of the machine made for a partial deafening noise, pervading city-wide, with some proportion far out across the vast countryside. The thundering sound of the black helicopters rumbling overhead dispensed a heavy vibration the girls could feel underneath their feet, until the loud, disrupting noise began to fade into the distance, toward a formidable rise of distant foothills.

The rest of the walk home for the girls was confounded in a gulf of silence. There was nothing left to be said, after Koh's defusing answer earlier. It had a devastating effect on them, in a confused state of mind; and they no longer wanted to talk about it.

When they reached the steps, the passing helicopters now far in the distance, with the popping sound of the rotary blades nearly at zero decibels, Koh spoke softly, testing the girls' loyalty, "Are we still friends?"

The girls paused before opening the front door, looked at each other for a moment, with nothing decisive in their stares; then Elise smiled a little, with acceptance, as did Monique, and said cordially, "Sure, Koh. We're still friends."

Once inside, things were normal; the fresh, clean smell, the soft, faint aroma of dinner cooking on low heat, the hint of what was cooking uncertain, but smelled delicious. The atmosphere was comfortable. All that was left to make it a perfect afternoon was that their ghosts didn't die. In leaving their bookbags on the sofa, for now. The girls checked the kitchen, where dinner's aroma remained soft, sauntering. But no one was there.

Listening for tell-tale signs of human presence; there were none. Except for the girls, downstairs were vacant.

"Where is everybody?" Monique moved over by the stairs, along with Elise, and looked up to the top, listening.

The quiet whirring of Wendy's sewing machine was in full gear. She was home, that's for sure. Miss Agnes must be out again, as she was nowhere about the premises; just piles of new lumber out back that had been put there recently, as the girls had scantly noticed, coming home.

The girls grabbed their book bags and scampered up the stairs, and headed straight for Wendy's room, where they shed their light burdens, leaving them on her bed.

"Oh, no you don't." Wendy immediately got on to them, pausing from what she was sewing on the machine.

"You take them to your room, right now; and then you may come back." That was her normal reaction toward the girls in keeping them in line. Only today, her attitude seemed a bit different, maybe preoccupied with something. Could it be a female-issue? After all, Wendy was 16. The girls hadn't entered that phase of their lives yet; and were thankful they had not. However, Wendy didn't appear mean-spirited or even cranky, by any means. She merely seemed distant as if there was something on her mind she didn't want to share with anyone.

The girls left Wendy's room, to put away their bookbags. Almost instantly, they returned and found Wendy calmly sitting on the end of her bed, seemingly in a far-away state of mind. Her sewing patterns, as usual, were scattered on her bed behind her, unorganized; but only she could sort them out correctly, in choosing the material she wanted to work on.

"You guys," she began in a somber, arid tone of voice, "You're twelve-years-old, which is old enough to know what's happening here. There's something critically important we have to discuss.

The girls sat beside her, one on each side, fully attentive. Anything she may say, they were braced for it, figuring nothing could be more jolting than what they already knew if it concerned their friendly, impish, little smart-mouths, ghost-friends.

"If this is about our ghosts-friends," Monique said prematurely, "we pretty much know the facts."

Wendy was surprised, "You do?"

Elise answered pensively, "Yes, we do. Koh explained why they can't become visible again, because, if they do, they will die."

"Is that all she told you?" Wendy asked.

"What else is there?" Monique was honestly frank.

"Of the three of us, *you* should be the one to know everything about them. You were the first to know more about them before Elise and I were."

Elise spoke in astonishment, "You mean there's more."

Wendy got to her feet. "Let's go outside," she said, staring out her bedroom door. The girls followed, looking to one another inquisitively, in a haze of confusion.

"Miss Agnes' not here?" Monique casually asked. Wendy shook her head as they walked out onto the porch, into the balmy afternoon.

"Where is she?" Elise asked.

It was apparent that she and Monique may have been stalling for time, in consideration of what Wendy had in store for them Wendy quipped with no life in her voice, "She's not here."

"We can see that," Monique smarted-off. Wendy turned to her with mouth open. She couldn't think of anything to fire back at her, at the moment.

"You wanna know what I can do?" Wendy finally said sternly, tauntingly.

Monique grew a little tense, without a clue what to expect.

"No, but I'm sure you're gonna show me," she said.

"You guys remember asking how fast I can run?" Wendy said, moving over to the edge of the porch. Neither Monique nor Elise commented; they just waited quizzically, not knowing whether to anticipate something abnormally fantastic, or terribly frightening!

"Well, check this out." After that, Wendy darted off the porch with such a burst of speed it was overwhelming. She headed straight toward the city, vanishing out of sight in a millisecond. Within two seconds, she returned, and not the least bit winded. Her smile was a little bit jubilant, but only for a moment, to prove to the girls not to ever tease her about her foot-speed. A huge, pressing matter was much at hand.

The girls, wide-eyed amazed, just stood there marveling.

"Oh, that's nothing," Jor was first to break into the long silence between them.

"You can fly if you want to."

"Fly?" Monique didn't understand, figuring everything about their live-in ghosts had been quite understood, with the final analysis being they weren't immortal ghosts, after all.

"That's crazy. Nobody can fly, except maybe ghosts. It's ridiculous."

"Only if you don't want to, like Motatu," Jor said.

"Be quiet, Jor," Motatu warned her.

"You see," Koh chimed in, "it's not that she *can't* fly, she doesn't *like* to fly."

"Blabbermouth!" Motatu shouted fiercely, with about an equal amount of anger in her voice as there was an embarrassment.

"So, are you saying, we can actually fly?" Elise wanted clarity on the matter.

"Like birds, airplanes... those sorts of things?"

"What's an airplane?" Koh asked naively.

"Never mind that," Elise wanted to be clear on Koh's previous statement about human beings flying.

"Are you really serious that we can fly?"

"Now that's a new one to me," Wendy acknowledged, Motatu as quiet as a church mouse. She was hoping that neither Jor, nor Koh, would continue reminding Wendy of Motatu's no-flying handicap since she and Wendy had spent the entire day together.

"I wasn't told anything about being able to actually fly, which I am totally in agreement with Motatu. I, myself are not fond of heights. And I have never flown in an airplane. I'm perfectly Okay with keeping both feet on the ground."

"You tell them, Wendy," Motatu was exceedingly overjoyed she had a friend in that category.

"Flying's for the birds. And I do mean *birds!"*

"So, everything you said we can do is true?" Monique asked, not exactly having fully understood everything.

Wendy said to Monique in hindsight, "You know, when you demonstrated your ability to jump out of that god-awful, deep hole; you probably could've kept on going if you'd wanted to. Have you tried your leaping ability since?"

"No, I thought it was a one-time thing," Monique admitted. Then she withdrew with a little cringe in embarrassment.

"But about flying? I'm not sure I'd be Okay with it. It sounds weird. No, I don't think that'd be cool, do you, Elise?"

The thought was also embarrassing to Elise, as she sided with Monique.

"Human beings aren't meant to fly under their own validity. It would look too awkward, too weird. We'd be laughed at."

"I agree," Monique said, "And I even agree with the big word she just used. It drives the point home with such…such," She looked to Elise. "Big word needed here. Help a sister out."

Elise's eyes searched the room as she struggled to come up with the perfect, *big word*, "Ah…ah…ah…*Force!"* she suddenly shouted.

"*Word*!" Monique shouted excitedly. "Right on, sis!" Then she thought, "It's not that great a word." That was sarcasm.

Then she decided, triumphantly, "But it worked! Big word!"

"Girls! We got a more serious issue to try and resolve," Wendy urgently stressed. "Now, let's go back inside, to my room. Miss Agnes will be home in a little while."

Back in Wendy's room, the girls wanted to sprawl on Wendy's bed, but they couldn't because of her many patterns of pieces of clothing occupied all the space. But there was a sofa chair and carpet. Very clean carpet. But the urgent meeting did not come with the comforts of home. They had to make their own seating arrangements. So, they took up where they left off, sharing the end of the bed beside Wendy.

"It really doesn't matter that they can't show themselves again. Just so as we can hear and speak with them should be fine." Elise was trying to make do with a not-so-desirable situation when she preferred it remained as it was if living with a ghost was a choice she couldn't control.

"Oh, but we can see them," Wendy said in contrary to Elise's and Monique's dismay.

They perked-up, staring at Wendy, with the look of hope in their faces.

"We can?" Elise was first to spout-off. Monique's deep, wet-brown eyes beamed with elation.

"But how?" she wanted to know. "They told us— "

"Believe me," Wendy insisted. "You can see them. Just go stand in front of the mirror."

That was puzzling. The girls hesitated, not understanding. *Was it as simple as that? No wave of a magic wand?*

Koh and Jor could've told them that, without taking them through all the confusion, and death penalties-stuff.

Wendy went on to say, "Remember when I told you that my reflection in the mirror was replaced by a ghost that looked just like me, only it was blue?"

Monique abruptly hopped off the bed and ran across the room, over to the mirror over the dresser, to see for herself. Wendy and Elise followed. Aside from her reflection, which she could plainly see, Monique panned the mirror from side to side, top to bottom, believing that her friendly little imp would soon pop out into clear view.

"Jor?" So far, nothing happened, Monique's patience wearing thin. When Elise and Wendy arrived, now the three of them stood before the mirror, staring at only their reflections. Wendy stood there, calm, with casual interest, her soft gaze satisfied with her reflection.

"Okay, what's the deal?" Monique piped. "I only see myself."

"Same here." Elise was as disappointed as Monique, they both staring at Wendy, dissatisfied.

"You guys are not listening," Wendy urged, "You're not paying attention. Just look at yourselves in the mirror and BE QUIET! Then I'll explain."

"Tee-hee-hee," the invisible images softly giggled at Wendy's outburst, which they found amusing.

"I hear them, but, where are they?" Monique simply didn't understand, and neither did Elise.

Finally, Elise, figuring she suddenly knew the answer, decided to share it. "Oh, don't tell me this is one of those moral issues, like, *even though we can't see them doesn't mean they're not there,* is it?"

Becoming a little agitated, Wendy shouted, "You're looking at them! Doggonit, you Guys!" She hesitated, gathering her poise, "We have absorbed them. They live *inside of* us! That's what they meant by *living with us!*"

"GAHH!" Monique was terribly frightened by that shocking enlightenment.

"Inside us?" Elise went pale, glaring at Wendy in disbelief, who tried to stay calm as their older sister and their guidance.

With the girls gaping at her, hoping in some way she could magically fix this recurring, creepy nightmare, she went on to make her point, "Motatu explained the situation to me, today. She said that once we agreed to let them live with us..."

"We agreed?" Elise immediately protested.

Then both Elise and Wendy glared at Monique accusingly, as she retaliated by yelling, "I thought it was a dream. I TOLD YOU THAT!"

"Alright!!" Wendy was compassionate, "We're all in this together now. It doesn't matter whether only one of us agreed; we all gave consent because we're considered a whole unit, working together."

Wendy then sighed, and in conclusion, she added, directing her attention to Monique, "Well, how fast do you think I can run now?"

Monique had no comment.

Elise murmured to herself, "Faster, stronger, better."

Then suddenly, she shouted aloud, "I get it! Faster, stronger, better! That's what we've become now. I so get it!" There was glee in her shout.

"Oh boy." Wendy rolled her eyes to the ceiling in agitation then sighed, "Now she gets it."

"Oh, my god," Monique suddenly realized. "We have superpowers!"

She suddenly grabbed hold of Elise under the arms—beaming with excitement—and lifted her clear off the floor with hardly any effort, shouting in her face, "We have superpowers! Do you get that?!"

Elise kindly slapped her on the back of her hand and calmly uttered, "Put me down."

Monique put her down then said, "You don't weigh much, do you?"

Elise just stared at her.

"Guys," Wendy began, feeling an extreme weight of responsibility now resting on her shoulders since she was the oldest. This strange and unusual awakening was a bittersweet new reality.

"Guys listen to me," she went on to say, "This is nothing you can take on and off, like clothing. What we've become now is forever."

Elise and Monique then climbed down off their cloud of bliss, bringing their full attention to Wendy.
"Forever?" Elise said in deep thought.

"That's a long time," Monique said in realizing exactly what that meant: no turning back, no matter how grave the situation may become. *Forever!* That certainly was a long time.

Wendy went on as best she could, within mind the immensely volatile situation they've inherited, "That is a long time. Motatu explained that once we've been absorbed, the process is irreversible..."

"Wait," Monique begged to differ. "I thought you said we absorbed them."

"It doesn't matter. We've all been absorbed," Wendy said under so much pressure, and frustration. "Now, be quiet."
Jor murmured under her breath to Monique, "How does it feel to be told to shut up? Embarrassing isn't it?"

"The bathroom-door," Elise said with recollection, getting everyone's casual attention, "It wasn't a freak accident," she recognized. "I did it. Only I wasn't aware, at the time."

She turned to Monique, theorizing, "And what about your eyes?"

"What about them?" Monique didn't get it. "Jor, you should know: You and Koh both agreed that... What was it you guys said about readjustment?" Elise went on to say.

"Oh, my eyes," Monique then realized the problem she had in seeing naked people. She was a little embarrassed. "I could see through things, like...clothes."

Jor explained, "You have extremely keen eyesight now."

"All of us?" Wendy asked. The images, now inside them, agreed simultaneously.

"Yes."

"Yes, all of you."

"All of you."

A final concern came from Monique, the first to come in full contact with the image Jor. "Now that you've tricked us; how dangerous is it you're living inside us? And how come you can't come out, and it is like it was before?"

"Let me try and answer her concerns," Motatu volunteered to explain.

Jor remarked gladly, "Go ahead. You're better at this than I am anyway."

Motatu began, "Once we are permitted to coincide with you, both our molecular structures intertwine and become one in all aspects of our entire physical system. We become one individual, just with special modifications. What I am, you become; and you are what I become. And you can't very well tear yourself apart and expect to continue to function in the cycle of life, do you?"

For better clarification, Wendy asked, "So this is permanent, right?"

Motatu spouted, a little annoyed, "So many questions! We make you faster, stronger, and...and better! Why you, all the time, look a horse's gift in the mouth?"

Wendy and the girls laughed.

Motatu, puzzled by their hilarity, asked, "What's so funny, why are you laughing? It's true what you do."

Wendy said, her laugh trailing off, "We were laughing at your misplaced metaphor. It's *gift horse,* not a horse's gift. Horses don't give gifts."

Chapter 8

After a short while, the air of mixed emotional excitement began to ebb. Wendy moved over to her sewing machine and started dawdling uninterestedly, with some loose material she'd left there; Monique returned to Wendy's bed and sat back down on the end of it, a solemn look on her face as she leaned back, resting on her elbows.

"Now what'll we do?" Elise said as she moved idly away from the mirror.

"You're not happy?" Koh asked, not understanding Elise's dampened mood, "I tell you what, why not help people who are weaker than you? You can fly, or you can run fast. And I mean fast, like Wendy. You have great eyesight; you're in great shape, and nothing can harm you. Like if you fall very hard, it won't hurt you. Or if you fall into a well, like Monique."

"Hey!" Monique cautioned her. "That's rude. You don't make fun of someone who fell into a well."

Then the girls went quiet, immersed in their own private thoughts. They looked across the room at each other from different locations. Wendy was behind the sewing machine, disinterested in sewing anything; Elise was in the cushion chair, while Monique had gotten comfortable on the bed by lying on her back, with her blue-jeans knees raised. This was going to be a long night.

Overhead, in the late afternoon, more military helicopters flew over, the chopper blades creating a rather disturbing sound with their loud popping noise. They weren't black helicopters; this time, they were much larger, with a dark brown and tan camouflage finish, and were heavily armed.

They were doing field exercise. With their scientific devices in place, the special team of scientist went about conducting evidence that proved the presence and activities of visiting extraterrestrials did exist.

The weather was overcast without the threat of rain. It was a little windy and a thin, gray haze came with the morning, now about to dissipate as noon approached. The outlook favored another mild day of spring.

A gathering near the lakeshore consisted of part military and special government agents. Colonel Seth Gordon, Army, and head of operations were in command of a company-size element, the Fourth Army Division. A Tactical Operations Center was in place as a defense post, on full alert.

A meeting took place in one of several quarters designated for conference rooms and strategic planning.

In the meeting, Agent Ed Milburn, and his team of co-workers, agents Rooker and Connelly, were in a discussion of awareness. Connelly spoke; using her expertise on aliens of many kinds. She was now delving into the existing aliens at hand.

"According to the reports turned in to us from the sheriff and his deputies of Medfield County, it appears what we have here are, what we call, *alien biological entities*, interpreted as A-B-E. Among these types, it's commonly known that they'll need a host to survive in this realm for over a long period of time.

"What about the consistencies of each report?" Rooker fervently raised the question, "Didn't each deputy's, along with Hollister's, individual reports collaborate with each other's?"

"Yes, indeed," Jillian said.

Ed spoke up, "These alien entities appear to affect certain emotional behavior from humans, is what I read the report."

Sitting in his chair with his elbow propped on the table, Ed reached over to his left and took up one of the reports off the stack before them. He began to scan it.

"Yes, here, it says, 'The overall experience was heartwarming, is best I can describe.
They looked, and sound like sweet, innocent little kids."

Ed went to the stack of reports again, drawing out another. He then read a selected part of the report. "I didn't have the heart to harm them in the slightest fashion. Even though they barely have formed, their persona, aura—call it what you like. But, in all sincerity, I believe these creatures are completely harmless."

Ed had read enough. He laid the paper aside, making his decision. His tenure as a special agent had given him an education on trust. And during his experience as a special agent, he'd learned emphatically not to trust anyone, other than yourself. But sometimes, even that was doubtful. A long time ago, a wise fellow once told him that the true measure of character is what a person will do if no one finds out.

"You know, I must tell you, I'm getting bad vibes from these reports," Ed made the announcement. "It has all the ingredients of a hostile alien-race to try and take over Earth. The warming, the emotional sedation you get at a close encounter with these beings.

It has all the warning signs of deception. First, they lure you into their confidence, with whatever it is about them that gives them the ability to sedate you: But, I'll lay you odds that is their primary weapon, which means they, undoubtedly, depend on that as a major part in their victory."

"What would you recommend to the president?" Susan asked, sitting across the table, opposite him. Jillian still had the floor after her speech.

"Well…," Ed hesitated, stretched a little, then looked them in the eye and said pompously, "That would be entirely up to the Commander-in-Chief. But, for the most part, the aliens are in control of their own destiny, whether it's good or bad—depending on their behavior—wouldn't you think?"

Susan responded, with Jillian favoring her thinking, "Just remember, our priorities are to try and establish communications with them before we bombard them back to wherever they came from."

"I completely agree," Jillian replied, angling over toward them in concentration, "If we act aggressively towards them, we could be opening a Pandora's box. They're here now, so we just as well."

She broke off her speech, and looked toward the entrance, as Colonel Seth Gordon entering was a subtle interruption. He walked directly over to them in somewhat anxious strides, clad in his combat-uniform.

"What you got, Colonel?" Ed was hoping for something of vital interest. And he wasn't disappointed.

"I think we've found something you need to take a look at." The colonel didn't lag, waiting for them; he just turned briskly and started walking away in hurried strides, with Ed, Susan, and Jillian hurrying along behind him. The lake was vast, deep, a shimmering blue. The weather was calm, nearing mid-day; the sky was serene; the landscape a breathtaking vista out there in the wide-open spaces.

Along with a rise beyond the roadway a short distance from the lakeshore, some members of the science crew were in the process of pruning selected, leafy branches from a tree line atop the rise.

At a glance across the way to the crew working in the trees, it didn't appear worth the time wasted watching them, which was good, thought Ed. The deception to fool the populace, and the media worked. Nothing looked suspect.

"This way, please," the colonel said to Ed and his crew.

He escorted them across the way a bit, to a portable lab made of pre-fab and Plexiglas where, inside, a lab crew was on hand- busy analyzing samples of cut, leafy twigs that held an unusual soft bluish-green tinge.

"Here, look at this." The colonel dismissed a lab tech, who was checking some plant-samples through a microscope. As the lab-tech moved on to another area, Ed looked through the microscope, his findings puzzling.

"What's this?" he murmured.

A tiny smear of a gooey substance extracted from one of the many plant-samples gathered emittedd the soft bluish-green tinge; but, amazingly, under the microscope, Ed clearly noticed a slight pulsation, like it was a breathing, living organism, much unlike the source of a live plant.

He withdrew, glaring at the colonel, bewildered.

"What's it means?"

The colonel seemed proud to announce, "It's the dispensation of an alien life-form."

"May I have a look?" Jillian anxiously stepped forward. The colonel moved aside obligingly, with a vague, accommodating smile.

"Be my guest," he made welcome. Jillian looked through the microscope and was suddenly overwhelmingly amazed by what she saw.

"This is fantastic! It's pure energy!" She withdrew, gaping in astonishment.

With disappointment, the colonel spoke, "It's unfortunate, though, that the pulsation only lasts for a short while. Then it becomes completely lifeless."

"That's to be expected," Jillian was not discouraged; she was gratified, as she exulted in her conclusion. "Gentlemen," she continued while nodding her head towards Susan, "and you too, Susan. We have alien-visitors somewhere close around."

Susan acknowledges, "The next step is to locate them. Unless, of course, they've already found a host. Then it could become like looking for a needle in a haystack."

"Even if so," Ed was optimistic. "Eventually, whoever the host or hosts are, they're bound to show their hand."

Jillian concluded, "And now comes the wait."

"If there's anything I've learned about our government is that they're not very good at keeping secrets; they're only good at keeping them away from dumb-asses. Which they don't matter anyway."

Chelsea and Jim were on their way back out to that government facility, which was, allegedly, wasting government funds on needless vegetation development.

"Are you calling me a dumb-ass?" Jim sparked jovially. He was wearing a baseball cap promoting an adult beverage. The caption above the bill read: *Drinking beer doesn't make you stupid. It made Budweiser.*

Chelsea laughed in noticing the humorous jest on the front of the cap, as she replied, "If the cap fits, wear it."

After a moment of silence, Jim went on to inquire, "Seriously, why are we going back out to this boring place? Do you actually believe you gonna find something they're doing that's completely contrary to what they're claiming to be doing?"

"Do you have the gear together for filming?" Chelsea merely asked him.

From over on the passenger side, he looked over his left shoulder, into the back seat, where video equipment was piled in the seat. "Yep," he said. "No worries."

Chelsea smilingly commented on Jim's familiar intonation in confirming their gear was aboard, "Hakuna-Matata."

"Hakuna-Matata," Jim returned with recognition. "That was from *The Lion King.* I liked that movie."

They finally approached the gate, Chelsea slowing down, coming to a stop. The guards at the gate this time were different. Sergeant Milton wasn't there. The man in uniform, who approached the driver's side of the car, didn't appear as accommodating as SGT Milton. This guy was wiry, with a thin face, unfriendly air about him.

"I'm Chelsea Freeman, and this is my associate and cameraman, Jim Placket." She showed the spindly guard her proper ID. He wasn't impressed but gave her no problem in clearing her to proceed.

"Is there anyone you need to see?" he asked going beyond his duty.

"Mr. Milburn," she said, putting away her ID, back in her purse. Jim had gotten out on the passenger side and started walking around the front of the car, to join Chelsea.

"Ma'am," said the guard, "I'm not sure, but I think he left a while ago with his staff, the two ladies. And I'm not sure when they'll return. Did you have an appointment to meet with them?"

"Well, yes, in fact, I did. I'm supposed to get some footage of the work they're doing here," Chelsea explained.

"I understand," the guard said. He was an E-4, one rank below a sergeant and he was starting not to seem so harshly ill-mannered. Maybe nature was a bit cruel to him in designing his outward personality appearance. Perhaps she did judge the book by its cover. He turned out kinder than he first appeared.

"Well, I guess it'll be all right for you to wait if you like. I wouldn't know what to tell you about filming, though."

"Thank you kindly," Chelsea said. She looked around to Jim, who had elected not to have a voice in the matter. He was just there to accommodate her in whatever manner he could and run the cameras. She glanced at her wristwatch.

10:17a.m.

It would be lunchtime soon. "Well," she said decisively, "it'll be lunchtime in a little while. But we could take a minute to look around inside. It's important that we check to see how much space we'll have to set-up our equipment."

Chelsea was very convincing. The guards at the gate were becoming very helpful.

Gradually, he became more tolerant to look at. "Oh, sure," he welcomed them in, "Just park your car right over there and go on inside. Someone'll be there to assist you."

"Thank you," Chelsea said with a generous smile, then slowly drove away to the parking lot, where several government vehicles—a mixture of sedans and SUV's—were parked.

After they parked, she and Jim, calmly, went inside the compound. Surprisingly, no one was immediately there to greet them. Jim was at a loss.

"Now what do we do?" He looked about, feeling a little bit intrusive. "Where is everybody?"

He looked to Chelsea for suggestions- she had none. But, in truth, unknowingly to him, she wasn't there to do any filming. Her cover had worked. That small piece of property she'd left there earlier was the real reason she returned. Walking into an empty room, where she'd hidden the tiny piece of vital equipment, couldn't have been more convenient to retrieve it.

"Maybe they're all out there somewhere treating some poor, sick plants. How should I know?" His naïve disposition was almost irritant to her, as she then strode across the spacious room, over by the door, intending to collect the special item she'd left underneath the small shelf, nailed to the doorframe.

The floor was untidy, spangled with scattered spring-green leaves, tiny bit of twigs that had been snapped off bare branches left lying around. But Chelsea wasn't fooled, as she deemed those government agents had gone through a lot of trouble for nothing, as far as she was concerned. And she hated a trashy floor, with leaves scattered everywhere and those bits and pieces of broken twigs that rolled under her feet when she accidentally stepped on a few.

What she didn't want, or need, was for Jim to crowd her. Like a little puppy would its mom, he followed Chelsea to the door, impeding her chance to take back her property- his innocence and docility getting on her nerves. There was nothing more urgent than getting out of there, with her belonging, right now!

"So, what'll we do?" He stuck close to her blindly inconsiderate. "Do we wait for them? There's no telling how long it might take before they return."

That gave her an idea. "Hey, you know you may be right." She handed over her car keys to him, which he was surprised she did that.

He'd never driven her car, but didn't think anything of it, which was one of his biggest problems: he didn't think!

"Go bring the car around..."

He didn't give her the chance to finish before he butted in, "What are you going to be doing?"

She was about to lose it. She got in his face intimidatingly, their noses almost touching, although he had her in height about a couple of inches. "I'll be killing myself, if you don't do as I say and go get the car, *now!* I'm going to try and raise someone, to get a cancellation on this silly filming!"

That was a lie. She had no intentions of getting a hold to anyone; she only wanted him gone long enough so she could recover her hidden video camera.

Jim left to get the car somewhat anxiously. The closest he'd ever get to driving a luxury car was his uncle's 2010 Chrysler. That was right about seven years ago, and it wasn't considered a luxury automobile; too many people owned one.

While he was gone Chelsea went over to the little shelf on the doorframe, leaned down a little, with a hand feeling around for the tiny item she'd left there.

Suddenly, her heart throbbed in her chest from a rush of startling disappointment. She bent down even lower with a thorough look where she was certain she'd left it. *Not there!* She stood upright, looking aimlessly about in desperation, close to panic. It simply wasn't there!

"May I help you?"

That startled her. She turned quickly, meeting the stare of a young woman in a white lab jacket with her nametag pinned on it. She'd appeared in the doorway from the far side of the huge room. She had gentle features, short, light hair, and she wore a wry smile, with a vaguely curious stare at Chelsea.

She stammered, a little bit of nervous guilt hampering her immediate speech, "I...ah...I think I dropped something out of my purse."

"Oh? What was it?" The young lady offered help in searching for whatever it was Chelsea claimed she'd lost.

Jim pulled the car up outside and lightly tapped the horn, which mildly distracted the young lady, whose nametag read, Penny Tyler. Up close to Chelsea, she looked well-groomed and smelled nice.

"That's my ride." Chelsea was ready to ditch the search; the pressure was so great.

Just as she started to leave, Penny said to Chelsea's amazement, "Is this it?"

Penny was standing there, holding Chelsea's most treasured item—under such desperate circumstances right now—between her index finger and thumb.

"Yes," Chelsea admitted, tentatively reaching for the tiny item. In doing so, she maintained subtle eye-contact with Penny, trying to read her gaze as briefly as that fleeting moment would allow.

"Thank you."

"You're welcome. It was just lying there on the floor, by the door." A bland smile, as Penny surrendered the precious item to Chelsea, never suspecting a thing. She *owed her one*, Chelsea was thinking, relieved to make it out of there without much of a hitch. She was so grateful to recover such a precious *jewel* that she never bothered to relieve Jim from behind the wheel of her car, as they now cruised along the interstate.

Finally, she sighed with relief from all that nervous pressure, staring at Jim with an accomplished gleam in her eyes, "Well... that's that."

"That's what?" came Mr. *Naïve*. He was without a single clue.

A tight-lip, condescending smile creased her scarlet lips. "How do you like the way my car handles?" she simply asked, refusing to let him upset her, after that great achievement.

"I like it!" he smilingly expressed his content with the vehicle. Chelsea, momentarily, held him in an amiably soft gaze. The only thing he could hang his hat on, in one aspect of his character, was the fact that he wasn't bad-looking. Strong shoulders, moderately muscular because of he worked-out, tall—sort of.

Chapter 9

Mind-wise, they were still in limbo. Elise and Monique were headed to the bus stop, under a cloud of immense frustration, laced with uncertainties; which was whether to tackle this incredulous, new reality head-on or leave it alone. All this thinking in hopes that it remains dormant for the rest of their lives—hoping that maybe someday it'll go away on its own.

But not a chance, the girls realized. This was much too *real*! And, now, in the real world, they must come to terms that this is something they're stuck with indefinitely and has created a constant decision-making process.

They walked through the grove solemnly, no conversation between the two, when, normally, they'd be chatting, laughing. Each day of classes was filled with new adventures in learning.

"I guess Wendy was right," Elise finally admitted, "We'll have to get used to it."

"But what'll we do with it?" Monique exerted in frustration. "We can't be seen flying through the air, like some freaked-out bird that looks human!"

Jor intervened, "You don't have to fly. Do like Motatu, just run really fast."

"Oh... I dunno." Elise was skeptical of that also. She cringed in continuing, lightly stammering, "Um...it's sort of freaky, too."

Koh spouted, a little irritated, "No one can see you when you're running really fast! Now get a life. Deal with it!"

Elise got a bit testy, retaliating, "Shut up, Koh. You can't talk to me like that.

I'll have you know that—" Koh rudely fired back, "you can't tell me to shut up. I'm not Jor. And I have a mouth, and a right to talk. And furthermore..."

"Furthermore, what?" Elise smarted back, angry. And it went from there, the two of them back and forth in an intense argument, from inside to outside.

"Besides, Koh, no one was speaking to you, if I remember correctly— "

"That's your trouble. You can't remember much, can you?"

"*Oh!*" Elise exerted, insulted.

"Guys!... we're wasting time," Monique had tolerated them long enough, "Stop arguing or we're going to miss our bus."

Jor chuckled, "Then fly to school."

Monique rolled her eyes in displeasure, "Not you too." They resumed walking to the bus stop.

Finally, Koh said to Elise, in a surprisingly benign voice "Are we still sisters now?"

Elise, suddenly confused by the retracted hostility in Koh's voice, "What?"

Koh replied, still soft-spoken, "Well, the three of you are at each other a lot, and you are sisters. And you love each other. That's why it's okay that you argue sometimes, right?"

Elise was then beginning to understand Koh's brash, verbal outburst. She was touched. "Koh, you mean you did that on purpose?"

Koh hesitated, then said quietly, "Yes. So, are we still sisters?"

Instead of a direct answer to Koh's question, Elise had something else she wanted to be cleared up. "Koh, that was you the other night who said you loved us, wasn't it?"

"Yes." Koh's voice was tempered, tender.

Jor piped, pretty near embarrassed over the sentiments between Koh and her host, "Oh, get on with it! You sound silly...all that mushy, mushy talk. Answer her question: Are we sisters or not?"

"Do we have a choice?" Monique pointed out curtly.

Jor shouted with enthusiasm, "Yay! We're sisters. And this time, I *know* what it means!"

At each passing moment, the girls began to understandingly accept their bountiful reconditioning, unconditionally. With Wendy's wisdom and help, they were sure to get through this. God only knew how.

"Oh!" Elise abruptly shouted. "The bus is here. We'd better hurry, or we'll be left!"

"Not again," Monique whined. "We'd better run!"

The last small group of kids had just about finished loading on the bus, and it was ready to drive away. Without carefully thinking it over, the girls got excited.

"Hurry!" Elise shouted.

Their feet took one step forward and, in a flash, they streaked through the shallow woods like a couple of bolts of lightning, arriving at the bus before the driver had time to close the door.

Only one kid, Bryan Alan, had paused and looked back through the open door, just in time to catch a fleeting glimpse of the girls, as they tended to have just materialized out of thin air. It happened so fast that he simply didn't trust his eyes.

He shook his head in disbelief, then muddled his way to the rear of the bus, though still slightly dazed and a little confused.

The bus driver, a portly, elderly black guy, spoke to the girls while closing the door, "I see you made it. You kids must have run fast to catch-up. I didn't see you at first," he chuckled, bringing the coach-load of kids safely into a shallow flow of traffic.

After having realized their careless mistake, Monique and Elise had little to say to the bus driver; they just smiled at him friendly-like and were a little embarrassed.

"That was close," Monique said to Elise as they made their way toward the rear.

A few kids in front of them slowly moving in selecting their seats. The short-lived thrilling adventure they shared a while ago, in their race to the bus stop, had brought them to realize the importance and seriousness of whom they had become. With that in mind, the weight of concern and latent skepticism were rapidly on the decline. The entities inhabiting the girls' bodies were beginning to shape their entirety into accepting this enchanted makeover.

As they moved along the crowded hallway, on their way to class, they were in quite a placid mood, laughing, chatting, Elise saying to Monique, "That was kind of fun *and* weird!"

"Weird isn't the word," Monique stressed. "It was super...colossal-weird!"

Elise cocked her head to the side, stared at Monique incomprehensively a moment, then decided, "Okay, I give you that as a big word."

"Thanks," Monique replied.

"But you know," she added as they rounded a corner to a connecting hall right before their classroom, "Wendy's right. We must maintain restraint. We nearly messed up bad. What if someone would've seen us?"

Elise replied, making a joke, "Then we would have to kill them."

As they were near to enter the classroom, Brittany and Natalie appeared among the bustling kids headed to classes. She and Natalie had just finished haggling with some smaller kid—naturally—as he was attending his locker. The jammed hallway was virtually smothering, to get to Elise, and Monique before they entered their classroom.

Brittany, snidely grinning, rudely pressed her way through the crowd of students—with Natalie close on her heels—anxiously squeezed through, to get to the girls.

Natalie, with a short attention-span, inquired, "Brittany, what do we want with them, this time?"

Brittany, just slightly ahead of Natalie, remarked, "Just follow my lead."

Dumbfounded, Natalie responded, "I am following your lead; I'm right behind you."

"Oh, brother," Brittany sighed, annoyed. At times, Natalie was such a bore. Her idiocy deserved an award for the most incompetent. Why did she put up with the girl? Oh, that's right; she lived true to the adage, misery-loves-company.

They made it to Elise, and Monique right as they were entering the classroom.

Brittany was just barely able to reach out and touch Elise on the shoulder, getting her attention. She turned around to a gross disappointment. Immediately, her blithe attitude turned sour. Monique stood her ground right beside Elise, while other students inattentively moved passed.

"We have some unfinished business to attend, you two. I'm not forgetting what happened in the bathroom, the other day," Brittany was saying in a threatening tone of voice.

Natalie mimicked her in a weak, dependency fashion. Otherwise, she had no gall of her own. "Yes, that's right... unfinished business."

They were irritating to Elise. "Not now, Brittany!" she scoffed.

Elise's bold rejection of the two girls had angered Brittany for an instant, as she grew rigidly enraged, imposing on the girls' space. Now, it was the four of them, stiffly staring down each other. But then suddenly, as Brittany had the thought of believing that her superior size over Elise, or Monique, would easily gain the advantage over both, something strange and unexpected took place.

Brittany jumped back with a yelp from a sudden start, now gaping at Elise apprehensively. Without her champion Brittany, Natalie was at a lost, with no gumption, no courage, and no will of her own.

"Brittany, what's wrong?" Natalie's voice held hints of pleading like she was half-frightened.

"Let's get out of here," Brittany said, failing miserably to match her voice with what anger she could barely maintain over the wash of fear that had suddenly come over her.

Natalie had no choice but to *follow her lead*, as the two of them left the girls alone. But somewhere along the congested hallway, Brittany thought it was safe to announce to Natalie her concerns, as she said, "There's something very weird about those two."

"Why do you say that?" Natalie was confused as they moved along in no rush to get to class.

Brittany, too abashed to admit to the smallest measurement of fear she'd gotten from her constant gaze into Elise's hard stare, dared to risk telling Natalie, "You mean you didn't see it?"

"See what?" Natalie had no idea.

"Her eyes," Brittany said, a rise of anger in her voice.

"No. What about her eyes?" Natalie's response purely innocent.

Brittany brushed by her, heading into the classroom, murmuring, "They looked like a cat's eyes!"

"Cat eyes?" Natalie stood there a moment, stupefied. Then it came to her that she was about to be late for class.

"Brittany!" She ran after her.

"Why'd she freak-out like that?" Monique was curious to know, whispering to Elise once they were seated in the classroom. They had seats beside each other, and the class period was just getting underway. Mrs. Rachel Garland, their English teacher had just entered the room.

"I have no idea," Elise said, innocent of the fact.

"Tee-hee," Koh snickered quietly, which caused Elise to react with sudden nervousness.

"Koh don't do that," she seriously whispered quietly, looking around with concern, hoping no one was observing. No one was.

Monique leaned over to Elise and said, "Why's she laughing?"

Straightening up in her seat, Elise answered, "I dunno. Koh, what's so funny?"

"Brittany," she whispered very softly, not possible to be overheard.

"Brittany?" Elise didn't understand, "What about Brittany?"

"Koh, you didn't. Tell me you didn't!" Elise said with excitement, and so was Monique.

"You fixed it, so I'd look through your eyes? And what did she see, your alien-eyes, which look like a cat's eyes?"

"No," Koh disagreed in what was true to her.

"I don't have a cat's eyes; I have my own eyes like you have yours. They just happen to be different. And, besides, she was picking on you, and we're sisters. We have each other's backs, don't we?"

That was more congenially touching to Elise and Monique that they couldn't remain upset with Koh for acting on behalf of her *sisters*. Elise finally conceded with timidity because of her softheartedness.

"Well, since you put it that way, I guess you did okay. I would have probably done the same. But, remember, we *must* maintain restraint. No one ever is to learn who we are now. It must be *our* secret at all time."

"Got it," Koh promised. School had let out for the day, as they were strolling across campus in the area where student-traffic was very shallow. They were conversing about Brittany's freak-out. No sooner had Koh made her promise, Brittany, and several older girls came upon Elise and Monique, surrounding them and blocking their way to their bus. They all looked mean, disrespectful, nondescript in attires; and their tacit approach was as if they were ready to do battle.

Monique sank into a deep depression, sighing despondently, "Aw, man."

"Well, whadda you have to say for yourselves now, huh?" Brittany was very brave with her posse behind her. She walked upon the girls, with vile intent.

"You two have some explaining to do, don't you think?" There was serious contempt in her incorrigible approach.

It had come down to this: either fight and risk exposing their enchanted abilities or fly away. Well, they had one other choice. They could run. What were they to do?

"Brittany, just go away and leave us alone," Monique asserted her solution.

"Yes, make it easy on yourself." Elise was running out of patience, not a game for a fight, however, just tired of the likes of Brittany. And she stood ready to put an end to this, for the last time, despite the risks.

Brittany moved in threateningly.

"Let's take their bookbags and scatter their stuff all over the place," she said to her posse, as they started moving in on her command.

Elise and Monique drew closer to each other, preparing to do whatever was necessary. But they had to be careful not to seriously hurt any of the girls, as they were blindly unaware of the vehement task they'd taken on.

But no. Interference intervened. A sizable group of students dutifully crashed the goons' party. Four older girls—around Brittany's and her friend's ages—came forward in defense of Monique, and Elise.

"Hey," The girl who boldly came up to Brittany was fourteen-year-old, Yulanda Bishop, well-trained in Martial Art; and she didn't like bullies!

"I'm only going to warn you once. You leave these girls alone, like forever! Or you'll hear from me. I promise." She spoke in a thick, dead-serious, angry voice.

The rest of the kids who came to the girls' aid stood around to make certain the bullies left the area, which they did gradually. Brittany begrudgingly hung around, though timidly. She knew she was taking one heck of a chance, with Yulanda Bishop still there.

Finally, Brittany cleared the area and headed home.

"Wow," Monique marveled.

"Thanks for helping us, Yulanda," Elise was happy to add.

Yulanda smiled cordially at them. "Anytime, girls," she said,

"I hate bullies. If they ever bother you again, you let me know."

"Thanks, we will," Monique said with a grateful smile.

After Yulanda left, Elise and Monique boarded their bus stress-free.

"I didn't know you knew her," Monique made known.

"I've watched her demonstrate Karate in the gym a few times. She's really good," Elise said as they moved down the aisle, in search of a seat.

"Cool," Monique said, "Looks like the problem with Brittany is finally over."

"Let's hope so," Elise said in good spirit. They found an empty seat and sat down, as the bus was gradually pulling out into the traffic lane. A huge truck had been out back of the foster home, unloading building material, while Wendy and Agnes were away. It was the second such truck that been there today. The first was earlier that morning when both Wendy and Agnes were home. Wendy was left with only the assumption that remodeling was the situation; Agnes hadn't mentioned a thing about it, one way or the other. She and Wendy had been gone since shortly past lunchtime and hadn't returned as of late.

Agnes had business at the Federal Building, on a matter concerning the foster home. Wendy had gone along to do some shopping for more patterns for her sewing purpose. Their transportation was a state-issued vehicle, a white, used 2010 Chrysler Town and Country SUV.

It was when Wendy was done shopping, coming out of the department store with her purchases: two bags of an assortment of clothes, with other needed sewing items, new spools, and a threader, with extra needles. The van was a couple of blocks down the street, parked out front of the government building.

The van was left unlocked for her convenience in case she was done before Agnes. While loading her packages on one of the back seats, she heard a loud crash some were along a back street, up the way a piece. It was a loud booming sound, like a huge explosion. Then, almost instantaneously, a crowd of people started running toward the explosion in a rage of excitement.

Wendy, out of stark curiosity, left the van and followed a fleeing group of people headed in that direction. She didn't run to keep up; she went around a corner, to the back street where the explosion had occurred. Thanks to her gifted, keen eyesight, she could clearly make out the results of the tumultuous explosion.

The top of a high-rise, the commercial building had burst into flames. People were trapped from the tenth-floor to the very top, which was a twelve-story structure, as towering flames with billows of black smoke pervaded for several blocks. Sirens of emergency vehicles soon filled the mid-afternoon, speeding to the grim, emergency scene.

Wendy began pacing frantically with indecision when this wasn't the time trying to decide who's to live, and who's to die; the fire was rapidly rampaging out of control.

"Wendy," Motatu spoke in a quiet, personal manner, hard-wired into Wendy's mind like it was her own conscience.

"There are people trapped in that building and could use your help."

Wendy, strenuously frustrated. It was a sheer pain to just stand there, watching, and doing nothing to help.

"What about us? Doesn't it matter that we need protection from those who'd wish to harm us? If our government knew about us, we'd be locked up in a cage for them to study. We would lose our freedom. We'd become their property."

"Wendy, you and the girls have the powers to do whatever you want. And you and the girls are good and pure. You can't be swayed to do evil. That's why we choose *you,* and your sisters."

That was surprising, coming from Motatu. "You chose us?" Wendy was astounded, "You mean you purposely picked us out of all other choices? That's amazing! It's fantastic! Why?"

"Because we are infallibly compatible with values, compassion, and love," Motatu was thoroughly convincing.

"There is no evil of any kind that lives within you or me. Or the girls. We represent what is good, and our love is pure. But we are fighters, with the capability to destroy worlds."

That was a bit disturbing to Wendy. She didn't understand.

"Why would you entertain the idea to destroy a world?"

"That cannot be decided on a whim," Motatu made clear, "Your powers will not function against you."

That was a hazy understanding, with tentative satisfaction. She wasn't quite clear on that explanation.

"I wouldn't want to destroy any world," Wendy made clear, "I guess what I'm saying is that we just want to be left alone, to live normally."

"Heroes aren't selfish. They do what's necessary and want no reward for the deed," Motatu said with sincerity.

The flames consuming the building were getting worse, raging. The intense heat was felt all the way out to where Wendy stood at quite a distance away. Her enhanced, sharp hearing picked up screams from potential victims trapped inside the burning building. "You can approach this in a manner that you won't be seen.   Just use and trust your powers," Motatu concluded.

"That may be easy for you to say. You've had these powers...no telling how long. I'm sure you'd know exactly what to do. This is all new to me," Wendy said as a disclaimer, thinking of herself as being justified in her complaint, "And I don't think I'm being selfish."

The screams of the desperate people began to plunge into her soul. And the fire was intensifying, the smoke dense and black, choking.
"You're hesitating because you're afraid," Motatu said, "Don't fear. I am with you. Now go quickly. They need you."

Wendy struggled momentarily with her conscience. Motatu had gone silent. It was all up to Wendy, who finally jetted away at light-speed, toward the flaming building and those hapless people trapped on several of the highest floors near the top.

"Remember," Motatu gave her a friendly reminder, "the flames won't hurt you. Time your speed to the task at hand, and we'll get through this without hitching."

During risking this infernal damnation, Wendy found it a little difficult to stifle a mild chuckle over Motatu's mispronounced metaphor.

"I think you meant to say, *without a hitch*," she said, a little mirth in her subtle voice.

As the flames grew more intense, the billowing, black smoke became denser and suffocating. So far, the victims needing emergency rescuing had managed to stay just barely ahead of the deadly, devouring flames. Soon the stairwells became impassable, as heavy metal beams started collapsing; devastating smoke inhalation was causing survivors to pass out under the heavy stress of laboring to breathe.

Three young professional women were trapped on the tenth floor. With flames and toxic smoke closing in, blocking the entrance to the room they were in; they had no way out, except through a huge bay window, which would send them to certain death far below.

Their screams were bloodcurdling; their desperate want and need to survive were unmeasurable as they continued screaming, pressed together in a *final* embrace near the window.

Wendy, unnaturally fleet of foot, raced up a flight of stairs amid deadly flames leaping out at her with fiery tongues. She passed through them at blinding speed, which made her normally solid physical structure appear transparent.

"Blow, Wendy," Motatu's soft whisper instructed her, "Blow out the flames in your path, and all around you. You have the power to freeze this inferno in areas wherever you need to."

"Oh, really?" Wendy wasn't dubious of Motatu; together, they were just too incredibly amazing!

"Well, okay... if you say so. Here goes."

She took a deep breath then let go while flashing up the flight of stairs beyond warp speed. Instantly the path before them became frozen-over, and so went the flames and the deadly smoke, leaving only hissing mist dissolving into fading clouds of white phosphorous plumes.

The emergency crews, in great numbers below, as well as the gathering mass of spectators, were immensely awed—some gawking with apprehension—at the birth of this apparent miracle. High atop the building, where the fire did most of the damage; in a state of disbelief, a captive audience witnessed, first hand, something the mind would never comprehend.   A   hush came over the massive audience as a cloud of engulfing bewilderment. Firefighters ceased spraying their hoses at the permanently distinguished flames.

Rescue helicopters appeared on the scene, as the charred ruins on, and near the top of the building, had been secured for a safe rescue. High atop alongside the building, heavy, thick frozen residue looked like an ice storm had struck the building only in those areas. Realistically, it somewhat appeared haunting against the gloom of lingering white phosphorous mist.

During the rescue of nearly a hundred people, not a single life was lost, and no serious injuries were reported. Wendy, done with the monstrous task, sought a way out without being seen.

She was on the tenth floor, where the three yuppie-girls waited for rescue.

The three girls, waiting impatiently, paced about on thin, melting ice on the floor, with precarious footing. They were neither awed nor mystified by the miraculous distinguishing of the fire; they merely assumed it was modern technology responsible for the mechanics behind the successful operation. As Wendy did some last-minute searching for survivors, with her sharp and penetrating eyesight on hand, at her disposal; at passing glances—wouldn't you know it—she happened to spot the three young girls in that room, beyond the closed door.

Now, Wendy was left trying to figure out a way to get to them without any vivid exposure. That wasn't going to be easy, she realized as she thought it over.

Through the closed door and the outside wall, to inside the closed room, she saw a large trash bin. It was virtually empty and large enough for the three girls to fit inside it, with a little bit of cramped space. In Wendy's rushed decision, it was the only solution she could come up with. The tenth-floor had sustained the most damage, which was where the fire had started earlier. The elevator was inoperable, and the stairs were unstable, brittle, with huge gaps, the entire structure ready to collapse with the slightest pressure applied.

"You can do this, Wendy," Motatu was reassuring, "Look the situation over thoroughly. I can hear your thoughts; they are the same as mine. Go for it."

Wendy realized with what she had in mind would undoubtedly scare the girls, but she would just have to risk it.

She flashed, crashing through the closed door with an awful bang, sending ruptured kindling, splinters of shattered pieces of wood flying about. The girls, altogether, screamed while hitting the floor, covering their heads by folding their arms over them. But before they could process the abrupt interruption in their minds, they were, in a flash, lifted off the floor, placed inside the large trash bin, and rushed out of the room, down a rickety, condemned flight of stairs, and onto the street outside.

The girls' screams were short, as they were jolted into the whirlwind of a mesmeric state of mind, while being placed safely on the ground, in the trash bin—which then toppled over from their combined weight. Spectators, including emergency personnel, only got a fleeting glimpse of what appeared as an apparition that quickly vanished into thin air.

Finally, a medical crew, along with other officials, and some spectators, gradually began gravitating over to the girls to give them assistance. Everyone closes enough to the bedazzling occurrence concerned themselves with what had just happened. They became wary, with skepticism, looking around and about, as if fearing that, perhaps next, a piece of the sky just might fall on them.

The girls were helped free of their confinement inside the trash bin by a couple of police officers, and then delivered over to a medical team, where they were treated for smoke inhalation, and checked for other possible injuries—which there were none.

During this thought-altering upheaval, dense murmuring swelled from the many in rapt curiosity. They shared opinions, questions, fears, optimism, serious concerns. Was this a prelude to what was coming? And what was it that was coming?

"You guys didn't see it?" one of the three girls admitted while being treated by medics.

Her friend, standing close by, was leaned over to her for clarity. She shook her head, "No, Theresa, I didn't see anything. I just felt this big rush of a strong wind. The next thing I knew, we were in that...that...," she stammered nervously with a shaking finger pointing, "that trash container and was brought out here by... *something.*"

The three girls were close together, discussing their clouded views on what they had experienced.

"Well, I saw this face...and hair, but only for a second. Then it was... gone," the third girl said, her voice declining in realizing how silly she must appear to her two friends after that inconceivable remark.

But there were others bewildered, searching for answers, and speculating on their own, as the buzzing among them swelling.

"Was that an alien? Did you see that alien?" a male voice was clear in the mix of other speculative comments, "What was that? The building just froze-over at the top, like someone, just threw a sheet of ice over it. Did you see that?"

"Angel," an elderly lady declared, "It was an angel." The verbal search for answers continued among them in a haze of confusion.

Chapter 10

When Wendy returned to the van, Miss Agnes was waiting behind the wheel. She didn't appear impatient during the wait for Wendy, but the solemn-look on her face was clear to Wendy that something of a serious concern was heavily on her mind.

Wendy kept Miss Agnes in a look of concern as she closed the door. Miss Agnes simply started to drive away.

"I'm sorry for being late," was Wendy's benign apology.

A vague smile touched Agnes' lips, the silver hair, lovely in texture, pushed back on her head and pinned together in a ball; and the caring-look in her soft gaze made clear her loving-grandma disposition.

"Oh, you're not late, honey," she said, "It'll be a little while before the girls are in from school."

She entered the flow of traffic with caution then headed across town, toward the interstate.

Miss Agnes' silence along the way wasn't normal. Whenever she and Wendy took trips into town, or anywhere else, they kept up a lively conversation. And Wendy loved telling little wholesome, family-friendly jokes that made Miss Agnes laugh. But today, something was wrong, and Wendy could only assume the worse as if she didn't have enough stress on her young mind already.

"Miss Agnes," Wendy broke the silence, no longer able to just sit there over on the passenger side, constantly shifting glances at her, "is there something we need to talk about?" Wendy recalled a similar behavior from Agnes when it was thought Elise was up for a possible adoption. It took Agnes quite some time to let it be known to the three of them.

She looked over at Wendy. Through her dark-rimmed glasses, Wendy could tell that her soft, hazel-blue eyes looked a little stormy from stress, which was a show of sadness. Whatever it was she kept from Wendy must've been so heartbreaking.

As Wendy sat back in her seat, has decided not to further press whatever was the issue, Agnes said, "They're closing the foster home."

Wendy's heart sank, and her stare over at Agnes held a thousand aches. She was rendered speechless.

While driving along the interstate, Agnes continued to explain what was necessary, though much to Wendy's dismay. It consisted of when and why, but left Wendy with a very important question, "Will we be separated?"

The look on Agnes' face offered no encouragement. "That hasn't been decided yet, but it's possible."

"The property is being taken over by some land-developers," Agnes said. "They're going to tear down the old place and build a shopping mall in its place. But it's still a little while before all that takes place. I'm almost sure you'll have the rest of the summer together."

"What about you, Miss Agnes? What will you do?" Wendy was deeply concerned about her; she and the girls have grown quite attached to Agnes. Even if, somehow, they were placed together in another foster home, without Miss Agnes, there would still be a huge void in their young lives, which would be a callous move on those in charge.

"Well, honey, I'm retiring after this," Agnes said. She chuckled under her breath.

"I'm getting old."

"Nonsense," Wendy respectfully disagreed, "You're just fine."

"Oh, don't forget that next year, on your birthday, you'll be emancipated." A friendly reminder from Agnes.

But that was even more bad news for Wendy. Yesterday, things were running along smoothly, considering...

Oh, what a difference a day really does make, she was thinking, in the wake of her already building stress.

After the girls got off the bus that afternoon, they strolled along, educating themselves, concerning things about the entities inside them that they should be further aware of beforehand.

"Can we do that trick you guys do by changing ourselves to look like anyone we want?" Monique asked Jor, who hesitated, thinking it over.

"Um...not exactly," she began to explain, "But, you can do objects."

"Objects?" Monique didn't understand.

Neither did Elise, as she said, "Why would we want to look like some silly object?"

As Jor tried to answer Elise's question, Koh said, "I got this. We're a complete, single unit now. As raw energy, shape-changing is unlimited. But once we become a solid, living and breathing organism, the process of shape-changing would become more difficult, not impossible, just more...tricky, you might say. The solidity of our new structure is more confining."

Jor added, "But there's still an advantage with objects. For instance, if you look at an item of clothing that you liked... Well, you can own it."

"How?" Monique asked as they were then walking through the grove, within the shade of foliage cascading over them.

"Look at Elise," Jor said laughingly. At a glance at Elise, Monique was amazed. Elise had on the exact clothing as she had on—the same color top, jeans, and snickers. They looked like twins, except for their obvious difference in skin-tone. It was hilariously weird; the transformation was like magic.

Elise laughed, "How'd that happen? I didn't do it."

"I did," Koh laughed, "By simple concentration on any item of clothing you like."

Elise and Monique were enthralled over this discovery.

"This is great!" Elise shouted, glad-face. "We can have any style of clothing we want."

"And Wendy doesn't have to bother making us anymore, which most of the time she messes them up," Monique carelessly criticized.

A little farther on, Elise suddenly held up in her pace then said to Monique, with the sentiment, "Wait. We can't do that."

Monique, holding up beside her, asked, "Why?"

"Because..." Elise drawled. "It would hurt her feelings. And besides, if we started dressing up in expensive clothes, people at school would start asking questions...thinking we have lots of money, not to mention how jealous some of the kids will get, especially that Brittany Stewart."

Monique stomped a foot, agitated, "Doggonit! I hate it when you're right! But, wait," Monique suddenly thought., "Can Wendy do the same thing?"

"Sure," Jor made clear. "You all can."

"That's good," Monique was happy to learn as they continued through the grove, "She shouldn't be left out."

"Remember," Jor added. "All three of you have the same powers. Just Motatu and Wendy don't like to fly."

"Flying's too weird," Elise said.

Koh and Jor laughed quietly.

Once they cleared the grove, they discovered Wendy sitting on the porch, in one of the chairs. She looked a little depressed, sitting there with her head down in her hands.

The girls looked at one another quizzically for a moment, continuing while wondering what was wrong with her. Normally, she was in good spirit. They didn't get it. Before they'd passed through the grove, Elise had on her own attire—a skirt, and an impressive copy of an Adidas top, made by Wendy. Monique's beige blouse was a product of Wendy's also.

Wendy casually regarded them as they walked up on the porch by raising her head, greeting them in a rather sullen fashion, barely uttering, "Hi, guys," with a weak toss of her hand to them.

"Why're you so happy?" Elise quipped. She and Monique walked over to her caringly, Elise slipping an arm around Wendy's shoulders, concerned.

To look them in their innocent faces was hard to do, as her gaze shifted away solemnly.

"Are you okay?" Monique asked empathically.

Wendy nodded with a vague, arid smile that barely shaped her lips.

"We nearly beat-up a girl today," Elise said to spark her spirit.

Wendy glared at them. "Are you serious?"

"No," Elise laughed. "I just wanted to see the change in your expression."

Then it was back to her misery. She sank back in the chair, her depression unchanged. "Guys, there's something you should know," she said regretfully.

"Who died?" Monique felt a rise of impending disappointment. A great disappointment. The kind you didn't get over soon. "Are you about to get adopted?"

"No," Wendy replied, that time, with a little chuckle in her voice, thinking how Monique loved to kid around.

"Well, then am I? Because, if it is, I won't go. I swear it!" Monique fervently declared.

"No!" Wendy stressed, almost to the point of laughing as she got to her feet, which was an indicator that they should follow her upstairs, and to her room. And they did.

Miss Agnes was in making dinner as the girls headed upstairs to Wendy's room. Once inside, she closed the door, then leaned against it a bit, gathering her thoughts. This time, her bed was free of patterns lying about, so Elise and Monique sprawled out on the clean bed, braced for the anticipated bad news.

Wendy then moved idly away from the door, concentrating on where to start. It wasn't easy. She could've used Miss Agnes' help, but she was busy making dinner.

Wendy took a breath, sat down on the end of her bed, with the girls sprawled face down, with their heads turned to her attentively. The explanation was brief and paraphrased, to make it plain and simple. When she was done, they knew the whole story. Neither was acceptance of the news, including Wendy, but they had no choice but to digest it anyway. It was a hard pill to swallow.

During a couple of weeks that past, Wendy, and the girls did very well in their readjustments. In realizing their continued stay at Lily Field Foster Home was now limited, they sat out to concentrate on an alternative method in which they were to survive and continue functioning normally. Their biggest concern, however, rested on the outcome of their re-establishment. Would, by some miracle, they'd remained together, not separated?

"Wendy, once you're emancipated, maybe *you* could adopt us," Monique suggested idealistically, with a cheerful grin.

They were out walking in the countryside, not far away from the orphanage, along with some shallow wooded area. It was also a rural district, where there were widely scattered residential homes, along with a few government-subsidized farms. The air held a vague smell of distant dust from tractors plowing in the fields, and the sky was becoming dismal with building cumulonimbus—better understood as thunderclouds.

Elise added a little elation, "You sure could. That would make you our mom."

Wendy leaned forward in the girls' faces, with the stern remark, "Don't you ever dare call me mom!"

Monique dared to tease, "Why not... Mom?"

Wendy flew into a jovial rage, suddenly giving chase to Monique, but only in their normal, gangly clumsy, *human* fashion, Monique squealing, frolicking at a disadvantage, as Wendy kept yelling futilely, "You get back here! I'm not playing with you!"

The fun-chase—laughing, giggling—was momentary; then off they were again, walking along while chatting; they'd managed to drift some ways off their intended course, which was to stop at the corner store, near the orphanage, for some snacks from a vending machine—Wendy's treat, because she had all the cash from her sewing earnings.

But, instead, they finally ended up near the lake some five miles east of where they had begun. The lake was beautiful at that time of the year; sparkling, deep blue water, with gentle waves splashing along the shoreline. Far out across the way, the blue water held a sunlit glitter that tended to pervade beyond infinity. It was a formidable, breathtaking scenery, worthy of photography, or a landscape painter's paradise. However, the sky was still dim by heavy clouds growing darker and denser. Far off in the distance, the occasional soft rumbling of thunder was mildly carried across the gentle waves.

"Maybe we'd better head back," Wendy wisely suggested, studying the deep gray sky a moment.

"Oh, it's not gonna rain," Monique said under hoped. "We hardly get to spend time together, like now. Let's stay a while longer."

Jor shrewdly announced, "If worse comes to worse, you can always fly."

All eyes went to Monique accusingly, where Jor was hiding inside. Monique miffed, "I didn't say that! But, I guess it's comforting to know."

"Okay," Wendy agreed. "I guess staying a little while longer won't hurt. There is something else I'd like to tell you guys."

Heart-dropping time...again. Monique and Elise prepared themselves for another disappointment.

"Haven't we had enough bad news happen to us? When will it end?" Monique griped.

Wendy moved over to a boulder protruding out of the ground, in a grassy area along the shore, and took a seat there. The girls joined her, choosing their own protruding rocks close by, as there were quite a few scattered about.

Monique, sadly ready for another grand-slammed disappointment, "Okay, let's have it. Should we, maybe, consider really beating-up someone?" That was a joke. But Monique was just about teetering on the verge of a harsh seriousness.

"Maybe I should've told you guys about what had happened a couple of weeks ago," Wendy began. She was sitting there, staring in thought, far out across the way.

"What happened a couple of weeks ago?" Elise asked, very attentive to up-coming explanations. Monique, on the other hand, was disillusioned from any further stress. She lay in the grass, closer to Elise than to Wendy, looking at the gathering, heavy gray clouds in the darkening sky, trying to set her mind adrift to avoid the pain of yet another tumultuous disappointment she feared

Wendy was about to share with them.

Wendy leaned over toward Monique lying in the cushioning grass, to make sure she had her attention.

"Monique are you listening?" she asked. "I'm listening," Monique responded unattentively while dawdling with nearly a handful of dandelions.

Wendy gave her a fleeting glance in disbelief then continued, "You may have seen on the news about a fire that occurred downtown, a couple of weeks ago."

"Who watches the news?" Monique said, inattentive.

"We should start," Wendy suggested.

"Who we've become; it wouldn't hurt if we kept up with current events." Wendy looked away, her mind bombarded with thoughts. Then she brought her gaze back to the girls. "Two weeks ago, there was this huge fire, and...I was needed."

"Why?" Elise didn't understand, sitting on a smaller rock close to Wendy, with her arms clamped around her raised knee. Monique...still more attentive to the dandelions, lightly blowing off their delicate fuzzy caps, and watching them flutter in the soft wind.

"Because we have these...*gifts,*" Monique said, then added, "You know what the 'O' in orphan stands for?"

She went on to answer it herself, "*Organized* Disappointments."

Wendy said immediately, "There's no 'D' an orphan."

Monique raised up, stiffened, and shouted, "That's the disappointment!"

Wendy leered at her then continued, "There was this building in flames. People were trapped. I had to save them."

"Of course, you did." Elise saw no error in Wendy's judgment.

"How did you save them?" Monique said. She was more attentive, having relaxed, braced on her elbows, with her head turned to peer at Wendy.

"I blew out the fire," Wendy said, a subtle, small amount of pride in her tempered voice.

Monique sprang to her feet, wide-eyed. "All by yourself?" She looked around excitedly, aimlessly, and in realizing she couldn't look either Jor nor the other two entities inside them, in the eye; she resolved to yell into the open, "Jor, can we do that?"

"Sure." Jor was calm, collected. "You don't have to shout."

"Wow!" Monique was impressed. "Then what happened? Did anyone see you?"

"I don't think so," Wendy said, looking back to that fateful mishap.

"I was very careful... and very fast!"

Then Wendy took a different approach to the subject, as she'd been giving her bizarre rescue a lot of thought and had arrived at a decision—hopeful that would help them to settle into this new reality of themselves and to live among society with a successful co-existent achievement.

She continued, "I think I have an idea, which may be a solution to our situation."

The girls were ready to listen. Even Monique was done with the dandelions, as she moved over and sat beside Wendy, sharing the bolder. Ever since she could long remember, she'd regarded Wendy as her pretend-mom, and then, later, her pretend-big sister. Now, the three of them had become a self-appointed family.

Wendy went on to say, "What we now give us the right to stick together, no matter what. If we must take matters into our own hands, then we must. We need each other now more than we ever have. If we are forced, by the State Department, to be separated; we cannot allow that to happen, even if we have to become fugitives...on our own."

Monique wanted to be clear, "Outlaws?"

Elise chimed in, bemused, "I thought were the good guys."

Chapter 11

A different type of helicopter flew over as the girls had started their extensive trek back to the orphanage. It was sure to become a washout, the way those dark clouds appeared before they reached home.

It was a commercial helicopter, with *WCGN TV NEWS-CHANNEL 5* stenciled on the outer body, flying at an altitude low enough that the girls could clearly read the lettering. But it passed over so quickly they scantly noticed, except for the noise of the rotary blades, though the chopper and the noise soon fading in the distance.

The girls were walking alongside a dirt road that led through some woods shortly ahead. Conventional traffic no longer used it, only heavy-duty, motorized farm equipment. The girls were about to disappear among deep shadows of trees, heading through the woods, when the faint sound of a repeating horn rose from a far distance out across the lake.

The source of the repetitive beeping was so far away that it was invisible to the naked eye, but it was a mechanized object—like a boat of some kind. And it was becoming annoying, and disturbing to the girls, as they paused from continuing through the woods, listening intensely. They soon realized it was a distress signal, coming from far out across the lake.

"Is someone in trouble out there?" Monique was first to acknowledge.

Then the three of them turned around, exercising precaution as they moved attentively back toward the lake, to the continuous beeping sound carrying across the subtle waves. With their ultra-keen eye-sights, they focused on the direction the, almost, rhythmic beeping arose.

They saw the object; it was a party barge with people aboard, but some were in the water—kids too—splashing about. Ordinarily, that was common; but April wasn't the time, during the warming season, for swimming.

"That's trouble," Wendy was certain.

"Look closely," Motatu suggested. "Look close, through my eyes."

The three of them looked closer through the eyes of the entities inside them, and magnification was clear up-close and finely defined. Some small children and adults alike were in the water without any life-preservatives; and the people still aboard was doomed as well, as the boat was slowly sinking, taking in water from the rear. The girls' keen hearing also picked up the screaming in dire stress from the passengers. In a matter of minutes, the struggling survivors would become a memory, if some miracle didn't take place, and soon.

Monique reacted pitiably, instantly misty-eyed, to cloud her sharp vision.

"We gotta help them," she whimpered.

"I know," Wendy said. "This is what I was afraid of."

"We have no choice," Elise said in mistaking Wendy for being selfish and unwilling.

But she wasn't. "I know. Let's go, and make it fast," Wendy kindly urged.

They hit the water like torpedoes, skimming across the lake toward the pending disaster at jet-speed.

"Submerge!" Wendy shouted as they rapidly closed in on the troubled area.

"You guys," Motatu assured them, "we'll help you to breathe underwater. *Don't worry!*"

"We know. We trust you," Elise yelled, to add a little bright-side to the *grim situation: "Be happy!" (a Bob Marley popular hit tune).*

At blinding speed, the girls disappeared underwater. A young teenaged girl was sinking for the last time, with her mom desperately holding onto her, trying to keep her precious child afloat, but was fighting a losing battle; their blood-curdling screams for help unheard, as the extreme emergency cries among others heightened.

Suddenly, at the noise of a rush of water, the mother and daughter were abruptly catapulted safely back aboard the barge as another force of rushing water restored the sinking boat back to its upright position; and was drained dry of excess water simultaneously. Underneath the barge, Wendy repaired a gaping hole in the bottom, near the rear, with lasers from her eyes.

The spectacular phenomena persisted until all passengers in the water were safely air-lifted and placed unharmed back on board the barge, by some unseen, divine intervention. The only fleeting hints the driver of the boat *thought* he saw was formless images vanish into a thin, lingering mist, which had been brought on by the previous disturbance in the water.

The young man shook his head disbelievingly because he was still under tremendous stress, dazed, his mind in disarray. Ask him, once he was cleared of total insanity, and he might disclose that he'd seen the images of something in the half-forms of three teen-aged girls—two of them very young—simply vanish into thin air, just above the surface of the lake.

The helicopter from earlier had returned just prior to the conclusion of the blissful melee in the water; the pilot caught only a small portion of the disruption on film, perhaps not enough deserving to view. He was on a reconnaissance mission, assigned by the news team he worked for. This was unexpected. If anything, news-worthy caught on film of this event was pure luck.

The girls returned to shore dripping wet, the noise of the helicopter a little annoying as it began fading in the distance, leaving the area.

"I hate getting wet if I'm not in the shower, or it's not swimming season," Monique complained, pressing water out of hair with both hands, "Maybe I should shake like a dog, to get dry."

She was joking; however, Wendy took immediate action in protesting, "No, don't do that. That's ugly."

"Ew...gross!" Elise frowned with distaste.

Monique laughed, "I was just kidding!"

As they resumed their trip home along the dirt road, the fading noise of the distant helicopter aroused cautious-Wendy's awareness for the first time. "Was that helicopter here while we were out there?" She was speaking of the raucous water-rescue.

Elise shrugged her shoulders; Monique, uncertain also, replied, "I'm not sure."

"Great," Wendy worried. "That's all we need...to have our pictures taken."

"Taken of what?" Monique raised the question. "No one saw us."

Their triumphant results allowed Elise a jubilant, little chuckle as she commented, "They may've gotten pictures of lots of people freaking out."

Wendy complimented the girls, along with feeling a spiritual reward from helping those innocent people back there, "You guys did a heck of a great job back there. I'm very proud of you."

"Don't count yourself out," Monique said thoughtfully. "It was all of our doing."

A wan smile from Wendy. Then she said, surrendering to the innate compassion she held for others; plus, the added benign influence from the entity inside her, "I realize that. That's why we need to prepare for long-term involvement in society. Instead of hiding or trying to run away from who we are now; we must embrace it, put it to good use.

"But, we gotta remember, we can't serve as global police; we have to understand we can only do so much."

Once they were home and walking up the steps, Wendy shared with them one final detail. "There's one other thing we have to consider," she said, "I'll explain it to you, once we're upstairs, which we must get started on right away."

Elise and Monique looked at one another as if thinking, "When will it end?"

Miss Agnes was in doing the laundry, as the automatic washing machine was going out back, on the encased back porch. It wasn't time for supper, as Saturday afternoon was still early— only a couple of hours' past lunch. It was pouring down rain, so much that visibility was restricted to only a short distance ahead. The murky sky held a deep gray, half-light, insufficient for safe travel by automobile, yet traffic flowed right along precariously, with headlights blaring in the heavy spray of rain.

The girls were in Wendy's room, relaxing on her bed, as usual, while she sat at her sewing machine, busy putting patterns together. When they had just come in, Miss Agnes had handed Wendy some clothing items that needed mending from a few outside customers. There was no rush on the orders, and Wendy had promised to have them done in a few days. Right now, a matter of urgency was bearing down on her.

"Today, we were lucky; the other week, I was," she said, paying more attention to working her pattern into position to begin stitching than to the girls.

"This is an idea I've been contemplating for some time now. After today's incident, it's clear to me now that this little idea of mine just might work."

"So, you're actually making our costumes," Monique found amusing.

Wendy laughed over at them. "Take it as a joke, if you want. But it worked for all superheroes; Batman, Superman, Wonder Woman. And how about Supergirl? She has her own TV series now."

Elise pointed out frankly, "But none of those characters are *real*. And we'd still look like idiots, flying, no matter what we were wearing."

"We'd look like idiots in clown suits," Monique giggled.

Wendy said in hilarity, "I'm not trying to glamorize your appearances; I'm only trying to fix it, so you won't be so easily recognized. No one said you *must fly!*"

Elise's mind shifted back to that near tragedy on the party barge, and on a serious note, she said, "I sure hope those people made it off the lake safely."

Monique blurted, sounding uncaring, "Are you kidding? Didn't you guys hear that boat hauling ass once we left?" She laughed in further saying, "I think that driver believed he'd gotten lost in the Bermuda Triangle!"

Both Wendy and Elise gaped at her with jaws dropped, stunned! Elise was first to respond, "Potty-mouth!"

"Monique!" Wendy was astounded, "Where did that come from?"

But, after a while, struggling to stifle their laughs, both Wendy and Elise let it rip. And the three had a belly-laugh, with Elise and Monique rolling on the bed, holding their stomachs. Wendy had to suspend her stitching, to catch her breath, as the three of them enjoyed a side-splitting, gut-busting, good laugh, at the expense of Monique's Potty-mouth and insensitive comment. And, deservingly so, that relieved a huge amount of pressure off them, temporarily.

Chelsea had stayed up late nights, studying the film she'd caught on her favorite, tiny toy, that miniature camcorder she'd left in that makeshift, government facility. She'd gotten nothing interesting, for the most part on film, except during a portion when the camera must have fallen, or accidentally knocked to the floor.

Up until then, there was nothing but scrapings of broken twigs, loose leaves, and other discarded debris, like bits of paper, and broken pencils. Nothing that readily caught the eye. However, near the end of the recording, something of a vague interest did appear on film but was cut short, as the filming mechanism quit working, which must have been caused by the jolt when it hit the floor.

What little Chelsea could gather for her efforts was something brought in on a small tray, by one of the workers, that held a high gloss of a bluish-green hue as she passed before the hidden camera. It didn't appear like an ordinary plant. If anything, it closely resembled some type of carnivorous plant, which is not indigenous to this Country. What little glance she'd gotten of the thing, in some sense, it appeared alive, though lying dormant. Perhaps it was the intense glow it emitted. Plus, she only got a glimpse of it. The one thing she was certain of, however, the government wasn't just out, treating vegetation. They were on to something big! And she wanted in on it.

It had been about two weeks since that major fire in downtown Grand City. As far as public knowledge, the so-called mysterious appearance of ghosts, to assist in the rescue of those hundreds of potential victims, was dissolved before any rumors of supernatural beings, or aliens had gotten off the ground. It was chalked-up as anxiety attacks, accelerated stress. As for the three girls, they decided between themselves not to delve into the bizarre, for fear of jeopardizing their job security, and magnificent careers. So, Wendy did very well in covering her tracks.

Chelsea had missed-out due to an assignment out of town on that day. In the driving rain, she took a trip back to the government compound, hopeful to stumble upon something deserving of her friendly visit, since the media was made welcome to come at any time. Jim rode along for company. The one thing she never quite got the hang of was driving in a heavy downpour, which it was, at the time, with no let-up in sight.

The hard rain ahead dispensed a heavy, dark gray mist and dense spray, making it extremely difficult to navigate the roadway, even at a slow speed. Motorists in a rush went by her and Jim, condensing the hazardous conditions even worse, risking a higher rate of speed.

"Jerk!" Chelsea yelled to the windshield in futile anger at the spurious guy ahead, in a Silverado.

He went through two yellow lights about to turn; and right through a red light. Luckily, the intersection wasn't as busy.

"Why do these blithering idiots wait for in climate weather to drive like a bat out of hell?"

Jim chuckled, "You want me to drive?"

"A fine time to ask," she grumbled under her breath.

He went silent, refocusing through the windshield, on his side.

They finally arrived at the modified warehouse, through the heavy rain and dense mist. But it was to Chelsea's great disappointment; Jim sat there over on the passenger side calm, poised.

The place was abandoned. Vacant, densely hazed in the deluge, the entire area resembling a ghost town, like in some forlorn villa, set within the gray misty gloom and driving rain.

Chelsea drove up to the metal gate, which stood open and deserted, quietly creaking in a slow swaying motion caused by the movement of a subtle wind.

"Oh, this is just great!" Chelsea scoffed. She sat there, frustrated.

"What'd you hope to find out here?" Jim asked.

No reply. She just put the car in reverse offendedly, but with enough poise to back out cautiously.

"Did you know they had left the area?" she asked Jim.

He shook his head. "No, I didn't. But earlier this afternoon, I spotted a line of government vehicles headed out of town, from the air. I was on this recon like you asked me; that's when I happened to see them headed north of town."

She stared at him accusingly. But, in realizing she was only to blame for not telling him in the first place where they were going, her stare softened, and she looked away.

Jim said, after a brief silence, "Did you hear of anything that may've happened out at the lake this afternoon?"

"No, I haven't."

Chelsea looked straight ahead, soberly concentrating on her driving, and on the road ahead, in the sudden, late afternoon. After Jim didn't reply right away, she stared at him, wondering why he didn't continue. He'd opened the door to a curiosity, but then just left her hanging.

She finally went on to ask, "What happened at the lake?" In her mind, she was thinking, "*You dodo!*"

"Oh, nothing," he said.

"It's just that...," He had to rationalize what glimpse he'd gotten on the return trip to the lake.

"Well, I was in the chopper, panning the area—I spotted three teenaged girls walking along, by the way. Anyway, I saw this party barge on the lake, full of people, like they were on some sort of excursion. Then I left the area, but only for a moment. When I returned, something was happening with the boat. It looked as if it was caught in some...weird, huge...," He couldn't quite get it together, gesturing with his hands, holding them apart, facing her.

"Some giant waves," he went on. "It was the craziest thing, I thought, that I'd ever seen. But it lasted only for a moment, like some type of huge undercurrent rose from the depth. It was really crazy!"

More interested than not, Chelsea held him in her stare, uncertain what to think of his account of the incident he'd claimed to have witnessed.

"What happened to the boat?" she asked, her interest increasing.

"Nothing," he said with a slight shrug of his shoulders. "It just kept on going, after settling down. And it was full of people... kids, and families."

If there was any truth to what he'd just explained, maybe it was worth a further look in to, Chelsea was thinking.

"What was their reactions?"

"I couldn't really tell that high-up," he said.

"You didn't drop lower, to get a better look?" she asked disappointedly.

"No, I just got out of there, since everyone seemed okay," he casually replied.

"Of course, you did," she murmured her sarcasm, with mild disgust, buried under her breath.

"Well, did those three girls you mentioned—the teenagers— seemed to have noticed what went on with the boat?" she went on to ask, despite his idiocy.

"No, they were too far away, walking along the shore," he said. "The party barge was way out in the lake. I doubt if they could even see it that far out." Then he cocked his head in thought, as he recalled something about the girls' location that he figured was rather odd.

So, he said, as an afterthought, "But you know, when I think of it, those girls appeared to be a long way from home, wherever they lived."

"Oh?" Chelsea shifted a glance over to him without much interest, "Why?"

"Well, they were in the middle of nowhere, just walking along. I mean it was miles to the nearest settlement. And I saw no vehicle of any kind near that they could've been riding in."

"Well, it could've been anywhere." Chelsea didn't claim that as a probable cause of interest. There's so much brush and trees...it could've been parked a mile away, among some trees—who knows?"

She was done with that issue. But then a thought occurred to her, just sort of a wild thought, so she decided to ask, "You didn't happen to take pictures of what happened with the boat, did you?"

Jim answered, unabashed of his thoughtlessness, "No, I shut the camera off before I returned to the scene and forgot to hit the on button again. But I did get pictures of the girls when I first flew over."

"Naturally," she said with a very low opinion of him, thinking, why did she keep him on as a photographer. Certainly, there were other good helicopter pilots out there somewhere.

"So, you filmed three teenaged girls out for an afternoon stroll, but didn't think to catch the so-called weird incident with the boat-load of people being tossed about during some...some freak-wave, you say?"

Then she muttered again under her breath, "Pervert!"

"Huh?" He didn't hear her.

"Nothing," she said begrudgingly.

"If by now, they've obtained hosts, it would be impossible to detect them by any devices we have," Jillian explained to her crew.

Having wrapped up the assignment in Grand City, the team of Special Government Agents returned to Headquarters at GSW, where they would resume a continuous watch to locate the aliens, and to form an investigating team to scout areas near and far. Colonel Gordon, his staff of officers, and special coordinators attended the conference, as Jillian continued her briefing on this top priority issue. She had the floor, idly pacing lightly with poise and concentration.

"Ladies and gentlemen, there's no pertinent reason to think that these entities have been dissolved into raw energy by this atmosphere. They're experts at finding hosts. Their purpose for being here is to find a host. Our population here, alone, would supply enough...subjects to fulfill that task."

Agent Rooker pointed out, "So, the hosts themselves would be the catalyst to expose the aliens."

"That's correct," Jillian confirmed.

"There's been disreputable reports on a bizarre incident that happened at a fire downtown, a couple of weeks ago," Ed made mention.

"It was believed that three young girls, with brilliant careers, were, apparently trapped on the tenth floor of the building aflame. However, it was reported that they ended up safely outside, in a large trash bin. Some elderly lady claimed an angel was responsible for getting them out safely."

"Was it reported how, or why, they ended up in the trash bin?" Jillian raised the question, somewhat curious.

Ed groped, then replied, "No… My guess is delirium. In such a mass of confusion, that old lady could've imagined anything of a supernatural nature."

"Did anyone with credibility speak to the lady?" Susan asked, "like a news reporter?"

"I never saw it appear in any newspaper, or on TV," Ed concluded.

"Mm…Angels, huh?" Jillian sort of mulled over the idea to herself.

Then she continued, "Entities doesn't necessarily have to be evil by design, especially this type. Remember the sheriff's and his deputies' reports; every report specifically pointed out that the believed aliens were warm, friendly-natured, and were like children—little girls."

"Oh, get out," Ed laughed. "That's ridiculous. Angels? *Ha!*"

Jillian went on to further make clear, "For what we do know about outer space; there are tons of mysteries out there that we don't know. They could be metaphysical beings."

Jillian's stunning remark jolted Susan.

Are you serious? Are you suggesting they're angels?"

A gleam of confidence in Jillian's stare at Susan, and Ed as she confirmed her belief, "There may be angels."

Colonel Gordon, a mundane type of person all his life, interrupted in a stern belief, "People, as far as we know, there could be an invasion fleet on the way as we speak! Enough of this nonsense about angels. According to the myth, lest we forget: There are also *devil's angels!*"

Ed said as kindly as he could get the words out of his mouth, "Colonel, it's your job to defend against an invasion."

"Sir," the colonel replied, "the military is ready."

Chapter 12

Since it was the weekend—and a wet one, as rain continued to fall—the girls were up over half the night, being fitted for special garments designed by their big sister Wendy. To Monique and Elise, she had this hair-brain idea to make them outfits suited for their special abilities. It would hide their true identities, Wendy felt certain. Monique had accused her of making them *flying* suits, which she totally rejected the idea.

"They're not flying suits; now hold still while I measure this." Wendy held up to Monique's chest a piece of black cloth cut into a top just her size. She'd already sewn together with a pair of black, skin-tight pants so snugly-fitting that they looked like a second skin.

"I'm not wearing this." Monique was annoyingly dis-agreeable. She was more difficult than Elise in cooperating with Wendy. "Monique... Gosh, girl. Just hold still!"

"Alright, I'm holding still." Monique finally quit fidgeting long enough to try on that disgusting, too-tight-a-fitting top.

"There." Wendy beamed at her, smiling to that small accomplishment.

"I think it looks great," Elise said, hopping off the end of Wendy's bed. Then she sashayed over to Wendy and Monique, who were over by the sewing machine where a pile of unfinished, loose patterns lay about the sewing-desk.

Elise held up, critiquing Monique at arms-length away, nodding her head in agreement. "Not bad, Wendy..."

"Liar!" Monique pouted, shifting her fervent, disagreeing-look to each of them. Elise had on red, a complete bodysuit of a glossy, apple-red. Under intense light, like the sunlight, it had a tenuous fluorescent effect.

Monique then shifted her attention only to Wendy, asking, "Where's your suit?"

Then, with thought, she said, "Oh, that's right, you don't fly."

"That doesn't mean I don't need a disguise," Wendy said. "Don't worry, I've already finished with mine. Once we're all done, we'll check them out together."

Monique settled down considerably, having decided to fully cooperate with the majority. Well, she was in a difficult situation anyway; she had no choice.

It was nearing three o'clock a.m., when the three of them finally stood before the mirror, looking at themselves over of Wendy's sewing technique. She did a great job, which said a lot, coming from her worse critic, Monique.

"Not bad, Wendy. It'll make a nice un-scary Halloween costume," she said.

"It's not supposed to be scary," Wendy made clear. Then, after carefully looking them over, Wendy noticed something not quite satisfying to her.

"Mm… Something's missing," she said. It was about the girls' snug outfits. It wasn't the shoes, for they were all barefoot; that concern would come later.

Elise in her nifty, apple-red skin-tights; Monique in midnight black. Both outfits were stunning, gave them a completely different personality, with a lurid appeal. Wendy's outfit, for the purpose, was complete, a brilliantly-designed royal blue, with white lightning bolts on the arms and legs, enhancing her lovely, young figure; and she looked drop-dead gorgeous in those skin-tight.

"What's missing?" Elise said, puzzled. "I think we look great. I admit, before we — "

"Capes!" It suddenly came to Wendy.

"Capes?" Monique and Elise said simultaneously.

"Yes, I think it'll be very effective for you guys," Wendy said affably.

Jor spoke through Monique, "It'll become you when you're flying."

Monique took a rigid stand. "We're *not flying!*"

"Okay, you're not flying," Jor conceded. "You don't have to be mud stuck on a stick."

"What?" Monique frowned, confused.

"A stick-in-the-mud; she meant the old saying, you don't have to be a stick in the mud." Wendy made clear.

"Oh," Monique laughed.

Jor spoke "Whatever. Just do the cape...thing."

"Gotcha," Wendy went back over to her sewing machine and got busy.

Nearly an hour later, Elise and Monique stood, once again, before the mirror, decked-out in spiffy capes that reached the calves of their legs. Elise's was a solid red, while Monique's was solid black. They wore a waistband; Monique's was silver, Elise was yellow-gold that matched her satin blond hair. Monique was simply dashing in her black and silver. The three of them stood before the mirror, reviewing themselves for the final time, Wendy's contrasting, white waistband the perfect choice with her royal blue bodysuit, with the white lightning bolts streaking along the arms and legs.

"Shoes," Elise said. "What about shoes?"

"Or boots." Wendy had a better idea.

"Fashionable boots...I saw a pair of *SEVENTEEN* that'll go perfectly with this outfit. They're silver. Here, I'll show you," Monique said elatedly.

She ran over and got the magazine off the nightstand beside the bed, opened it to the page the silver boots were on and showed them to Wendy and Elise.

"Hey, those are cool," Elise marveled.
Wendy agreed, "Oh, they *are* cool."

Jor again, "Now, here's what you do: Take a good look at them, then concentrate."

Wendy waited with an anticipating-look on her face, then was amazed by the magic right before her eyes.

"Whoa," she said. "How'd that happened?" She wasn't there when the entities exhibited that bit of talent to Elise and Monique.

"Sorry, Wendy," Motatu explained. "It's transformation. I never told you about that."

"No, you certainly did not," Wendy was astounded, gaping at the gleaming silver boots, now snug on Monique's feet. "Can I do the same thing?"

"Sure," Motatu assured her.

"What I have in mind is not in the magazine," Wendy made known.

"Have you ever seen the kind you want... just anywhere, at any time?"

"Let's see..." Wendy looked away in concentration.

Then she said excitedly, "Oh, oh...I remember now! It was a month or so ago. There were these perfect, white boots at JCPenney's! Can I have them? Or is it too late..."

Motatu delighted to inform her, "It's never too late. Just remember, then concentrate."

Within a minute, the transformation was complete. Wendy stood there in those gorgeous, white boots, comfortably hugging the calves of her legs. She bounced up and down on her toes in a childish excitement. "They feel great!" she shouted.

Laughing, Elise needed no further instructions. She already knew the procedure, as within moment, she was wearing spiffy, yellow-gold boots she recalled noticing while window-shopping downtown, some time ago.

At the results of their fantasies coming true with the aid of their unusually talented, *special* guests; they busted a happy dance-move, rocking away all over Wendy's cluttered bedroom, the uniforms flashing their brilliant colors.

The noise of them carrying on so late brought a knock on the door.

"Girls?"

That was Miss Agnes! They quickly ceased the vivacious celebration, in hopes she wouldn't come barging in, the way they were dressed.

"Quickly...think back to your regular clothes," Jor speedily warned them. Morphing back into their normal civvies was a cinch, as Miss Agnes respectfully only poke her head in the doorway after she'd opened it.

The girls were seated on the end of the bed, with a feigned-look of innocence on their faces, as if to fool the wise, older lady into thinking she'd made a mistake in hearing noises that weren't there.

But Miss Agnes, knowing better, merely gave them her usual warm smile, saving them the trouble of lying, "You girls have a good night."

"Goodnight, Miss Agnes," they kindly said together.

She headed back downstairs.

The girls high-fived each other before sinking into a blissful night of slumber.

Wendy yawned, half-stretched then told the girls, "All right you guys, off my bed and to your own room. It's been a long night for us."

Monique and Elise dragged themselves across the room, toward the door.

"Goodnight, Wendy," they both said, languidly heading out the door.

"Goodnight, guys," Wendy said, Elise closing the door behind them.

Jor said as the girls were headed to their room, "Tomorrow would be a good time to practice flying."

"No flying!" Monique shouted, abruptly interrupting her.

"We'd look silly!" Elise agreed as they went inside their room for the remainder of the soggy wet night, soft rumbles of distant thunder infrequent on such a rainy night.

Monday morning, it was back to school. The girls had finished breakfast and were headed for the front door with their backpacks strapped to their backs. The early-morning news report was airing on the big-screen TV set in the living room as the girls were about to head out the door. Miss Agnes was in her favorite, leather recliner with a half-folded newspaper on her lap. Wendy was in the kitchen, tidying up after breakfast. Everything ran along routinely until the news broadcasted on television made a distracting announcement, while running footage.

"Eight-year-old, Amy Holland and her five-year-old, younger brother, Timothy are still missing since early Saturday this past weekend..."

The doleful announcement grabbed both girls' attentions as they walked by. Their initial reactions were to pause and stare at one another, though careful not to attract Miss Agnes' attention.

Trying not to appear conspicuous in listening to the news broadcast, they dragged their feet, watching a balding guy on TV go on about two kids lost in the woods, which took place over the weekend.

"The authorities have employed   friends of the family, neighbors, and family members to join in the search."

As the announcer continued with explicit details, the story became darker, hopeless of a happy conclusion.

"With the heavy rain over the weekend pelting the land like a monsoon. There was flash flooding in low areas, some wind-damages to farms, along with a few residential homes—noncritical—but in the area, the two children were reported missing."

"Hey, you guys...you gonna miss your bus," Wendy appeared from the kitchen, distracting them.

"What's so important on TV?"

Monique and Elise each looked over to Miss Agnes. She wasn't paying attention to much of anything. She was leaned back in the recliner, nearly asleep, with the newspaper on her lap, her glasses pulled down on her nose.

"Nothing," Elise said to Wendy as she and Monique continued out the door.

Wendy was never the wiser about the news broadcast, nor had the gripping story reached the newspapers, like the one Agnes cradled on her lap.

"There had to be something to ruin the whole day! Do you think they'll find them OK?" Monique lamented, glassy-eyed from a stir of emotions

"It's hard to say." Elise was being truthful when you consider the atrocious weather condition over the weekend. They looked at one another, sharing the same sentiments for the lost children. But they also realized that no power on Earth, or in outer space—without knowing the kids' location—would benefit the cause. What loomed the largest was the doubt that, because of the brutal weather, such small children stood the smallest chance to survive an unforgiving savagery of nature.

"We shouldn't kid ourselves," Monique came to terms in realizing the odds were stacked against them, which included everyone involved; the authorities, the family members, friends, and neighbors.

It became clear that Elise could read Monique's thoughts, as she had taken on a far-away-look in her stare.

Then she brought her gaze back to Elise, who said, "Monique, I understand... But we wouldn't know where to start. Remember what Wendy said, that we can't be the world's police."

"We're not cops, and this isn't the whole world." Monique was being difficult. "It wouldn't hurt to look. We're much faster..."

Koh added affably, "And you can fly. Remember that; it makes a huge difference."

This time, the girls didn't fidget over the idea; they remained calm, thoughtful, as Elise finally commented, "Too bad we never even bothered to test ourselves in flying."

"I guess it would make a difference," Monique admitted with regret.

"Even if we did decide to help in the search, we wouldn't have time to practice flying," Elise pointed out.

"No better time than now."

The way Monique sounded, Elise knew she wasn't about to give up on the idea of trying to find those two missing kids. And rightly so.

The way Monique felt was simple. What was the use of having those powers and not use them to help those in need... especially the severity of this case?

"But what about school?" Elise was confused, although knowing that the lives of two missing, young children were, without question, much more important.

But what about the trouble they'd risk getting into, with the added pressure to maintain their crucial secret, just by missing school?

Monique looked down the way in which the school bus would come. No sign of the bus; only two private vehicles, a car, and a rustic pickup truck. They soon went by slowly, clearing the way.

"If we leave now, with any luck, we could return to school before classes began," Monique was persistent.

She was determined to at least try, with an insistent-look in her intent gaze at Elise, as she was wanting to surrender for this just cause.

"What about our school supplies," Elise hesitates, "our bookbags?"

More stalling? Monique stared at her, then looked over to some bushes. "Over here, in these bushes," she said, moving toward some thick undergrowth. "They should be safe here."

Monique removed her backpack and placed it under patches of some low branches on the bush, where it was well hidden.

"Here, hand me yours." While still kneeling beside the bush, she reached a hand out for Elise's bookbag. After receiving it, she carefully stored it under the bush, right next to hers, making sure their properties were safely tucked away.

She got to her feet, and they both just stood there at a temporary loss. The roadway was vacant, no traffic. Not even a kid on a skateboard, bicycle, or afoot. The sky was overcast with the spread of heavy, gray clouds, a residual reminder of the past weekend's deluge.

"Now what?" Elise asked. "Where do we start?"

"Follow me." Monique started to walk away, with Elise right behind her, while neither of them had the faintest idea in which direction to go. There they were: two great-achieving middle-school students, at the very top in their class, on the verge of ditching school for the very first time, since beginning pre-school. Unheard of, unless they were on a mission of mercy that involved the lives of two innocents, young children.

Their nervousness intensified the farther they walked through a small neighborhood, where the spread of a lay of homes was scattered about, along with a drab, rural district. There was a short span of rustic silos, old feed mills; a single-story brick building served as both City Hall and the cozy, sleepy, little villa's police department and court.

The girls were hardly at risk of anyone recognizing them passing through this little hamlet because of its sparse population. During the work-week, no one was hardly ever home, except for a few soccer-moms, the elderly, and small children too young for even kindergarten.

"How did it feel when you jumped out of that dry well?" Elise asked Monique, they both showing signs of increased nervousness uninhibitedly.

"I mean … did it, in any way, feel like flying?"

"I guess, sort of," Monique answered.

They'd come to an area where the ground started on a downward slope, and they ended up in seclusion farther away from them, rather, quiet, vintage neighborhoods. This was a bit isolated, sustaining a rather wet residue from the downpour over the weekend. The area, tattered with pits, some fallen, dead timber, and somewhat treacherous footing in places where there're uneven stretches of forbidding terrain.

"Maybe we should change," Monique suggested as they gingerly walked along to maintain their footing.

"Girls," Koh chimed in. "Whenever you're ready, you can rise to the air. This walking is a waste. You could be miles from here by now."

The very thought of flying brought back that small dose of nervousness they'd just barely dismissed, but still held on to most of the jitters.

"Well, you ready to try it?" Elise failed in trying to show stability, as she was very tense.

"Right," Monique said, in a poise to leap. "On the count of three. One— "

"Wait! Wait, I'm not ready!" Elise shook like a leaf in a breeze. "Okay. Okay. One more time."

A middle-aged man, walking his golden retriever a short way out the back of his home, was returning. He and his dog were adequately concealed from the girls' view due to heavy patches of undergrowth and strands of trees in the secluded area. From his vantage point, he had a clear shot at seeing the girls, as he was purposely spying on them from behind a tree. They were clad in their spiffy, colorful costumes Wendy had designed for them.

The elderly man thought they looked rather charming in their pre-Halloween outfits; so, he decided to continue observing them, while wondering what the occasion was. Should they come to his place on Halloween—wife or not—he'd make certain he had plenty candy for them. They were so young and precociously attractive, those outfits fitting so snug. He kept observing them.

"Ready now?" This was the third take. The girls took up positions to jump, with Monique on the count, "One-two. You ready?"

"Yes, ready," Elise...so anxiously.

Monique rushed the count, "One-two-three, go!"

They leaped but fear hampered their ability, as they only accomplished a six-inch clearance off the ground covered with spreads of fallen, wet leaves.

"Darn it! My bad," Elise confessed. "This time for sure."

"OK, here we go." For the umpteenth time, they got in position to leap. Monique, once again, began the count.

The man and his dog remained unnoticed by the girls, as he was getting an eyeful, grateful his dog didn't bark. But golden retrievers are usually self-restrained, and friendly. For his personal entertainment, the man didn't dare leave that secured spot, for he reveled in the idea of admiring these two, cute, little girls, pretending to be superheroes, their colorful costumes a soft sheen in the dull, morning light. What two remarkable, little super girls they're pretending to be. He chuckled to himself, wantonly focused on them.

Still, they hadn't gotten off the ground. Monique was becoming exhausted merely from counting, alone. "One last time," she said.

"OK," Elise agreed, nodding her head. But then she shouted, "Wait! Let's hold hands."

"Good idea." They took hold of each other's hand, poised to leap once more, after several failed attempts.

The old man continued to avidly enjoy this. He ogled them, his eyes proverbially bulging. He was there for the duration, if they remained, pretending to fly.

Monique was counting amid him watching, "One-two-three, *go!*"

That time, they bolted to the air, disappearing out of sight within seconds, far beyond the clouds, high up into the distant sky!

The dog instantly started barking excitedly; the old man, having too much happened to the mind, fainted dead away, collapsing to the ground beside his dog.

They eventually dropped out of the sky, below the mass of deep gray clouds, to a very low altitude, rocketing across vast landscapes, while keeping their eyes peeled for any sign of the missing kids.

Nothing, so far. But it would take a few passes over the landscapes for the girls to get used to being airborne; they had to learn how to man their guidance system, speed, and agility while flying. They cruised right beside each other, occasionally joining hands for reassurance, and building confidence.

"Whadda you think?" Elise asked. There was a forgiving air about her, with a smile in her voice.

"It's OK," Monique said over to her as they flew over a ridge lined with a thick layer of the forest below. "So long as no one sees us."

"How do you like the thrill of flying?" Elise further asked.

"It depends," Monique said. They were coming up on the lake, which wasn't far away. More forest, hills and deep valleys, and ridges.

"Depends on what?" Elsie asked.

"If those two kids are found alive and well, I'll tell you," Monique asserted.

Finally, they reached the lake. And, there it was, vast, shimmering. Blue. And deep.

"Let's put down somewhere, to have a look around," Elise suggested.

"Great idea," Monique agreed, "but how?"

"How do we land? Good question," Elise realized.

"Flying's all about *will*," Koh told them.

"Figuring it out through your mind is the key to master flying. Just decide where you want to put down, then do it. Now, let's put our minds together and pick a spot."

After passing over the lake, a clearing was dead ahead.

"Down there," Monique said.

"Then let's go," Jor said, poised, and collected.

Monique and Elise then separated, the two now less nervous, but realizing it was a challenge. So, in slowing down their flight-speed to a self-maneuvering ease, the girls managed to land without too much a problem to maintain balance. Once on the ground, in looking back, it wasn't such a horrific experience after all.

"We're going to have to clean that up," Elise insisted about their clumsy landing.

"You'll get the hang of it before long," Koh said to them.

As quiet as it was kept, Monique and Elise were simply bursting with pride, after their successful first flight. But, even with that in mind, still, their silly pride wouldn't allow them reconciliation of their previous prejudice about flying.

Chapter 13

Police and other rescue helicopters were in the air, covering a wide area in search of the missing children. A small group of concerned citizens gathered along with family and friends, and a host of professional rescuers, including several police departments, dedicating their unrelenting services to assist in finding the two lost children.

The huge search party, with air-support, combed every inch of ground, in vast areas the two children were believed to may have wandered off to, with negative results. The lengthy, intensive search was beginning to tire individuals, forcing them to succumb to logical thinking. To survive such a violent downpour over the weekend would take more than a miracle, even for a trained survivalist.

Dona and Jeffry Holland were the missing kids' parents; they had an older daughter in college, Tyler Holland. She was home on spring break when the tragedy took place. Jeffry was out, combing the wilderness with the massive search party, while Dona could not withstand the oppressing stress, at the very thought of not seeing her two children ever again.

Earlier, her daughter, Tyler, had driven her to the emergency room for medical treatment, as she was coming apart from worry and excruciating anguish from the fear of losing her two youngest children. The last report from her husband by telephone was no sign of the children. And this was Monday morning, after two days of intermediate thunderstorms, dangerous lightning, high wind-gusts, along with a torrent of heavy rain.

But she refused to accept the logic, and the obvious results of a useless hunt for her kids, who couldn't have possibly survived.

She lay in bed, under heavy sedation, having hopeless dreams that her children had returned to her. But when awake, the dreams were only agonizing nightmares. At one time, when Tyler had come in the bedroom to check on her mom, she saw her mom abruptly awaken from one of those dreams, calling to her children, and vainly reaching out to them. Tyler had given her another sedative and sat with her until she fell asleep again.

An exhausted police officer came over to Jeffry, the father of the children. He was completely stressed-out, his clothes filthy from dirt and grime—as was pretty much everyone else from the grueling, relentless search, which had been on-going since the rain started late Saturday afternoon.

The officer approached Jeffry with the look of deep empathy etched in his gracefully aging face. "Jeffry, pretty soon we're gonna have to let these people return to their own families." The sound of the officer's voice labored with sympathy, which Jeffry understood. He expected terminating the search was only a matter of time anyway. He was grateful to everyone involved; however, he couldn't bring himself to abandon the search, no matter how long it lasted.

He insisted on a resolve. He needed closure, one way or the other. But there was nothing encouraging in sight; dense and shallow forest surrounded the search party from all directions. Nothing but gloom, hopelessness, and despair closing in.

It was approaching mid-morning; the girls could tell by the position of the sun. So much for getting to school on time. But they had made their choice and would just have to deal with it later. In the meantime, they were becoming flustered because they had no idea what they were doing. They had absolutely no information on the missing kids, let alone their home address.

Elise stood in place, with arms folded, a gradual look of discontent in her eyes. Since they were declared-sisters, she could get away with blaming Monique for moving strictly on emotions alone. But as she opened her mouth to speak, she changed her mind just that quickly, not uttering a word.

Monique wasn't paying attention, she was scanning some brush, strands of trees when she suddenly remembered she could see through things.

"Elise!" she shouted over to her, Monique's gaze limpid with her idea.

But Elise, a little irritated, beat her to the draw, airing her mild frustration, "Don't call me Elise, when we're like this. Call me Koh. That's who they'll understand is doing this and won't be trying to track us by knowing us by our real names."

Koh sounded off a little offended, "I'm not a *that!*"

Elise, "What?" She didn't understand Koh's outburst.

Koh made clear, "You said, Call me Koh. *That's* who they'll be... whatever else, you said. Then I said, I'm not a 'That!' It's she's who..."

"Aren't we're a little edgy?" Elise noted. "Okay, I apologize. I'm sorry to have offended you. We good?"

"Tee-hee-hee," Koh laughed, gratified.

"We're good."

Elise suppressed a grumbled as inaudible as possible, uttering, "Big baby."

"Can we get on with this?" Now, Monique was getting irritated.

"Let's split up. I'll take this area, and you that one over there." She pointed to some woods that stretched seemingly endlessly to the northeast. "We'll meet back here in a little while if we don't find anything."

"Agreed," Elise said, slowly lifting to the air, to Monique's surprise. She didn't take the time to remind Elise how much they supposedly loathed flying. "Oh, forget it," she murmured, watching Elise lazily adrift over a patch of woods nearby, enjoying her flight.

As Monique headed into some nearby woods, Jor started to speak, "Monique, remember you can search the area best if you-"

Monique interrupted her in mirth, "Don't call me Monique, when we're like this. Call me Jor..."

Jor got the jest and laughed, "Tee-hee... Gotcha."

Monique entered the woods. The deep woods. Darkened by dense, heavy shadows. The deep gray, half-light for the day couldn't penetrate the close-knit massive foliage surrounding her. Without Jor, she realized, she'd be terrified this far into the wilderness, with no sign of human-life within miles. If she let her mind wander, this would be a scary situation anyway. Therefore, she could only imagine how terrified those little kids were, stuck out here all by themselves. If they were still alive.

In the back of her mind, she'd began to fear the worse as the only alternative in this situation. She stood in place, scanning, panning immense areas by looking through Jor's eyes, which transformed Monique's eyes to appear like those of a cat. She could see through trees, vast obstructive areas of undergrowth that made up this on-going stretch of forest.

Speed, agility...faster, stronger, better, she was thinking. But to put it to good use... Was it too late, in this case?

It was the authorities' duty to keep up the search, if nothing else, to locate the bodies of the two lost children, which was a most undesirable task of such an emergency. The huge number of volunteers were dismissed in groups, by State and local authorities. Sheriff Hollister and a few of his deputies had joined the search, once its boundary had reached Medfield, the small town he patrolled.

As the search dragged on to a hesitant conclusion, many from the search party offered to stay on for sentimental reasons, as quite a few were friends of the family. But it was ordered they disperse by the professionals in charge, to allow them to complete the task of their obligations... discover any remains, should that be the case.

Monique had wandered randomly about, checking out areas after areas, and coming up empty. She and Elise joined each other, as recommended earlier, with no news, good or bad. "Shall we go back now, so Wendy can kill us for skipping school?" Though Elise was only vaguely concerned about that.

Monique hated to admit Elise was being practical in her suggestion, but the thought of those lost children kept eating away at her conscience. "One more pass," Monique said with a heavy heart. She also feared that this one last pass might reveal something they weren't prepared to accept, like the *obvious*.

"I guess we may as well head back," Monique sadly complied.

They slowly lifted to the air, both with mixed emotions, somewhat overwhelmed by the ability to fly. They never thought it would be so ecstatically thrilling, despite the embarrassment it would be, should they ever be discovered in mid-air by anyone.

One final look down and around, thought Monique, as through Jor's eyes, she scanned briefly an area ahead of them. She and Elise were close beside each other, in mid-air, just above tree-tops, where the fresh air greeted them, and their visions were clear of obstructions; holding their positions on a fallible cushion of thin air.

Then something of a vague nature caught Monique's eye. Among a bed of congested undergrowth, she spotted a rise in the earth, with an opening in front of it, like a small cave. At a closer, penetrating stare through interference, she clearly discerned two small forms of a separate kind from nature sort of heaped together within deep shadows, just slightly inside the sizable mound of dirt, rock, and gushing earth. A short way farther out front of the mound, a crystal-clear brook gurgled over wet rocks, some fallen, broken tree limbs, flowing all the way to a mountain stream quite some distance away.

What Monique had seen inside the opening of the mound, at a glance, it looked like some...discarded...clothing, maybe worn some time ago, as they looked drab, time-worn.

In landing near the opening of the mound, her keen sight cut through the dimming shadows, to where the apparent clothing—

"Oh, my god. Elise!" Monique suddenly shouted from a serious rush of excitement.

Elise was at her side instantly, they both now staring into the hole in the mound, aghast. They looked to one another, each too afraid to advance on what they saw curled-up together on the damp, dirt floor inside the mound.

Two small children, male and female were cuddled in filthy rags, lying very still in the shadows. Scattered about and alongside them were a few candy wrappers, their hair caked with mud, their faces smeared with dirt and grime.

"Wake them; they're not dead," Jor informed the girls.

"Use my touch. It should revive them," she added.

Monique and Elise moved in dubiously, and with extreme caution, they both daring to touch either one of the sleeping kids— if, indeed, they were only asleep.

Elise lightly shook the boy, but quickly withdrew with no response. Monique took the girl gently by the hand, but then let go. After which, the little girl squirmed just barely, but enough to show life-signs in her body. Then the boy stirred, just a hair.

The girls beamed at each other, very relieved; but with hesitation, they were careful not to frighten the children with their presence.

"Hello?" Monique's voice so tender, caring. "We're here to take you home."

Her overwhelming emotion was close to rendering her into tears of triumphant bliss, and relief, as the two no-longer-missing kids were now in the arms of safety, along with a free ride home.

The little girl, now, laboring a bit to refocus on reality, was finally rid of those haunting nightmares over the past, horrific two days. She'd looked after her little brother, the minute she'd caught up to him after he'd wandered off the other day, when they were out back, playing in the yard.

The little girl tried to sit up but was too weak to manage now. Monique assisted her to sit up as then her brother awoke. Elise was there for the youngster, lifting his small upper torso to rest on her chest.

"You okay?" Her smile was warming to the boy. He nodded in a week, almost disoriented fashion, his head falling to rest on her shoulder.

The kids were suffering from exposure, hunger, and exhaustion. There was no telling how long they'd been without food and water, even though the tiny stream of clear water was right at their disposal.

Finally, the little girl managed to ask Monique, after a moment gathering composure, "Who are you? Is it Halloween already? Was I asleep that long?"

Monique chuckled, happy to answer any questions the little girl found necessary to ask, "I'm Mon— "she caught the mistake she was about to make, correcting herself. "I am Jor. What's your name?"

"Amy," the little girl said. "He's my little brother, Timmy. We got lost."

"I know," Monique smiled, delighted to have found the kids alive and unharmed, except for a few minor bruises, you might say. "Do you know where you live?" Then, regarding Elise, Monique said to the little girl, "This is my friend, Koh. We're here to take you and your little brother home."

Elise smiled at them while maintaining attention to the little boy. She was grateful to Monique for remembering *not* to call her by her real name.

"I'm not sure I remember where we live, from here," Amy said, looking around, confused. Then she asked, wanting to understand, "How are we getting home? Do you have a car?"

Oh, brother. Monique and Elise stared at one another at a loss. Neither knew exactly what to say to them, now, *found* children. They'd have to wing it, take their chances. Missing school suddenly didn't loom as large now.

Monique stood erect from slightly bending over to the little girl, whose stance was yet a bit weak from loss of vitality in her system, after their long stay in the woods.

"Sorry," Amy said for having to lean on Monique that bit for balance.

"It's Okay," Monique said, her mind distracted, trying to figure a way to *approach* this next issue of getting the kids home.

Elise attempted a more direct approach. "You guys ever ride a roller coaster? Well, get ready. You're about to get one."

Little Timmy was okay with it; he wasn't old enough to question the whereabouts of the thing; just show him the way to it. But Amy was old enough at eight years old. She saw no sign of a roller coaster; and in the middle of the woods, the idea sounded strictly ridiculous! "Where is it?" Amy was curtly frank.

"Well, would you like to close your eyes, and let it be a surprise?" Monique's slight hesitation was all about giving *herself* the courage to lift off.

"No," Amy said frankly, her little brother shaking his head. "Where is it?" she went on to ask, that time, looking about the tops of trees as if hoping to see the giant thrill-ride towering over the forest from some direction.

"The longer we wait, the later it gets," Elise reminded Monique, who was very aware of the situation; it was only one thing bugging her: the kids' home location.

"Oh, I got an idea," she said, a bit more motivated.

"It's gotta be the first suburb we come from this direction. Once we get there, I'm sure Amy will recognize familiar surroundings. Maybe he will too. Most young kids are very astute, these days."

Elise knew her sister too well; she was stalling.

"Astute? No more big words. This is not the time!"

"OK," Monique readily replied.

"OK, you guys." Elise drew a breath, girding-up her courage.

"Are you ready for the roller coaster?"

"Where is it?" Amy kept insisting.

Little Timmy was anxious, bouncing up and down in place, like a kid on caffeine. "I'm ready," the little fellow said, excitement in his child-voice.

"Okay... Here we go," Monique said, lifting Amy up in her arms, which surprised the little girl.

"Whadda you doing?" She was a little embarrassed. Monique wasn't that much bigger, nor older than she, and lifting her up like she was a baby?

Little Timmy was five-years-old; it didn't matter to him, to have Elise lift him up in her arms. He liked her, thinking she was pretty, with the shiny, yellow-gold hair. That bright red costume she had on made her look like a real superhero, and so did Monique in the shiny black and silver. But he liked Elise best because they were together.

As Monique cradled 8-year-old Amy snug in her arms, she protested this action; it felt weird. Her older sister Tyler stopped lifting her in her arms, right after she'd turned six-years-old. This was a little extreme, thought Amy, as Monique insisted, "You seriously might want to close your eyes for this one."

Timmy loved being in Elise's arms; she was pretty, soft, and warm.

"This feels weird, Jor," Amy was so not comfortable. "Nobody's picked me up since I was five."

"Believe me, I understand," Monique made clear.

"So, do you wanna close your eyes now or later?"

Before Amy could respond, with both kids secured in the girls' arms, they bolted to the gray sky—once again—this time in triumph.

Amy squealed from the sudden shock, with both arms, now, tightly clinched around Monique's neck. Every now and then she dared to peek at the dense forest below. Roller coaster was not to be compared to this. They were flying with Angels!

Little Timmy, thrilled to the max, was in disbelief—even at his young age, as he eventually asked Elise, "Are you an angel? And are you taking us to Heaven? Did we die?"

Elise, now as Koh, issued a soft chuckled, flying with the young tyke.

"No, to all the above," Elise was pleased to announce. "We're taking you and your sister home, to be back with your family. I'm sure they're very worried about you."

Amy had heard her little brother and was puzzled over their present situation. She spoke to Monique, "Are you really angels? Because ordinary people don't fly. We can't."

Monique murmured, inaudible, feeling a bit embarrassed, "Don't remind me."

"But this is so cool!" Amy was so enamored! "We're actually flying!"

Monique perked-up, smiling cheerfully, "It is? Yes, it is cool, isn't it?"

Amy then, feeling so much gratitude, deliberately hugged Monique around the neck, elated to be in her angelic arms.

"You *are* angels. You came and got us! Nobody knew where we were, but you did, and you came and got us." Amy grinned while staring at Monique immensely enthused and grateful!

The girls began to slow down considerably, once they approached a suburb. They were still out of eye-sight range, but they had to be very meticulous in selecting a secluded place to bring the kids down safely, and without being noticed.

"That's where we live!" Amy suddenly recognized the neighborhood.

"Amy will you guys do us—me and my friend—a favor?" Monique humbly asked the little girl.

Amy was more than happy to do the *angels* a favor. The question was, what could possibly be the favor she could do for an *angel?* She gladly complied, "I sure will."

"Try not to tell people too much about us, OK?" Monique explained.

"Can I tell them you're angels, and that you found us in the woods and brought us home?" Amy wanted to know, not understand why that was such a big favor.

The girls brought the kids down with a soft landing within a clump of trees, just down the street a piece from where they lived.

"That's our house up there." Amy pointed to a lavish two-story home, with a beautiful garden, a manicured lawn, and neatly trimmed hedges, a little better than a block up the street.

"You can tell them we brought you home," Elise said to Amy. "But we must keep our secret special because too many people will try to find us; and we must remain sort of a secret, especially to our friends."

Monique added convincingly, "Yes, we must have lots of privacy, so we'll be free to help others who may need our help." If that wasn't convincing enough for Amy, the girls were out of made-up excuses.

"We'll keep your secret, won't we, Timmy?" Amy gladly agreed.

"Well, we have to say goodbye now," Monique said as they prepared to return to the dense, misty gray sky.

"Wait!" Amy called out to them. "Can't you walk us home?"

Amy didn't understand, but they didn't dare venture any farther inside her neighborhood.

"I'm afraid not," Elise said. "We really must be going. There's lots more work we have to do."

"Oh, yes, that's right. You're angels. You must stay awful busy, helping people. Now, I understand." Amy was finally agreeable. She then waved to them, taking her little brother by the hand and started down the street, for home.

"Bye," she waved to them as they then lifted slowly to the air from that area of seclusion.

"Bye!" Little Timmy waved excitedly to him and his sister's *angels*.

"Bye, bye," both Monique and Elise waved to them, then hit the after-burners, jetting far and away, vanishing into the gray haze, in the distance.

Chapter 14

Several law officers of a special police force were at the Holland's home, getting together with Jeffry on their next maneuvers regarding his two lost children. It was right past mid-morning, approaching lunch-time; but due to the grim circumstances, no one was hungry.

The house was quiet, clean, with soft, light-gray shadows cast by thin shafts of the half-light outside, through cracks in the drapes at the windows in the living room. The small group of officers, along with their host, Jeffry, were seated at the breakfast table, having only coffee. It was a somber occasion, for there wasn't a word uttered between them. The task at hand spoke for itself.

The oldest child, Tyler, was in the living room, curled-up asleep in her father's easy chair. She'd been up the previous night with her mom, who was now asleep in bed, under heavy sedation. It'd been trying for the whole family; stressful- so closely near the breaking point. The tomb-like quietness justified the laden oppression felt by everyone.

Suddenly, the front door burst open, startling everyone to their individual degree; the officers reacted sharply, bounding to their feet, with hands in the ready position to draw their side-arms, if necessary.

Tyler awoke abruptly- quickly alert, while Jeffry, maintaining his seat at the table, looked toward the door in reaction to the sudden interruption.

Little Amy, and her younger brother, Timmy, came tearing into the living room, in filthy rags, but as happy as could be.

"Mom! Daddy!" Amy shouted, ecstatic to be home.

Little Timmy raced alongside his sister, in a reckless-abandon fashion, to get across the room to his dad, who had bounded to his feet, anxious to receive his son, with glad arms opened wide. The officers were stunned and overcome in disbelief, though extremely relieved.

Jeffry gathered his beloved two children in his arms. Tyler was among them in an instant, anxiously grabbing for her siblings to hold and caress to no end.

"What's all the noise —"

An enormous burden of oppressive stress was abruptly lifted from Dona, the instant she appeared in the doorway of her bedroom-tomb, to the sudden eruption of celebratory noise in the living room.

"My babies!" she shouted in an escalated dash across the room.

Disbelief overwhelmed her in her ecstatic flight, her bare feet hardly touching the carpet-floor in her swift movement, as she felt resurrected by a huge surge of healing power. She suddenly felt like a champion, revitalized, rejuvenated!

She raced over and scooped up little Timmy in her arms in a clinch she relished to never let go.

"My babies! My babies!" she wept. "You've come home!"

Amy was next.

In letting little Timmy go, she grabbed up her youngest daughter in such a blissful embrace, swinging the child around in her arms, not daring to put her down right now, smothering the child with kisses.

It took a while for the settling to take place. Before the officers took their leave, they lingered a while, as a professional courtesy, to listen to the kids give an account of their incredible survival.

Like most kids, Amy, and her little brother were jamming words together excitedly, speaking at the same time. Little Timmy, trying to catch his breath while speaking so intensely, stammered, "We...we were sleeping, and the angels came..."

Amy interrupted, breathing excitedly, like her brother, "Yes... the angels came and got us, and brought us home..."

"And they flew us in the air," Timmy said, still bubbling with excitement.

"Angels?" their mom sobbed, holding tightly onto her children, as they were seated on the sofa.

Realistically, their mom half-way listened to their fantastic story, not actually caring what they said right about now; she was only so ecstatic to have her children home. And the oldest, Tyler, wasn't that concerned with how the children returned, just as long as they didn't sustain any permanent damages, and they returned safely. As for the police officers; as professionals, it was their duty to take into account what the kids had to report on their experience, no matter how wild, and incredulous their stories may appear.

Little Timmy maintained his views and interpretation, in giving an account of what happened out there in the woods, with just him and his sister, alone.

"We were flying, and I saw our house. And the angels brought us here..."

"That's right, mom, dad," Amy confirmed her brother's account of the situation.

"They said they came to find us, and they did. And they brought us home. They flew us in the air with them!"

This miraculous event still overwhelmed their mom; and it, perhaps, would be some time before she becomes truly focused on listening to her kids. However, their dad was beginning to hear them in the light of suspect; and their older sister was becoming confused. But the kids insisted they flew with the angels.

And that's the way it appeared in the newspapers the next day, the missing children were returned home, safe and unharmed.

"I didn't tell Miss Agnes you guys missed school yesterday because it was for a good reason." Wendy had walked onto the porch with the girls, as they were about to head out to their bus stop.

Monique asked her, "Did you mean what you said when you said we may become fugitives?"

"Yes, I meant it," Wendy returned solidly.

"We really have no choice, *if,*" she emphasized, "the State decides we're to be separated."

Then Wendy took a breath, shifting to a different subject.

"So, what was it like flying? Those kids just about ratted you out, if it wasn't for your costumes. See? I told you it would work."

"We never said it wouldn't," Elise said. "And flying was cool."

"Cool, huh?" Wendy stared at her dubiously.

"It was cool," Monique said. "Amy kind of made me feel better about flying when *she* said it was cool. I mean the way she said it, it meant it *so* was cool! Now, I don't feel so embarrassed to fly."

"Me either," Elise admitted.

"Well, let's hope you've done enough flying for a while," Wendy cautioned them, as they had started off the porch.

"You guys have a great day at school. No ditching this time, maybe for some stray animal." That was a joke, and the girls laughed, walking away, then said together:

"Bye, Wendy."

"Bye, Wendy."

She waved to them as they gradually disappeared beyond the grove.

"How'd she finds out we ditched school?" Elise wondered.

"You didn't tell her, did you?"

"Why would I do that?" Monique was surprised Elise would question her loyalty.

"I thought maybe you did."

"Me?"

"Forget it. Wendy has ways of finding out lots of things," Monique reminded Elise.

"Since we never ditched school before, the teacher may have called."

The headline in the newspapers that the two missing children had been returned to their family was received from recent police reports. It was the topic of discussion among faculty members at the middle-school the girls attended. It also became a topic of interest to the students, especially the part about angels. At some point, discussions among the students nearly got out of hand, as a split majority shared differences of opinions about angels, although the headline was clear in not giving credit to the kids, who had given the outlandish story to their parents, with the police on hand at the time of their return. The reading of the article following the headline clearly stated the part about the metaphysical beings strictly came from the kids, as they saw it.

"There are no such things as angels!" Brittany spat, for spiteful reasons, shifting a mean stare at Monique, and Elise, as if accusing them of believing that there were the possibility angels did exist. The mass of students was milling around in the halls, taking their time migrating to their respective classes, buzzing with the heavy discussion.

"OK, students," came a female voice of authority. "Let's move along. Let's clear the hallway!"

An increase in gradual movement ensued among the students. When Elise and Monique entered their classroom, one of their classmates, Trevor Lewis, asked them, "Hey, what happened to the two of you, yesterday? You guys don't miss school. Did something happen? Were you sick?"

Monique teased him, though with an appreciation for his concern in her smiling, wet-brown eyes, "Let's not get nosy, junior."

Trevor leaned over to her and quietly, while smiling, softly whispered to her, "You'd best be nice to me."

Monique bit, "Why?"

Elise waiting beside them, as the fair-looking youngster at thirteen, sort of curly, dark brown hair, replied, "Cause, someday I'm gonna be a rich millionaire; and you may need a good husband."

That did it. Monique and Elise cackled.

A notable look of feigned disappointment in the young lad's face, which both Monique and Elise thought he was rather cute, as he piped, "Aw...c'mon. It ain't that bad, is it?"

Monique surprised him with a little kiss on the cheek, then she and Elise walked away, leaving him utterly astonished. He felt his kissed cheek amiably, beaming at the cute girls walking away.

"Can I turn the other cheek?" he called out to Monique, blushing.

Chelsea hadn't been paying attention lately. When she reported working that morning, she was sorely enlightened by the headline in the newspaper that was on her desk. In just skimming over the article, the checkered flag went up in her head.

She didn't take the part lightly where the once missing kids had declared being rescued by angels. Put two and two together, and you get government-cover-up. There was something to their story. Even exposure to the elements wouldn't have the two of them sharing the same illusions. But, in realizing she couldn't approach the family directly to interview the kids, she had to plot another course of action, which she already had in mind.

She whipped out her cell phone, found her contact, hit the call button, and waited.

"Jim, meet me at the helipad in thirty minutes." She hung up and left her office in brisk strides.

A half-hour later, she and Jim were airborne, with Jim at the controls. They headed for the wooded areas, in the general direction the kids were first reported missing. Just over a rise, they came upon a clearing, where below, a dirt road ran for quite a distance, winding, and twisting along stretches of land, finally disappearing into some thick woods a short way from the lakeshore.

On a whim, Chelsea asked Jim, "Would this be the place you said the barge was having some kind of trouble; and where you saw those girls walking?"

They communicated with each other through tiny microphones on their flight helmets.

"This is the place," Jim confirmed.

"How far is the nearest town from here?" she asked.

Jim thought a moment, then said, "Mm...some five, maybe eight-miles. East of here is the town of Medfield. Back where we just came from is Grand City. It's a good ten miles behind us."

Chelsea took up a pair of binoculars from in the seat beside her and started scanning the areas below.

There was nothing of interest down there. Patches of forests, dense and shallow, pervaded over endless landscapes; the vast lake, right in the heart of this formidable, scenic lay of the untapped countryside. Pure nature in her rarest form. It made for a deep, depressing sensation of absolute loneliness, a lost feeling of hopelessness.

There's nothing out here, she was thinking.

"Nothing," she said aloud, though barely audible, that lonely, sinking feeling getting the best of her emotionally.

She took down the binoculars from her eyes as a thought occurred to her, and she said to Jim, "You said those girls you saw were in this area, walking alone?"

"Just strolling alone leisurely, without a care in the world, seemingly," he answered casually.

"And you didn't see a vehicle of any kind, this far out, in the middle of nowhere?"

"That's what I told you earlier. There was no vehicle, just those three young girls."

"Which way did they seemed to be headed?" Chelsea didn't know why, but something about that just didn't quite sit right with her. It didn't raise a red flag or anything; it was basically a passing thought.

But her interest tended to increase, although it could have stemmed from the eerie, lonely feeling this deserted place gave her. She couldn't imagine anyone purposely taking a trip this far out, even with a vehicle.

"Well, from all I could tell, they were out here all by themselves," Jim said.

In looking back, he came to a bemusing conclusion as he added, "Come to think of it, they were headed down that dirt road that went through those woods. Once I left the area, I wasn't paying much attention, but after I cleared that jungle down there, the next thing I came upon was that orphan home that's been there for years."

"Maybe that's where they're from," Chelsea said as a wild guess. Jim was doubtful, the way he figured it.

"I don't see how," he said. "That orphanage is a good ten-miles through those woods, out to the lake; it's much closer to walk to town from the orphanage than out this far."

That still didn't raise a red flag. Chelsea dismissed the conversation and went back to sight-seeing through the binoculars. Having noticed how persistent she'd been looking through his binoculars, Jim asked her, "Are we getting close?"

"Close to what?" She hardly regarded his question, never removing the binoculars from her eyes, as she answered him absentmindedly.

In the distance, and direction they were heading, she spotted black helicopters headed to a point unknown, at the time. They were partly the verification of her hunch. What she had read in the newspaper about those missing kids' report about angels; she did not take it lightly, and neither did she believe the government did either. She couldn't get out of her mind that glowing plant-like thing she'd caught on film, despite its poor clarity. The feds were on to something, and it wasn't about vegetation treatment. This was big, and it had Pulitzer award written all over it.

"In a few more miles, we'll be at 12-Mile Junction," Jim alerted Chelsea to their present position.

"Just keep flying," she told him.

The arrangement in which the rhythm of her voice came across to Jim, he was reminded of a certain intonation, as he began singing, "*Just keep swimming, just keep swimming...*"

"What are you doing?" She took the binoculars from her eyes a moment to stare at him.

He laughed quietly, "It's the song that little fish, Dora, sang on the Disney movie, *Finding Nemo*. Don't you remember?"

"When I was a child, I behaved like a child." Chelsea, unfeeling, shared with him one of her firm beliefs. "Now that I'm an adult, I've put away childish things. And, in answer to your question: No, I've never seen that movie."

"Dang, woman," Jim protested, "Lighten up."

"Follow those helicopters over there." Disregarding his frivolous complaint, she abruptly pointed passed him, out the window, on his side of the helicopter, to those distant helicopters. Jim, following directions without question, accelerated, slightly changing course, then sped away, giving chase to those black choppers far in the distance.

"Don't get too close," Chelsea cautioned him, "They must not become wise that we're here. Just stay in close enough range and follow them. This is free airspace; we can go wherever we want; we're on a news-hunt."

Jim said humbly, "Anything you say. You're the boss."

Chelsea didn't find anything conclusive to her hunch. However, she wasn't that far off the beaten-path; just looking in all the wrong directions. As for the black helicopters, they were merely doing training exercise, only with the purpose that was a government Top Secret. They were on alert. And they stayed to the north, far out of the area the missing children were found. That

Charles H. Woods
211

wasn't a deterrent for the news anchor lady Chelsea Freeman; on the contrary, it boosted her confidence she was getting close to something. Something, maybe not of this world, that the government either feared was a threat to National Security, or some otherworldly ally they'd been preparing for since Roswell.

Whatever the case, she wasn't giving up on her intuitive suspicion. She was a bonified successor in her line of work. She didn't give up!

"Let's head back," she told Jim; and immediately, Sky-Cam responded to a manual command, turning about then headed toward downtown Grand City. Jim said to her, "You gotta another idea?"

If she'd told him yes, he wouldn't have had any clue. But, in his own way, she was thinking, his innocent ignorance made him kind of lovable. He didn't have a mean bone in his well-put-together body.

Within the days that followed, the city, and surrounding areas tended to become conscious of something that may be out of the ordinary. It began at the increase of murmuring rumors that something a little bit strange may be at hand. A little while back, an elderly man named Alfred Sweeney had sort of went off his rocker, complaining on a constant basis, in a muddled state of mind, that he saw two little girls in spiffy new Halloween outfits leap into the air and kept on going; that they were fast, and that they disappeared high in the sky, out of sight. His condition got to the point where his wife, Bernice Sweeney, was forced to take him to their doctor, who ultimately recommended a psychiatrist for mental health treatment.

The Holland family eventually began receiving calls from the school Amy and her little brother attended. Timmy was in kindergarten, and Amy was in the third grade. What had triggered the calls to their parents was the consistencies of the kids' stories about angels collaborated with each other's to the letter. The many times they had told the story to their classmates, it was always the same and never wavered.

That's what was so amazing to their teachers. And it had gotten to the point where their mother, Mrs. Dona Holland, had met with her kids' teachers on several occasions on the matter. The final meeting resulted in the teachers' recommendation of a child psychiatrist for them.

Dona, when finally regaining her full capacity to realize she hadn't been dreaming all this time after her kids had returned, had awakened to the reality that, perhaps, something did seriously need to be done about their mental instability.

She recalled finding some of their artwork left behind while they were at school. To her astounding discovery, both children had drawn stick-figures, depicting themselves being rescued by images representing inconsistency of what we perceive as angels; from the halos over their heads to wings. What was odd in Dona's mind was the color of the wings, and each angel had on a different color outfit. Instead of all white, one wore black, trimmed in silver, the other wore red, trimmed in yellow-gold.

The kids, perhaps, in sort of an unusual stretch of the imagination, even so much as to give each angel a nationality by illustrating that one was black and the other white—both females.

Dona had brought with her the kids' sketches she'd found in their rooms. She shared them with each teacher she met with, at two different times. They were about to wrap up the meeting with the last teacher, Mrs. Kathy Brenner, Timmy's kindergarten teacher.

"You gotta know they went through an awful lot, being lost out there in those woods; and in all that terrible weather.

Sometimes nightmares can follow you for so long they can become a reality to some de-"

"I understand that, Mrs. Holland," said Mrs. Brenner sincerely.

Dona gathered her composure, realizing her son's teacher was only voicing her deep concerns for the innocent child; and Dona Holland appreciated the lady's concern.
But Dona only wanted to point out, "Can you imagine what those two children went through, to survive? And there's one other thing that's most important of all"—she hesitated, almost in tears reminiscing the brutal, unforgiving elements her children were exposed to, during those lengthy, horrific hours they'd spent in that wilderness, "Someone, or *something*, rescued my children and brought them home, safe and *unharmed!* And the strangest part about it: no one ever came forth, to admit to saving my children. Whoever's responsible, the Holland family's forever in their debt!"

She then showed her children's sketches of their supposed rescuers to the teacher, who gazed at the child-drawings without a comment. But, in comparing the separate sketching, their cohesive similarities prompted reasons for the further investigation.

Finally, Mrs. Brenner decided to ask, "Mrs. Holland, may I keep these?"

It wasn't clear to Dona what her son's teacher wanted with the drawings, so she gave her permission, "Of course."

Worthwhile news does travel, whether by word-of-mouth, electronically, hands-on information, or by any other conventional means. When a thorough investigation was launched in and around the providence of Grand City, by special government agents, Ed Milburn, and his staff were on the job. They'd collected information of interest through doctors' reports, mental health physicians, not to forget the cooperative police departments; even school employees who served as student counselors, and principals.

Mrs. Brenner had shared the Holland kids' child-like drawing she'd gotten from their mother, with Maggy Smith, the elementary school counselor. She did it out of concern for the children.

"This is interesting," Maggy was somewhat awed to learn from Mrs. Brenner how young Timothy, and his older sister—who was assumed old enough to know the difference between make-believe and reality—stuck to their stories about angels rescuing them.

It was especially bewildering that the kids went so much as to give complete details in the way the angels were dressed and their specific nationalities. It was as if they were naming two young female individuals—one black, one white—in costumes, for whatever reason.

"I must admit," Maggy confessed, "I don't quite know what to make of it."

"Unless there's some truth to all this," Kathy Brenner waived her doubts momentarily to adhere to the possibility that sometimes things can happen that we just don't understand.

"Listen, Mrs. Brenner," Maggy kindly requested. "Would you mind very much if I took these drawings with me? I'd like to show these to doctor Stacy Embers.

She's a pediatrician, who's also practicing Child Psychology. I work for her part-time."

"Do you think it'll do any good?" Mrs. Brenner said. "Mrs. Holland swore that no one showed up with the kids; said they came home all by themselves. That's when they told their parents about the angels."

"That doesn't sound like anything related to pent-up rage, or unresolved anger when kids are exposed to either mental or physical abuse. This is really weird."

"I know," said Mrs. Brenner.

Couple that with Alfred Sweeney's story making the news via a doctor's report, and the Holland kids drawing attention to the feds, due to the passing-around of the descriptive sketches of their angelic heroines. Now, you got tabloids circulating in and around the areas accusing the government of a massive cover-up.

But not to the point of a city-wide alarm. Tabloids are usually regarded as entertainment. Less than a quarter of the population of any area give those publications credibility.
They mainly attract UFO buffs, who often make up their own fantastic tales of alien abductions, and plenty of alien-related encounters.

Chelsea never chased rainbows, shadows, phantoms, or the like. She'd always been sharp. Alert. Her feet planted solidly on the ground; and all her wits about her. You may call it an overreaction in chasing those black helicopters. No. It was just leaving no territory to chance, within the scope of her determined investigation.

She was chasing a realistic dream. She was amid doing some leftover homework from hindsight. The footage Jim had captured of the three teen-aged girls walking alongside that dirt road, out by the lake, although she couldn't finger a reason for reviewing the film at the time, it stirred the competency of her intuition. She had gone over this before in her mind.

There was no significance, off-handedly, to be gained from watching this film. However, she sat on the edge of the sofa in her swank apartment downtown, with eyes glued to her big-screen HD TV, having transported the footage to be shown on screen.

At certain points in viewing the footage, she stopped the action, rewind and start again. Sometimes in the middle of watching, she'd slow it down, hit the zoom button, bringing pictures of the girls up close. She didn't recognize them; she'd never seen them before. They looked clean, healthy; they were charming. She couldn't figure it. Yet, she had a compulsion to just sit there, watching the film repeatedly.

"We'll have to treat these personal interviews discretely," Ed instructed his staff of two ladies as they cruised through neighborhoods of gated communities, trying to sight any unusual activities among residents.

"Anything from someone talking to themselves, or someone trying to climb a tree backward," Ed realized he sounded redundantly facetious, but he'd never encountered an entity in possession of a host. Neither of the three in the car, with Susan at the wheel, Ed on the passenger side, and Jillian in the back knew what to expect behavior-wise.

Jillian added her share of sarcasm from the back seat, "You don't expect them to come up and show you their ID's, do you?"

Ed chuckled, "It would help."

Susan said not a word. She just kept driving, following orders, like a good agent, keeping her eyes peeled.

Finally, though, she did speak, "Do you think I'd be wise to have a brief conversation with the old guy who said he saw two little girls leap into the sky?"

She peered in the mirror at Jillian in the back seat, directly behind her. Their eyes locked for a moment.

In bringing her head around to face the front, she virtually read Jillian's thoughts from the knowing look in her eyes.

Chapter 15

There was still plenty of daylight before sunset when Timmy and Amy got off the school bus out front of their home. Their mother, standing in the doorway, so grateful to see them running toward the house once again. She vowed to keep a much closer watch on them. It was such a harrowing experience, going through what she had those couple of days.

"Hi, mom!" Timmy rambled passed his mom, brushing against her slightly. She loved his little clumsy rush by her, smiling so happily.

"Hi, honey," she said. Amy was next. She'd stopped running before reaching the front stoop.

"Hi, mom." She leaned her head to one side to receive a little kiss on the jaw from her mom.

"Hi, sweetheart," her mom returned, in closing the door shortly after the kids were inside, and rambling up the stairs, to their rooms to put away their things.

Dona was in the kitchen, getting supper ready. Their dad would be home from work soon. He was a computer analyst for a high-tech, communications company in a downtown office building. Since their kids were back safe, maybe they could get on with their lives, once again, as a happy family.
Tyler had returned to the dorm at the college she attended, as spring break had ended.

Through the window over the sink in the kitchen, Dona happened to look out back and spotted the kids playing in the yard. That's where they were last seen the day Timmy had wandered off, chasing a stray puppy. His sister had gone after him was how they'd ended up lost in the woods. Beyond the backyard wooden fence, through the gate was a steep slope that emptied into a gully. Once across the deep ditch, along with that part of the community, was the edge of a dense forest that stretched all the way into no-mans-land. Once there, it was easy to become disoriented and lost because of the darkness from deep shadows that lived there among crowded strands of trees so closely knitted together.

Dona raised the window and yelled out to the kids, "Do not leave this yard! I mean it!"

They called back, "OK, mom!"

"OK, mom!"

What the kids were doing got their mom's attention, and she paused from what she was doing in the way of making dinner to curiously observe them.

They were running around with makeshift capes of towels they'd gotten out of the clothes hamper in the washroom, out back. Timmy had on a towel as close to red as you could get. It was a deep red-wine color, along with khaki pants with a solid red shirt. Amy's towel was gray, and she wore dark green pants, with a yellow top.

They were running around in the yard, with arms extended forward, pretending to fly.

Their mom heard Amy shout, "I'm Jor!"

Little Timmy spoke, and his mom clearly heard him, "You can't be Jor. She wears black. That's not black!"

Amy said as her defense, "I don't have anything black I could wear. Besides, you don't have on all red. Koh was wearing red and sparkling yellow, just like her gorgeous blond hair."

Their mom reeled in her stance, as she was leaned over the sink to peer out the window at the kids. She gathered her poise and withdrew from the window, muddled a few paces over to the breakfast table and sat down in one of the chairs at the table, with a distant, vacant look in her stare. Supper was delicious; however, Dona wasn't hungry.

She hardly ate a bite. What haunted her she'd seen her kids doing in the backyard earlier. The way the game they were playing specified what they'd told their mom and dad about the two angels who brought them home. No, who *flew* them home. They even recalled their names: Jor and Koh. Those names weren't common, by any stretch of the imagination. And the clothes they wore; one wore all black... and the other wore all red. And there was something about gorgeous blond hair. The kids' accuracy in remembering those exact details was almost spellbindingly surreal! They couldn't make that up.

It was late.

The kids had been long since sound asleep. Jeffry went to bed shortly after supper. He was beaten after a grueling day at work. Dona remained wide awake. She couldn't sleep. Those haunting names her kids new so well. Who, or *what* was Jor, or Koh?

She paced the floor restlessly, in her gown and bathrobe, under the frail night light in their bedroom. She thought of waking her husband; then again, she knew he was tired and needed his rest; so, she continued pacing. She may not fall asleep for hours, the kids sound asleep in their rooms, content that *angels* brought them home.

Angels, they insist. Not some old man in an old pick-up, with a pile of stinking garbage in the back, smelling like rotten bananas and sour peaches. But angels, they say; like angels from Heaven, whose names are Jor and Koh. It couldn't have been Gabriel and

Michael. Those angels everyone's familiar with.

"Honey...," From across the room in the bed, her husband spoke. She was pacing closer to the door, between the vanity.

She went over to the bed caringly, "Honey, I didn't mean to wake you."

"It's okay," Jeffry said, raising up in bed then resting his back on the pillow.

"What's wrong, aren't you tired?"

A vague smile barely creased her lips as she came over to the bed and sat down on the edge, on her side, holding him in a gentle stare. She pondered over whether to let him in on her concern. Yes, it was a concern, not fear. Whoever brought her kids home could not be anything of an evil nature, no matter if they were little green men from Mars.

"Maybe I shouldn't let it get to me," she said. But he knew that was only a prep to keep him up half the night.

He popped up, getting comfortable with his back braced against the soft pillow.

"OK, out with it," Jeffry kindly insisted, slipping a gentle arm around his lovely wife. She had medium-length, deep brown hair, her soft blues were like two tiny pools, exuding warmth with gentle caring.

"Have you been wondering how the kids got home, after spending the weekend, lost in the woods, with all that bad weather?" she began.

"I try not to think about it too much," he was humble to say, "But I can't help it." He looked away in thought, serious thought.

"It's beyond me. I hate to admit it, but sometimes, when I think about it a lot, it frightens me. I mean they just showed up out of the clear blue. Honey, we combed every inch of those woods and turned up nothing. I mean absolutely nothing. And, suddenly, without any warning—like maybe you'd think one of the search helicopters spotted them—they show up."

She dropped her stare, having plunged into deep concentration. As her heart rate increased, she took a breath, gathered herself then went on to say,

"Honey, this afternoon, after the kids had gotten in from school, they were out back, playing. You wanna know what game they were playing? Superhero. Now I know that's not far-fetched," she looked away, briefly gathering her poise, then continued. "But the names; they were pretending to be the angels they insisted who had brought them home. And they called their names, Jor, and Koh. Do you remember them telling us the names of the angels?"

"Ah...no," Jeffry shook his head regretfully, "I remember they told us something, but we were so excited to have them home..."

Dona cut in, "I do... Well, once they called their names, I remembered.

"Honey, Jor, and Koh are *real!*" she concluded emphatically.

He looked at her with reverence. Without saying a word, his stare at his wife was ingratiating. He'd never felt such relief. He hugged her in gratitude, and it sort of surprised her.

"You don't know how glad I am to hear you admit to that. I've put every logic piece of evidence together in my mind since they came tearing through the front door that day."

To make a long story short, he earnestly told her, "Honey, I've concluded: I believe them, and I believe you. And, unless someone comes forward and clearly explain what *did* happen with our kids out there; I'm going with the angels." The honesty in his voice gave her comfort, as she became glad-glassy-eyed.

Later that night, Dona stood before the window, looking out at the stars on a clear night. They were bright, as hard as diamonds, millions of them. The universe so vast. It went on forever. *So much space out there,* she was thinking, *with millions and millions of worlds. There's no way we are alone!*

She looked around at her husband, who was asleep in bed. She left the window, with a vague smile of contentment. Before getting into bed, she paused, looked back toward the window, and murmured inaudibly to herself, "Goodnight, angels. Thanks for bringing my children home."

The idea of locating the hosts of the alien-entities was not by conducting personal interviews. That would certainly lead to a dead end. A man or animal on the run develops a sharp insight to avoid the pursuer. Other means to track these otherworldly fugitives would be more likely successful by a sneak attack.

Alfred Sweeney had collapsed after reportedly having seen two pre-teenaged girls, one of color, the other Caucasian, leap into the air, wearing what he described as colorful Halloween costumes. To follow up on the story, special governments agents received access to Alfred Sweeney's medical history record. It cleared the man of ever having mental issues, but this method of tracking the aliens proved ineffective to the cause. It would take a millennium to check the medical record of each citizen in this city alone, to determine whether their mental capacity would lend credibility to anything strange, or out of the ordinary that they may report to the authorities.

"Poppycock!" Ed shouted, fervently agitated over this government bureaucratic nonsense.

"Now, here's what we're gonna do."

"Well, what?" Jillian, a little impatient. They were at Headquarters.

Ed closed the medical-file folder with a harsh snap, "We're going to smoke them out."

"Smoke them out?" Susan didn't quite get it. Ed said with assurance, "Since they're so eager in helping others; let's give them jobs."

"Huh?" Jillian thought she'd gotten the idea; suddenly, she was at a loss.

"Follow me." Ed then started for the door, calmly at ease. Quizzical Susan, and Jillian followed instinctively.

Wendy heard bits and pieces of the conversation downstairs between Miss Agnes and some lady-representative from the State Department. She was up in her room, taking a break from creating on her sewing machine. Her bed wasn't cluttered with rolls of cloth, like normal; it was relatively clear, nicely made. Only a few patterns were laid out.

She was tidying up her room, with the door open. That's how she overheard voices coming from downstairs. She could've taken full advantage of her, now, super-improved hearing, provided by Motatu, whose spirit resides inside her; but her suave mannerism far exceeded the slightest notion to disrespectfully eavesdrop.

What little she understood came from Miss Agnes as she was saying, "Is it necessary they have to separate? They've been together since they arrived here some years back. Monique was first to arrive as an infant. She wouldn't know a thing about the outside world without Wendy and Elise. They've created their own little family. And Wendy's been looking after them since they arrived. It'll be such a miscarriage of fairness, to split them up now."

"Well, unfortunately, Mrs. Greene, it's out of my hands. I do want you to know that I truly understand, but it's just nothing I can do."

The lady was sharply dressed, in a black, medium, low-cut, dress, with a string of cheap pearls around her neck. She was African American, thirtyish, very articulate, a suave disposition in her neck.

"Well, could you tell me how long before this place closes down?" Miss Agnes asked, as the lady, Miss Valerie Stanfield, had stood up to leave. She was holding onto her purse, along with a rather thick, black binder filled with important papers and documents.

"Right now, I'd just be guessing. Tell you what…just hang tight for right now. You should get a notice to vacate in plenty of time… I'm guessing two, maybe three months." Then Miss Valerie Stanfield bustled across the spacious living room, and out the door, with Agnes accompanying her only to close the door afterward. When the State representative had left, Agnes turned away from the door, with a doleful look on her face; but it was more of a painful look, from Wendy's vantage point.

She stood in the soft gray shadows at the top of the stairs, having absorbed enough of the downstairs conversation between the two ladies to fully understand the grim situation.

As Miss Agnes was headed back into the living room, Wendy was staring down at her from the top of the stairs. Their eyes met in silence. Agnes then knew the child must have heard them downstairs. Words of comfort or encouragement wouldn't come to Agnes to say; she could only send up her sympathy and compassion to Wendy by the caring look in her soft stare.

Wendy's mask was stern, a look of unfeeling. A moment of a deep-seated rage was kept to herself, not for Miss Agnes to know. Wendy then left the top of the stairs and returned to her room. She had a decision to make, the biggest decision she would make in her life. The one thing that was so intensely demanding was the three of them, herself, Elise, and Monique, *must* stay together; not altogether for their sake, but for the entire world!

The girls left for school on a brisk, soft, cool morning, a gentle, spring breeze sauntering across fields of tall grass that looked like waves on an ocean. The sky was clear; birds fluttered about in the trees, chirping in a frolicking fashion. Monique and Elise strolled through the grove in a celebratory mood, after that adventure they enjoyed a while back in saving those innocent kids, who had gotten lost in those miserable woods, during that terrible weather. The residual effect of that time left the girls comfortably settled in their new roles as helpers to those in need—just like the comic superheroes. It was a nice feeling. Their greatest challenge from here-on, they figured, was keeping their alternate egos firmly a secret, as sometimes it made them feel giddy, like the excitable, little school girls they were.

On a sour note, however, they were still without the knowledge of their approaching, harrowing disappointment Wendy had been keeping from them for over the past several days. She just couldn't find it in her heart to break theirs, even though she knew the time would come when she'd have no choice, which would be soon.

But, for now, she sat at her sewing machine, in discontentment, while idly stitching together creative new civvies for the girls, which she'd successfully copied from the teen-aged magazine *SEVENTEEN*. Agnes was getting ready to leave on an appointment, regarding her retirement; she was also to meet with state officials in regards to the girls' disconcerting situation.

When she left out the door, the noise of a large, diesel truck, pulling a flatbed trailer, got her attention only for a moment. It was backing in an unloading-position around back, with a stack of more building material. Agnes got in the SUV parked out front and drove away, the diesel rig reminding her of the limited time the girls had left to be together as sisters.

The day was going as normal at school through lunch period. The students had settled in their classes for the remainder of the time left before school let out for the day. Principal George Mavery received a telephone call in his office at 1 p.m.

Within seconds after listening to the voice over the phone, he went pale, shouting, "Who is this?"

The voice, a coarse male-voice replied, "Just get those students out of the building in a hurry! That bomb is set to go off in thirty minutes!" Whoever it was then hung up the phone.

Principal Mavery—mid-forties, a man in good physical shape—hung up the phone and left his office with panic on his face. He met Miss Sylvia Pike, a young, math teacher, in the hallway, as she was coming from the teachers' lounge. She was on her way back to her classroom when she and the principal nearly collided.

They both reacted quickly to avoid the collision, as she moved aside to give him room to pass. He lightly grabbed her by the shoulders with a quick reflex in his hast to get to the emergency alarm down the hall.

"Excuse me. Get your students out of the building *now!*"

She took no time to think; she just left in a huge rush to get to her students.

At the abrupt sound of the fire-alarm, students immediately fled the classrooms, scrambling through the hallways, and spilling out of the building in droves.

Once outside, they were brought to orderly procedures under the directions of professional city officials—police officers and fire department personnel.

As students were being instructed to move at a safe distance from the building, members of the Bomb Squad moved into the building, carrying their gear; owners of some private vehicles were anxiously concerned that they were parked too close to the building, that they would be in the way of a possible explosion. Policemen had sealed off the area of concern, with officers standing guard to prevent trespassers.

Among the congested gathering of students, Elise, and Monique had managed to ease through and between the massive gathering, undetected, to an outer edge of the crowd, where they could try and sort this thing out. All the attention from the body of students and faculty were on the emergency at hand, not on the girls. That gave them the freedom to maneuver as needed.

"Well, whadda you think?" Elise asked Monique, the two of them looking-on indecisively. Suddenly, they began to realize that responsibilities of this magnitude were more easily said than done. Rescuing little kids stranded in the woods was a cinch, compared to this. What would they do? What *could* they do? It was spread among the students, profoundly, that a bomb had been planted somewhere inside the school; some of the mischievous, little misfits reveled in the idea of some free time away from school, while many students were crushed over the idea of having their learning institute destroyed by some mad bomber.

Monique replied, after giving the serious matter a thorough going-over in her mind, "I'm not sure what we should do, but I am sure that we should do something, and not just stand here and do nothing."

They then looked around and about themselves in search of an area where they wouldn't be easily detected by wandering eyes of anyone—on, or off campus. But in realizing the high risk they'd be taking of themselves, they were hesitant in making a move that could save the possible destruction of their school.
They stood there, neutral, now understanding how it feels being in such a difficult situation. It didn't sit well with them, as they were having a difficult time deciding. Finally, an idea came to Elise that she shared with Monique.

"Look through Jor's eyes, I'll look through Koh's. Maybe we can see the bomb from here."

"What good will that do? We can't do anything about it from out here," Monique made known.

Elise humbly agreed, a look of defeat in her faltering stare, "Yes, you're right. If only we could get inside the school without anyone seeing us."

Then another idea came to her. "What if we changed… just in case?"

"We'll only be a major distraction, and get laughed at," Monique was overly cautious, and afraid.

"Well, then what?" Elise was out of ideas, stomping a foot, flustered.

"I don't know," Monique stressed, lightly stomping her foot in frustration.

As the mystery build, caution and concerns mounted. The students who rode buses were escorted aboard by authorized personnel and driven away. The walkers were instructed to vacate the premises quickly but orderly.

In watching the kids leave the campus in masses, Monique had an idea. She looked around for Elise—

She was gone...disappeared at some point.

Monique did a complete three-sixty, in place, trying to locate her. She was not among the thinning crowd of students; she was nowhere in sight.

"Elise?" Monique was dumbfounded. Finally, she went wandering about in search of Elise.

Inside the school, the bomb squad was mystified. They had searched every nook and cranny and found nothing remotely like any type of bomb, homemade or professional. Ultimately, they concluded that it was a student prank to get out of going to class. The bomb squad consisted of two experienced men, late forties, clad in dark, protective clothing, a sidearm, and other proper gear to work the task in disarming a deadly charge.

After having made a complete sweep of the building, they were headed toward the exit when a flash of something of a bright red caught their eye.

One of them—as they both held up at the same time—asked the other, "Did you see that?"

The other man replied, "I'm not sure. I thought I saw something move around the corner down there."

"Something red?" the first one said.

The other nodded, "Yes. But it was quick, like a flash of light."

"Uh huh. Let's go have a look."

Monique had made her way, undetected, around to a far-side entrance to the school, near the cafeteria. Right before going inside, she morphed into her costume, which altered her recognizable appearance. She was the stunning image of a hybrid superhero. She could convince anyone she was an alien, with humanoid features, especially if she looked through Jor's cat-like eyes, which she did, to save time searching for Elise if she was inside the building.

And she was. Monique spotted her in the Science room, and Monique could tell she was looking for something unusual in the manner of a bomb. But how would either of them know what a bomb might look like?

Nevertheless, Monique decided to assist her by entering the school through the side entrance. Once inside, she moved with caution, making sure she didn't run across the two men who had gone inside earlier. In that somewhat luminescent black and silver attire that fit like a glove, Monique moved carefully along the empty corridor, staying close to the wall for added precaution, her reflex, quicker than any creature's known to man, if needed, poised to react in an instant.

In nearing a corner, she heard voices. She held up, listening. She was paused next to a row of wall lockers. The voices were approaching. It was the two men of the bomb squad, as she overheard one of them say to the other, "Did you happen to see..." The man hesitated rather timidly as if he was afraid to admit to something that might lose his friend's respect for him.

"What is it, Tate?" His friend paused, looking Tate earnestly in the eye, "We've worked together for over fourteen years. And we've gone through quite a lot; some good; some not so good. But we've worked things out, always, right?"

Tate nodded in agreement, then went on to say, "I was just wondering what'd you see, other than that flash of red light."

His friend reacted with an expression as though *he* was holding back something in the relation to what he thought Tate was hiding. He said, "Exactly what was you about to say?"

"About the flash of red light? I saw something else."

"Something else?" Now, Tate's friend, Jesse Cobb, was playing cat-and-mouse with him, which was somewhat intimidating.

Tate girded up his courage, saying outright, "Hair, Jesse. I saw hair. Blond hair! Like on a little girl's head."

Jesse didn't reply. But after a silent moment, he said in a soft, subtle voice, "So did I."

As the two men drew closer to her stilled position, Monique had only one alternative: clear the area. And she did. In a flash, back the way she'd come, and had vanished out of sight, as they made the corner simultaneously. Down the hallway, a few loose pieces of paper lifted off the tile floor as if a small, phantom-draft had just passed through when no breeze of any degree was present.

Monique took a different route to the science room. As she was going in, Elise was coming out. They nearly slammed into each other, as they both shrieked sharply, startling one another.

"Oh my gosh!" Monique's shriek prominent.

Elise reacted, open hands pressed forward for bracing, "Whoa, watch out!"

"Don't do that, Monique. You kinda scared me," Elise said, they both catching short breaths to the degree of their little scare.

"I should tell you the same thing," Monique returned.

Jor said, "You guys be careful of being afraid. It can work against you at a critical time."

Was she serious? thought Monique, and Elise. What did she mean? Elise decided to probe a little deeper into the seemingly small matter. "Whadda you mean, we should be careful of being afraid? Everybody gets scared every now and then."

"Just be careful how much you become afraid. It can suspend your ability to perform at your highest level," Jor explained.

Koh added, more informative, "Listen. Never tell her I told you, but fear is the reason Motatu doesn't fly, not because she can't. We're hoping she'll get over it soon enough."

"What frightened her?" Monique curious to know.

"It's a long story," Koh said, and Jor added, "Yes, it's not important right now."

Monique said, a quiet laugh with humility in her voice, "She's the fastest on foot that I've ever seen. She really doesn't need to fly."

"Maybe not," Elise said. "Flying is fun, once you get the hang of it."

Koh teased her, "Oh, but miss smarty-pants will never fly, says you. What happened to the kids lost in the woods? Did you suddenly reconsider, or did an overbearing *desire* get in the way, huh?"

Elise snickered softly, a little abashed to admit she may've spoken too soon on the matter, as she joked, though honestly, "I don't want to talk about it."

Koh and her sisters, Jor and Motatu, laughed knowingly, "Tee-hee-hee-hee!"

It was warmth and caring in their laughter that opened the hearts of Monique, and Elise to the fullest extinct of their acceptance of the smart-aleck, though amiable, little imps.

But enough of the fun and games. Monique went right to the point, "So, did you find anything?"

Elise threw up her hands, "Nothing. I scanned everywhere. I saw nothing   that came close to look like a bomb, whatever it supposed to look like."

"You didn't run into those men in here, did you?" Monique went on to asked.

"No, I came close," Elise admitted. "But I don't think they saw me. I was a little too fast for them to even get a glimpse of me."

Monique was relieved to hear that. She then suggested with seriousness in her voice, "I think we should get out of here. I nearly ran into them when I was on my way here, looking for you."

"Let's go," Elise agreed, the two of them cautiously starting to make their exit, while wisely checking the way, to make sure it was clear, with the use of the eyes of the entities.

As they reached the hallway leading to the front exit of the school, they were suddenly pressed to make a speedy decision.

Tate Johnson and Jesse Cobb, the two men of the bomb-squad team, were only a few steps before walking right past them in the hall, as both girls were standing smack in the middle of the doorway to the Science classroom.

Monique and Elise flashed more quickly than the eye could follow, with a quick, short burst of their super speed. By the time each man—as they were closing in on the girls—started to focus on what was ahead, the girls were gone, that same phantom breeze lifting more loose, light trash slightly off the tile floor in the hall.

Only this time, a lingering presence of something lasted, but just for a tiny puff of a moment. However, the men—despite the quickly-fading vagueness of whatever—noticed it, with more of a clear distinction than not.

"You smell that?" Jesse asked Tate while sniffing the air. "Oh, wait. It's gone now."

"But I did smell something." It reminded me of my daughter, when she was, oh, about twelve. It was like a little girl's cologne, or perfume—lilac! That's it! It smelled like lilac," Tate asserted.

Jesse then brushed it off as something logical, "Could've been cologne a female student had on to today."

Tate rejected Jesse's logic. "No, Jesse. That was a fresh scent, not half a day old. It was like whoever was wearing it just walked by."
Bob was done with the discussion. It could've been ghosts of students past, as far as he was concerned. It was over and done in a manner of a split second. And no sign of any strange glimmer of hair, this time.

As they were walking out the exit, Jesse asked Tate, being a bit sarcastic, "So, what are we going to report, that we smelled a little girl's cologne, with hair?"

Tate fired back, "We want to keep our jobs, don't we?"

Jesse smiled with a subtle shake of his head with recognition as they continued over to the lieutenant, to make a report of their negative findings.

Elise and Monique had morphed back into their regular clothing, on their way out a side-exit. But first, Elise had to retrieve her backpack she'd left leaned against her locker when she first entered. In doing so, Monique remembered she had to do the same thing, only she'd left hers outside, by the ramp through which she'd entered.

It was still there when they returned, lying beside the concrete steps, on the ground. "There it is."

After they cleared the ramp, Monique went over, stooped, and picked up her backpack, with Elise waiting.

As Monique straightened-up, while strapping on her backpack, she and Elise both were blatantly interrupted by one of the teachers, "Just what are you girls doing here?"

She was Emily Beecham, assistant principal and was on her game. It was rare that a *kid* could slip one by her. To the students, she was known as the all-seeing; the all-knowing, dragon-lady.

Monique stammered to the mild scare as she turned to face the gentle beast, "I just came to get my backpack."

Her smile was meek, with a hint of embarrassment.

"You two know you're not supposed to be here. This is still a red zone. Until we get the all-clear sign, no one is to be in this area," she scolds them in her own grumpy, but caring manner.

"Now, the two of you, get going."

"Yes, ma'am."

Elise and Monique lit out across campus, holding on to their backpacks by the straps in front. They weren't terrified of the assistant principal; they respected her authority. They knew she was a kind older lady underneath that false meanness she displays. The girls were in a bland mood, now slowing their hurried strides after having crossed the campus. Some stragglers were slowly dispersing, which made the girls unnoticeable, strolling along.

"That was kind of close," Monique said, she and Elise relieved that they'd gotten away cleanly.

Across the way, hidden from view, among nature, and other structural inhibitors, the three federal agents sat in their sedan, keeping a watchful eye on the declining masses of the children on campus. They'd been there since the opening bell—the beginning of the upheaval of students and faculty members, scrambling for safety in mass droves. The team was spying on the event through binoculars, carefully monitoring the dissipating situation gravitate to an end.

The ladies took down their glasses from their eyes, focusing on their supervisor, Ed, who maintained his focus on the stragglers leaving the campus, through his binoculars.

"Anything? "Susan asked, sitting behind the wheel as Ed sat beside her, on the passenger side, pointing his vision through the windshield.

"Not... yet," he dragged the words out of his mouth, his preoccupied attention still on the campus. He did a complete sweep of the campus through the glasses, picking up the last of scattered students walking along, skateboarding and on bicycles.

"Then why are we still here?" Jillian asked.

He removed the binoculars from his eyes and stared at her. From the sound of her voice, he got the inkling she was in opposition to this scheme. For all the wasted efforts that he'd put into this plan, it was a total wash.

Before he replied, he did a final sweep through the binoculars. That time, the pan was broader, as he brought into focus from long-range two young girls walking along together. They were alone, headed alongside a roadway with no traffic, so far. Ahead of them was nothing but the distance that seemingly went on forever; not anything lively, like a farm, or some lived-in-houses...nothing but fields and trees, flanking each side of the macadam blacktop. He removed the binoculars from his eyes for the last time, looking at Jillian, who was seated in the back seat, saying to her, "Are you holding onto your theory that we have angels?"

Jillian leaned forward, to look him straight-on in the eye, undeterred, and said, "For all we know, any alien—as what *we* refer to them being—could very well be of a metaphysical nature. We already assume their intelligence level far exceeds our own; and, in many cases, we categorize their abilities are superior to ours. That's why we fear the unknown. Who's to say that these biological, little space beings aren't here as friends?"

"Ha!" Ed laughed scornfully. "So, you're suggesting we let down our defenses, and welcome these creatures with open arms, and docile our way straight to Hell!"

"I'm not suggesting any such thing," Jillian argued in defense.

"It's exactly what you're suggesting," Ed emphatically confirmed, to his belief.

"Ed, did you see anything remotely suspicious?" Susan asked as a damper to the building of a brewing, heated conversation.

Ed settled down, turned in his seat, facing the front. He let out a sigh and replied to Susan, "No, nothing. The last thing I noticed was two little girls walking by themselves, along a road that looked deserted. From what I saw, it looked like they have some good ways to go to school, on foot. I didn't' see a sign of any life for miles ahead."

"You wanna fly?" Elise asked Monique, on a whim.

Monique thought a moment, then smiled, "Why not? When you got it, flaunt it, I always say."

"No, you don't," Elise said frankly.

"And where'd you get that from?"

Monique was honest, shrugging her shoulders, "I don't know." Then Monique laughed as the two of them switched into their radiant, skin-tight body suits, with dashing capes, a stunning sheen in the bright sunlight. Finally, in tucking away their backpacks under their arms, they were ready to meet the sky. What they hadn't noticed was a vehicle approaching from the rear. They weren't paying attention because vehicles seldom traveled that particular road.

So, inattentively, the girls moved to about the middle of the road with anxiety, ready for take-off, while the speeding vehicle in the rear coming up fast. The passengers in the car were carefree teenagers, coming home from school. It was Friday, which meant Friday-night party time! Two guys up front, and three girls, and a guy crammed in the back seat.

They were whooping and yelling, drinking cans of beverages, with the CD player blasting While reaching behind his head for another beverage to be handed to him from his girlfriend in the back seat, the driver allowed his eyes drift off the road ahead a moment.

"Do we need to count, this time?" Monique asked Elise.

"No," Elise said. "I got this— "

At that moment, the boy on the passenger side in the car saw the girls in the middle of the highway, too late, as he screamed to the driver, "GIRLS!"

The driver screamed, slammed on the breaks, swerving to avoid the girls; the passengers in the back, screaming, grabbing things to hold onto for dear life, as, within those fleeting moments, the girls bolted to the air like a couple of rockets, right at the moment of impact, disappearing far, and away, into the distance within seconds.

The car skidded through where the girls, were standing, just missing them only by a hair. It came to a halt at the edge of the road, on the other side. Everyone was shaken, but uninjured. But every one of them was in a state of disbelief, over this mind-bending, supernatural event.

The passengers, including the spooked driver, got out of the car, dazed, disoriented, and nearly in a state of shock. Eventually, two of the girls and a guy passed out. Those left standing were incapable to render any assistance, for the moment.

Chapter 16

The Am-Trak left the station on schedule, with a scarce number of passengers onboard. It originated at a northern point, headed southwest, soon to be cruising along the rails toward the velocity to gain. The day was slightly breezy, though without intermediate wind-gusts; the northern plains spread across the land in vast proportions. The Montana sky was big, bright with sunlight, and soft pillows of white clouds lay adrift against the infinite spread of the big blue. It was the weekend, Saturday. Am-Trak sped along the rails, across the wide-open countryside—south-bound—giving the passengers a breathtaking vista of farmland, and small towns, remnants of the Old West.   Wendy had yet to tell the girls about the short time remaining of their stay at the foster home. She'd been hesitating, trying to find the right time to do so.

But there was no *right-time.* And they had to know, soon, before the difficulty of the task became too great. So, that Saturday, she treated them to pizza at an Italian restaurant downtown, with money she'd made from her sewing skills. Grand City was lively with shoppers, as it was business as usual, on the weekend.

They were seated at a corner table, by a window that looked out over the passing, shallow traffic, and the bustling side-walkers going about their shopping routinely.

Inside, the restaurant's tantalizing aromas of a variety of Italian dishes were soothing to the smell and inviting to the appetite. A frosty picture of lemonade came with the order of a large pizza that Wendy had ordered for them.

Elise and Monique couldn't wait to dig in when a sprightly, young waitress finally brought over a large pan of piping-hot, pepperoni pizza to their table. The girls rubbed their hands together, anxiously anticipating the first, delicious taste of their first bite.

Across the room, on the wall, near the ceiling, was a big-screen HD-TV airing a golf tournament, on low volume. As the girls, including Wendy, began eating, she decided this, of all times, wasn't the time to deliver bad news. In fact, after carefully thinking it over, she decided not to discuss their impending short-lived stay at the orphanage; they were already aware of its closing. Why rub salt in the wound? The girls previously had mandated a course of action they'd take, should the State deem that separating them is necessary. What was important at hand was to discuss how they'd maintain on their own.

"You're the best, Wendy," Monique managed, between bites. Then she wiped tiny strings of cheese from her mouth with a napkin.

In pausing, she added, "So, will you please reconsider being our mom?" Monique then withdrew, cringing, anticipating Wendy lashing out with a harsh word or two. But she didn't, the three of them sitting in a semi-circle at the small table, across from each other.

Elise was first to voice her show of surprise. "Wendy?"

She couldn't think of anything else to say. Monique timidly came out of her cringe, staring at Wendy, who beamed at her with a loving, vague smile. The girls stared at each other, puzzled. They didn't get it. Wendy sitting there without a single comment?

Wendy's stare wandered vacantly across the room, over to the big-screen TV on the wall. Something was airing on the screen, other than people playing golf; maybe a commercial, as Wendy said to the girls, "Whatever happened with the bomb-threat at your school; did they find anything?"

"No, false alarm," Elsie said.

Still idly gazing at the TV screen across the room, Wendy continued, "I saw on the news yesterday that two other schools were under the same investigation.

Monique asked, a little excited, "Did you see us?"

Wendy directed a tenuous, suspicious stare to her. "No," she said. "Did you do anything to attract attention to yourselves? Because you never told me you got involved..."

Elise quickly interrupted her, "OK. We did look around as Koh, and Jor, but we didn't find anything. And we weren't seen by anyone."

Again, Wendy surrendered her attention back to what was airing on the big screen across the room. The face of a news-announcer pretty much filled the screen, leaving only room for footage of a speeding train barreling along the tracks, with a few helicopters above matching the train's velocity.

Ordinarily, she couldn't hear the announcer that far away on low-volume. Therefore, she was unable to determine what was taking place with the train and several helicopters speeding along a desolate-stretch of real estate.

Aboard the train, the engineer struggled desperately to bring the powerful locomotive under manual control, as the computer system was offline, due to a malfunction shortly after leaving the station. Communications, along with the speed controls were inoperative, leaving the crew members, and passengers at the mercy of the fate that lay ahead; members of the crew worked frantically in using their mechanical skills to bring the vastly advancing problem to a speedy resolution, but, so far, without results.

Wendy, sitting there, staring, engulfed in curiosity, brought the action on TV up close by looking through Motatu's eyes, and adjusted her hearing likewise.

The news anchor man's announcement was then clear to Wendy, and the action thereof was also limpidly clear.

"The Am-Trak's communications system is down; also, the speed mechanism has apparently malfunctioned, as the train continues to increase its velocity, as I speak. News helicopters and Air Police are tracking the event as it unfolds..."

"Wendy?" Monique called to her, a little puzzled.

Wendy didn't answer; she was preoccupied, staring, and listening to the developing news on TV, across the room.

Someone suddenly burst through the front entrance of the small restaurant, anxiously shouting to the few customers enjoying an undisturbed afternoon delight, "Hey, everybody! A runaway train is headed this way, with passengers. It's bound to derail at any moment! It's speeding out of control!"

He was a spindly, young man, average height, and casually dressed, with thin, light-colored hair.

Less than half the customers left out of the restaurant, along with him, to see if they may witness the destructive climax of the ill-fated Am-Trak. They were in a section of town where the railroad depot ran along the southern edge of the city, close by; but the obstructions from buildings and other city structures prohibited a clear view of the passing train, from their vantage point, should it happen to make it that far.

The shout, breaking the girls' tranquil mood, got their attention abruptly. Spontaneously, they bounded to their feet, fully alert, glaring *knowingly* across the small table at each other. It was a foregone conclusion what they should do next.

"I was watching that situation develop on that TV across the room," Wendy said to them.

"Why didn't you tell us?" Elise asked, not understanding.

Wendy didn't answer her directly. "Let's get out of here," she said instead.

She then left the money on the table for the unfinished pizza they'd ordered, and the three of them left the restaurant in a bit of a rush.

They weren't noticed on the streets, as the people who were aware of the pending disaster headed their way. Some hopped in their vehicles, while those on foot scampered off towards the depot, which was over ten blocks away.

"What'll we do now?" Monique put the question before Elise and Wendy.

There was an alley up the street a short way. It was densely shadow-darkened, trashy; and, under ordinary circumstances, it was totally uninviting.

"This way," Wendy led the way toward the darkened indention of the alley.

Ten-year-old Justin Crenshaw, and his two younger siblings; Dianne, just turning nine, and Nichelle 6-1/2, shared a seat to themselves. Justin, the oldest, was the self-appointed commander over his siblings; whatever he says goes, and he'd insisted on the window-seat, now looking out across the vast plains as the train moved along with increasing speed.

"Man, we're really moving!" Dustin marveled, his two sisters excitedly climbing across him, to get a look out the window with him. He didn't give them much of a displeasing rejection; they deserved some measure of pleasure, even if they were silly, little kids, with hardly any intelligence at all.

Their mom and dad were in the seat directly behind them, to keep an eye on their every move. A scattered mix of passengers was beginning to get a little bit nervous. Some others were coming down with mild anxiety attacks, at the increasing speed. Overall, they remained seated, though buzzing with building concerns. The sensation of constantly increasing speed was nearing the point of alarm.

Without Chelsea's advice or permission, Jim Placket took the Sky-Cam helicopter, upon his own to join the others in pursuit of the runaway train. It passed through Grand City at a high rate of speed. Jim made certain the camera was on, filming every bit of the scene below, not missing an inch of footage. It wasn't time she reported in for her evening broadcast; she was home, going over the footage of the three girls walking along that gravel-and-dirt road, Jim had filmed some time ago.

In the far distance, about twenty-minutes ahead, Am-Track would cross over the massive late, along with a bridge. Rails had already begun to buckle under the weight and centrifugal force the train presented at such a high rate of speed. A derailment was imminent. It was only a matter of time.

In the distance, coming up from the rear of the speeding locomotive, three foreign, brightly-colored images were closing fast. Two by air, one by land were traveling at such an incredible rate of speed that their countenance was virtually invisible. To the naked eye, the three fast-moving figures looked like streaks of blues and whites, mixed with a combination of bright red, and yellow then black, with glaring Titanium silver.

On their extremely rapid approach, in the bright, afternoon sunlight, the glittering colors emitted a glare, almost fluorescent, though not harsh to the eyes, just luminously distinct.

They went past the helicopters in a flash, and in phantom-quietness. Jim and the pilots of the three other helicopters only caught a fleeting glimpse of the odd figures, moving at blinding speed. UFO? No one got a long enough look at the things, or objects, to decide what, possibly, could they have been. They were like a light gust of wind in color, ripping passed at an enormous speed.

The three girls, Elise, Monique, and Wendy, materialized in full forms some distance ahead of the speeding train, where they plotted their strategy.

"What about those helicopters up there?" Elise cautioned, "They're bound to try and take our pictures."

"There's not much we can do about that now," Wendy was aware. "We gotta stop that train before there's a catastrophe. And we don't have much time. If we move fast, maybe they won't get any clear enough pictures to do them any good."

The train was coming.

Fast!

The girls braced for the inevitable impact. They all closed their eyes, somewhat in a cowardly fashion, though standing their ground. As the train drew very close upon them, Monique panicked, cocked her leg, assuming a karate stance then violently kicked the front of the engine, as it was about to either slam into them or run them over.

It did neither.

Instead, it buckled under Monique's superior might, with a loud explosive boom, rumbling to a screeching halt, looming huge before the girls, dispensing a white phosphorous cloud of dense vapor, along with a loud hiss. The train was dead, but the girls combined their strengths, bearing against the multi-ton engine to bring it to a dead stand-still, the monstrous engine having sustained irreparable damage. It leaked diesel fuel, and other oily fluids, leaving that awful smell in the air.

"It stinks!" Elise complained, slightly holding her nose.

Monique was skittish, overcome with concern. She stammered nervously, "I...I didn't mean to kick it so hard. It was right upon us..."

Wendy teased her, "Oh...they're gonna be looking for you. Now you've done it."

"Shut up!" Monique shouted curtly, then grumbled, "Stupid, fast-running train. If it hadn't been for— "

"Let's go, you guys," Wendy quickly urged them, as there was no time to linger. They had to assume that everyone onboard was okay, as the helicopters were closing fast; and, now, emergency land-vehicles were approaching, to attend the jolted, rattled passengers aboard the disabled Am-Trak.

With the helicopters bearing down on them, and, of course, the land-vehicles, also; the girls had to skedaddle, quickly!

"Guys, we gotta go, now!" Wendy insisted.

Monique said, feeling solely responsible for the wrecked train, "I hate leaving them without the chance to explain what happened. Maybe we could leave them a note—"

"Monique!" Elise shouted. "Forget it. It's not our fault."

"I know," Monique argued, "It's all my fault."

Oh, the frustration. Elise gave her a little shove, indicative that they get flying, "Monique, get up there!"

They lifted to the air at low altitude, Monique still complaining, "Don't call me Monique, remember? It's— "

"Higher!" Elise yelled, disregarding Monique's protest. With a sudden burst of speed, they bolted to a much higher altitude, kicked in the afterburners, and were out of sight in seconds. Wendy flashed and vanished out of sight quicker than a wink. Three official helicopters landed in a vast field nearby, but Jim elected to fly back to the TV station "because of the unauthorized trip he'd taken, despite the unusual turn of the event with Am-Trak. He had on film the evidence of a train wreck, but no evidence of what had caused the collision. The way it had appeared from the sky to the four helicopter pilots, the speeding Am-Trak had seemingly slammed into some sort of an invisible forcefield. They never saw anything foreign, or otherwise on the tracks, except the train.

"Is everybody all right?" the captain of a firefighting squad said to a bewildered engineer, who sat there in the operator's position, behind the controls, frozen in place, and pale from the shock of his life.

Other rescue personnel came pouring on the scene, to assist the dazed and confused passengers as they got off the train, which was still hissing and leaking fluids. The heavily damaged engine was leaned lopsided on the track, facing South. None of the crew members on the train could give a full account of what had intervened to save them, and the passengers from a woeful fate. They were only grateful.

Two of the choppers were properties of the FBI, one was an official Police helicopter, then Sky-Cam from WCGN Television News, which had left the scene. The girls had found a spot in the middle of nowhere, to come together in a brief meeting.

Monique and Elise landed swiftly but softly, having proudly mastered the art of flying. Jor and Koh were commendable in their quickly-developed skills. In a vast field tattered with scattered trees, erratic placements of bushes and gross underbrush, the girls leisurely strolled idly along, sharing ideas of what the future may hold for them.

"Does this make us fugitives now?" Elise wanted to know.

Wendy, now, feeling protective toward the girls, said in thought, while walking with her head down slightly, "We've sort of been fugitives since the day we became who we are now."
Elise paused in thought, a smile on her lips to a surge of intrigue.

"Can you guys feel the rush?" she said with a distant look-away in thought, as if looking forward to whatever risky challenges lay ahead for them.

"She's around the bend," Wendy said of Elise's warped judgment.

"It does make for a huge challenge, don't you think?" Monique grinned with acceptance.

"You've lost it, too," Wendy was convinced of the two. They went on to take some time off, finally relaxing in the comfort of a grassy place along the shadowy edge at the entrance to a shallow forest.

Jim entered Chelsea's lavish apartment by invite, lugging the camcorder under his arm. It wasn't heavy, just somewhat a bulky, old camera that Chelsea had been intending on updating soon but hadn't gotten around to it. She was in the living room, surrounded by luxurious furniture, beautiful plants, and fresh, clean carpet. The air held an exotic scent of Tropic Potpourri.

Jim brought over the camera, placing it gently on a folded bath towel, which cushioned the weight of the camera on her smoke-stained, Plexiglas coffee table.

"You know," she said to him after he'd safely placed the camera on the coffee table and moved away, "I've been studying the footage you took of those three girls walking along that dirt road, that day. And it occurred to me, just how far did they live from that spot out by the lake? In studying their leisure behavior, they appeared to be there all by themselves. There never was a sign of any vehicle; which I don't think there ever was. So, why, or what were they doing out there so far away from any community? And how far did you say that orphan home was from the lake?"

"Oh, a good ten miles or so," Jim was certain.

"And the next town, or civilization?" Chelsea asked.

"Medfield," Jim said.

"Oh, I'd say about six to eight miles. But, from what I observed of them, they never went in that direction. If anything, I'd say they lived somewhere close to Grand City. But why's that so important to you? How is it you seem more concern about those girls than whatever happened out on the lake, that day."

Chelsea casually waved it off, "I don't know. Maybe it's my maternal instinct kicking in. And don't ask why because I don't know, only that I'm a woman." She took a break from her self-criticism, turning her attention to the camcorder on the coffee table. "What you got for me?"

Her voice was mild, but with a little interest.

Jim moved over and stood by the camera, with a little show of confidence in his subtle demeanor. "You know about the runaway train that passed through here a little ago, don't you?"

"Vaguely," she said. "I was busy. What happened?"

"What happened? I'll tell you what happened," he said in a raised, excited voice. "Probably the biggest, and the weirdest thing that ever happened in this town; and probably the whole world, as far as that matters."

Chelsea's stare at Jim widens to capacity from curiosity. They were both standing about center of the living room, somewhat face to face. "Well, C'mon," she said anxiously. "Tell me!"

"Just a minute." Jim rushed over to set up the camcorder, breaking it down, getting it prepared for showing the film. Chelsea took a seat on the sofa, wearing casual slacks and blouse. She was slightly leaned forward with anticipation, waiting for Jim to play the footage.

"This is going to blow your mind," he added, anxiousness in his movement, and his voice, as he got everything set to go.

He hit the on-switch, sat beside Chelsea at a respectful distance on the sofa, and they began watching the footage.

"Just what am I supposed to be looking for?" she said, interrupting their viewing of the short film.

He went, "Shush...it's coming."

She observed the train moving along extremely fast. Nothing, so far, caught her eye. She was beginning to tire, just watching. She sighed wearily, leaned back on the couch.

"Any minute now, wait for it... wait for it..." Then Jim shouted, "There! Did you see it?"

She only saw on film that the train appeared to stop suddenly, which was amazing of itself.

"It stopped, so what happened?" she asked, staring over at him, a little puzzled.

She went on in recognition, "I noticed it seemed rather sudden. And, unless something's wrong with the film—may be a glitch or something. But trains don't stop on a dime. They're just not built that way. I know; I've ridden them."

"That's just it," Jim said frankly.

"That's the big mystery. But that's not all. Keep watching."

"There's more?" At Jim's advice, Chelsea sat up straight, leaned forward a bit, gazing directly at her big-screen, HD TV.

"Watch," Jim said. "The camera's gonna pan to the front of the train."

As it did, Chelsea nearly comes unglued, she was so shocked. The front of the engine was totaled. It looked as though the train had slammed into the side of a stone-face mountain.

"What happened, what did that?" she asked, gaping awe-struck, and in disbelief.

"No one knows., With me included, there were four helicopters tracking the desperate train, as it was headed for certain disaster. Then some sort of unseen force suddenly stopped it. Whatever did that was very powerful. But we never saw anything, other than the train; we only heard this earth-shattering sound, like a huge explosion, and the engine started vibrating violently and came to a halt. Smoke, steam, and fluids were everywhere. But there was nothing we could see that caused the whole thing."

"What are those streaks of what looks like smears of different colors that keep interfering with the picture, every now and then?" Chelsea made mention.

"I'm not sure. Probably sun-glare," a short laughed. "Kinda looks like the wind in color, huh?" Jim laughingly concluded.

Chelsea didn't comment; she just sat there in deep thought, realizing this just may be the turning point she'd been waiting for. Then, for an instant, she figured it was another one of his incompetent bungling that caused the camera to lose focus on what it was that stopped the train.

Cleverly, she finally asked him, "Jim, what were those other helicopters doing there? Were they from the media?"

Jim went over in his mind, making certain he'd been clearly observant.

"Oh, no," he answered right away. "Two of them were of the FBI, and the other one was from the police department."

What Chelsea suddenly had in mind needed no further discussion that Jim would understand. This time she decided to go it alone.

"Jim," she told him, "leave the camera with me. You can pick it up later."

"Sure." He was very cooperative, getting up to leave. "I can get it later."

She walked him to the door then softly closed it behind him. Then she turned away slowly, immersed in deep thought.

Chapter 17

A team of FBI agents was on the scene, investigating the Am-Track mystery. Pictures of the damaged engine were taken for a more thorough examination, later, and to be placed with other classified documents. Also, passengers onboard the train were interviewed briefly; but no one claimed to have seen anything worth reporting to the federal agents.   Susan and Jillian stood aside with Ed while they looked at the horrific damage the engine sustained. They were awed and largely baffled over what possibly could have caused such irreparable wounds to tons of steel.

Susan said to Ed, incomprehensive of the mystery staring them in the face, in broad daylight. She's known how shrewd he'd been in the past, "Ed, this isn't another one of your ploys to draw out the aliens, is it?"

Ed laughed, "I assure you I wouldn't go to the length of endangering people's lives on a hunch, which could blow up in our faces. There was never a bomb placed in any of those schools, just a harmless threat."

Jillian said, "But you believe this was done by the aliens?"

Ed turned to her, as she was standing to his left, and said, "Belief? I'd bet a year's salary that we positively have aliens among us. Those sporadic reports on strange-happenings... those kids lost in the woods, being flown home by angels? And the old guy who witnessed two little girls leap into the air and fly away. Not only are there aliens; they have *hosted.* Our next assignment, ladies, is to find those girls!"

"And just how do we go about doing that?" Jillian put it to him frankly.

He looked her in the eye and replied honestly, "I don't have a clue."

Susan said to Jillian convincingly, "Don't worry, Jill, he'll think of something, I assure you; he always does."

Chelsea's astute investigation brought her to the police department in downtown Grand City. The desk-sergeant, Larry Meeks, a heavy-set, balding guy in his late thirties, recognized her as soon as she approached the desk.

"The news lady," he greeted her cheerfully. "It ain't often we get the pleasure. What can I do for you?"

Chelsea was appreciative of his kindness. She said, turning on the charm with her delightful smile, "Did you people have a helicopter on the scene of that runaway train, the other day?"

The sergeant was happy to announce, "We sure did. Got some pretty interesting pictures too."

"Oh? Is it possible I could see them?" she asked.

"Well, we got it on film," the sergeant told her. "We haven't made copies of still-shots yet."

"Is it possible I could look at the film?" she asked.

Sergeant Meeks said to her delightful surprise, "For the news lady? I think that can be arranged."

He picked up the phone on his desk and said to someone on the other end, "Logan, we got *the* news anchor lady, Miss. Chelsea Freeman, at my desk, as we speak. Uh huh. She wants to view the film on the runaway train."

He paused, listening; then his smile was the reassurance of ensuring good news. He hung up the phone, beamed at her, smiling, and said, "Go on back, he's waiting for you."

"Great," she thanked him, then started walking to the area he'd directed her.

On an afterthought, he said to her, which she paused to listen, "Hey, are you gonna mention my name on the news? It's Larry Meeks. Sergeant Larry Meeks."

She chuckled in walking away, "I think I can arrange that. Thanks a lot for your help." She left through double doors that led to some place in the back.

Chelsea watched the film in a dark room, along with a couple other courteous police officers—two males and a female. What she saw was the exact same thing she saw on the film Jim had taken. At the point of impact, there was nothing defining the cause. But the same multi-colored glare was on that film, as well.

The same sun-glare at the exact same place in this film, too?

Chelsea was thinking. Was this ironic, or what?

However, as baffling as it was, it couldn't have been a coincidence, to the letter. And she knew the FBI wouldn't allow her a look at their files. So, she assumed there would be no different than what she'd already seen.

While the film continued, she sat there, pondering until the notion came to her that something beyond the natural order of things abounded. She left the police station and returned home, where she began studying the film Jim had left her, with the utmost scrutiny. She wondered if the feds were that smart.

It was another grueling day of classes at school.

During the changing of classes, Elise ran across Brittany at the lockers. For some odd reason, she didn't seem herself. Elise became curious, daring to approach her; she looked sullen, sort of in a dampened mood.

"Brittany?" Elise cocked her head to the side, staring curiously at Brittany. She only responded with a casual, but solemn glance at Elise then moved on.

"Brittany?" Elise went after her, despite their deplorable differences. They were alone together, which was unlike usual. Monique wasn't there, and neither was Brittany's posse, Natalie, or any of the other girls she hung with.

Brittany whirled around, glaring at Elise with nothing kind toward the girl in her stare.

"What?" That was harsh, with a bold hint of displeasure, and a show of rude impatience.

Elise shrugged her shoulders while holding her books down to her tiny waist, staring innocently up into Brittany's hateful, stormy eyes.

"If you going to bite my head off, forget it!" Elise scoffed.

"It was just that... Well, you look like you've lost your best friend. I was just concern, that's all. It's not every day you don't pick on us for something. I thought maybe you'd come down with something."

"So, you're saying, you care what happens to me?" There was a glimmer of softness in her eyes—for just a moment, mind you. But it was there.

"Of course, I care," Elise made clear. "We hate each other, but not to the death, I would hope. I wouldn't want you to die, to get you out of my hair."

"So, you're asking me to be your friend?" Brittany was testing the water.

"It wouldn't hurt to try, even though it may be impossible." Elise had her doubts.

"So, you don't trust me," Brittany miffed.

"I never said I did!" Elise fired back.
Brittany swiftly turned around, and resumed walking away, leaving Elise with, "Just forget it!"

Elise was peeved, murmuring, "Try to be nice to some people..."

Then with a certain burst of irritation, she yelled, "You're right. Forget it!"

Something wasn't right with Brittany. She was always a bully, although her bark was far worse than her bite. She'd nothing but mean words to say to Elise, and Monique, and many others. But, this time, Elise had noticed she seemed deterred by something other than her mean streak. Maybe she was changing, had changed; or wanted to change, which was it? The girls elected to walk home after classes that afternoon, the day was that perfect, serene. A warm breeze, hardly a breeze at all, sauntering across nature's gardens near and far; leaves gently rustled in the trees and surrounding foliage on such a becalmed, mid-spring afternoon.

Monique and Elise lagged after most of the groups of walkers, kids passing them on bikes, skateboards, and scooters. With about two miles ahead, the girls were in no hurry, taking in the vista of nature's natural wonders against industrial structures, scattered about along the way.

"Brittany's whacked," Elise declared to Monique about their nemesis Brittany Stewart.

"I tried being nice to her today, but she wouldn't— "

"I know," Monique interrupted her, knowing what Elise was about to say. "She was insulting, as usual, right?"

Elise looked away in thought, then decisively replied, "No, not really."

"Huh?" That was a surprise to Monique, "You mean she was actually nice to you?"

"No, she was bitter, as usual," Elise said.

"Then why bother to tell me how mean she was? Everybody knows she's a pain—all the time," Monique spoke harshly of the girl in question.

Then, at a glance behind them, while on the subject, Monique spotted Brittany walking at a leisure pace, but would soon catch up to them because they were dragging along much slower, as Elise was saying, "But not this time. She acted as if something was bothering her..."

"You better make it quick," Monique warned, "because here she comes."

As Elise looked around, Brittany walked right by them without the slightest glance their way. She continued straight ahead in an idle, preoccupied fashion as if she was immersed in some deep meditation over something certainly unknown to the girls.

They looked at one another, mystified. Monique quipped, "Was that Brittany? *Our* Brittany?"

"See what I mean?" Elise pointed out.

"I guess." Monique was stumped as Brittany move ahead with lackluster.

"That was not Brittany," Monique was in disbelief.

"I know," Elise agreed. "She's being really weird."

At that moment, Natalie appeared from a short distance behind them, and paused long enough to ask, "Have you seen Brittany?" She was a bit winded having hurried along, trying to catch up with her friend.

Elise and Monique pointed ahead simultaneously, as a curious Monique asked, "What's wrong with your friend?"

Natalie, with a bland disposition without Brittany's hands-on influence on her, said, to the girls' lack of understanding, "I think she's trying to kick me to the curb."

"Why? You guys been friends for..." Elise groped for words to finish her statement.

"I know," Natalie sighed dolefully. "I don't know what's gotten into her. She's been acting strange all day. I can't figure it."

"Well, there go your chance to try," Monique said having spotted Brittany dart through a small group ahead.

After Natalie saw her friend some ways ahead of them, she pressed on, picking up her pace once again. "Thanks," she was polite enough to say to Monique in leaving the girls alone, to catch up with her friend.

"Natalie's not such a bad person if she'd stop hanging around that Brittany," Monique commented observingly.

When Natalie caught up to Brittany, Monique, and Elise saw them pair-off in what appeared like a heated discussion. Brittany was braced stiffly before Natalie, berating her with harsh words, it seemed, while Natalie, seemingly, was trying to calm her down.

Elise and Monique looked-on baffled but didn't interfere, even with their ultra-keen hearing, or their extraordinary sights. They were self-disciplined enough to respect others privacy.

"I wonder why she's getting on to Natalie?" Elise said. "She's as harmless as a kitten."

"I know," Monique said, enlightened. "I believe you; Brittany's acting very weird." "Did you know yesterday was my birthday?" Brittany yelled to Natalie in her face.

Dumbfounded, Natalie shook her head in guilt. "You never told me your birthdate," she innocently replied.

"That's not an excuse!" Brittany scoffed. "Evidently, I never told my folks neither!"

"What are you talking about?" Natalie didn't understand.

"What parents forget their kid's birthday? That's impossible."

"You're right," Brittany curtly returned. "My folks *are* impossible!" After that hateful flare-up, Brittany stormed away in quick, angry strides.

As the girls watched the incredulous scene come to an audacious, premature conclusion, they shared their mixed emotions, as Elise was first to comment, "I now kinda wish we had listened-in on what they were talking about."

"Brittany seemed very upset about something," Monique said. "Whatever it was she was so mad about, Natalie looked so innocent."
"I suspect that Natalie was being naïve over something Brittany expected her to do that she didn't do," Elise speculated.

"That sounds about right, knowing the two of them," Monique settled for that assumption, as the two of them continued along.

Natalie waited a moment, confused. Then, decisively, she ran after Brittany, who had strayed from the thinning groups of kids. She was headed toward a deserted part of any settlement, where there were scarce, forlorn building structures, such as houses, and the like. The area was unpopulated, only a ghostly remnant of a past life from long ago. Deep shadows, punctuating the lay of the land, were like hordes of phantoms haunting recluse remains of a lost civilization.

Trying to navigate her way through unfamiliar territory, among rocky mounds laden with brush and tall weeds; gushing earth, steep slopes and stretches of barren wasteland, pitted terrain with a few dangerous cliffs; Natalie became increasingly desperate. Brittany was nowhere in sight. It was as though she'd simply dropped off the face of the earth. The quiet, the emptiness was almost apprehensive.

"Brittany?" Natalie calling out to her only echoed on the edge of the wind in despair.

Time after time, she called out to Brittany, but to no avail; only an empty, quiet no-return, with a quiet breeze hardly rustling the leaves in trees and foliage around her, imminent of a lost cause.

Natalie was on the verge of panic, at this time, she screamed out the girl's name, "Brittneee!"

Natalie finally realized there was nothing to be gained by yelling into the emptiness surrounding her, and the wind. Brittany was nowhere to be found. Natalie then turned away, intending to head back to where there was life, and out of this dead zone.

She hadn't gone very far when a far-away echo of someone crying out became barely within range of her hearing. It was faint, very weak, barely audible. But she heard it.

"Brittany?" She wasn't sure exactly what she'd heard, but she was willing to gamble that the sound was significantly different from anything Mother Nature produced. That was a *human* voice.

"Brittany, where are you?"

There it was again; that time, more distinct, *"Help me!"*

Natalie lit out in an aimless direction, to track down the location of the distant voice.

"Brittany, where are you?"

"Here... down here!"

"Down here?" That was puzzling to Natalie, looking around at somewhat of a loss. "Where?" she yelled, flustered.

"Down here. Hurry!"

That was more precise. Natalie rambled through prickly thickets, carefully through dense brush, across the erratic terrain, to a clearing. That's where she held up, stymied. She saw no one, and that's what had her worried. Brittany's voice had come from this specific direction; but Natalie saw no one, only a cliff edges a few paces ahead of her.

"Brittany?" She tested her direction-finding skills.

"Natalie, I'm down here!" That was Brittany, dangling over the edge of the cliff in front of Natalie.

Natalie moved with caution to the edge of the cliff, her mind reeling to the idea of taking such a risk. She was deliriously afraid of heights. But Brittany was her friend, despite her shifty mood-changes. That's what made Brittany who she is.

On her hands and knees, Natalie crawled as close as she would dare to the edge of the rocky cliff wall, where she then lay flat on her stomach and looked over the edge. She was horrified at what she saw, gasping with overwhelming fear.

Brittany was hanging on to a protruding root jotting out of the dirt-bank near the top of the cliff. The root extended from a small tree not long on any support. It was dried-out to merely a stick of a piece of wood, and brittle, ready to break apart with the slightest amount of added pressure.

Natalie withdrew from looking over the edge, and sat down in the dirt, near the frail life-support Brittany only had to hold onto. Her feet dangled freely, in midair, with over a one-hundred-foot drop below to jagged rocks, sparse groups of trees, and a tiny, shallow stream. The situation was a nightmare, hopeless, and downright horrifying.

As Natalie chanced to look over the edge of the cliff once more, the two girls' eyes met in excruciating despair. Brittany knew her time was very short, only a matter of a few waning minutes. Natalie could no longer restrain the tears that began flowing from her eyes.

"Hold on, Brittany," she sobbed desperately, vainly extending a useless hand down to Brittany, which couldn't have been for nothing but a gesture of farewell to a friend.

Elise spoke to Monique, as they were walking alone, having finally separated from the other kids, "Do you hear that?"

Her keen sense of hearing had picked up what sounded faintly like a distress call for help, then...murmuring.

Both girls then paused to listen, with Monique saying, "I hear the wind in the trees."

"Tell the stupid wind to be quiet and get out of the silly trees!" Elise shouted while concentrating.

"Now I hear it," Monique said. "Someone's in trouble!"

Natalie had exhausted her futile efforts to find anything which might help her friend to safety. So many tears in her eyes fogged her vision to see clearly, as she'd muddled tear-blind to find any means of support. Numerous times she'd called down to Brittany to hold on, but the girl was running out of time, and they both knew it.

Finally, Natalie could do nothing but sit by the edge of the cliff—which was the closest she could get to her friend—and with her knees drawn up to her chest, rocking back and forth, stark-raving mad in denial, with her arms locked tightly around her lower legs.

Brittany called up to Natalie in a weak, whimpering voice, for the final time, "Natalie...I'll miss you..."

Natalie sobbed painfully, "Don't, Brittany. Please...just hang on."

"I can't— "

Just as Brittany had attempted to respond to Natalie's frivolous urge for her to hang on, she was abruptly hampered by an unseen force that gently snatched her free from the failing root she'd been hanging on to. This immensely swift proceeding took place within the blink of an eye. Brittany didn't have time to think, or reason in any fashion. She felt a gentle tug underneath her arm-pits, a quick, solid lift, and she was afloat in midair, but only for a second before she was gingerly, ever so softly, placed atop the cliff, right next to Natalie, who sprang to her feet in sheer fright.

She squealed, but it was more like a squeak, as the traumatic shock was so sudden and debilitating, it rendered her speechless, diluted of reality. Ultimately, her stance became weak and she collapsed to the ground in a heap. Brittany sat there like a stone statue, propped in a still-sitting-position, unblinking, unthinking, frozen in a state of apprehension.

"Oh...," Monique was empathetic, "I feel so sorry for them."

She and Elise were in an intense vibrating mode, which made them invisible to the naked eye. They were only an arm's length from the pair, after having delivered Brittany safely out of harm's way, just moments earlier.

"If we don't do something, they're going to totally freak-out," Elise felt the same pity.

"I think, maybe, they deserve a sign," Monique suggested.

"I think you're right," Elise agreed. "But let's do it quickly, then get the heck out of Dodge."

Within the next instant, they became visible to Natalie and Brittany; but their images were so vague, and unaccountable, they appeared as a couple of apparitions in stunning, fashionable costumes.

Natalie and Brittany could only look-on with gaping eyes, in disbelief, and apprehension, after Natalie had regained consciousness.

"Take care, guys." "And be careful," Elise and Monique kindly said to them. Then, with a tremendous, aeronautic burst of speed, they bolted to the air and out of sight in a flash.

When Natalie and Brittany were finally settled enough to try and make the attempt to start home; they moved vaguely, and indirectly in the general direction of where the home was. For the time being, they weren't sure what was real, and what was not. Their minds were still muddled, unclear, unable to rationalize. A no-such-thing had just happened. Other than logic, and the law of gravity, Brittany should be deceased; Natalie should be walking home alone, bearing the horrible news of her friend's demise. But they were together, walking along as if nothing of such horrendous magnitude had occurred.

While dazed, disoriented, and confused, Natalie finally said, with no certain terms, "Do you still think there are no such things as angels?"

Brittany didn't reply; she just stared at Natalie with a vacant look in her eyes.

Chapter 18

Natalie saw Brittany home safely. It was Friday the weekend coming up. Brittany's near-death experience had humbled her considerably. In their approach to the neighborhood, Brittany's home was in sight, only a few blocks down the street. Natalie had been obliging by not chatting, rambling on, like she normally does. This time, she was quiet, reserved, concentrate. After what they'd both gone through, some quiet-time was essential. They were still in the process of collecting themselves in the aftermath of having visited with...*angels.* As they drew closer to Brittany's home, they noticed several vehicles parked out front of the house. Her parents' vehicles were parked in the driveway.

Upon noticing them, Brittany knew, firsthand, why the extra vehicles were there, as she drew on her strength to say to Natalie, "You want some company for the weekend?"

Ordinarily, Brittany was a recluse. She preferred being alone when she wasn't at school, harassing other kids. And even though Natalie had spent time with her over the weekend, whenever Brittany was in a tolerant mood—which was seldom— she'd never shown the humility to make such a request to Natalie for herself.

Natalie, the docile child as she was, responded in delight, "You are asking *me*? Why, of course. Spending the weekend together would be great!"

They were on the walk-way, coming up to the front stoop of a posh, two-story brick home with a two-vehicle garage, with only a single-wide, automatic garage door.

"You sure it's okay with your folks?" Brittany asked, showing a polite attitude Natalie hardly knew she had.

"My folks are out of town," Natalie said. "But even if they weren't, it'd be OK for you to stay the weekend."

"I'm mostly alone on weekends," Brittany said.

Even if her reasoning for the surprising request was a selfish one, Natalie delighted to have her over as a company.

"Well, you're welcome at my house any time," she said to Brittany, then added, the extra vehicles out front stimulating her curiosity, "What are all these people doing at your house?"

Brittany shrugged her shoulders, but she had an idea why; she only kept it to herself as they entered through the front door.

The minute the girls came through the door, they noticed right away the living room was suspiciously shadow-darkened; not suspicious of Natalie; only to Brittany. But before she could turn to Natalie and warn her, they were blasted in the face by shouts from people springing forth from hidden places within the shadows throughout the living room.

"Happy birthday!"

That was more startling than appealing to Brittany, as her reaction was far less enthusiastic, and filled with disappointment.

After getting over the initial start, Natalie, with a hand held slightly to her heart; and in catching small breaths, she related to Brittany, "You see? They didn't forget your birthday."

"You don't understand," Brittany said. "Look around you and tell me who do you see."

Natalie didn't get it. She looked around at the guests, as they were all adults. Oh, except there were two other kids besides Natalie and Brittany; a young boy about eleven, chubby, and munching on a hamburger, sort of a sloppy eater. Then there was this gangly, little girl, early teens, accompanied by her mom, a frail lady, tall, and thinly, almost succumbed to anorexia.

These people were only her parents' associates; her dad's hunting and fishing friends, social drinkers; and her mom's co-workers, card-game partners, along with a few others Brittany wasn't that familiar with.

"Who are all these people?" Natalie was befuddled. "I don't see anyone we know from school."

Brittany, *knowingly,* hesitated to admit, "Because there aren't any."

Natalie went silent. Brittany's arid tone of voice painted a clear picture of the reason behind that abrasive comment. And Natalie knew what she knew: they had no friends.

Brittany's mom came over to her and Natalie, with a lively smile, "Honey, aren't you and your friend going to join us? The party's in your honor. I know it's a little late, but it's your birthday party."

She smelled of a delightful perfume, "Evening in Paris."

Her name was Lyla Stewart, a spry, flamboyant type of person nearing middle-age; her husband, Josh, average height and build, three years Lyla's senior, a straight-laced, no-nonsense, penny-pincher. Brittany's belated birthday celebration came by his unwillingness to support, what he claimed, was a waste of necessary finance. Her mom had ended up footing the bill, which was why the acknowledgment of Brittany's birthday was delayed. But the essential point of this whole scenario was the undeniable fact that the Stewart family was dysfunctional. "Maybe later, mom," Brittany said, taking her friend Natalie upstairs.

Her mom yelled up at her, "Don't forget, you have to be here before we can cut the cake!"

"I'm spending the weekend with Natalie!" Brittany yelled back to her mom, unfeeling. She replied under her breath, in surrender, "Whatever."

Natalie lived across the way, in the next neighborhood, about six-tenths of a mile, clear on the other side. The walk would be refreshing. After grabbing a few items of clothing, they were off. Brittany didn't bother with any cake, and neither did Natalie, although she would've loved to have, at least, one small slice.

They were walking along in the shades of trees lined alongside the streets, on their way through the neighborhood, to Natalie's house. It was so noticeable to Natalie that Brittany was deeply preoccupied with thought. Finally, Natalie was compelled to break the silence by asking,

"Are you all right? You sure you're okay with spending the weekend at my house?"

Brittany's response was strange, unlike her normal behavior. Instead of a direct answer to Natalie's question, she said, "Do you know the names, Koh, and Jor?"

Natalie stared at her peculiarly. "Huh?"

A faint smile barely spread Brittany's lips, her distant stare looking straight through Natalie, into a far distant vacancy, as she continued, "The names won't get out of my head."

Then she shifted her stare to Natalie, looking her intently in the eye, and said, "It was them, you know."

Brittany then went quiet.

"*Them*? Them, who?" Natalie was still baffled, although she realized the bedazzling, upheaval discontentment Brittany must be suffering through. She was there, as well, to see the phenomenon unfold right before their eyes. And Natalie also recalled being the one who'd fainted. So, not by a long-shot was either of the two cleared of insanity; they were both a trauma case.

Brittany finally replied, under a great weight of depression, "The angels. They are real, you know."

If Natalie hadn't been there to witness the whole bizarre episode unfold; it would be simple for her to declare that her friend, Brittany, needed psychoanalyzing. "I know they're real. I saw them too, remember?"

Chelsea had gone over the films she'd obtained from both the city police department and her own employee, Jim Picket at WCGN television station. It would have been ironic, should the exact same glitch had occurred in both camcorders, leaving certain, colorful smearing interference in both the exact same areas on the films. But that wasn't the case, as Chelsea had discovered by repeatedly viewing the films. It had come down to super-slow-motion, to stop-action at certain points in the films. To her jubilant amazement, she found a resolve.

The colorful smears turned out to be imaged, dressed in colorful outfits in relations to Halloween costumes, very skillfully designed by an expert seamstress. Two of the images appeared airborne while a third image seemed to be afoot, as if in a high-speed race against a speeding locomotive; and the fleeting image was winning. When carefully managing the flow of the film with slow-motion and stop-action, Chelsea pieced together a complete composite of what exactly took place, involving the run-away-train that afternoon. Thus, her suspicion was gratified. What she suspected was aliens; what she hunted was aliens, and what she ultimately had found was the closest things to aliens as there will ever be. Otherwise, these were *aliens! Her aliens,* as far as she was concerned.

She'd paused the film, holding the images in place, as they appeared as three young girls—in human forms, dressed in dazzling uniforms—addressing the very front of the train, after having brutally forced the mammoth engine, made of tons of steel, to a violent halt.

After having achieved her long sought-after resolve, Chelsea sank back in her comfortable sofa, enjoying the end of this gripping mystery, reveling in the thought that these aliens— whatever type they were—could *stop* a *train!* They were like cute, little superheroes, in their spiffy outfits. Then, offhandedly, she recalled the article she'd glanced at in one of those tabloids on the magazine stand in the supermarket a while back. She read about the old guy who claimed he saw two little girls leap into the air, dressed in superhero costumes, just like the ones on film.

Could there be any relations? Of course, she was thinking. Now, what to do to establish communications or a friendly relationship with them? She didn't figure them to be of a hostile nature; they stopped the train to save lives. Her main concern, following this fantastic discovery, was how far along was the government in tracking the aliens. Should the feds encounter the aliens before she does, it could mean disaster for her cause. She didn't dare broadcast her findings on television; there were still loose ends to be tied together. Other than that, while the public may not take it seriously, it would alert the feds. She was at an impasse, stuck with waiting it out. She had no other choice. Luck was her only ally now.

Her cell phone rang. She took it out of her purse next to her, on the sofa, and answered it. "Yes?"

It was Jim with a little bit of news.

"Chelsea, about those three little girls; I think I've solved the mystery."

He did a pass over the foster home, in the helicopter while on the phone with Chelsea. "You ever hear of Lily Field Orphanage—or foster home?"

"What?" Chelsea was beside herself in frustration. By him chiming in with idle talk about some kids in an orphan home was a distraction. She was hot on the trail of *her* Pulitzer Prize. Those three little girls are long since a fading memory.

"Those girls," Jim stressed. "I think I've found where they live. There's a Lily Field Foster Home directly along that dirt road, out by the lake, for about 8 to 10 miles. And there's nothing, no houses of any kind. And the orphan home is the only, the closest place to the lake. Anything else, like the city, another residence, even Medfield, are much too far away to walk that distant."

Oh, that man was so exhausting. But, the poor thing only thought he was helping.

"Thank you, Jim," she was polite.

"You've been a big help. Now, meet me at the helipad in about an hour."

"You going to fly out to the orphan home?" Jim thought Chelsea would follow-up on the info he'd just given her.

"What for?" she said, disinterested.

"We're not? I thought you'd want to know...," disappointment in his voice.

The halls were buzzing with students preparing for a lunch break. Elise and Monique had decided to have their lunch outside;

the cafeteria was in disarray, with students pushing and shoving, causing confusion in the lunch-lines, and at tables with very little space left for kids milling around to sit. And the noise decibel was incredibly loud.

The girls chose a picnic table under several close-knit trees, assuming they'd be alone. But that idea was thwarted when a few other kids came over, to the girls' tolerant dismay. They really didn't mind the company, as they were all classmates, twelve-though-thirteen-year-olds.

As they opened their lunch sacks, and boxes, mixed, delicious aromas were faint, elusive in the air around them. During their chatting, a kid, Brad Tatum, 13, blurted out to Elise, and Monique, meaning no offense, "Hey, what's it like being an orphan?"

A dark-haired girl, Connie Austin, sitting beside him, nudged him in the side with an elbow, cautioning him to mind his manners, "Brad…"

"It's OK," Monique said in a lively voice. "I never knew my parents. As far as I know, I never had any."

"That's impossible," Brad argued the point.

Monique stared him in the face, from across the table, "Dumb-ass, I know that!"

That got laughter, which ceased almost instantly, as Brittany was then spotted by nearly everyone sitting there, on her approach.

"Oh, my god," a girl named Michelle Harris—whom everyone referred to as Mikki—murmured in stark dismay.

"Here comes the *beast.*"

Several kids immediately got up and left the area, leaving Monique, and Elise there with only a couple other kids, Brad, and Connie left to *defend the fort.*

As nervous tension mounted, the closer Brittany got to them, Monique muttered under her breath facetiously, "Maybe we should've let her fall off that cliff."

Elise stared at her, surprised by that cruel remark. Then Monique smiled with the wisecrack, "But, we saved her, so there...all's forgiven. Let's kill her now."

As Brittany approached them, Connie and Brad were poised to bail, as Brittany said to them, "You guys don't have to leave."

Her voice was subdued, reduced to an unfamiliar humbleness no one was ready for, as Connie, and Brad left anyway, inconsiderately abandoning the two orphans.

Brittany took a seat at the table, across from the girls. Her stare at them was becalmed, no hint of malice of any sort. Then her stare faltered, and...yes, she was a little glassy-eyed.

"Well, whadda you want?" Elise boldly asked although she realized the residual trauma the girl must be suffering; she and Monique being the ones who'd rescued her from certain death. But Elise couldn't afford to let on to that effect.

"Nothing," Brittany said.

Then she lifted her misty stare to them, stammering, "Look. I know how you guys must hate me, and I don't blame you. You can go on hating me for the rest of your lives, I'll understand. All I want to say is..."

She became overcome by emotions and quickly got to her feet. But as she was about to bolt, she had second thoughts; turned and went back over to the girls, circling around to their side, and stood between them from behind.

"So, where's your posse, Natalie?" Monique piped uncaringly.

Brittany merely answered, "She's not here."

Then, on an emotional whim, she leaned over them from behind and gathered them in a duel embrace. In other words, she brought them together, with arms around both. The hug, the girls felt, was sincere, apologetic, filled with warmth.

Monique cringed, a little dubious toward Brittany's show of sincerity, as she commented, still in the girl's embrace, "We like you too, Brittany. But can we not keep this up among all these trees? They may get the wrong idea and start spreading vicious rumors."

Brittany cackled, letting go of them. She said to Monique, her spirit suddenly lifted by Monique's witty remark, "You are unbelievably hilarious!"

The bell rang to start the afternoon classes. Brittany walked along with Elise, and Monique, feeling a bit out-of-place because of her past demeanor. But the girls were comfortable with her, only Brittany felt obligated to them.

"Look. If you guys feel uncomfortable with me along, I can get lost," she made clear.

That did it. She was becoming annoying. Monique and Elise paused, staring intently at her. Brittany waited sheepishly, responding to their judgmental-look at her, "What?"

"Brittany, stop feeling sorry for yourself." Elise just lets her have it, continuing, "So, you've changed. Let it be a good thing. We'd rather be friends, even if we don't hang out together. We could always be there for each other if needed."

"Yes, that's a good idea, don't you think?" Monique added.

Brittany's vague smile was distant, although she took in everything they said. And she regarded their presence in an amiable sense but was preoccupied with those angels on her mind. She nodded half-consciously to Monique's final suggestion.

As they were walking up the concrete steps to enter the building, Brittany asked frankly, though in a lulled, far-away thought, "You guys believe there are angels?"

That got their attention, as the girls looked at one another *knowingly*.

Monique was first to reply, "What brought that on?"

Nothing more was said from either, as they continued down the hall, finally mixing with the heavy flow of students-traffic.

Later, as Brittany was headed to her class, alone, Natalie popped up. "Where've you been? I've been looking all over the place for you."

They were right outside about to enter their classroom.

"Nowhere," Brittany said, then suddenly thought to ask Natalie, "Hey, you haven't told anyone about what happened, have you?"

There was a serious, deeply concern-look in her stern gaze at Natalie.

"No, I haven't. You told me not to, remember?" Natalie assured her. "But why shouldn't people know? Those kids who were lost in the woods said there were angels who brought them home, even though nobody believed them. But I'll bet you they were the same two angels who came to us. Don't you believe that?"

Chapter 19

Though far and, pretty much, in between, rumors of angels began to gather strength. Among the populace of Grand City, those who have had close encounters with the mysterious beings took their stories to the local authorities due to the mind-bending unrest it created. It wasn't fear that drove them to that decision; they were gratified. The hard disheveling of such a reality was what took a toll on the mind.

The newspapers, along with the radio, and television began using the stories as a stimulant for business—to attract patriots, more listeners, and investors. Soon, nonbelievers were caught up in the act of star-gazing. They weren't expecting any Earth-shaking event; it was just their innate curiosity at work.

Government Agents, Ed, and his staff, Susan, and Jillian had scrutinized the film just as Chelsea had. They knew the aliens had obtained three hosts. And they knew that eventually there would be a confrontation. The president had given the order to proceed with Operation Annihilation if no suitable terms are met. But under no condition would the aliens be allowed to co-exist among humans, which meant, for the most part, annihilation loomed larger than life. The military was on a daily alert, and on secret maneuvers.

Chelsea was in a race against time. She'd become so deeply involved in staying one step ahead of the government, in her search for the aliens, that she'd taken a leave-of-absence from her job as a news broadcaster. Her replacement was a suave gentleman, very apt in that line of work. She would have no interruptions, pursuing her task at hand.

It was early evening, nearing twilight. The sun was low on the horizon, a large, bright yellow-orange emitting its final brilliance of the day. Grand City was awakening to its night-calling. Neon lights began spangling their inferior glow throughout the lay of the city.

Chelsea was home, studying the films she had in her possession.

After long hours of going over parts of each film, she suddenly had a hunch so incredible the enlightenment was dizzying.

"Of course," she shouted aloud. Enthusiasm overwhelmed her, as it came to her very clearly.

She took up her cell phone and called Jim, her heart racing with excitement. Finally, "Hello… Jim?"

She waited, "Yes, it's me. Fire up the chopper and meet me there, immediately!"

She hung up, sprang to her feet, grabbed her purse, and left the apartment in a huge rush. She was dressed just fine in fashionable beige slacks, with an accommodating, white blouse, and a light, waist-jacket.

While the feds may have their own film to study; they didn't have the films her sweet, lovable Jim had. There was still the chance she'd succeed ahead of them. A great chance!

Miss Agnes was home relaxing after a busy day, concerning the closing of the foster home, and her retirement. She was near exhaustion. The girls had just left the movie theater and were standing around, trying to make up their minds where to get some snacks, even though they had pretty much stuffed themselves on movie-popcorn and candy bars. During her short tenure in school, Wendy recalled one of her schoolteachers' remark, *"Kids can eat the darndest things and never gain an ounce!"*

Under the canopy of neon lights, and streetlamps, the city was luminescent with plenty activities, such as night-shoppers that filled the streets; restaurants were busy, and numerous parties with live music graced the hot spots of town. The city was alive with generating patrons' energy!

"Well, how 'bout it, you guys, what'll it be?" Wendy was open to suggestions, so long as they stayed within her budget.

"Burgers," Monique said. Then she and Wendy turned to Elise for her vote.

As she was about to speak, Brittany and Natalie appeared, and some stragglers from their school tagged along, which made it seven of them to idly mill around. But, with Brittany's new attitude adjustment, it was a pleasant gathering.

"You guys down for some food? My treat," she made welcome, her passing glance casually regarding Wendy stimulated a vague memory from long ago.

"Don't I know you?" she asked Wendy, who had her about two-inches in height—much better-looking, and so much better built.

Wendy said with slight recognition, "You were just entering middle-school as I was leaving."

"Did you graduate?" Brittany asked, a gesture to continue a friendly conversation. And it felt great being part of a pleasant gathering, without the negative vibes and berating insults.

Wendy shook her head, "No, I study online now. I'm only sixteen."

Brittany smiled at Elise, and Monique and said without any harmful intent in her voice, "Are you in charge of these brats?"

"Kinda sort of," Wendy replied, with a little smile to the friendly jest. But she was a little confused by Brittany's warm approach. She was the crude bully the girls use to mean-mouth. But Wendy decided to see what happens, not be the spoiler of a casual, rather mirthful gathering. The girls had told her about having saved Brittany that day from falling off the edge of a dangerous cliff. Even though she never knew her rescuers, her brush with death that close could cause such a genuinely blissful change in her life. With baring that in mind, Wendy trusted Brittany's show of good nature to be real.

Natalie, on the other hand, was indifferent due to her docile nature; also, she was co-dependent; always wanting to please others more than being self-reliant. She understood Brittany's shift to a tolerant, benign person; she was there at the edge of the cliff when the old Brittany failed to return home with them. She felt good about the new Brittany, and about herself.

"How about some ice cream?" Natalie blurted, bubbling with a glad spirit.

Monique frowned disapprovingly, "Ice cream?"

Nobody said anything to suggest otherwise.

"Okay, then it's ice cream," Brittany said affably. A glance at Monique, and Elise, who looked undecided. Brittany then added wisely, "Or whatever else you guys would like. Remember, I'm treating."

They headed for the nearest McDonald's, which was just down the street a short way.

Along the way, Brittany, Wendy, and Natalie hung back a little, as Monique and Elise moved on ahead with the other two kids, Dannielle and Pixy- a couple of spry, young pre-teens.

Scantly observing the kids in front of them, Brittany commented decisively, after going over the observation in her mind, with taut scrutiny, "You know there's something about those two that's..." She hesitated, looking to Wendy, who was without a clue.

"What?" Wendy asked.

Brittany continued, "Well...different."

She stared at Wendy again, this time conclusively. "And you too."

Wendy was surprised. *"Me?* Who are you talking about? There're four girls ahead of us."

"I'm talking about Elise, and Monique," Brittany made clear. They had moved among the four girls, with Brittany closest to Monique, as she continued, "I can't put my finger on it,"

"Monique jumped, pretending startled—with a surprising wisecrack no one was expecting, "Don't touch me!"

Everybody laughed, including Monique just being her farcical, quick-witted self.

Brittany softened her speech to continue quietly, only for Wendy, and Natalie to hear, "Seriously, you guys have a this...this thing about you. It's an aura that tends to make you guys sort of glow. Like I said, I don't know why, but you just do."

Wendy stared at her, humorously thinking that the entities inside them must be showing. It was a sound observation if

Brittany was psychic. But she wasn't and thank goodness for that.

Then Wendy noticed Brittany staring at her quizzically.

"What?" she asked curiously.

"You're Wendy, right—with W-E-N-D-Y?" Brittany said, vaguely remembering her name.

"It's *Windy*, with an 'I'-N-D-Y," She laughed, "I guess I was born on a windy day. My mom's half-Cherokee. Anyway, that's the way it appears on my birth certificate. But, Wendy with an *'E's* OK. It's the way everyone spells it."

"I think it's neat. It's different, which is cool," Brittany said.

Speaking of different: Brittany was different and what a change! Wendy recalled that not too long ago, Brittany had referred to her as Pocahontas, which was intended as a racial slur. But, this time, Brittany smiled at her, and it was pure. Then Brittany dropped her head in remorse, and murmured with recognizable guilt in her voice, "I owe you guys a lot."

A sincere stare at Wendy in continuing, "I'm not trying to buy your friendship. I just want to be your friend."

The look in Brittany's eyes and the sincerity in her voice convinced Wendy she was in mental anguish from her past, despicable lifestyle. And she wanted so much to mend her ways and to be accepted guiltlessly among her peers. Her near-death experience had given her a complete make-over.

The two of then hugged briefly, while Natalie stood aside emotionally, silently, and jubilantly teary-eyed.

Outside the city, and across a vast lay of empty spaces, darkness pervaded, as the night was without a trace of the slightest moonlight. The stars were thinly spangled against the night, restricted from their immense spread across the heavens because of a moderate overcast, leaving limited windows in the cloud cover for the stars to prevail.

Chelsea had Jim to trace the distance between the lake and the orphanage, in the helicopter by way of the dirt road, as a means of checking out his findings. They were accurate. In the pitch blackness of night, Jim flew over that suggested stretch of ground repeatedly, with the highly intense glow of the spotlight mounted on the chopper.

Chelsea was satisfied with a point. Next, she wanted verification of the foster home, and that those girls in question did indeed reside there. After several passes over the orphanage, to her chagrin, the place was dark, a total blackout from the air. There was no sign of anyone living there. And it was still early, with no reason for a building that size, housing so many orphans that they all be in bed, and asleep, at this hour. But there wasn't a sign of life anywhere about the place. It was easier to assume that the orphanage was abandoned.

"What's the name of this place?" she asked Jim through the mike on her headset.

"Lily Field Foster Home," he returned.

She instantly took up her laptop on the seat beside her, opened it and began looking up information about the place, online. She found it and became baffled. According to the info she'd found online, the home was still active, though due to close soon, not now.

She closed the laptop and said to Jim, "Let's head back to the city. I'll look further into the matter, later. I just want to say that you've been a great help."

She smiled at him from under her headgear. "Even though you weren't aware."

The noise of the helicopter flying over mildly disturbed Agnes, as she'd dozed off in her recliner. There were courtesy lights on in the home, soft lamplights, the overhead kitchen light; but the heavy drapes were drawn closed at the windows, throughout the place. That's why the place appeared completely dark to Chelsea, from the helicopter.

As the chopper flew over, the noise dissipating the farther it moved away, Agnes came to the door, opened it, and peered out into the night sky, just in time the see the flickering, conventional red light atop the helicopter fading in the distance. Chelsea had just missed the one opportunity that may have sealed her confidence that she was on the right trail. But trusting the information she'd found online provided her the initiative to not give up.

Next time, she was thinking. *Maybe tomorrow.*

Agnes closed the door and returned to her recliner. In knowing the girls would be home soon, she was trying to wait up for them. But, it is the weekend, they had a 10-o'clock curfew, so long as they were with Wendy. She'd never kept them out past curfew. But Agnes was exhausted, and it was only seven-thirty. She had provided them with cab fare, so there was no worry over them getting home safely. She sank back in her seat and got comfortable.

Moving into the parameter of the city lights, Jim headed the chopper for the television station and the helipad. Within minutes, he and Chelsea would be safely on the ground. But in their final approach, something high in the night sky caught both their attention. A bright flare was moving toward the city at a high rate of speed. Not a meteor; it was much too close, and it was huge!

"What is that?" Chelsea cried out fearfully.

"I don't know!" Jim answered, just as alarmed as she was.

"Get us out of here!" she yelled in her mike to him. "That thing is headed straight for us!"

Jim quickly diverted the helicopter hard to starboard, and fled back across town, as the huge flare became identifiable as flames having engulfed a Boeing 747, headed for a climactic destruction right in the heart of the city.

"Oh my god!" Chelsea yelled, overcome by sheer panic, and fear, as Jim had taken them safely out of harm's way.

The flaming jetliner was in a nose-dive, headed for downtown, where the girls, with Brittany and her reformed friends, were enjoying an evening out on the town. They were walking out of McDonald's just as the flaming, catastrophic disaster passed over. People were screaming and scrambling all over the place in a mad panic, fleeing aimlessly for cover.

For the girls was a nightmare, as they looked-on, petrified over a secret now bulgingly at risk. Monique and Elise gathered close to Wendy, solely depending on her decision—whatever it was.

"Oh, my goodness," Wendy said under her breath, gaping up at tons of a doomed aircraft embroiled in roiling flames.

"I was afraid this day would come when we could no longer keep to ourselves... Guys, from here on in, we must do what we have to, to stay together."

Elise muttered, nervous and flustered, "Stupid airplane. Why'd it had to fly over *our* town, and catch fire?"

Monique was already in a desperate rush, conversing with Brittany; she didn't have time to address the other three girls,

"Brittany, you must keep our secret."

Natalie and the other girls stood there, dumbfounded. Brittany didn't understand either, "I don't know what you are talking about but, of course, I'll keep your secret. It is what friends do."

"Thanks," Monique said then quickly rejoined her invulnerable crew. They were in the mix of screaming mobs of panicking citizens, fleeing blindly under a gripping horror.

The imperiled jetliner was on its final descent, certain to destroy many building structures, along with hundreds of lives, including the passengers aboard the flaming aircraft.

"There's no time to try and explain to anyone," Wendy desperately urged the girls. "We have to go, *now!*"

"Elise…Monique?"

Brittany was at a complete loss, as was Natalie and the other girls. Brittany pressed to try and understand, "What's up with you guys? What secret you want us to keep?"

But at that fleeting instant, the enchanted trio flashed, morphing into costumes simultaneously, leaving Brittany and her friends tremendously shocked!

Elise and Monique bolted to the night sky, vanishing out of sight, streaking in the direction of the flaming airline. Wendy, in a flash, vanished through the scrambling mob within a split second.

Aside from Brittany, and her friends, some members of the frantic mob had caught an instantaneous glimpse at the preternatural display from the trio, and were stymied, in an overwhelming state of disbelief.

Wendy raced to the summit of the tallest building in the immediate area, just as the flaming Jumbo jet flew over. She then went into a tornadic spin then launched herself like a slingshot into the air, where she gracefully landed on top of the fast-moving plane, among the searing flames. Elise and Monique having just arrived lifted the nose of the aircraft from underneath and began flying it away from the heavily populated areas of the city, and suburbs.

Amid the scorching flames, Wendy repeated the tactics she had that day to put out the fire in that downtown high-rise; she extinguished the flames with a heavy dose of frost breath.

Aboard the plane, the pilot, and crew members were stunned by the sudden calmness of the troubled aircraft. Although the exterior of the jetliner was a catastrophe, it held intact. But the most amazing aspect of the whole ordeal was that the plane-ride had suddenly become incredibly smooth as if the mechanical failure had miraculously been restored. But it hadn't.

The crew up front peered out the windows on both sides of the Jumbo jet, and to their bewilderment, of the four, giant turbine engines, not one had a life. They were all dead. The huge airline was on a ghost-flight. The intense flames had torched the wings; half the tail, which played an intricate part in the guidance system, were charred. There was no logical reason the aircraft should be airborne, in its critical condition. But it was.

While Wendy rode atop the plane, Elise and Monique maintained its balance and smooth-flying from underneath. What went unnoticed by the girls was the damaged engine on the end of the left wing. It was a heavy piece of loose, scrap-metal, barely dangling on to the unstable bracket.

Finally, it tore loose and went spiraling down through the atmosphere, where far below were busy sections of the city still in danger of a dead aircraft.

Charles H. Woods
293

Monique was underneath the side of the plane the engine had fallen from, and she happened to catch the mishap in time.

"Elise— "

"It's Koh, remember?" Elise corrected her.

"Sorry!" Monique said.

"The silly engine just fell off the wing!"

"Can you get it?" Elise yelled from the other side of the airplane.

"Can you handle this alone?" Monique wanted to make certain.

"Don't expect any help from Wendy. She's riding on top, after putting out the fire. She's not flying these days!"

That was jovial. Elise said, "I got this! Go get the engine. Hurry!"

Monique shot away like a rocket, chasing the falling engine, as it tore through layers of clouds on a downward plunge, on target to cause inescapable tragedies below.

Wendy called to Elise from atop the plane, "Was that Monique I just saw leave the plane, what for?"

"Call her Jor!" Elise screamed up to her. "That's the agreement! Remember that?"

"Well!" Wendy expressed her lighthearted disapproval of Elise's grumpiness "I am sorry to have offended you."

Elise, not impressed, "Oh, be quiet. She went to get the engine that fell off. It could hurt someone—really bad."

"Oh, my goodness!" Wendy was suddenly enlightened. She chanced to lean toward the edge of the plane to look down. She saw only clouds idly adrift below the aircraft.

Somewhat of a disquieting calmness vaguely began settling over the jaded city dwellers, as the horrific happening with the disabled airliner seemingly had past. Many who had witnessed the incredulous event still milled around in a daze of confusion, suspiciously looking up at the black sky sparingly. As emergency vehicles came on the scene—the police, to direct traffic, after numerous fender-bending, the fire-rescue teams, and Paramedic squads—a young mom with her three, young children, ranging in ages from a three-year-old to five and eight, were rushing for their vehicle across the street.

The mom was carrying a bag of grocery in one arm while holding the hand of the three-year-old, who was her son, Kevin, in the other; then there were her older two little girls, Anna, 5, and the oldest, Myra, 8. As they stepped off the curb, screams in horror and deep gasps from people nearby reacted to a fatal disaster just seconds away from striking the mom and her three children. The hideous remains of a dark metal jet engine were hurling down on her, and her kids so rapidly, and so close she had only time to scream, lose the bag she was holding, and gather her precious children in her arms for the final time.

No! Quicker than suddenly, out of nowhere, a dark something unidentifiable as anything tangible streaked down out of the night sky at the speed of light. It grabbed the falling engine in mid-flight, halting its momentum to an abrupt dead-stop just inches above the mother and her three children.

Whatever it was that saved the young family took a moment in brief, while firmly cradling that hideously monstrous engine in tiny arms, and said to the lady, who was losing consciousness fast, "Sorry, ma'am. My bad."

Then the thing in black left a fleeting human impression of a little black girl wearing some black cape and tights; but the image faded so quickly, as it took to the dark sky, with that hulking bulk of a ton of charred metal, at blinding speed, leaving a shy, charming, little smile for the mom and her kids to not soon forget.

A group of caring witnesses rushed to the young mother's aid, with concern for the children as well. The woman's stance was weak, unstable as she reeled, and had to be stabilized by a gentleman close by. The kids were OK, not old enough to comprehend the melee surrounding them.

As the nurse of a medical team checked the woman's vital signs, an inebriated, in descript, older man muddled over to them, carrying a small, crinkled brown bag with something in it, in his hand.

He leaned in as close as he could without tipping himself over in the woman's face, the stench of his whisky-breath nauseating to her, as he said, "Ma'am, this may not cure what's ailing you; but it'll sure let you not give a damn," offering her the bag with what was in it.

A small, mixed group of people kindly ushered the man on his way. The populace began to gravitate together slowly, cautiously in small groups, settling into a state of disbelief, and rapt curiosity. Murmuring among groups of people filled the streets.

"I knew it, I knew it, *I knew it!*" Brittany said, on the verge of totally freaking out. She and her astounded friends stood outside the McDonald's restaurant, gawking at the starry sky, stupefied. Brittany was on the edge of collapsing, like Natalie had that day out at the cliff, which would not have been cool, or acceptable, even by her friends who stood there, frozen like statues, on this warm, eventful, late evening.

"I knew it was something, I knew it was something," Brittany kept rambling on, mainly to herself, she was so lost in this gripping mysticism.

Finally, tears came to her eyes as she continued in her state of guilt, and other mixed emotions. She couldn't get over the fact that the two young girls she used to pick-on so abrasively turned out to be angels.

Yes, *angels!*

And they came and saved her. And they saved those other people she'd been hearing about. They are here to help us, she became convinced as the tears now flowed freely; and it didn't matter who noticed.

When Natalie saw Brittany crying for the very first time since she'd known her, it brought tears of compassion to her own eyes. The other two girls joined Natalie, who had embraced Brittany; and the four of them huddled together, teary-eyed in the marvel of this weird, but blissful, celebrating new reality.

"We have angels," Natalie sobbed in good cheer, her wet cheeks aglow under the city lights, as she continued her gaze at the dark sky. Then she brought her attention to the girls and added, "Elise and Monique are *angels!* And they can fly!"

"Did you see her?" The mother's name was Freda Maxwell, and she kept uttering in a daze, sitting there with the nurse, "Did you see her smile? It was so beautiful, so pure, and sweet. And she flew away with that god-awful... thing."

"Yes, we saw her. And we saw what she did." The nurse wasn't only trying to console the young woman; she was being as truthful as she saw it.

Freda's eight-year-old daughter recalled, "She's one of the angels who came and got Amy, and her little brother, Timmy, out of the woods, when they got lost that day."

That was said with conviction, as it was easy to understand, to little Myra.

Chapter 20

The crew and passengers aboard the plane had settled into a quietude, closely in a state of apprehension. The ride was that quiet, and smooth, as if nothing had gone wrong, although it had. The Boeing 747 was a wreck, charred on the outside like it had just been through an intensely-heated inferno. Yet it flew like an untarnished, brand new aircraft.

The captain sat in the pilot's seat calmly, but with discontent, expecting the big explosion, which would devastate the entire plane. But then, at a glance out the window, to his left, he reacted to a startling sight.

Something... No, a person...a little girl, in fact, in black tights, and black cape...

Was this *real?*

She was re-attaching the missing engine to the wing, using a welding method with lasers from her eyes. *Incredible!* Mind-boggling!

He looked away overwhelmed with apprehension, his mask pale from the shock.

"Captain, what's wrong?" His co-pilot paused from trying to get the landing gear down—with no results—to stare at him, "You look like you've just seen a ghost."

"You'd think so too," the captain said, his mind stuck in overdrive in disbelief. "Have a look for yourself, Charley—out the window."

The captain was barely able to lift a finger to point in the direction he'd suggested.

When the co-pilot looked out the window, he instantly withdrew, the moment he caught sight of the *impossible* on the edge of the severely-damaged left wing. In changing a second look from both the captain and the co-pilot, the *nonexistent image* took flight in midair and ducked to somewhere underneath the bits and pieces of what was left of the Jumbo-jet.

"Where did it go?" The co-pilot struggled to maintain his sanity. And the captain was not far from that same difficult task.

"My guess is whatever *it*, or *she* was, is somewhere underneath, flying what's left of this plane." Those words came from the captain as if he never said them on his own; that they were just silly thoughts, using him as a conduit to speak.

"What's going on?" The navigator never saw the bizarre occurrence; he'd been busy at his assigned post. The communications guy was fighting a losing battle with his job, still.

"Don't ask so many questions, Victor," the co-pilot responded out of fear, frustration, and disbelief. "Just keep flying this heap of junk until we no longer can."

"What the hell does that mean?" Victor fired back.

"You guys know something?" The captain said with gathering faith and confidence.

"I think we should just shut-up and keep flying. Somehow, I believe the angels are on our side. Either that, or it's a leap of faith."

Charley stared at captain London dubiously but was unable to argue the point. So, he just sat back and began working the gadgets, in sheer vanity.   Pressing right along in maintaining the balance, and a smooth flight from underneath the plane, Elise said over to Monique, who was on the other side, "I wonder where this flight's headed."

"Why don't one of us go up and ask?" Monique suggested.

"Good Idea," Elise said. "Do you think Wen-I mean Motatu is up to the challenge?" Elise corrected herself.

Monique thought it over, then said, "I don't know. She can't fly, remember?"

"Yes, that's right," Elise agreed.

Motatu piped from alongside the plane, so Wendy could get a peek at them, "I heard that." She was perched alongside the plane, like a fly on the wall, very balanced, and secure, in stark defiance of the law of gravity.

That amazed Elise, and Monique. "How are you doing that?" Monique asked.

"I can do other things besides flying, I'll have you know." That came from Wendy, with Motatu's approval, bursting with pride.

"Good," Monique congratulated her. "Then you can go up and ask the pilot what's their destination."

"They're gonna freak," Wendy warned.

"Who cares?" Monique said, unfeeling. "We need to know."

"If you say so," Wendy said, starting to move alongside the plane, toward the front.

"I say so," Monique said in a grumpy fashion.

As Wendy moved alongside the fuselage, a ten-year-old with his mom, caught sight of what appeared to him a teenaged girl with beautiful, dark hair, and was wearing a neat, blue costume, as she moved past.

"Mom, someone's out there. Look," the boy said to the lady sitting on the aisle seat, next to her son.

She looked around, out the window, but didn't see anyone, or anything, only clouds and sky. She'd been preoccupied worrying over their present disposition, which didn't seem promising.

"Honey don't talk like that," she told him.

Her ten-year-old, sometimes a bit naïve, to a certain degree, responded earnestly, "Mom, it's the way I talk. How do you want me to talk?"

His mom, nearing forty, only stared at him, hopeful he'd grow out of his, sometimes, lack of clear understanding—if they survived this increasingly tacit dilemma.

Having made it to the window on the pilot side of the aircraft, Wendy sat alongside the plane like a human spider, her lustrous, dark hair blowing freely all around, and about her head, with a harsh, brisk wind in her face.

She took a small breath for courage, then tapped softly on the glass. At that barely audible tapping, the pilot, Captain Paul London, turned his head and looked out the window. And he had company; all the crew members up front looked out the same window.

A rush of fear overwhelmed each of them, as they reacted simultaneously as if they'd been seized by the boogie man. "My

God!" one shouted. Another, "Jesus H. Christ!" Yet, another looked, then shouted, "What the devils is she doing out there?" Then he caught himself, his mind reeling, "Jesus! What the hell am I saying?"

"How can they hear me through the glass?" Wendy asked Motatu.

She said, "Just speak in your normal voice, it'll penetrate the shield. You can do that; it's one of your gifts."

Wendy trustingly said to the pilot, "Where are you headed?"

The captain didn't know what to think, or believe, in hearing her voice so clearly through the glass; none of this was possible on this side of reality. "What?" he found himself responding without reason.

"Where are you taking this airplane?" Wendy spoke more emphatically.

His response began as a rigorous stammer from his absence of logic, "Dah, dah, dah, dah...Dallas..."

"Dallas, Texas?" Wendy wanted to be certain.

Captain London nodded from instinct, then looked to his crewmen as if he didn't realize what he was doing, speaking with an impossible figure in the guise of a young, human girl? Outside the plane?

Along the way back to their watch position, Motatu commented, "Some of your cities sure do have strange names?"

"What do you mean?" Wendy didn't understand the question, just as she'd crawled back underneath the plane to make the announcement of their destination to Monique, and Elise. But Motatu was first to blurt, "We're going to dah, dah, dah,

dah...Dallas!"

Both Elise, and Monique were confused, "What?" they said together.

Motatu innocently replied, "I know...silly, right?"

Wendy laughed, "Motatu...that's not what he meant."

Motatu argued, "Well, that's what he said!"

"Oh, I get it," Elise laughed. Then she said, putting on her best Southern accent, "Dallas, Texas, here we come, Yahoo!"

"Koh," Monique said, remembering their code-names, "your Southern accent stinks!"

Koh came back, offended, "Hey, get your facts right."

Then she yelled begrudgingly, "*I didn't say anything!*"

On the final approach to Love Field in Dallas, the huge, charred, 747 looked like a dead ship in midair, silhouetted against the gloom just outside the stretching limits of the city lights. It started dropping altitude at a normal descent, finally putting down in a vast, vacant field just outside the many strips of runways.

The tower wasn't expecting this type of an arrival; neither was Air Traffic Control. It was a rather spooky event to unfold in such a macabre appearance. It was like an unholy, satanic miracle, other than some angelic intervention. But it was here, as rescue squads of various sorts raced to the scene, with emergency lights flashing, sirens blasting.

Once the girls noticed all that attention rushing toward the downed aircraft, that was their signal to clear the area, which they did successfully, under the cloak of darkness, just outside the perimeter of the many airport-lights.

They'd moved to the edge of the darkness, where the lights didn't reach. For a moment, they watched the passengers safely disembark the plane by way of the emergency, rubber ramp. Murmuring among them was quiet, hinging on whether they should be grateful for the safe arrival, or fly into a panic over the dark, perhaps, forbidding mystery that brought them here. The horrible wreckage of the plane proved undoubtedly that some wicked force had no intentions of the aircraft ever arriving, period.

To some of the more skeptical passengers, the thought even occurred that maybe they'd *crossed over* and that this dream-like escape was just that: a dream that they'd survived.

The girls were thoughtful about Wendy's idea. They had done a good thing—a great thing—by saving all those innocent people. To abandon them to wander about for the rest of their lives, perhaps, under the canopy of such a dark, frightening mystery wouldn't be justifiable to a good deed. It was a tough decision to make; the weight was on her shoulders.

"On second thought, guys, we should make our presence known," Wendy finally decided, regardless of what circumstances that lie ahead for them.

"Are you sure?" Monique asked. "We've already blown it back home. By tomorrow, everyone will know who we are."

"I say, let's do it," Elise said, giving it, plenty thought. "It was bound to happen. It was only a matter of time. And besides, we're about to be on our own anyway."

"Which is another issue we must face," Wendy said. "I never told you guys, but, a while back, a lady from the State Department was by while you were at school." Wendy took a breath then

Charles H. Woods
305

continued, "From what she said, it looks like they are indenting on separating us."

Monique blew her top, "Well, then we'll just fly away to some place, where no one will ever find us! Then they'll be sorry."

"Well, let's not concern ourselves with that, right now," Wendy said. "We've already agreed that we won't be separated.

"C'mon, guys. Let's get this over with and go home. I'm not sure that we may be in a different time-zone."

"Oh, yes, I forgot about the dumb time-zone," Elise said.

There were some hundred-plus passengers aboard. Once they were off the plane, they grouped together laden with the great mystery as to who, or *what* had brought them there. To gaze at the aircraft's horrific condition was terrifying. Slabs of siding hung loose, leaving huge, gaping holes along the fuselage; the right wing was barely intact. The tail section had melted almost beyond recognition; the landing gear never worked, as the hulking airline, by some unnatural force, was put down on its metal belly, in that vacant field, beyond the tarmac. It was outright disturbing, frightful to look at.

As medical teams arrived and began checking out the one-hundred-percent survivors, they were amazed to bewilder, to find all onboard the ill-fated flight suffered no injuries whatsoever. It was as if they'd arrived under normal conditions. *Impossible,* was the final opinions of doctors on the scene. And that drew the media in droves.

They crowded the scene with cameras flashing, mikes shoved in the faces of many of the survivors. The captain was among the crowd, somewhat of a stand-out, pressing his way through, with a pale, dazed-look on his solemn face. His muddled steps drew the attention of a medical team, along with the media.

He looked disoriented, in a mild state of shock.

Wendy and the girls could see the whole developing situation unfold very clearly from their vantage point. Instead of a gratuitous celebration, everyone who was aboard the plane was in a state of unrest, confusion, and apprehension.

"You notice the way everyone who was on the plane is behaving?" Wendy seriously observed. In her mind, it was scary. Then it came to her a way to maybe soften, if not dismantle, the disconcerting impact.

"C'mon. I think I got an idea," she said.

Jor sounded dubious, coming from Monique, "You *think?*"

Wendy got on to her, "Just go with it!"

Jor, displeased, "Dang, woman, what an attitude."

Motatu, a little irritated, "Jor!"

Jor went silent. Koh laughed, "Tee-hee-hee."

Jor shouted, "Shut up, Koh!"

The childish bickering agitated Elise, "Guys!"

As they moved into the dimmest portion of light from the airport, their attractive costumes began to emit a soft luminescent appeal to the eye, so fitting for what they do, and for this unique occasion.

"Who are they?" Someone in the crowd spotted the girls, and that drew other attentions.

A hush, with curiosity, settled over the crowd, as the girls timidly braved their volunteer approach before an unnerved audience seeking answers to this tumultuous miracle.

The girls moved in together sheepishly, more nervous than they'd thought; Wendy hopeful to establish an understanding, and friendship by a natural truce. Murmuring increased, along with curiosity among the large gathering, as the girls were now vivid in the full frame of light. To the audience, they looked no different than normal, young teenaged girls, their stunning, limpid costumes the only minor distraction. Otherwise, what purpose did they have to be this far from *home?*

A couple of police officers approached the girls, who stood out front, clearly separated from the large gathering.

One of the officers asked them, "What are you kids doing out here? Aren't you girls sort of a long way from home? Where do you live?"

"We don't live here," Wendy said. Then came the dreaded part, which put the three of them on alert, though, hopefully, not in jeopardy.

But Wendy didn't get a word out quick enough before the ten-year-old, who was on the plane, came rambling toward her, pointing, and excitedly shouting, "Mom...everybody! It's her! She's the one I saw on the plane, on the wing!"

If no one else aboard that ill-gotten flight was willing to attest to the bizarre nature of its *impossible* arrival, the captain was grateful to the young boy for sharing that bit of honesty with everyone, especially with him. It proved to be no longer unsettling for him to accept what he'd witnessed was indeed real. He also recognized the little girl in black, standing with the other two. The one in the red outfit wasn't familiar, but it didn't matter. He was convinced she was just as part of the wizardry aboard the plane as the two he'd seen.

As the crowd began to form a semicircle around the oddly-clad little girls, slowly, tentatively, they looked-on, oblivious of what to think of their out-of-season masquerade. Muttering among them was mostly of compliments, abated admiration of the costumes' skillful design.

"Who were their tailor?" came out-spoken from the gathering.

The boy's mom took hold of his hand and brought him away from being too close to this new attraction. "Mom, I know what I saw," he ranted. "It was *her,* the one in the blue suit!"

The captain vaguely stepped forward at the risk of having to find a different job, after this vulnerable stand on behalf of what he believed was real.

"The kid's right," he said to everyone's shocking amazement, the boy's mom suddenly gaping at him at a loss for words.

The captain, desperate for the courage to continue, "I wouldn't have believed it myself. But..."

He turned and looked back, for a moment, at the shabby remains of what was once a state-of-the-art, luxury airline.

Then he continued, with all the attention on him now, including the officers detaining the girls, "Just look at the conditions of that aircraft. Does that look like a machine equipped to carry...anything across the continent? Ladies and gentlemen, we originated out of Minneapolis. The plane was intact, working to its full capacity. But we encountered a problem that devastated the flight. In short, we would not have made it here, if not been for those young girls, whoever they are!"

The captain dropped his head, assuming persecution to soon follow his ludicrous stand. But instead, a disquieting hush settled over the crowd like an oppressive, pending doom carrying the mental weight of a massive, dark cloud.

An elderly lady, out of such fear and frustration from the horrid flight, lurched forward to ask the girls, "Just who are you? And why are you dressed like that?"

The girls could feel the potent staring from everyone there. Stage-fright is hanged; this was much worse.

Then Wendy spoke in a meek voice, almost unqualified to be clearly understood, "We only wanted to help, so we brought the airplane here. It's where your captain told us you were headed."

A male voice from the crowd asked emphatically, *"How?"*

"We flew you here, OK?" Monique was anxious to get going while trying to recall in which direction they were to take.

Chuckling, along with an increase of murmuring of unrest, with leaks from outstanding voices announcing uncertainties:

"Flying, who's flying?"

"No one can fly!"

"Are they aliens?"

"Hybrids..."

"What are they?"

"Guys show 'em," Wendy said.

"Was that your idea?" Elise asked at a rush of crude excitement that coursed through her.

"Yes, but there's more. When you do your demonstration, take off for home, fast," Wendy explained. "I'll be right behind you."

"You don't fly," Monique reminded her.

"I know where we live," Wendy stressed. "And I know how to get there from here. You think you're talking to a kindergarten?"

One of the officers spoke to the girls condescendingly, "You expect us to believe you are superheroes, just because you're wearing those fancy, little costumes," he laughed.

Elise wisely pointed out, "You weren't listening to the kid, or the captain, were you?"

As the officer opened his mouth to speak, the girls—Elise, and Monique—hit the sky-ways, leaping into the air with a burst of blinding speed. Everyone was tremendously overwhelmed, as gasps from riveting astonishment emitted from the bedazzled audience filled the night air at that instant.

After that super-fantastic display, it may take some of the witnesses—if not all of them—days, or maybe years to recoup from this preternatural demonstration.

As they were left reeling, for the most part, Wendy went on to further point out to them her reason for hanging back a spell, "I just want all of you to know that we're only here to help, whenever, or wherever we can. We are your *friends*. So please keep that in mind. Now I must leave you..."

Wendy was ready to depart, but the police officer—feeling nervous, and ashamed—wanted her to understand something.

"Forgive me," he said. "I didn't know."

His face was pale from a blatant show of captivation.

Members of the media were jammed close around her, pointing microphones in her face, and bombardments of questions, with flash cameras going off all around her, while she was saying to the officer, with sincerity, "I am your friend."

Her voice was calm but penetrating, forgiving. Then, in moving to an area roomier very nearby, with a small host following, she made her get-away.

"I gotta go. Remember..." was the last they heard, or saw of her, as in a flash, she was gone.

As a deeply emotional quietude ensued, the co-pilot came over to the captain to point out, "Paul, we never learned whether they're aliens, hybrids, or what?"

The captain looked him in the eye, with a distant stare and said with a heartfelt sentiment, "How 'bout angels?"

The co-pilot wandered away with his head down in deep thought. The mom said to her boy, "Honey, I'm sorry I didn't believe you."

"It's alright, mom," Dustin replied. "Sometimes, even when you don't see it, that doesn't mean it's not there."

Wisdom to the wise. You're never too old to learn. The woman looked at her young son in a different light.

Chapter 21

They were all over the newspapers, TV, and radio. The cat had been let out of the bag! It was no longer a secret or myth. There may be angels was a fact! Grand City had the *Angels!*

And so, stories about the mysterious beings had become nationwide. Although there were skeptics; the main body of the source had been proven authentic to the tune of three young girls, origin unknown, who've been quietly busy helping those in dire need.

Headline-articles carried different stories, reaching back to grab even outlandish claims from the recent past that these extraterrestrials had the capability to fly! And that they used their special powers to help other of less fortune.

Citizens of downtown Grand City had the luxury seating to watch the phenomenal event take place when a Boeing 747 passed over in flames. A fierce panic ensued as a huge number of the populace began scattering all over the city. But just before a major disaster struck, which would've killed quite many innocent people, the trio of super-human beings took to the air, like the comic book character Superman, and the Power Puff Girls, to save the day. And they did just that.

Correspondents from Dallas confirmed the fact that the severely damaged Jumbo-aircraft landed safely just outside Love Field in Dallas with all passengers, and crew members onboard not having sustained the slightest injury and landed safely by those three phenomenal beings.

Those were the headline stories throughout areas involved, all the way to Dallas. Grand City was buzzing with the breaking news. There were those, however, who assumed this was the end-times, that not long would there be trumpets blowing and the Rapture. Those extremists, very few in numbers, fled to the wide-open spaces, took up cabins in the woods, to become survivalists.

Ed Milburn and his staff were scrambling to set up security outposts, with the on-full-alert standby Fighter jets patrolled the skies on a regular basis, while military units were on constant training maneuvers.

At downtown Headquarters, Ed met with his staff, and other federal agents, with an agenda. Since none of his staged mishaps worked, it was time to use other tactics—a full frontal attack.

"Haven't you been keeping up with the latest news reports?" Susan wasn't entirely in agreement with him.

"Well, let me say this...," She produced a newspaper she'd just gotten off the newsstand, prior to this meeting. She shared it with Ed, Jillian, along with other agents who basically sided with Ed, even if he was careless in some of his judgments. Which, on very few occasions, he had.

"Look at this."

She showed him the headline briefly, then began reading the article underneath, paraphrasing, "It says here, they have shown nothing to the public but kindness, and a willingness to help others. Also— "

Ed was thrilled to show her up by producing his own edition of the latest news on the situation at hand.

"No need," he said in an ogling fashion, "I have my own."

"What I think we all need to take in consideration is that these aliens could be very young," Jillian raised an interesting observation.

But everyone just issued her a blank stare, waiting to make their own decisions, after she'd made her point.

She felt belittled, a hint of withdrawal in her faltering stare as she continued to make her point.

"I'm referring to the three young girls—the aliens' hosts. People, as far as we know, we could be waging war against *children,* who means us no harm!"

Ed said arbitrarily, "So it never occurred to you that their appearance as mere children is their primary weapon of deception?"

Jillian went silent and reclaimed her seat at the conference table with a gleaming Cherrywood finish, in a small, closed room.

A slightly heavy-set, female agent, sitting next to Jillian quietly said to her, "I remember when he used to work as a covert operative."

Jillian stared at her, enlightened. She didn't know that about Ed. She and Susan were strictly employees at GSW, with a whole different job-description from Ed's, on this critical assignment.

Chelsea was livid after looking over the headlines from her own editing department at the television station she worked. The news of the aliens she'd been on the hunt for had made a vivid, public appearance, while she was away with Jim—her helicopter-pilot—trying to avoid the dangerous path of a flaming jet-airline on a collision course with certain death.

Still, on administrative-leave-of-absence, she sat at home, in her lush apartment, figuratively kicking herself for not being as alert as she should've been. But then the one thing she figured was in her favor brought her to her feet, rejuvenated...just as her cell phone rang. She went over and grabbed it off the smoke-glass coffee table:

"Yes?" she asked over the phone.

"Chelsea?" It was the editor of the television-news department.

"Are you aware we have aliens in our midst? The story broke early last night. Maybe you should get down here. This is something I think you'd be interested in chasing down for an exclusive."

"I'm well ahead of you, Mr. Goshen," Chelsea said with spry in her voice. "I've been about my own plans, concerning the present situation."

She hung up and started getting ready to hit the shower, feeling good about preparing to initiate her infallible idea.

"If you have any trouble at school, like a mob of students ganging up on you because they know who you are, get home immediately," Wendy instructed the girls, as they were preparing to leave for school.

"Gotcha," Elise said as she and Monique were walking off the porch, headed for their bus stop. They were a bit more than surprised that the kids didn't storm their foster home after that bold, spectacular exposé they put on before a live audience over the weekend. Even though the news reports stated the lack of knowledge of the aliens' origin—or their whereabouts—the girls feared that Brittany and her cohorts might have spilled everything they knew by now. And that's what Wendy was mainly referring to.

But there was something of a dire nature simmering in the back of her mind as she stood at the edge of the porch, leaned against one the huge, old-style-crafted pillars. She stood there watching the girls as they disappeared beyond the grove, the morning bright with sunlight under a clear blue sky.

"You'd think that by now, Brittany, and her posse would have told everyone about us," Monique said as they drew closer to their bus stop.

"Hopefully, they died," Elise quipped.

"We should be so lucky," Monique returned with a smirk.

Elise laughed, "You *are joking.*"

Monique, a feigned-look of seriousness in her stare, "Were you?"

They began snickering as they reached the bus stop just in time. The bus was coming.

The campus was buzzing with students bustling there and about, rushing to classes; some milling around, with silly horse-play among some of the energetic boys nearing puberty.

The girls were a little skittish in considering they could be singled out as the *supernatural heroes* who rescued Grand City from near devastation, the other night, by that inflamed, Jumbo-jet that passed over.

As Monique and Elise got off the bus among the many other students, they were a little confused between disappointment, and relief that their secret seemed well intact. The campus atmosphere was, however, buzzing with the excitement that there were, indeed, angels in Grand City; while Elise and Monique moved among the students, almost as if they were invisible.

In the crowded hallways, somewhere along the way to their class, Brittany pops up, "Hi, guys!"

Charles H. Woods
317

She was right on them, aglow with spirit, staring them straight in the face, with a beaming bright grin on her narrow face. She was rather cute, for a change, now with the hostility in her nature finally gone, replaced with the nature of an amiable, friendly person deep down inside.

But her mere presence raised the eyebrows-of-suspicion from the girls, fearing it may be a trick to fool them into thinking she was on the level, while she was cooking up some scheme to destroy their sanctity in dwelling peacefully among the normal flow of humanity. They would soon find out.

"Hi, Brittany," Elise politely returned, Monique, holding Brittany in an alerted gaze.

"You guys notice everything's cool? Well, everybody knows about the angels," Brittany said, suppressing the urgent excitement in her voice.

"Only they don't know *who* they are, except *me!*"

Oh, this was dangerous, the girls feared.

"Are you sure you can handle keeping our secret a secret?" Monique asked.

"Are you kidding?" Brittany said jubilantly. "I wouldn't dare tell a soul. That's what makes it so great! And Natalie and the others feel the same way. We've talked about it, and we all agreed it's much better this way. We have angels as our best friends!"

She looked toward the ceiling, with her hands clamped together in the praying gesture. "Oh, this is *so* going to be good," she boasted.

Natalie, and the other two girls on the highly intense scene, the other night, came pressing through the crowd ecstatically up to

Brittany, and the girls. They were all gleaming with blithe adoration, at the very thought of knowing the two girls' extremely important secret.

Natalie, bursting with elation, said in a giddy voice, "Guys, you're just...*super-cool!*" She kept her voice secretive, as she'd promised, under the pressing circumstances. "And we want our special friendship to last forever! And that no one shall ever find out!"

The other two girls, standing idly by, grinned with sincere approval, which convinced Monique, and Elise to trust them, tentatively to a point. Should that work out, perhaps, they'd be home-free. Right now, they had no choice but to trust them, and under no certain conditions.

Wendy was alone. Miss Agnes had been away since morning. It had been this way for her over the past several weeks. She'd been busy settling the closing of the foster home and preparing for her retirement. Wendy was upstairs, in her bedroom, relaxing on her bed, scanning through a different fashion magazine, other than she and the girls' favorite, *SEVENTEEN.* Her spirit was down, and she wasn't in the best of mood.

A knock on the door downstairs was faint due to the length of the distance it had to travel, to be heard all the way upstairs. But Wendy heard it, and lay the magazine aside, got off the bed and went downstairs to get the door. In opening it, a mild surprise greeted her.

The lady outside at the door was a stranger. She was fashionably-clad, mildly attractive...vaguely familiar, though. The shiny, luxurious-looking vehicle, parked in the yard, Wendy assumed was hers. She carried a spiffy purse strapped to her shoulder.

"Hello," the lady spoke in an elegant, likable voice, "I am Chelsea Freeman from channel 5 News on WCGN."

She politely presented Wendy her courtesy, business card.

Wendy took the card.

"Yes," she said, moving aside to let the news lady enter, "I've seen you on TV." But Wendy had no idea why the news lady was there. Did she know about the closing of the foster home? Was that newsworthy?

"Is the guardian here?" Chelsea asked as Wendy escorted her into the spacious living room.

"No," Wendy said. "I can't tell you when she'll be back. She's out on business. This is a foster home. You are aware of that, right?"

"Yes, I am," Chelsea answered.

"Won't you be seated?" Wendy kindly offered.

"Thank you." Chelsea took a seat on the sofa; Wendy took the sofa chair across from her. "Are there any other kids around? It looks kind of...empty," Chelsea laughed benevolently.

A little tip-lip-smile. "No, it's just the three of us left."

"The three of you?" Chelsea leaned slightly forward, a seriously interest in Wendy's answer.

"Yes," Wendy gratified her with the answer. "Elise, and Monique. They're now at school."

"At school, yes, of course." So far, Chelsea felt she was on the right track.

"And how old are they?"

Unknowing to Wendy, she was a pawn, playing directly into Chelsea's hand, as she replied, "Well, Monique is twelve, and Elise is also twelve but will be turning thirteen in a couple of months."

"And how long have the three of you girls been orphaned?" Chelsea asked, readying a pad and pencil to take down some notes, as Wendy began to explain.

The middle-school students poured out of the building like water out of a pail, once the final bell rang that afternoon. Elise and Monique strode along without interruptions from their *secret* admirers, Brittany, and the girls—no longer her posse now, as they'd been reformed.

"I feel kinda guilty," Monique began.

"About what?" Elise wanted to know. They were leisurely moving toward their bus.

"The girls," Monique made clear. "Maybe we should do something for them, to show we appreciate them for being so... loyal?"

A flat-out guess.

"What do you have in mind?" Elise was willing to support her idea.

"Well, we should ride the bus home," Monique suggested. "I'll explain it to you on the way."

Elise had no objections as they boarded the bus that afternoon, "Whatever you say. Sounds good to me."

After getting off at their bus stop, the girls waited until the coast was clear before putting their plan into action. The few kids who shared the bus stop with the girls had moved on ahead, going home. The girls were alone.

"This should be good enough," Monique said to Elise as they moved down the path a bit, completely away from highway traffic.

They stashed their backpacks safely away in some nearby bushes, where they were well hidden, then morphed into those stunning costumes of black and silver, red and yellow-gold. Dogs barked faintly from a near distance on a normal afternoon, as the girls leaped into the air, put on a burst of speed, and was gone in seconds, as quiet as a couple of phantoms on a bright afternoon haunt.

"Oh, we know them, all right...," Brittany and the girls were walking along amid other kids, bragging to them about being acquainted with the Angels, up close and personal.

"Get outta here!" Thirteen-year-old Tommy Ross wasn't impressed with the girls, figuring they were lying to get special attention. "You guys are full of it, thinking anybody would believe you."

"But it's true!" Natalie sternly claimed. "We were there when they flew after that airplane!"

Dannielle Cramer and Pixy Jennings added their two-cents as material witnesses, as they were also on the scene, right before, and when it hit-the-fan!

"We saw the whole thing!" Dannielle swore. "We don't have to make things up. We know them personally. And they're our *friends!*"

"Yeah!" Pixy added with emphasis. "You people are just jealous because *you* don't know them, or never met them, but *we* have!"

Her boastful smile irritated those among them, who, even took them the slightest bit serious. But Brittany and her placid crew were only scoffed, jeered, and laughed at.

Some kid in the group-gathering shouted ecstatically, pointing above them, "Look up there!"

As everyone looked up, two of the Angels were swooping down out of the sky, right above them. *Unbelievable!* Their dazzling costumes a fluorescent gleam in the bright afternoon sunlight.

They feather-landed right before them, where everyone had a clean, clear view of them. Gasps of stark astonishment filled the air in that small area the kids occupied, as they stood frozen in disbelief, gaping in awe.

"Hi, guys," Jor said in a friendly voice.

Then the two of them lifted just slightly off the ground, and glided forward, toward the group of kids. They floated over to Brittany's and her friends' positions, as they stood close together.

"Brittany, right?" That was Koh. "I thought I recognized you from the other night."

Then Jor said to Brittany, Natalie, and the other two girls, Dannielle, and Pixy, "You guys OK? It got kinda scary there for a while. But did you know we had to take that silly airplane all the way to Dallas before we could put it down, to save all those people?"

Then Jor chuckled, "But it was fun, the way those people were freaking out. Why do they do that? We only did to help them."

Then Jor and Koh turned their attention to the general audience and said, "Will you guys please tell your friends, and the people you know to not freak-out every time we stop to help them because that's why we're here."

Kids heads were nodding spontaneously, from sheer instinct, as they were incapacitated, dumbfounded, awe-struck, weirded-out, and overwhelmingly amazed, and bedazzled! To be standing before two metaphysical beings. No, Angels are the most astounding highlight of their very lives!

"Well, Brittany, Natalie...you guys, take care. We gotta go." Koh bolted to the air, giving everyone the thrill of their young lives.

"Later, you guys," Jor said then followed Koh with a burst of speed.

"Bye!" Brittany waved to the girls in flight like they'd been casual friends for quite some time. Natalie and the other two girls follow suit, waving to the now empty air. Tommy Ross sat on the ground, in the grass, licking the wounds of his hurt pride, and self-centered ego for being so wrong in his disbelief of the girls, despite that no one else believed either. He took it more personal because he was the most ardent in defying them. He now looked at them differently because they had a friendship link to the Angels, the most popular, the most revered beings on earth! How could he ever overcome this jolting reality? And they are so cute! The rest of the kids began to slowly scatter, swamped with the reality that those four students from their school had made an impressionable contact with superhuman beings—if they were human. If not, even better. Aliens. Friendly aliens. The fact remains; four of their peers were friends of the Angels!

Chapter 22

They feather-landed short of entering the grove, where they'd left their backpacks underneath some bushes. Morphing back into their civvies, they collected their school supplies then continued through the grove, headed home.

Giggling, they high-fived each other, feeling good about themselves, figuring they had done a good thing.

Elise said affably, "Looks like your idea worked. I think now it'll be easier for them to maintain our secret."

"I kinda figured they'd be hard-pressed to keep quiet about meeting us in person," Monique went on to say.

"But this way, dropping by just to say hello in front of their friends should make it easier on them in keeping our secret." She flashed a healthy spread of gleaming white teeth with her charming, little smile.

"Very good, ah..." Elise thought a moment, then continued, "Monique."

Monique glared at her. Had she forgotten...

"It's OK to call you Monique," Elise reminded her. "We're not in costumes."

Monique stood corrected but was a little embarrassed to admit it.

Though, after a short pause, she finally murmured, "I knew that."

Elise stared over at her, as they walked side-by-side through the grove. Finally, she decided to voice her disagreement, "No, you didn't."

After a short silence, they both giggled.

Once through the grove, at the sight of a strange lady standing on the porch with Wendy, the girls slowed their pace, wondering who she was.

"You think this might be it?" Elise was worried.

But they didn't notice any distinct markings on the shiny new car in the yard to suggest the lady on the porch with Wendy was a state official. The lady was dressed to look sophisticated.

"I don't know," Monique replied, quizzically looking ahead at her, and Wendy, who didn't appear disturbed by any means; but didn't appear calmly complaisant, either.

As Monique and Elise approached, a bit precariously, they caught Chelsea's eye. She beamed with delight, placing the two girls as the missing pieces in her self-created puzzle. A perfect match, she decided.

The girls' final approach was rather vague, holding both the lady and Wendy in their stares as they walked up onto the porch. Chelsea was elated to greet them, extending her hand in a kind gesture.

"Hi, I'm Chelsea Freeman, correspondent at WCGN-Television."

Elise was relieved in her response, "Oh, you're the news-lady on TV."

"That's right," Chelsea was happy to announce. The three shook hands briefly. Elise and Monique properly introduced themselves.

As they chatted out on the porch—Chelsea preparing to leave—she had a final request from the girls, including Wendy. "Would it be asking too much of you if I could get some pictures of you girls?"

Her request was much too genteel to turn down. She was dapper, charming, and persuasive.

The gullible little, innocent girls agreed, along with Wendy, who had been entertaining the news lady for the better part of the early afternoon. When she was done with taking their pictures, Monique and Elise went inside the house while Wendy accompanied Chelsea to her car. And as she was getting in behind the wheel, with the driver-side door open, Wendy asked out of aroused curiosity, "What are the pictures for? Does our being orphans make us newsworthy?"

Good question because all the while Chelsea was alone with Wendy, she never established a valid reason for her visit. She drank coffee, and they chatted, but never about anything specific. She was made aware of the foster home closing; and finally, the possibility of the girls being separated, placed under different foster care for each. Wait a minute, Wendy was thinking.

She stared at Chelsea, who issued a tittered laugh, then glanced at her watch, "Oh, gosh," she said.

"Look at the time. I must be going. I have an early appointment, this afternoon."

That's the way she left it hanging in closing the door, starting the car, and backing out of the yard.

"She never made much sense of her entire visit," Wendy told the girls, once they'd gathered in her room, later that afternoon.

Wendy needed to meet with them on a matter of this urgency: her visit by the news-lady being suspect.

"But I don't see what harm she could cause. She doesn't know anything, and I didn't tell her anything that may arouse her suspicion about us. Everybody there saw us in costumes, the other night; and pictures were taken. We could be anyone, as far as everybody knows."

"Why would she want *our* pictures?" Monique raised the question.

"Good question," Wendy said.

"I have no idea. What's been bugging me about the whole thing is the way she acted when I told her it was possible we could be separated."

"What happened?" Elise asked she and Monique sprawled on Wendy's bed, while she sat on the end, facing them.

"She seemed to become upset, for some reason," Wendy said.

The three of them went on an assignment to try and locate a suitable place to re-establish a safe environmental place of residence. Miss Agnes hadn't returned yet, so the girls thoughtfully left her a note, not what business they were attending, just that they'd return soon.

Elise and Monique took to downtown as Koh, and Jor, ripping through the air at low altitudes, like a couple of rockets- their colorful costumes glinting in the bright, afternoon sunlight as they passed over the city, with the streets filled with bustling pedestrians, and motorists. They were highly vivid to the eye, flying at half-mast among the tallest of buildings.

A roar of cheers erupted among the many people watching this spectacular showcase, along with fervent chanting, and fanatic waving of hands, "Angels! Angels! Angels!"

The girls then descended to an altitude low enough to give the public a brief wave of their hands, which brought even more bursts of cheers exploding in the air. Then they jetted up and away with a burst of speed.

The feds had a spotter among the people on the streets, and he radioed-in on the ecstatic commotion, from the government vehicle he was sitting in.

"I just saw the *Birds* in flight," he said to Headquarters downtown.

"I wouldn't have believed it if I hadn't seen them with my own eyes."

Ed Milburn said over the radio, at the command center, alongside Commander Seth Gordon, "Is it the three of them?"

"Negative. Just two of them," the agent said.

"Colonel, do we have any choppers in the air?" Ed turned to the colonel and said.

"Yes, we do," the colonel said, reaching for the hand mike to radio the pilots of several heavily armed gunships a flight.

Jillian was in the area close enough to overhear the colonel and Ed in their clandestine discussion. She stormed over to them, enraged. "Are you going to just shoot them down, like clay pigeons? What about our priority to try and establish communications with them?"

"They will sue for a piece negotiation, once they feel the might of our military power," Ed boasted.

The girls were cruising alongside one another, close enough to hold hands, enjoying the brisk, cool wind-force in their faces, and hair. In moving aloft, with a bird's eye-view, taking in the beautiful vista from high above was a thrill beyond measure. And they once thought they wouldn't like flying. They grinned to one another occasionally, enthralled beyond description.

Then out of the sky behind them they were struck fiercely without warning. A military helicopter, heavily armed, had opened fire on them with a devastating mechanism, in military terms, known as the Wart Hog, one of the most powerful weapons in the modern day, military weaponry.

The girls were immediately startled but hardly phased. They looked behind them and shockingly discovered the huge, metal monster spitting fire at them, like some maniacal, armored dragon.

They pivoted in midair—such a dynamic maneuver, very impressive to the on-looking citizens below—and went in separate directions within a split second, leaving the helicopter firing point-blank into an empty sky. The Angels simply had vanished far beyond the distant blue.

The pilot and battle-crew gawked in amazement, hurled into an apprehensive state of disbelief.

The pilot, now in a daze of bedazzlement, got on the horn to radio the negative results from the attack. "This is Red Badger One, to the base. The *Birds* got away. And, Sir…you won't believe how."

The colonel came back with agitation in his voice, "Try me!"

There was a slight hesitation from the pilot; then he finally replied, with fearful humbleness in his voice, "They're impervious to our weapons. The Wart Hog had no effect on them. They repelled it as if it was a joke."

The colonel became flustered, extremely angry. He paced restlessly, with the radio mike in hand, fuming. Finally, he lifted the mike to speak. His military pride was seriously injured, for the moment.

"Abort," he said, his voice over the radio noticeably subdued.

"Sir?" The pilot didn't understand the rigid colonel's defeated attitude over the radio.

The colonel raged, "I said *ABORT, lieutenant!"*

Susan and Jillian approached Ed—their supervisor—and the colonel, with the avid displeasure of their actions.

Jillian, acting as spokesperson, scoffed, "So, now they're simply birds to you men, huh? You just shoot them down as if it was nothing...just some unwanted debris, floating in the air— "

Ed became incensed, already infuriated over the first misfire, as he turned to the ladies insistently, "You two...in my office. *Now!"*

Once in his office at Headquarters of the military compound, he released his fury on them.

"Listen...the two of you can return to GSW if you no longer want to be part of this operation. But we're not going to risk National Security of this Country, or any other part of the world, over some silly, emotional whim you ladies keep throwing at us!"

He then stormed out of his office, leaving Susan, and Jillian to make their decision.

Jillian stared at him as he was leaving. Then, turning to Susan, she said, unmistakably convinced, "That man's a covert operative, planted in our midst to carry out such a diabolical plan against a life-form that has shown no hostilities toward humans, whatsoever. They've only demonstrated a willingness to help, when they could've just remained hidden, never to become involved—if their purpose was a malicious ploy to take over Earth."

"I can't help wondering why they would, seemingly, only select children as their hosts," Susan was serious to know. Then she went on, "Unless they are children themselves, as a life-form we may be totally incapable of understanding."

Jillian suggested a gut-felt decision to Susan. "I think you and I should return to GSW. It's nothing else we can do here. I feel our best place now is at GSW. I can't quite explain it, but I'm almost certain that this visit from the aliens is not the end of it."

They rented a vehicle, and headed back to their home station at GSW, as it was a three-hour drive over the mountains, along with flat grounds, and across open plains.

The girls landed, starkly bemused, in the wide-open spaces somewhere along a mountain range, far outside the northern city limits, amid clearings that created huge gaps in a scattered forest surrounding them. The city skyline was in a haze against the far distant sky.

The girls came together amid the desolate wilderness. Elise was first to acknowledge, "What was that all about?" She was scantily checking herself over for possible nicks and tears in her costume. She found nothing of the sort.

"I don't know," Monique said.

"Were they shooting at us?"

"I'm not sure," Elise noted. "Something felt like... tiny pebbles."

"I know," Monique was puzzled. "Was it a bee-bee gun? I didn't really feel anything."

"Are you OK?" Elise was further concerned.

"I'm fine," Monique said. "Are you?"

"Just fine," Elise assured her.

But both their pride, and emotional fortitude were slightly bruised, as they simply couldn't understand the vicious assault on them, launched by their own, supposedly, protective military. It was very saddening as moisture collected in their eyes, standing alone in such a remote, isolated surrounding.

Monique finally said, out of curiosity, trying to belay her distraught emotions, "Well, we'd better not go back to town, dressed like this."

Elise agreed, "That's for sure."

Koh said as an urge to give them confidence, "You're OK. So long as you show no fear, you can't be hurt."

Elise was thinking. "You guys keep bringing that up. What is with this...*fear?*"

"Yes, I'd like to know that too," Monique was curious to know.

Jor said, "It can, and in most cases, will hamper your abilities to function, period. You can overcome it. And It'll be tough, but it can be done."

"Oh boy," Elise said to digest that bit of strange news from the entities. Then she went on, "Well, Wendy said we are to search for a good place to live."

Monique said, looking about, befuddled, "What kind of place that'd be, way out here?"

Elise laughed, "I'm sure she didn't mean in some jungle. We had no choice but to fly out here, remember; the helicopter with the bee-bee gun?"

Wendy took to the streets along a derelict side of the city. Dressed in plain clothing, she wandered about the drab district, checking the area for possible settlement, among vagrants, thugs, and destitute families of misfortune. She was as conspicuous as a light in the dark, specifically noticed by passersby, some with rejection-stares. She was so obviously out-of-place that she began to feel the pressure just from people staring; and she was only wearing jeans, sneakers, and a top.

The kind of place she was searching for, perhaps didn't exist anywhere. The district was a shabby place, entirely. Lived-in homes were jaded and damaged in some ways. Plywood was nailed to partly cover some broken windows of many homes, while others were lacking windowpanes.

What she and the girls were needing was a place with the power on, but was abandoned by the population, and the city's ordinance. By which, she never intended to relinquish her sewing talent; and she would need another usage, like for bathing, and preparing food. But this was her very first step outside the foster home to make it on her own, along with two other responsibilities. She mustn't give up, however; her success in her attempt was imperative. There was no turning back.

Some guys came along in a convertible. It rolled up to the curb, alongside her. There were five of them in the car; two up front, counting the driver, and three in the back. They were older teenagers, for the most part. The driver and the guy in the passenger seat look a bit older, maybe early to mid-twenties.

Even in the topless vehicle, Wendy noticed a thin, gray haze of misty smoke basically encircled the occupants, along with a pungent smell she vaguely recalled from long ago, when she was attending public school. Marijuana, it was. Pot, weed; yes, that's what they called it back then.

"Hi, sweetheart. Need a lift to somewhere?" the guy in the passenger seat spoke to her, a lewd gleam in his stare. They were nondescript, up-to-no-good thugs out joy-riding; and pleasure-seeking was on their minds. And Wendy was apt enough to perceive that.

"No, I'm fine," she returned beyond her barest civility, and without the courtesy *thank-you* in her reply.

Wendy knew she was the perfect stranger in this little squalor, and the obnoxious interference from these five degenerates was a staunch factor in her decision to leave this place.

The guy on the passenger side persisted, "Hey, cutie, we are going your way."

"No, you're not."

Wendy sensed trouble brewing from these guys, as she tenuously looked about for a means of escape with little effort. It

Charles H. Woods
335

wasn't so much as looking out for herself; it was the five misfits she regarded in her consideration. They had no clue of the critical situation that was building to overcome them. The guy on the passenger side took her annoyance as a joke, as he nodded to his friend behind the wheel, which he then whipped the car up on the sidewalk, atrociously blocking her path.

With so much negative thoughts running through her head, this abhorrent, bad move by these guys only ticked her off. She was running in seething anger. As the driver and his friend on the passenger side got out the car, Wendy smartly ducked inside a shadow-darkened tavern, with only a few customers sitting about, inattentive to her entering, as she did it with poise.

That stymied the guys, for the moment, for they had other plans for her. What was wrong with waiting her out? She had to return home eventually, wherever she lived, where the guys' consensus.

"We got all day, cutie," the driver said, having poked his head just a bit through the door. He never saw where she'd gone; he just knew she was inside somewhere. He withdrew and got comfortable with his friend leaned against the hood, and him against the driver-side door on the car.

The three guys in the back seat had also gotten comfortable, kicked back, relaxing, with folded arms behind the head, except for one. He'd crawled onto the top of the back seat, laid back, sipping on a forty-ounce. The tavern door opened, and out stepped a...stunning, young girl in blue tights, trimmed in white—a waistband and matching boots? Long, dark hair, almost like the girl who had just gone inside the place. But this little cute girl appearing suddenly was a huge distraction. They looked at her with a complete change of heart for the other girl.

The three other guys remained in the car, but sat up straight, giving her their gawking attention.

"Hello, darling!" One of the guys in the back seat, who made the comment, was leaned most forward to her than the other two.

"Did you guys see a girl go inside?" she asked them calmly, collected.

All five guys were very attentive to her.

The driver said, a lurid grin at her, "Honey, you should've run right into her. She just went inside as you were coming out."

Then he made mention of her dazzling costume. "Say, that's a really cool outfit you're wearing. Too bad it's not Halloween. You'd sweep them off their feet." He circled around her stealthily, looking over her spiffy attire.

"Man, that is something!" He ogled her, and she wasn't without that awareness.

As the two of them began to tacitly approach her, she wasn't intimidated in the least. She retained her composure, calmly saying to them, "She's a friend of mine, and she said some guys out here were giving her a bit of trouble. Was it you guys?"

The guy who was on the passenger side snidely replied, "What if it was, tuts?"

Wendy had had enough of their verbal abuse; their selfish, self-confidence and bogus mannerism. Growing vilely angry, although she kept her poise, she'd reached the end of her tolerant-level.

"Step out of the car," she demanded, sounding with the authority of a policeman.

The guys looked to one another, hilariously amused at her frivolous boldness. They even laughed at her.

"I won't ask you again," she said. "It's for your own safety unless you're willing to take a wild sky-ride."

Sky-ride? The guys looked to one another, their minds groping. What, on earth, did she mean by that?

"Okay, guys, let's amuse her. Get out of the car," the driver commanded them laughingly, as they began piling out of the back seat, onto the sidewalk. They grew close to invading her space in an obvious unrestrained lurid salaciousness. She was steadfast, poised and confident, as she moved away from them, over to their vehicle.

Suspending their ill-intent toward her, momentarily, they stood around awaiting whatever fun-thing she was about to display for their further amusement.

Before their very eyes, she stooped in her dazzling blue and white tights, reached an arm—only the one arm—underneath the car.

Now, the rowdy boys tenaciously geared up to make fun of her, watching her make a fool of herself.

What was she reaching for underneath the car, which weighed a couple of tons, at least? Unless her insane plan was to try and lift—

She did just that, bringing the one-and-a-half-ton vehicle clearly off the sidewalk, well balanced above her head. And she brought the extremely weighty vehicle out to nearly the middle of the streets, as the area was vacant of traffic, for the time being.

The once bad boys now completely rehabilitated from their wickedness, looked-on in limpid horror, as the girl in the blue and white costume said to them as her final warning, "I just want you guys to know not to mess with my friend."

Then she gave the car a heave and sent the vehicle rocketing skywards, to somewhere far away.

She then turned to the boys, and added, "Now, do you want to mess with *me?*" She jabbed her index finger in the chest, which was indicative of her warning.

The once tough gangsters cut and ran, scattering along the streets in a fierce panic—a couple of them screaming their lungs out. From that point, it was hard to tell which was which doing the screaming, because their backsides were facing Wendy as they fled rambunctiously into the caverns of this horrid side of town.

Wendy then flashed and was gone within the blink of an eye, leaving only a brief memory to fade with the ebbing of receding trash that was slightly lifted off the street as the young speedster went past.

But Wendy wasn't a super jerk, just because she had the superpower to be one; several miles away, along with a vacant area right outside a rural area, the vehicle she'd angrily tossed was on the decline from its long-distant flight. She arrived just in time to catch the falling car before it slammed into the ground. Then, with the extra baggage, she hauled it back to where she'd tossed it from.

On her brief return with the car, some stragglers were in the area, not paying attention. As she placed the vehicle gently on the street, an elderly couple returning from their heart-exercise walk happened to catch a glimpse of her just leaving.

They'd only get a fleeting glance of the blue-and-white clad, little miss, not enough to declare it was a person, just a quick stir of what they conceived as a puff of wind in color.

"Honey, did you see that?" the lady asked her husband, who depended on a cane for his physical stability.

"What I saw was what the wind looks like in color," he said facetiously, with a small grin. With his laugh trailing off, he added, "Just a Lil dust devil."

With a couple of hours left to GSW, they were traveling along a mountain road, at a high elevation. It twisted and coiled in places, like a serpent. Susan was at the wheel, Jillian was in the passenger seat. Neither one was comfortable being that high-up, even though the highway was a spaciously safe route to travel; there was always that chance of some freak accident.

"I was thinking about what you said about them being children," Jillian started the conversation about the aliens. "Who's to say that, since they're aliens, they can't be like humans? Can you imagine what we may appear to them?"

"I do think they're here for a reason," Susan said.

"Of course, they are," Jillian sternly agreed. "Look..." She angled left in her seat to face Susan behind the wheel. "I'm the first to admit I don't know the reason; but, from everything they've shown about themselves, hostility was never one of them. I don't know why, but I get this deep sense that they're not hostile, by any means.

"I think we're making a terrible mistake by attacking them," she concluded.

In rounding a curve, along with the accommodating two-lane highway, Susan had only time to jerk the steering wheel sharply to the left, to avoid colliding with an eighteen-wheeler in the wrong lane. The driver had dozed off, after having spent hours behind the wheel of the huge diesel rig and wasn't paying attention.

Both girls screamed at a rush of terror, as the vehicle they were in slammed through the aluminum guardrail on the left. The car careened over the edge of the cliff, airborne to some several hundred feet below, where a rocky bottom awaited them.

With their lives flashing before them, their deaths-screams continued as the vehicle spiraled downward in midair.

But an abrupt, senseless halt in midair occurred, causing the plunging vehicle to jerk with a mild thump. Then the descent continued at a much slower rate of speed. It floated down a short way, then, as if under its own power or—better yet—*its own* decision, the car began rising back to where it had left the cliff's edge.

It was gingerly put down on the shoulder of the roadway, safely out of harm's way. Inside the vehicle, Susan and Jillian were traumatically rattled, but in one piece, to catch their breaths, leaving their minds reeling in disbelief, with panic still susurrating in the back of their minds.   But it didn't take a brilliant scientist to finally conclude as to what miracle had saved them. Gathering their faculties, with a look through the window on the driver side, those colorful Angels, in their stunning costumes, were blandly staring back at them.

"Oh, my god," Jillian said, stifling a gratified sob in her voice. "I should've known."

Susan rolled her window down, as the Angels drew closer, to make sure the ladies were all right. "Ma'am, are you ladies all right? Please don't freak out. We do this kind of stuff." That was Monique, smiling pleasantly at them; Elise stood beside her, smiling as well, their dazzling costumes so hep, in the bright sunlight.

"Oh, we're not going to freak-out," Susan was most delighted to say. "We happen to know that you're the Angels everybody's been ranting about, here lately."

Jillian had leaned over in front of Susan, impeding her space behind the wheel, with a small camera in hand, aiming it out the window to the Angels. She was cheerfully smiling, beaming with enthusiasm, "Can I get a picture of the two of you? It's only for my personal treasure if you don't mind."

The girls were agreeable, knowing their pictures were already exposed to the public, but while they were in costume. Chelsea was the only person with a picture of them as orphans, for whatever reason. It was their understanding that she didn't know who they were, otherwise.

"Make it quick," Monique said. "We must be going real soon."

"How'd you happen to be out here?" Susan was puzzled. "This is quite a way from any populated area."

Elise said, to their amusement, "Sometimes we're out, just looking things over. We can also hear very well and see."

"Amazing," Jillian said, not wasting a second in snapping pictures of the aliens disguised as two, lovely young girls.

Monique added, "We heard you screaming, and we saw your car go over the cliff, so we came and got you." Then she tilted her head curiously, "Are you guys sure you're, all right?"

Jillian and Susan were so moved by the Angels' intelligence, and their flawless, amiable dispositions. They were indeed *Angels.*

"We're just fine, thanks to the two of you," Susan assured them, as Jillian was done with taking pictures of the girls, and withdrew from the window, giving Susan back her proper space. "Thank you, Angels," Jillian said to them, putting away her camera inside her purse on the seat, next to her.

"You're welcome," both Monique and Elise kindly returned at the same time. "We gotta go. See ya," Monique said as she and Elise bolted to the sky, giving Susan, and Jillian a firsthand look at their spectacular might, and super abilities.

At a lasting, stupendous impression felt by the Angels, Susan, and Jillian held their heartfelt, deep emotions a secret, even from one another. It was quiet among them in the car for miles, after they'd gotten started back on their way to GSW. Now and then, they'd look over to one another, with never a word said.

"I can't get the impression of their sweet, innocent smiles off my mind," Jillian finally commented, after a long-hours ride. GSW was just over the next rise ahead of them. The logo was in sight, high on a hilltop behind the huge establishment, on a giant billboard that read: "GSW, Ground Saucer Watch. Home of Sky Watcher, the World's Most Famous Telescope." A monstrous dome of a satin white finish, with the capability to make a complete 360-degree rotation, housed the giant telescope.

The compound was enormous; plenty of parking space; equipped with living quarters, plus living accommodations, such as a mini shopping mall, a supermarket, dry cleaners, and a recreational facility. It was home-away-from-home for the special-assigned personnel.

After they'd cleared the tight security at the main gate, with the guards wearing side arms, Susan returned a comment of her own. "They did seem to have such an aura about them. Ed talked about that as if they emitted some type of hypnotic spore, designed to lure their victims into a stupor, then take them to use as hosts for whatever diabolical purpose they're here for."

"We think these particular entities are life-forms of pure energy," Jillian shared her theory. "Therefore, they *must* have access to a host, or they'll simply evaporate into the elements, and become particles of molecular matter of all which is tangible or animate."

"So, they're simply fighting to survive. End of story; is that it?" Susan asked.

"I really can't be sure," Jillian admitted. "It's only a theory... the best I could come up with."

"But you've been pretty accurate with your theories about certain things of importance, over the past several years, so far," Susan complimented her.

Jillian then came straightforward with something completely away from the norm. "Susan, do you believe in metaphysical beings?"

"You mean, like the Angels?" Susan asked. "Well, they're here, aren't they?"

"Ah...yes, but, these are counted as aliens," Jillian made clear, then continued, "I'm speaking of the biblical term."

Susan answered frankly, "It doesn't matter whether we *believe* in them or not, for them to exist."

Susan claimed their assigned parking space, near the mammoth building's main entrance. She put the gear in park, shut off the engine; then she and Jillian left the car and headed inside the building, where they came across a man in a casual, blue-gray work-uniform, with some important papers, and a vanilla folder, stuffed with more documents, in his hands.

They were inside the main entrance when he spotted them headed for their station, and he hurried across the gleaming tile-floor straight over to them.

"Susan...Jill," he said in a rushed voice. Something exciting was going on with him. He was a little heavy on the physical side, average height, with a receding hairline; and he wore glasses.

"You're just the people I want to see. We've been trying to get a hold of you, but you were busy on the assignment with the Federal Agency about those aliens."

He then took out of his hand the thick, vanilla folder and handed it to Susan, his pink forehead gleaming with the residue of sweating. "Here, you can look these over on the way to the meeting." He sounded a bit winded in his speech, and mysterious, as the ladies stared at him: What meeting? they were thinking, Susan, holding on to the folder.

With his hand, he gestured she open the folder. She did and found large, glossy photo finishes of what appeared as a dark moon. In getting a gander at the photos from looking over Susan's shoulder, the two ladies were somewhat at a loss.

In noticing the inconclusiveness-look in their eyes, the way they stared at him, he went on to bring them partially up to date, "It's been in the range of the telescope for a few days now. We think it's headed this way." His voice was still rushed, and he was yet a bit winded from excitement.

"Brent, you need to calm down," Susan suggested thoughtfully. "I realize the urgency of this matter; but, man, you are really wired."

They moved across the huge vestibule, which had on displays a few artificial creatures of otherworldly culture, imagined by the designer. Brent took them on
the elevator, to the meeting room on the third floor. A small gathering of staff members was seated at a rectangular table with a highly-polished finish under the dim, regular lighting; added lights were from the computer-screens lined along the walls, with a person monitoring each one.

Susan and Jillian were briefly greeted by members of their team, and others, then took their seats to begin the conference. Brent sat across the table from them, as that was the only available place close to them.

The object of interest in the photographs was dispatched to a large screen on the wall before them. It was exactly like it was in the picture; it looked like a *dark* moon of some kind. There was no other defining factor about it, except that it tended to gravitate toward Earth's atmosphere.

"What is it?" Susan leaned over slightly, to ask Jillian sitting next to her.

"I pray it's not the set-up Ed predicted by the aliens of an invasion force," she said.

"As of now, we can't be positive where it's headed." A speaker had the floor, standing before the huge screen, with a pointer in his right hand. He was an Air Force captain in dress-blues, selected as technical assistant and advisor on this early development of a concerned situation.

"Could it be a ship of some kind?" Jillian asked.

"At this point, it could be anything in relations to some type of space vessel," the captain said.

"Is there any way we can determine its exact course before it gets too close to our atmosphere?" asked Susan.

The captain responded, "Jupiter-Two is our spotter; so, yes, we can. Our satellite is equipped to make a positive identification on any outer space intrusion at approximately some five-hundred-light-years prior to entering our atmosphere."

"How soon will it reach that point?" Brent raised the question. The captain: "At the rate, it's moving, I'd say in about three weeks." A tentative fear spread among the staff members. But no comment was made; just a gulf of silence settled over them

Chapter 23

Even though Chelsea didn't get the satisfaction she was after, she took the chance that she would, eventually. She paid a visit to the State Department on a matter she deemed was urgent.

She spoke with Miss Valerie Stanfield in her office, concerning this matter of urgency she had on her mind.

"Is it confirmed the three girls will become separated, once the orphanage is closed? Because I'm willing—and equipped—to take them into my custody, until such time they may be placed in a home where they won't be separated."

Valerie, with years of experience with adoption procedures, had never encountered anyone such as Chelsea Freeman. She was high-maintenance; a celebrity in her social standings. Why would she want the responsibility to maintain the welfare of *any* children?

"You're making a rather unusual request,"
Valerie said. "You're Chelsea Freeman, that famous news lady. You're single, and I'm sure you're very popular in your social group. But, I know," Valerie paused from being carried away with personal concerns.

"It's none of my business how you run your life. It just struck me kind of strange that a woman of your stature could become so condescending toward children. But, I'll consider the matter, just as a special favor to you. It's commendable that you're doing this, I want you to know," she concluded.

Chelsea spoke in closing, "I'd like this arrangement to remain confidential. I'm not up for all the attention it might draw, should word get out that I'm babysitting on the side." She added a jaunty smile at the end of her remark.

"I understand," Valerie assured her as Chelsea got up to leave.

Chelsea left her a gratified grin while walking out the door, feeling a little bit more accomplished.

She drove out to the orphanage; parked, got out of her car; walked up on the porch, and knocked on the door, using the brass metal door-knocker. No one answered. After knocking a few more times with no answer, she left the door, the porch; got back in her car, and drove away. The SUV that normally sits in the wide, gravel driveway was gone. Which only meant to her, no one was home right now.

Downtown was brewing in a mild state of unrest, as a small group of protesters marched along the sidewalks, bearing self-made signs complaining to the unjust treatment of the Angels by government hooligans. The protesters were only a few among the mass of citizens who witnessed the military war machine—that helicopter—firing on the Angels a few days ago.

They scarcely stood out in the mix of other pedestrians, going about their shopping, and other businesses. A guy in a terrycloth robe, long, dark hair, and a beard—a held-over from the 60's hippies-era—sported a make-shift, cardboard sign, carelessly written, that read: "Doom's day approaches. Repent now!"

There were other signs held up for reading from better organized, and better dressed, patrons of this great Country. Some of those signs were appealing and inviting to the Angels on a more personal level, like, "Come and live with us!"

"No violence against the Angels, they are our friends!" And more: "We love our Angels!"

The protesters continued their frail marching, though soon to become weary of their fruitless task. Eventually, they'd become thinner in numbers, and finally retire to their homes, after an exhausting, pointless demonstration.

Ed, and a partner, Federal Agent Tray Douglas, were parked in their government sedan across the street from a Taco Bell restaurant. In a private, low-keyed conversation, they kept a carefully, watchful eye on the scantily busy streets around them.

"How about some Tacos, Tray?" The gentle sauntering aroma from the restaurant had awakened Ed's appetite for a Mexican treat.

Agent Tray Douglas agreed, sitting over on the passenger side; and they got out of the car, and started across the street, through shallow traffic. They entered the restaurant where skimpy customers were seated here-and-there, and the aroma was deliciously prevalent inside.

Brittany and Natalie sat in a corner booth, with room to spare. They were speaking softly, in a quiet conversation, with the subject being exclusively about the Angels and their close-knit friendship. They were speaking in accordance to how close sparse customers was around them.

Natalie, carefully looking about, and only noticing two gentlemen in dark suits, sitting just outside the normal hearing range from them, said to Brittany in a normal voice, "I think it's so cool we know the Angels personally. If the kids at school knew what we know about them, they'd freak."

The two girls laughed, as Brittany said, "Not only would they freak over that; they'd really freak if they found out *we* knew the Angels' *real* names, and where they lived."

They laughed again, with Natalie adding during her quiet laugh, "This is just too cool! Just think, we can go and visit them anytime we want."

Brittany said just above a whisper, as the two of them shared the same seat in the booth, leaving a whole empty seat across from them, "But it's very important we keep their secret, no matter what." At a glance, she noticed the two darkly-clad men get up from their table, and leave the restaurant, without their orders. She thought it was strange that they would do that; but she shrugged it off, making it none of her business.

She glanced at her watch—the only present her mom had given her in quite a while. Her dad...only how to be rude, obnoxious, and dysfunctional. She said to Natalie, "I wonder what's keeping them?"

"If we let them *walk* now, we may not get this sure of a chance, later," Ed convinced his partner, agent Douglas. They stood outside the restaurant, near the entrance, contemplating a plan. They'd overheard enough from those two, young girls to hold them for intensive questioning, as it was strictly on behalf of National Security. And no one between the ages of a five-year-old to a full adult was exempt from interrogation when it involved a threat to the nation. "They were clearly speaking about the aliens, which they know them as angels. I say we pick them up, now," Ed was insistent.

He and Douglas went back inside the restaurant, and straight over to the booth Natalie and Brittany sat. Both men showed the girls their badges, as Ed said to them, "You two young ladies must come with us, please."

"The FBI, why?" Brittany became instantly frightened.

Natalie was near panic, dumbfounded, and very afraid, as they hesitantly, with increasing fear, left the restaurant with the two men.

Wendy, Monique, and Elise were coming up the street. They were to meet with the girls, Brittany and Natalie, at Taco Bell for an afternoon treat from Wendy and Brittany. Just up ahead, the Taco Bell sign was tall against the skyline.

But suddenly, Wendy caught sight of something that was instantly disturbing. She clearly saw Brittany, and Natalie getting in the back seat of a dark gray sedan. In drawing the incident closer with her magnified vision, she saw the vehicle had a government license tag; and that the two men with the girls were, undoubtedly, federal agents.

Confused, and alarmed after her shocking discovery, she wisely held up, insisting the girls do the same, and they did.

"Wendy, what's wrong?" Elise asked she and Monique puzzled.

"Look ahead," she told them.

As Monique and Elise focused on what was ahead, they were only in time enough to see the sedan leaving. Though, telescopically, they saw the backs of Brittany's and Natalie's heads, as they were seated in the back seat of the government sedan.

Monique gasped, confused, with incomprehension.
"What's going on?" she wanted to know. Desperately! Then a scary thought came to her, as she cupped her hands over mouth in dread.

"Oh, my god!"

"Yes...I know. My thoughts exactly," Wendy said as if she could read Monique's thoughts—which was one element not included in their special powers.

Monique went on to ask with reservation, "You think they might tell who we are?"

"I don't know," Wendy was skeptical. "They might try to scare them into telling."

She stared at Monique, worried. Then she had an idea, turning to Elise, and said, "Can you follow them? Don't do anything, just follow them. Find out where they're taking them, then come back and let us know."

"Why don't we both go?" Monique didn't understand.

"No," Wendy opposed the idea. "It's better this way. You and I'll be in reserve just in case we're needed." Then she pointed out to Elise, "Be careful. Don't let anyone see you and get back here as soon as you can."

"Gotcha," Elise said. She then slipped away behind a bush, just around the dark corner of a building nearby; and in return, she was in costume. The three checked out the less busy area they were in. No one was close enough to have noticed them.

"Go...quickly!" Wendy said to Elise, and she flashed to the sky like a bullet, high and away, and was gone.

Wendy and Monique took their seats on a bench people used while awaiting a City Transit to come along. While sitting there, Monique noticed the far-away look in Wendy's eyes, which wasn't comforting; it concerned Monique.

"Something's amiss with you, isn't it?" Monique asked, staring Wendy precise.

Wendy brought her attention to her and said with obvious contempt in her voice, "Where'd you get that word? Never mind; I'm angry!"

"Why?" Monique frowned, not understanding. "Is it what I said?"

"Those soldiers shooting at you guys. They had no right, which made me realize no one cares about us! They want to be rid of us, while we have nowhere to go; this is our *home*. Where else they expect to live? Probably what we should do is to fight back." That was mostly anger speaking through Wendy. She had no intention of waging war against the military. That would involve the entire Country.

Monique sparked in a childish delight, "Are we going to kick their butts?"

Wendy laughed softly, with recognition of Monique's gullible immaturity.

"No," she made clear. "It was just a misunderstanding. We can't go against our own Country."

But Wendy was smoldering over an unresolved anger no one knew about but her. And it began to drive her otherwise bland spirit into overdrive toward a different outlook on life for her, and the girls. Although she vaguely recalled her childhood; she was very clear on the fact it was short-lived. And what memories she could summon was never pleasant. Abandoned by her parents as a young child, she was left to fend for herself, from foster homes to foster homes, until she ended up here, although she never quite got over that lonely, empty feeling. But the girls, Monique, and Elise certainly made a huge difference by stimulating her innate compassion for others, and not holding the world at fault for her unwarranted misfortune.

The girls had never shown the slightest trace of bitterness over their parental abandonment, but, by the simple fact, they weren't old enough to recall much if any memories of their past lives. Foster care was all they've known; it was their way of life. And Wendy was an added delight as their proverbial older sister.

Now, Wendy had decided not to relinquish her responsibility for the girls, no matter what it took. And she began gathering confidence in meeting the unexplored challenge, with her new and powerful image. Only she had to be aware, and carefully manage the rage inside her, with in mind that absolute power corrupts.

"Wendy," Monique began, a timid look and uncertainty in her stare at Wendy.

"What is it?" It tortured Wendy that they were innocent of any wrong-doing, yet they were being persecuted for harboring three other innocent beings, just because of society's fear of the *unknown.* Then society should walk a mile in their shoes.

"Will we be OK?"

Wendy placed a gentle arm around Monique, with care and warmth.

"Don't you worry," she assured Monique. "We're going to get through this. Everything's going to be OK."

Those were comforting words. Even when Monique was a preschooler, Wendy had a knack for soothing her young, troubled mind, when it came to scary monsters under her bed.

"Don't you worry," was always Wendy's caring words. Then she'd follow with, "Everything's going to be OK." And it came true because Wendy said it. Monique always trusted, and believed in Wendy, regarding her as a mom-figure, and big sister. And during those awful rainy nights, with the loud, booming thunder, to scare the living daylight out of you; so often Wendy would awake in the middle of the night to find Monique curled up beside her in bed. To Monique, that was the safest place to be, short of Heaven. And Wendy was always receptive to her.

Elise took a dark, back route in her return, staying out of range of the city-lights' parameter. She landed in the shadows of the obstructions of tall buildings, and other structural inhibitors along the streets.   After donning her civvies, as if by magic, she moved into the lighted area where she'd left Wendy, and Monique to wait for her.

"Hi, guys," she said, unrestrained by any bad news she may have encountered. She strode up to Monique, and Wendy with a balmy attitude.

Wendy was expecting a grand slam of a disappointment, as she'd begun to worry about Elise/Koh. "What took you so long?" Wendy asked, she and Monique now standing to greet Elise attentively.

"Joyriding," Monique murmured, stifling a sneaker.

"I heard that," Elise quickly responded.

"Never mind that." Wendy was anxious to get an answer to her question.

A serious mask as Elise went on to say, "They took them inside this building... FBI Headquarters was on the front of it."

"Isn't that like a government police department? I know it's pertaining to law, and it's...," Monique groped.

"Federal Bureau of Investigation," Wendy said.

"That's it," Monique grabbed the credit, receiving brief looks from Wendy, and Elise, as Wendy then continued, "Did you see where they took Brittany and Natalie?"

Monique dropped her head in despair, idly pacing back and forth, muttering, "Oh...this is bad, this is bad. This is *so* not good."

Elise said while regarding Monique with tenuous interest, "They took them into this room...this kind of small room, not very big. And they just left them there."

"Is that all?" Monique blurted, clueless as to what to think.

"What should we do?" Elise asked Wendy, who didn't have the answer right away as she looked away in thought.

Beyond her rational thoughts, Wendy knew in the back of her mind that a show of force may be the only option. That was horrid to even consider. She was at a crossroads of indecision.

A dim light hung from the ceiling in the close room where Brittany and Natalie sat at a rustic table with a faded Walnut finish and the corners chipped down to the wood.

The waiting was about the scariest part. The two young girls have never experienced this kind of trouble. As troublesome as they'd been in the past, they've never been before the law of any degree that a disciplinary procedure was the resolve.

On the wall behind Brittany, but directly in front of Natalie, as they sat across from one another at the table, was about a 4X4-

foot mirror, with a closed door next to it.

"Are you scared?" Natalie asked Brittany, as Natalie was petrified.

"I'm a little worried," Brittany admitted. "But I'm not going to panic, because we haven't done anything wrong. They want us to tell them about the Angels because they heard us talking about them." Brittany then became a bit adamite. She leaned across the table, meeting Natalie's stare eye to eye, and insisted sternly, "Don't you tell them one word about the Angels. They saved my life, and they're our friends! And we promised them..."

"I know that," Natalie said, and for the first time with a little aggression in her voice. "I'm not a squealer. Besides, I'll bet that, somehow, they know we're here, and they'll come and rescue us like they always do when people need them."

"Well, we're not in any *real* trouble—like we're about to die or something like that. Those men can't do anything but ask us questions. They can't be mean to us like they do on television..."

The door opened to the small room, letting in a shaft of brighter light from the short, brightly-lit hallway.

The two agents, Ed, and Tray came into the room, their manly size, and heights imposing silhouettes against the backlight coming from the hallway, behind them. Brittany and Natalie braced for whatever impact the men brought with them.

Ed spoke in a frank, unfeeling voice, "One of you come with me. It doesn't matter which one."

The girls remained seated, each one tingling from an overwhelming nervousness, and...well, yes, fright, as suddenly, they weren't quite as brave. "Well?" Ed's voice boomed authoritatively. "Which one of you are coming along?"

Finally, Natalie sucked it in.

"I'll go," she said, nervous, and hesitantly rising from the metal chair she was seated. A worried glance back at Brittany, who seemed depleted of her last ounce of nerve.

Natalie left the room with Ed, and agent Douglas pulled up a chair and sat at the table, facing Brittany. She was a wreck, suddenly teary-eyed, and was about to come apart. "I don't know anything," she whimpered like a frightened six-year-old, away from her mom for the very first time.

"I haven't asked you anything," agent Douglas told her, no feelings in his husky voice.

Ed began with Natalie after they were seated in a more accommodating room with a view. The brightly-lit city skyline was through a bay window opposite them. "Would you like a drink of water?" Ed's voice was more humane, thick, but not stoical.

Natalie was withstanding. She shook her head, not letting him out of her firm stare.

Ed relaxed in his seat, figuring she might be a bit stubborn, by the way, she held her poise—for now. "Do you live around here?" he asked, an effort to set her mind at ease.

Natalie looked him in the eye. "That's a dumb question," she said curtly. "You saw us at the restaurant, minding our own business. Whadda you want?"

Ed chuckled, "A live one. Okay, what do you, and your friend know about them... Angels, you call them?"

"They're good," Natalie was frank.

Ed geared up, becoming serious while leaning toward her, with his elbows on the table, as they were seated opposite each other.

"Very well, young lady"—she was only fourteen- "Tell me about the Angels. Do you know them on a personal basis? Who they are when they're not flying around, doing daring rescues? How about where they live, their names? Yes, their names. That's a start. What are their names?"

"Sure," Natalie said politely. But that was only a false impression, as she continued, "It's Koh, Jor, and Motatu. But don't ask me where they come from because I don't know."

Ed was irritated, fuming! "Now you look here, young lady," his voice now firm, no more Mr. nice guy. He got more in her face bullishly. "Did you know it's a felony to withhold vital information if it's a threat to our National Security?"

Natalie matched his hard stare, braving his abrasive change in attitude. "Fourteen!" she scoffed, unafraid. "Which means I'm a minor, who hasn't done anything."

Ed returned angrier, "It doesn't matter if you're five, which is older enough, in this case, to be held responsible for keeping vital information that may cause the destruction of this *PLANET!*" That emphatic yell at his conclusion was meant to scare her into complying.

But Natalie, being naïve, and docile her whole life, was thinking of the conclusion of life, with no other alternative as an option, said to Ed in a subtle voice, "You mean if I don't tell you what you think I know about the Angels, the world will blow-up?"

"That's hardly likely," he said. "But it's not so impossible."

"Then why should I tell you anything?" Natalie was being earnest, innocently steadfast in her forward thinking. "If you kill me for not telling you what you want; and the world blows up anyway, but I'll already be dead, so what's the point. If I'm dead, I wouldn't care."

"What about the people you love?" Ed tried a different angle to get to the child through her emotions. "Don't you care about your family?"

Natalie belayed that answer for a more practical one. "With me already dead, and the world blows up...," She then bore up from her seat, stiffly leaned toward Ed, glaring him in the face, and shouted, *"Everybody's dead!* What does it matter?"

Brittany was a bay of tears. She'd frozen under duress. She may have spilled her guts if weren't for her continued weeping and violent sobbing. During the entire interrogation, she was unable to speak clearly due to her disrupting anxiety attacks. Finally, agent Douglas was forced to suspend the interrogation indefinitely, and seek permission to take the child home.

Ed and Natalie came into the room. Immediately, she and Brittany locked eyes; and, right away, Natalie noted Brittany's normally encouraging stamina had been reduced to a sniveling wretch. She didn't understand. Brittany was monumental with courage and inspiration. What had happened to her? She wasn't bruised in any way. But even Natalie knew they weren't allowed to strike kids. So, exactly what *did* happen to Brittany?

Ed said to his partner in a dissatisfied, contemptuous fashion, "Let's get these kids home."

Brittany began collecting herself to the tune of she, and Natalie's freedom. What had seemed like an eternity to Brittany was now like a delayed, but a short walk in the park. She was thrilled beyond measure to finally leave this dungeon of an unwarranted persecution.

As they were escorted out of the building, and over to vehicle designated to take them home; Natalie offered her shoulder for Brittany to lean on, but she wasn't having any of that. She was too embarrassed.

Ed was driving his partner over in the passenger seat, and the girls riding silently in the back seat of the government sedan. While driving across town, Ed said to his partner, Douglas, low-keyed, "I'll have to hand it to the kid. She has spunk. She doesn't scare easily." Everyone in the car, especially Brittany, knew he was referring to Natalie. Brittany sank away in despondency.

Eventually, Ed inquired about Brittany to his partner, "Anything useful from the other one?"

Douglas shook his head despairingly. "Nothing," he said. "She just whined like a spoiled kid."

Brittany knew that Natalie had overheard the quiet conversation up front, just as she had. But neither one uttered a word.

Chapter 24

Night-flying was for the birds. *No, bats*, thought Monique. As a natural law, most birds don't fly at night, bats do. Her mind was roiling with unsettled judgments. Through the dark quietness of night, she rose to the moon-lit sky high above the city skyline, and the parameter of the city lights, her black cape fluttering in the brisk wind, like a hundred bat wings doing a soft rat-tat rhythm against the calves of her legs as she soared through the night softer than a ghostly whisper.

Wendy and Elise maybe upset with her for leaving the orphanage in the dead of night, but her conscience wouldn't allow her to sleep. She felt at fault, along with Wendy, and Elise, that their innocent friends, Natalie, and Brittany, were being held by government law officials. Which Monique didn't think was right, in her childish thinking. Keeping a secret such as this shouldn't be against the law unless the feds were there for some other reason Monique didn't know about. Was that possible?

She saw the FBI building below, within the frame of the city now half-lit that barely reached the altitude she flew, her black and silver costume vaguely luminescent in the lesser light at her higher altitude.

She touched down in virtual seclusion near the back of the building, under the cloak of pitch dark. No streetlights or neon lights were close in the area. As for the night crew, everything pertaining to night duty was concentrated to the front of the building. The huge parking lot, with many assorted, government vehicles, was highly luminescent; and where the span of artificial lighting began to decline, a full moon casts its limpid, silvery glaze of night light pervading over areas not relevant to the city's watchful eye.

Within a bank of darkness, just beyond a pour of light spilling over from the next street across the way, Monique moved precariously around the dark side of the building, where she paused then lifted herself up slowly to black windows that marked that section of the FBI building being closed for the evening.

Through Jor's eyes, she checked the darkened areas thoroughly, in case the girls, Brittany, and Natalie had been locked away. For the most part, she only discovered vacant rooms and empty corridors for her menial trouble. She withdrew, abandoning the use of Jor's eyes, and softly landed back into the dark area sound the corner of the building. She was open for ideas as she sat on a raised cement block, near a weak, foul-smelling dumpster behind the building.

Jor said, displeased with their present position, "Monique, of all the places to pick for hiding, why did you have to pick the stinkiest place: that foul dumpster?"

"Remember, I'm *you, Jor* – whenever we're in costume," Monique instead reminded her.

"Oh, so that's it," Jor miffed. "Before *you* get into trouble; you'd throw me at the bus."

Monique laughed, getting to her feet. "Not *at* the bus, *under* the bus," she made clear.

Jor gasped, astounded, "Under the bus? That's terrible! You'd do that to your own sister?"

Monique found herself caught up in Jor's tedious, little mind-game, which was a distraction. "Jor, stop it! Nobody's being thrown anywhere."

Jor laughed, "Ha, ha, ha."

Monique rolled her eyes, feeling tricked by the smart-mouth, little imp, replying to her sigh, "Oh, brother."

In realizing the hour was late, Monique knew she had to do something toward a resolve, in the wake of her investigation. She wasn't satisfied to admit to a lost effort, at this point. Whatever else she should do wasn't clear to her, nor recommendable. Such a little girl just couldn't figure out what to do with all that power. It was terribly frustrating!

Oh, wait. She held up abruptly, as someone was on the way out the building through the front entrance. It was several people, three ladies, and two men in plain clothing, darkly clad. They were headed to one of the many government vehicles across the huge parking lot.

Monique waited in the shadows, and the darkness, trying to determine her next move, which she had no clue. Then, the idea came to her: *Just leave. Go home. Natalie and Brittany should be OK, even if they had to spend the night here. They were just kids. Surely no harm would come to them, Monique tried to convince herself.*

As she took flight, rising slowly, and indecisively to the dark sky, she looked about, collecting all she could comprehend below, within the vast scope of her ultra-keen eyesight.

The vehicle the people from the building had gotten into was now, slowly, leaving the parking lot, onto the street. Monique, conscious-weary, indecisively followed the vehicle from within a layer of soft darkness above, just barely out of range of the city lights. The vehicle was a sedan with a steel-gray finish. It finally turned off the main boulevard, onto a lesser-traveled back street, and continued into a region of the city disinteresting to Monique.

In looking back one last time in the direction the vehicle had gone, as she continued toward home, at sort of an unusual way of parking out front of a convenient store was another vehicle. It was a black SUV, with a sliding, side panel door standing open. No one was around that she noticed; streetlights poorly illuminated the area from a short distance away, and the dimly-lit commercial sign atop the front of the place.

For some reason, it was a bit of an eerie scene to Monique. There were several other vehicles in the area; however, they were mostly obstructed by the intrusive part of the night that overwhelmed what little frail light could get through. Bulky, shapeless humps, hidden in corners of the dark, only indicative of what make, and model of each vehicle.

Before Monique completely dismissed her curiosity of the, seemingly, isolated, subtle attraction below, the government vehicle she'd languidly been following showed up out front of the convenient store, and parked across the streets, where it was poorly visible under the frail stretch of light from far across the way.

Inside the sedan, one of the ladies among the three in the seat was about to get out of the car.

"This won't take long," she said to the others.

She was seated next to the left-side rear door.

"This constantly hunting aliens has given me a migraine. I gotta have some pain medication."

"Hold on, Connie. I'm coming with you. I need a trip to the ladies' room," the lady on the other side said, opening her door.

The one left with the two gentlemen up front said to the ladies, "Now don't you two take all night. My shift's about over, and I'm worn out. I gotta get some sleep."

Both ladies closed their doors, and headed across the street, under the frail lighting. In noticing the rather peculiar way the black SUV was parked, with the side door left opened, Connie made mention, slightly curious, "Why would, whoever they are, leave their vehicle on the sidewalk, in front of the store?"

"Whoever it is must be in a rush," the other lady replied, as they were crossing the street.

The pair of ladies crossing the street were Connie Morgan, and Sylvia Haden, government agents. The walk between the SUV and the entrance through the glass door of the mini-mart was nearly a tight squeeze, which was suspect to a degree.

"Why is it parked so close to the door?" Sylvia wondered.

When Connie opened the door, they were both seized by the strong arm of a husky, hooded guy in dark clothing, and a ski mask, wielding an assault, automatic weapon. At gunpoint, he ordered the two ladies in rather roughly and insistently.

Upon the rushed, shocking surprise, Connie, and Sylvia were instantly made aware that other innocent customers were being held, hostage. An elderly couple, a middle-aged gentleman, and a woman with two kids—both girls, in elementary school— were face down on the floor, being guarded by three other deadly armed, hooded masked men in dark clothing.

An extremely nervous, heavy set male clerk was ordered to open the safe behind the counter, on the floor right beneath the register. His nervous twitches, due to his overwhelming fear of the men, made it difficult for him to concentrate to even make it seem as if he was working the combination; because he didn't know it. The combination worked only by the sensor, operated by an affiliate downtown.

"C'mon, hurry it up!" The hooded masked man poked the nervous clerk under the armpit with the short barrel, automatic weapon, his patience running thin.

"I told you, *I don't know it!*" The clerk was sweating, bending over the safe in the floor, fearing for his life. "It's operated from downtown."

The masked hoodlum was heartless, bearing down on the frightened clerk, "If you want all these people to be killed, including yourself, keep stalling!"

"I'm not stalling; I'm telling you the truth," the chubby, terrified clerk insisted fearfully. The two government agents were useless without their weapons, which were in their purses. They didn't dare reach for weapons in such a crucial situation. It could be a fatal risk. They were better off lying on the floor with the rest of the hostages, and fully cooperative. The little girl—10-years-old—lying on the floor with her mom, and younger sister across the way from the two agents, had the gumption to bore up her head and boldly address the bad guys, "You guys better let us go before the Angels come; and they will fix you really well!"

Her mom suddenly horrified over her little girl's stunning outburst, gathered her tightly against her, tapping the child on the back of the head, urging her to keep quiet, the mom's heart racing frantically in fear for her children.

One of the two hooded gangsters standing guard over them scoffed at the little girl's futile outburst, "Keep dreaming, kid."

The little girl's younger sister spouted off recklessly, "She's not dreaming; it's true!"

Her mom quickly reached over and gathered her youngest on the other side of her and brought her in tightly, like she did the oldest. "Be quiet, you two!"

The atrocious hoodlum angrily trained his weapon on them.

"Keep your smart-mouths shut!" he said in a snide, vile tone of voice.

The mouthy kids were creating an angry unrest among the hostages, except the two federal agents. They were concerned about their secrecy. One slip of the tongue, or the discovery of their weapons, could put them all at a higher risk. The two agents remained very still, trying to maintain their composures.

The middle-aged man across from the mom with the mouthy kids shouted in fear, "For Pete's sake, kids, keep quiet, will ya?"

"But they'll be here, just you wait," the younger sibling assured him, and the rest of the hostages.

"Lady, will you keep them quiet?" he miffed, sweating for his life.

The two men and the lady left behind in the car began to grow a little concern. The driver looked at the time on the digital clock in the dashboard: 11:29 p.m. They'd been there for nearly 20-minutes.

"Wonder what's keeping them," he said. He looked around at the lady in the back seat, whose name was Agent Vanessa Sims— a black American. "Do you mind going in to check on them?"

"Not at all," she said, opening the right-side rear door, in getting out of the car.

As she was crossing the street, her thoughts, her quick stride were abruptly interrupted by an unexpected presence that dropped out of the night sky only a few feet in front of her.

A little girl dressed in black leotards with a silver waistband, matching boots, and a black cape signaled to her in a mute voice to remain calm. Agent Vanessa didn't know what to do, or to think, she was so mesmerized.

"Who..." she stammered, bemused. "Who are you...where'd you come from?"

She stood there, gaping at the odd little girl in the out-of-season costume, though it was very attractive, neatly-fitting, with a stunning sheen, straight out of *Hollywood.*

Then it occurred to her. "You must be— "

"I am Jor," the little girls said to her.

Jor sighed quietly, wearily, "Ho-hum, here we go... *Under* the bus."

The little girl, who was Monique, fought to refrain from giggling, ran across the street, and inside the mini-mart.

As the tiny bell over the door rang lightly, to an intruder's entrance, the four hoods reacted alertly. Each of them took up defensive positions in various, but close locations near the front of the store. Weapons locked and loaded, trained on the small intruder clad in black and silver, as she bravely pranced forward, to address the apparent volatile situation.

"What's going on here?" Monique/Jor inquired boldly, unafraid.

The oldest little girl bounded to her feet daringly, bursting with elated relief. "I told you the Angels would come! I told you!"

Monique's/Jor's passing glance swept over the hostages lying on the floor, finding the two little girls beaming at her in fervent delight. She smiled vaguely at them for a fleeting instant, then resumed her tentative glances.

The leader of the hooded gang stepped forward, with his weapon pointed at the small, what he thought was an insignificant person, disrupting his carefully planned heist.

He then relaxed, called out his men, and approached the oddly-dressed little girl.

"Hey, you're either a little early or late for Halloween. But I like the outfit. I think it's cool," He was an arrogant buffoon, hiding behind the weapon, the hood, and mask.

The oldest sibling shouted, excitedly bouncing up and down on her toes, "Oh, boy! Now you're gonna get it. I told you!"

"Jennifer!" her mother emphatically cautioned her, during her own gaping, curiosity over the little girl in costume.

The two federal agents were grossly at a loss, undecided whether to believe the little girl, Jennifer, that the girl in the costume was indeed one of the aliens they sought. During the distraction, agents Morgan, and Haden carefully reached inside their purses for their service revolvers, very gingerly placing their hands on the pearl handles.

One of the hoodlums, convinced the little girl in the costume was an idle threat, stormed toward the family of three, in a fierce approach, causing the mother to cringe in great fear. He shouted to the little girl, Jennifer, "You shut your mouth!"

The Angel yelled at him, "Don't tell her to shut up; you shut up!"

At that instant, Monique/Jor flashed with such quickness the eye couldn't follow.

Outside, agent Vanessa and the two gentlemen agents had started across the street to investigate, but, suddenly one of the plate glass windows shattered with a loud explosion, as one of the gangsters came flying through the broken glass, landing painfully onto the street out front. Then another came flying through the now open window.

The mysterious melee continued until the four gangsters were piled neatly on top of one another, sprawled on the street, out cold.

Surprise extremely caught the advancing federal agents, as they came rushing in—prepared for the worse—with weapons drawn.

"It's OK, you guys," agent Morgan told them, putting away her revolver, as did her partner, agent Haden.

The place was hardly a small shamble, the outside agents could see. But, in fact, something slightly worse than a tornadic whirlwind had mopped the floor with four would-be criminals, who thought they were a superior force against a handful of innocent victims. But they had fought with one of the Angels and had severely lost the battle.

Figuratively, before the dust had settled, the two little girls rushed to their angelic hero, bubbling with excitement, giggling with enthusiasm; the two of them grabbing a tight hold onto Monique's waist, hating to let go.

"Angel, you came, you came! We told them you would come, but they didn't believe us!"

The oldest, Jennifer, didn't have to express her love for the angel Jor verbally; her baby sister, Rachel, already had for the two of them. Jennifer just held on, ecstatically delighted the Angel didn't disappoint them.

Monique realized she must get home immediately, as she caringly, with gentleness, pried the girls' arms free of her waist.

"I'm happy you girls are okay," she said. "But I really must be going."

As she spoke to the girls, she could feel the eyes of all the adults were upon on her. Some filled with speculation, while others gazed in amazement. The federal agents stood, staring unblinking, temporarily mesmerized. This was their chance to at least make a valid attempt to capture one of their long sought-after quarries. But they just stood there gawking, marveling in disbelief that they'd gotten *this close*. They were stymied, powerless to move on such a glaring opportunity.

As Monique began warily making her way out the door, past those thugs piled in a heap on the cement sidewalk, the sounds of distant sirens grew closer. A grateful clerk, along with everyone else, walked out behind the Angel, almost with apprehension—except for Jennifer, and her little sister, Rachel.

Then they all witnessed the Angel take to the air in a gradual, graceful lift-off, climbing higher and higher, until finally, with a burst of speed, she vanished out of sight, far into the blackness of late night. Jennifer and Rachel eagerly jumping up and down, excitedly applauded their benevolent heroine.

The federal agents regarded the children, with personal, individual scrutiny. Then, in rejoining everyone else, looking up into the dark, in the direction the Angel—rather to them—the alien had flown.

Returning to their vehicles was done in moot silence, except for the two little girls; they were anxious, couldn't keep still

Charles H. Woods
373

walking along with their mom. This was more fun than spending the weekend with their estranged dad, which made for the reason they were late getting home on this night.

"You see, mom? The Angels are our friends," Jennifer said, a gaping smile on her face.

"I know, honey," her mom said, concentrating her gaze at the dark sky.

The five federal agents headed to their vehicle, across the street in the perse gloom, silently moving along until Agent Connie Morgan said to them, "Does everyone feel as I do? I mean, it's hard to describe, but... Well, while the alien was with us, I didn't sense anything like a threat. She seemed so... "

"Innocent, and benign; and, without a doubt, harmless to innocent people?" Vanessa added a look of agreement in her intent stare at Connie.

"Yes!" Connie immediately responded wholeheartedly. Everyone else kept their thoughts, and opinions to themselves. It was a somber flight home. Although she'd done a heroic deed, which was her nature, and the entity's inside her, Monique was in no mood to gloat. She wasn't satisfied knowing the whereabouts, nor conditions of Brittany and Natalie. They were entrusted with their greatest secret. Had they told? It wouldn't be so bad if they had; she, Elise, and Wendy could take care of themselves.

Under the frail moonlight, Chelsea sat in her car within the deep shadows cast by dense foliage, which darkened the area even greater under the night sky. She was parked across the property line, just out front of the foster home, spying on the place through a pair of night-vision glasses. The hunch she followed was so great that she'd pre-signed adoption papers for the three orphans left at Lily Field Foster Home. If it turned out to be a wash; then so be it. Maybe she would figure a way out. But then again, maybe she wouldn't want to; they were three lovely, young girls, well-mannered. That was dreaming. The risk of losing was her fear. Chelsea was convinced. This had to be the right move.

Something flashed through the binoculars, floating out of the moonlit sky. Incredible! She removed the goggles, gazing with the naked eye, through the darkness at a darkly-clad little girl float from the sky, in front of the orphanage.

Chapter 25

"That's exactly what I was afraid of! Now, I'm convinced my theory was correct!" Ed raved over the reports his agents turned in after they experienced a close encounter with one of the aliens at that mini-mart. It didn't matter that she'd singlehandedly captured four notorious criminals, and, perhaps, saved the lives of those innocent hostages, including two young children; he was bent on succeeding in ridding the earth of the three clandestine aliens.

"It is a purposeful act of inducement," Ed continued in a flare of rage. "It's their intent to lull their victims into a false sense of security; then they'll strike before we can mount a defense! Don't you guys get it? Every report we've gotten from anyone having come in close contact with those so-called *angels*, the results are the same. They virtually fall in love with them."

Agent Carl Weathers, a witness among the five on the scene of last night's raid by the alien, dared to be honest in his views of the encounter, "Speaking for myself, I didn't feel, nor sensed any lulled influence of my judgment, or emotions. I'm certainly not in love with a little girl. That's the way she appeared... A sweet little girl...maybe twelve, thirteen. She sacked the hoodlums, like a good football defense, would sack a quarterback. Then she left."

Ed was fuming but kept his poise. Nevertheless, he paced the floor inside Headquarters, incensed over the thought of losing his fighting forces to the, believed, the influence of those conniving aliens.

"Do you people know that, as we speak, a dark force of some kind is now headed toward our atmosphere?"

Charles H. Woods
376

A hush settled over everyone. Finally, agent Morgan said in a subdued voice, "No, we didn't know that."

"What does it mean?" Vanessa asked a look of creeping dread in her stare at Ed.

"Colonel..." Ed turned to col. Gordon, who was seated alongside him at the conference table, "How's our defense looking?"

"As soon the president gives the order, we're ready," the colonel acknowledged.

"Why didn't you guys tell me they were home?" Monique was a little agitated at Elise and Wendy but in a good way. She was so relieved. They were in Wendy's room, sprawled on her bed like normal. So was Wendy. They were in no orderly arrangement, just randomly lying about.

Elise was face down, with Monique resting her head on a pillow, in the middle of Elise's lower back; Wendy was lying, facing the foot of the bed, with her feet propped on the wall above the headboard.

"We followed the FBI-car when they were taking them home," Elise explained. "Then once the FBI-people left, Wendy went to check on Brittany, and Natalie, who spent the night with Brittany. The reason Wendy went was that she's sixteen. She can be out later than we."

"You were nowhere to be found," Wendy said to Monique. Monique, being the spoiled, little darling she was, spouted, "Did you look for me?"

"We had no idea where you were," Elise stressed. "You left here past bedtime, and just...disappeared. How were we to know where you were?"

"There were some bad guys trying to rob some people at this store. But I stopped them," Monique said triumphantly.

Then she went back to the subject of Brittany, and Natalie, asking Wendy, "Did they tell the FBI our secret?"

"No," Wendy was happy to announce. "Brittany didn't talk much, but Natalie said they didn't tell them anything, so they had to let them go. But I'm kinda thinking the FBI may come back."

"If they do, then what?" Elise asked.

"We'll deal with it, if it happens," Wendy said. "Right now, we have our own problems. Miss Agnes has been packing for the past couple of days. She suggested we start doing the same thing."

"Oh brother," Monique sighed at the return of being depressed.

The latest headline on the heroics of the Angels— is the story about the Angel that foiled the attempted robbery of a mini-mart downtown—had prompted Alfred Sweeney to turn himself over to the authorities for fear of his life, without the knowledge of his caring wife, Bernice. He was seated beside the desk, in the office of the sergeant who took down the man's confession, on a notepad.

"I'm a bad person," Sweeney told the officer. "I should be locked up."

"And why's that?" the sergeant asked a portly man about six-foot, thin white-blond hair, meaty face.

"Have you seen the Angels?" Sweeney said, sweating a bit nervously.

"Ah, yes, I've seen them sort of from a distance," the officer vaguely admitted.

"They're powerful, aren't they?" Sweeney rambled on.

The officer, whose name was Clint Daily, couldn't figure what the old guy was eluding to.

"Yes, they're very...powerful. Mr. Sweeney, what is it you're trying to tell me?"

Alfred Sweeney dropped his head in his hands, in dread, and remorse. Then he raised his head and said sincerely, "I have a this...this thing for young girls. I can't help it. I saw the Angels when they flew away that day, out at my place. When they hear about me, they're coming to get me. You gotta lock me up. Don't let them get me; they don't like bad people. Please, you gotta protect me. If I'm already locked-up in jail; maybe they won't..."

"Mr. Sweeney, I've run a background check on you," sergeant Daily said to him. "There's nothing to indicate you being a... 'bad person', at any time. Maybe you should see a psychiatrist."

Alfred Sweeney got to his feet wearily, in coveralls, and a red checkered shirt. He then dragged his feet in a hesitant fashion to leave. "Will I be protected, if they know I'm trying to get help?"

If this wasn't the strangest guy, the officer was thinking as he kindly ushered the old guy out of his office.

"You just find a psychiatrist. I'm sure you'll be OK," Daily said. "I don't think you have to worry about the Angels."

"They are something, aren't they?" Sweeney said as an afterthought, as the officer continued escorting him out the building. Then he paused to tell sergeant Daily, with a wan smile out of his own little secret admiration, "Aren't they the loveliest...most adorable?"

"Yes, yes. They are the cutest." Officer Daily was as kind, understanding, and agreeable as possible, with an urgency to get Sweeney to leave quickly, as he successfully walked the old guy to his pickup, with rather a forceful arm around Sweeney's plaid-shirted shoulders.

Once Sweeney had left the department, Sergeant Clint Daily stood there incomprehensively, staring in the direction the old guy had gone in his pick-up, wondering how he'd become so twisted, and confused after a brief exposure to the Angels. Everybody loved them. Maybe it was some incorrigible emotional strain for him to accept this upheaved change of reality.

The Angels continued to act on their good conscience, although sparsely appearing in the public's eye. A lesson learned, however, was to stay out of the way of a malign, hostile military, with a despotic madman in charge. They didn't know who; but someone of that facet didn't like the Angels, for some reason.

Downtown, a workman for the electric company was repairing some loose electrical wires dangling from a high-rise, commercial building. A freak accident caused it, involving a diesel rig hauling a giant piece of road-equipment that was too much an overload on a flatbed to clear the low-hanging wires. Deadly sparks from the loose wires exploded around the man in the highly-praised cherry picker on back of the company's huge utility truck.

As a crowd began to gather with a hard, empathetic concern, the transformer on the utility pole nearby exploded, sending deadly electrical currents through the frayed, loose wires the workman was attending. The fierce, jolting impact violently hurled the man out of the bucket on the boom, sending him plunging from ten-stories up.

The air filled with an eruption of gasps and screams as the crowd looked on in horror, powerless to intervene by any means of preventing the man from falling to his death.

The man let out a bloodcurdling scream just as he caught a fleeting glimpse of the ground rushing up to him. Pitiable screams from the horrified crowd filled the city streets for several blocks away, in all directions.

But the knight shining in blue and white came through in a flash. From out of nowhere, the blue & white-clad Angel caught the man in mid-fall, just a couple of feet before hitting the ground, and carried him ever so swiftly away to safety.

She placed him down gently on the curb across the street, where he was immediately surrounded by concerned citizens.

The Angel—Wendy—was only visible for an instant with concern for the man.

"You're gonna be OK. Just take it easy," she said to the traumatized man, as he sat there, laboring to catch his breath.

This was the closest look such a crowd had gotten of one the Angels. They surrounded her with applause. Wendy blushed, sheepishly accepting gratitude from the elated audience, the workman finally coming around to stare in disbelief at the young, very charming, little rescuer. He was speechless.

"I'm just glad I could help." Wendy was overcome with humility, bashfully trying to make her move through a thick gathering around her, as extremely excited admirers pressed close beside her, some urgently driven to feel the material of her stunning costume.

"Is this fabric from outer space?" a giggly, simple-minded, young female asked.

Not wanting to appear rude, Wendy realized she must leave them, and quickly. Each minute she was exposed to the public, she was at great risk.

"Oh, the suit," she said to the giggling, young lady. "No, it's not from outer space; I made it myself."

"Really?"

That was all Wendy heard from the silly, little girl. The next thing that exploded out of the air was a booming, male voice shouting to a buzzing audience from all the Angel-excitement, "Clear the streets! This is for your own safety! Step away from the alien!"

An older man, darkly-clad, shouted through a megaphone he held in his hand while riding in the passenger seat of a military jeep, driven by an Army PFC (Private First Class). The civilian was Federal Agent Ed Milburn, the relentless pursuer of the aliens.

"Clear the streets now!" he shouted insistently. "You are in danger!"

That astounded the crowd. They looked among one another, dumbfounded, oblivious to his command. Murmuring among them reached a considerable height.

"Danger…what danger?"

People were confused. "What's he talking about?"

"Is it her? She's an Angel…"

The confusion and curious murmuring continued to rise. Wendy was at a loss. She could've run away, but she stayed, undecided. Maybe it's good she stayed.

Perhaps, she'd get the change to explain especially to the dogmatic military.

"The Angel is no danger to us!" a male voice rang out from the crowd.

"Alien don't move!" Ed demanded of Wendy. "Hands in the air!"

This was embarrassing, thought Wendy, but she complied, moving to the middle of the street, among stopped traffic. The murmuring crowd lethargically began to disperse, though merged together in scattered groups, taking up positions on the sidewalks, near, and thereabouts.

As the forbidding situation intensified, several U.S. Swat Teams assembled, quickly taking up strategic positions in well-hidden locals nearby. Then small military units moved in, with weapons aimed, locked, and loaded.

This vile approach stunned the innocent bystanders, along with angering them, as distinguished voices of angry protesters filled the streets, on behalf of the Angel.

Such claims rang out like, "Why're they treating her like that?"

"What's going on? She never hurt anybody."

"This is bullshit!"

"The government sucks!"

Wendy stood there, waiting, with her hands raised above her head, clasped together. She was becoming weary of the useless waiting.

"Can I lower my hands, please?" she asked.

Hidden voices from Swat Teams surrounding her, vehement shouted from out of nowhere, *"NO!"*

But she did anyway, precariously. Nothing happened, just a gulf of tacit silence.

"Look, Mr. - Whatever your name is, or whoever you are; I'm *not* an *alien!*"

Chelsea rolled up on the congested scene, which appeared there was a rowdy unrest, with vile intent in the air. She immediately grabbed her high-tech camera to get some footage, amid this packed house, with hundreds already on the scene, filming, while she got out of her car.

She was hindered from clear passage to a closer location on the daunting scene by a band of military troops, bearing weapons—not as a threat to her. The weapons were part of their combat gear.

"I'm with the media." She flashed her correspondent ID.

The troopers, four of them just stood there.

"Look," she said. "I know there are news teams here, so let me through!"

Finally, one of the troopers, a sergeant, waved her through. "Be careful, ma'am," he said. "This could become hostile."

"I'll take my chances," she said in not so friendly a voice as she pranced past them.

She took up filming the girl in the blue costume, just across the street from her. And, with the camera rolling, Chelsea mentally took inventory of the vastly developing situation, her mind going a hundred-mile-an-hour, as she paid strict attention to what was going on between Wendy and the plainclothes gentlemen in the jeep. He was Ed Milburn, the agent she'd met, and had suspected he and his staff were hiding a secret of a great value from the public—mainly her.

"You are to surrender to me, now," Ed said to Wendy—*his* alien.

Wendy was perturbed, "What for?" She stood her ground, raising anxious interests from the huge gathering.

"So that you and those other two aliens can return to your own world. There's no room for you here."

Wendy folded her arms, miffed, glaring at the closed-minded idiot.

"This *is* my world!" Wendy scoffed, her patience rapidly growing thin over the misunderstandings, and ill-treatment she and the girls have been receiving from the military and the likes of government agents.

"I was born, and raised here..."

Chelsea took away her camera with a snap, and held it at her side, worried over what Wendy might let slip within the span of her anger.

Don't tell him anything vital, like your real name, and where you live. Chelsea desperately opposed her letting slip that piece of information.

Just give it a chance, she continued thinking, *I have everything figured out! Oh, we do need to talk...*

"You have an alien entity living inside you, am I right?" Ed asked. He maintained his seat on the passenger side of the jeep, extremely alert, suspicious of anything she might do, no matter how remote. Or minute.

"So, what?" Wendy miffed. "Look, Mr., all we've done was helped people who needed help. Is that a crime?"

Buzzing from the captive audience was on the rise from interest to her logical question.

Ed evaded the question, "Your crime is criminal trespassing.".

Wendy was becoming very annoyed with this imbecile.

"Mr.....," She groped, then shouted, "FBI-man, or whoever you are. *I live here!* I'm practically your neighbor!

The closest people to hear her became profusely befuddled: "A neighbor?"

"What she is talking about?"

"Whose neighbor?"

"I never saw her around before."

Two old men were standing together when one of them marveled, "Holy Mother of Mary!"

The other looked at him quizzically, asking, "Who was she?"

His friend replied honestly, "I don't know."

No, no, no, no, no! That's enough, that's enough! Chelsea's mind was reeling with fear that Wendy was giving out too much information. *Shut up, shut up, shut up, SHUT UP!*

"No alien's a neighbor of mine," Ed begrudgingly said to her. "Now, where are the other two, your friends? This is from our United States' Government: Give yourselves up!"

"No!" Wendy shouted.

Becoming more enraged, but tempered, as she strode over to the man in the jeep, along with the young, military guy, the driver. People cringed in ardent curiosity; Chelsea gaped expecting the worse.

Weapons locked and loaded from hidden places all around them, as Ed withdrew with dread at a rush of extreme alarm. He lay the megaphone aside, futilely crouching in the seat for a cover that wasn't there.

Wendy stopped suddenly short of reaching him, not understanding.

"What is wrong with you?" she yelled, stiffened in her stance just a few feet away from the jeep he was in. The young, now pale driver undecided on whether to run or sit there, gawking at a loss.

"Stay away!" Ed shouted, folding an arm across his face, to shield his eyes.

Wendy, and the people close to them, looking-on, were flabbergasted.

"Before, you tell me to surrender to you; now, you're—"

"Don't look in my eyes!" he raved.

"What? Why?" Wendy backed off, holding this despot in her puzzled gaze.

Chelsea was relieved.

But her relief was short-lived. Rumbling along the city streets, onto the main attraction was Battalion Commander Colonel Seth Gordon riding on top a modified, Sherman M-80 Tank. The modification of the metal giant consisted of a technical-advanced laser gun, extending from the upper body of the behemoth machine.

The tank rolled up beside the jeep, with the colonel, in full battle gear, looking down at Ed, who dared raise his head, in fear that the alien was waiting on the chance to zap him with those hypnotic rays from her eyes.

"Colonel don't let her look into your eyes," Ed stressed to the commander on top the tank.

"Why? What's wrong?" the colonel's commanding voice booming with authority.

"I received orders to report to this location, said an alien occupied this region."

His glance found Wendy, the odd little girls dressed in blue leotards like she was going to a costume ball.

"Who is she?" he went on to ask, his blue-gray eyes bleak in his stare at her. "Is she an alien, or a host?"

"Gathering from the information I got from her, she's a host. She says she, and the other two are our neighbors," Ed explained, but not near in the wretched voice he displayed earlier. His fear of her Medusa-touch cowered him somewhat.

"You should've seen what she can do."

The colonel pompously looked her over, noting the white lightning bolts striped along her legs and arms.

A degrading laugh, "Ha! Those lightning bolts... Do they mean you're fast as lightning?"

"She is," Ed verified the colonel's speculation.

Wendy was fed up. "You guys..." She didn't feel the need to regard them with courtesy to respect them as men.

"I don't have time for this. But know this: Leave us alone!"

As Wendy moved away to get clear of the massive audience, to a path for an escape, Ed, and the colonel yelled a warning to her.

"Stop right there!" That was Ed. "Did you bring the disrupter?"

The colonel said, "No, but I bought something that'll render her immobile, and unconscious until we can get her to a solitary confinement."

Then he turned to his gunner, whose head was poking up through open cupola, and yelled out the order, "Lieutenant, prepare to fire Geneva!" Geneva was his ex-wife's name. He'd claimed living with her was like living in Hades. Thus, he'd named one of the Army's fierce weapons after her, The Laser-taser.

"Sir, yes, sir!" the young, second lieutenant replied sternly. When the gunner ducked his head down inside the tank, the screaming crowd began a wild, chaotic scramble to get clear. A clear path for Wendy's escape was clogged with panicked civilians, scattering frantically to find cover.

"Wait!" Wendy shouted to the determined military men. A spark of concern from Ed, "Hold your fire! You may hit some innocent people."

"No problem," the colonel said. "It shoots a thin laser beam, only striking its intended target."

Wendy looked about desperately; wild scrambling was everywhere, people screaming, and fleeing. Chelsea, caught in the mix, with mayhem all around her. She would have run to Wendy but breaking across the street was impossible; fleeing people were all over the streets. The long, shiny bore of the Laser, Taser was brought into position, carefully trained on Wendy's upper torso. Still, no escape route. Maybe she could run in-place at supersonic speed, making herself invisible at such high velocity.

It was an idea, but...

The weapon was fired, striking her dead center, just as she'd quickly reacted to the aid of an old man in a wheelchair, who had rolled right in front of her. The effect of the violent impact was jolting, as she was catapulted a good ten feet along the rough cement turf. She lay still momentarily; the people close to her ceased their panic frenzy and went immediately to her aid. An older lady, along with a few other concerned citizens, wept silently in their rush over to her.

Ed stared over at the grim scene, uncertain.

"Is she..."

"No...just unconscious. She'll come around in a few minutes," The colonel was cocky, sure of himself."

Chelsea was finally free to cross the street, which she did—teary-eyed. By the time she reached Wendy, lying there, semi-conscious, Chelsea could barely see through her misty-fogged vision. This wasn't the way it was supposed to end.

"Hey, get a gurney! Get some troops over there!" the colonel yelled to his men, who instantly got busy following the order.

A military medical unit pulled along the curb, next to the emergency.   Ed remained with the jeep, on the other side of the street, gloating his success. Finally, he was thinking. Rounding up the other two shouldn't be a problem now that their leader had been captured.

But, suddenly, like the awakening of a deadly storm, Wendy awoke, shook her head, the concerned people around her giving way, puzzled, hopeful; Chelsea tentatively relieved, and hopeful. The troops on the gurney let go, stood back with apprehension. Ed and the colonel froze temporarily. Gaping, peering. Looking for one another, unsure. Wendy got to her feet, infuriated. She shook off the initial, mild shock; because she wasn't expecting anything of that nature to befall her.

People around her—her supporters, admirers, her friends—looked-on, wondering, glad within themselves she was back to normal.

But Wendy was boiling, nearly over the edge with violent rage. She glared at the military and the government. That's what the two men represented to her. She was so tired, and confused inside that, at this moment, she was ready to explode.

"*Why?*" she shouted to the cowering two men across the street, as she began to stalk them in a slow, ominous fashion, her angry stare, the eyes a seething, fiery red glare of a cat's.

A will to destroy roiled inside her, because no one cared for her, or her proverbial sisters, Elise and Monique. Innocent children, who didn't force their way into this world, and neither did they ask to come here. Some wicked, uncaring, selfish people brought them here to abandon, uncaringly!

"I live here!" she raged, gravitating closer to her withering targets. "You don't understand what it's like, do you?"

Someone needed to try and calm her down. She was a walking, revived killing machine if she so desired.

"She must be destroyed," the colonel said softly to Ed, as they stood beside one another, next to the Goliath weapon.

Ed agreed, "And the other two as well. She's enraged, which must be their behavior, eventually. They must be found immediately."

"We need to take care of this one first," the colonel anxiously suggested while secretly shaking in his boots. He looked back at the tank. The lieutenant was still inside.

"Lieutenant!" the colonel chanced to call out to his first officer.

Within seconds, the lieutenant's head rose above the cupola, "Yes, Sir.".

"Put the laser on maximum," he gave the order.

"Sir, yes, Sir." The lieutenant ducked back inside the tank.

"Tell him to hurry," Ed urged, reaching the desperation point, as he'd begun to sweat. But this time, Wendy was awake and alert. The instant she saw the bore of the weapon started pointing her way; her fiery red eyes, with a little moisture from tears she'd shed for her mental anguish, became filled with a fiery red glow of destruction.

"Not this time," she murmured fiercely under her breath.

She then let go a blast of red-hot lasers, in screaming anger, her body rigid with rage.

"She's firing at us! Get down!" Ed shouted as both men hit the dirt, barely escaping the laser blast from her smoldering red, cat-eyes.

The gunner and two more soldiers bailed out of the tank, scrambling up through the open cupola, as it gradually was becoming a melting inferno. After everyone had barely cleared the tank, the five lit out across the way, desperate for cover.

Still vexed, Wendy walked away, disconcerted. She wasn't up to splitting atoms with her ultrasonic speed; she felt destitute, dismal, struggling to hold onto a dwindling sense of worth. She didn't want to run fast, so she walked away, through passing stares filled with skepticism, shock, disbelief...

Someone was calling to her from back there.

"I can help you... the three of you! It's me, Chelsea! The news lady, remember? I want to help you!"

Chapter 26

Wendy sat down under a tree far along the outskirts of the city, by the side of a stretch of backroad. It was lonely out there, hardly any passing traffic; a quiet, soft, occasional wind rustled the leaves in the surrounding nature's garden. Birds fluttering about. It was serene, in a sense, but with a haunting silence.

After a while, there rose the distant sound of engines, very faint. Then it grew stronger, approaching. Finally, more distinct, rushing, like speeding vehicles headed her way.

That was normal; Wendy wasn't concerned. That stretch of secondary highway, like others, was often used as a speedway by careless teenagers drag racing. Or a shortcut used by motorists in a rush to get home after a long, hard days work.

Finally, two dark SUV's appeared, moving at a high-rate of speed, their gleaming black finish glinting in the sunlight. From a short distance, she noted the lettering along the side of each vehicle that read: U.S. Swat Team.

The occupants of both speeding vehicles, including the drivers, were peering out the windows at something they weren't sure of shortly ahead of them, alongside the road. One guy, sitting in the back seat behind the driver of the vehicle they rode, was leaned forward, anxious, and under stress, peering out the window with everyone else.

The instant they recognized the young lass in her blue & white tights sitting under a tree, beside the road, the guy went pale from fear, as it became an extremely anxious moment.

The guy tapping the driver on the shoulder, urging him to increase speed, "Oh god, it's her! Go, go, go, go, go!"

Wendy stood to watch the speeding vehicles go passed; this time, *she* was locked and loaded for a confrontation, just in case. But the two vehicles kept going at an increased speed. Wendy sat back down. She wasn't ready to return home; she'd gone into the city, to begin with, to pick up some material for outfits she was making for the girls—which she didn't get the chance to do—when this whole misunderstanding took place.

School had another hour or so before letting out. Besides, she could be home in a flash, so there was no rush. Miss Agnes was away on personal business.

She was ready to get on with the rest of her life; Wendy and the girls should be doing the same thing, instead of trying to protect, and safeguard unappreciative leaders of an uncaring government.

"Wendy?" That was soft, with an effect as if it was her conscience speaking just within an audible whisper to her. It was Motatu, and Wendy could feel the warmth, and the sense of carrying from within.

"Yes?" Wendy said softly.

"You have rage," Motatu went on. "It's OK to be angry. But don't lose yourself in your past life."

"How do you know about my past life? You're a newcomer," Wendy wasn't being mean; she wanted to know.

"But I do," Motatu's voice was gentle, with concern.

"I don't know *your* past life."

"Yes, you do. You're just not interested, right now. We have bonded; we're the same person. We dream—together. The same.

Wendy, we are one."

Wendy thought a moment, then said, "No, lately, my dreams' been about nothing just shadowy. Sometimes dark, meaningless."

"The darkness is in my mind sometimes," Motatu admitted to Wendy's enlightenment. "It's where I come from. It's not a world our planet; it's a place. The Plains of Souls. Good and Evil are separate entities. It's the division between the two that causes conflict. Good cannot become evil, under any circumstances, as light cannot become the darkness; and neither the darkness can become light.

"There was a great conflict on the Plains of Souls when the *Dark* thing came to comprehend the souls of every life-forms, even that which lives within the elements," Motatu continued.

"It sounds like you're speaking of God, and the Devil," Wendy said.

"We call it, Mamaron," Motatu said. "It's a force that creates life and its function. It knows all, sees all. It is omnipresent."

"Sounds like God to me," Wendy was insistent.

"God?" Motatu paused as if determining the meaning. Then she perked, "God! Yes, I understand. It is the term you use. That's good, for Mamaron is good, and it cannot become evil. That would corrupt and eliminate everything that *is*."

"Motatu, why don't you fly?" Wendy asked, as a final curiosity she'd kept hidden. Motatu was silent for a moment. Wendy thought she'd touch a sore spot, and she apologized, "I'm sorry."

"No," Motatu objected understandingly. "It's not for you to be sorry. On the Plains of Souls, it's like any life-form at its infant stage. We're vulnerable, susceptible to *influence*, which is not of a permanent design. It's like a child growing up. I was in the infant stage during the battle of the Dark thing. I had not yet developed the innate sense to fly, like every mature life-form on the plains.

"The battle was fierce. I was left behind, abandoned, and afraid, like yourself. But I was protected by Mamaron in a place of solitude for one millennium. The place was a tranquil dwelling, and there was no need, no reason to fly. So, I never attempted. With Koh and Jor, it was different. They could fly shortly after their infancy during the time they were born."

"Are you an orphan?" Wendy wanted to understand.

"No," Motatu made clear. "It is the way of Mamaron. We are born defenders of the great barrier, like the particles, and atoms in your elements; like the cells, and other important factors inside your body that fights off bacteria, and other diseases you may encounter. They are what they are, and cannot be changed or used for anything, other than its designated purpose.

"Just because you were orphaned, doesn't mean you're unaccountable. Your worth is as valuable as anything worthy of its existence. And that's *everything.*"

"Have you ever seen this...Mamaron?" Wendy asked.

"No one of the Plains of Souls has ever seen Mamaron," Motatu said. "It's not of any physical form; it is omnipresent; it's a part of everything, consumes all that is the great barrier. It *is* the great barrier, and more. Have you seen your... *God?*"

"No," Wendy said.

"Then it's Mamaron—the same," Motatu said. "We are of what Mamaron is, which is all that is *good*, and *evil* cannot abide."

"Why did the Dark thing come to you?" Wendy was curious to know.

"The Dark thing sent warriors to overcome the barrier; but it failed," Motatu said. "Some of the souls were displaced during the battle; we were among the scattered, but not *lost*. But beyond the barrier, we were not long to survive, unless we obtained a second soul."

That explained the need of a host, Wendy understood. She was firmly teachable, easy to comprehend; and was also book-learned, and wise, for her age.

"Why the need of a *second* soul?" was her question. Motatu laughed, "Not so much as the need for a second soul; we are mere souls at birth. But the consensus says we're entities— the same thing, where we're from. On this side of the barrier, we require a solid life-form, or we'll cease to exist."

"You mean in this atmosphere," Wendy was correct to assume.

Motatu laughingly admitted, "It's a killer!"

Wendy asked, after carefully thinking it over, "Are you from another realm? Because I remember studying in school about parallel universes, black holes, and the fourth, and fifth dimensions. The possibilities of their existence are overwhelmingly astronomical. One solid proof is, you're here."

Wendy suddenly realized the time. She got to her feet. The lengthy talk with Motatu was becalming, rejuvenating. Wendy felt much better. "Oh, look at the time," she said.

Motatu quipped, "I can't see it. You tell me."

Wendy joked, "Then look through my eyes."

Motatu piped, "I saw the time; I was only kidding. Get on with it."

As they walked along the back road, with still no rush to get home, Motatu said to Wendy as a word of encouragement, "Wendy, you're a good person. And you're a fighter, like those of the Souls of the Plains. There's no real evil in you or the girls. That's why you were chosen. Let the bitterness pass. Keep your aim toward the *light*. Mamaron will always be with you, or...*God*, if you prefer."

"You sound like a preacher," Wendy laughed, then added, after deeply thinking it over, "Maybe you guys are angels."

Motatu let it rest at that.

Wendy walked into a quiet foster home, greeted by puffy, cotton-soft, deep gray shadows, because the heavy, dark purple drapes at the windows, in the spacious living room were closed.

She went straight upstairs, exhausted from today's painful disappointment, in meeting what she could expect to be a misery for the rest of her life – she and the girls being what they've become. The girls had not yet gotten in from school.

In entering her room, the same shadow-darkness greeted her. Only it brought on a rather weighty somberness to intensify her already depressed state, at the moment. After lazily morphing into regular civvies, she crashed face-down on a soft pillow, burying her pretty face in it, while bringing her legs up to lie on the bed horizontally.

Finally, a faint, but constant, chirping of kids outside woke her. It felt like an annoying dream at first; but it forged out of her somewhat peaceful slumber into the brutal reality, the consistency was that annoying.

That was half-ways a bit refreshing power-nap, except for the rude awakening. Wendy got out of bed, left her room and went downstairs, where she looked out the front door, to a yard just about half-filled with kids from the girls' school. *What in blazes was going on? This never happened before.* The surprised expression on Wendy's face let everyone know her thoughts.

It got church-quiet, all eyes on Wendy. During which, Elise scrambled to her feet from sitting on the top step to the porch, beside a friend-girl from school, and rushed up to Wendy.

"They know," she said.

Wendy lost a bit of flesh tone from the sudden shock, as she gaped, astounded by Elise's frank remark. "They know? You mean like...they *know*, know?"

"They know we're leaving the foster home," Elise made clear. "But since we don't know where we'll be placed, they decided to come with us this afternoon, to show their friendship; and that they're gonna miss us."

The dark-haired boy, Tommy Ross—thirteen—interrupted her, "That's not all; they also know the Angels. They told us they *talked* to them!"

"Oh, really?" Wendy said in a *knowing* tone of voice, her criticizing-glance shifting to Elise, and Monique.

Monique, guilty by the sound of her voice, said, with a tittered laugh, "They want our autographs. Isn't that ridiculous, to come all the way out here, just for some writing on a piece of paper?"

Elise made the kids' trip sound somewhat legitimate. "They want yours, too. That's why they came all the way out here."

Wendy hid a considerable show of flattery, smiling a bit modestly, "Is that so?" She maintained standing in the doorway but was more relaxed. Tommy admitted rather bashfully, "I think I'm in love with them."

A few chuckles, and giggles among the kids. Then a little girl, Phoebe Carson—one of his classmates—said disrespectfully crude, "Silly... Angels don't fall in love with human-boys!"

Wendy cocked her head, with a feigned look of seriousness, stared at the young lass, and replied, "You think?"
"Wendee!" Elise drawled, blushing, trying to hide embarrassment.

"You mean, they do?" Tommy said in a raised, hopeful, shy voice.

Wendy laughingly said, "Just kidding." And she was. She was due for a little-lighthearted humor to ease the laden pressure she was under.

The kids finally dispersed and went their separate ways home. Brittany and Natalie weren't included in this group of kids; they'd gone home right after school let out.

Wendy and the girls had sat down to a relatively quiet supper Miss Agnes had laid out for them. While Elise and Monique pretty much stuffed themselves, they couldn't help noticing Wendy sort of picking at her food; and she hadn't said a word since they sat down at the table. It was luminously apparent she was bugging over something.

"Wendy, what's wrong? You're not eating," Monique said, pausing to look across the table at her. Then she joked, "Is it something I said."

A wan, vague smile barely touched Wendy's lips, with hardly a glance at Monique. "I'm fine," she said, barely audible.

Then she placed her fork on the table, beside her plate, dabbed her mouth with a napkin, lay it aside then gathered a breath. Looking straight across the table to Monique, and Elise, she said, "Listen, guys. We're going to have to be leaving here soon. Where we're going, I have no idea. But we must leave here.

"Miss Agnes will be gone in a few weeks; maybe even sooner." Wendy continued, "She just about has all her stuff packed. Some of it—especially the heavy stuff—is in storage already."

Monique slumped back in her seat, depressed. "Oh, well," she sighed wearily. "Here we go, fugitives on the run. Goodbye, comfortable bed, nice home…"

Elise, more practical, raised the awareness, "What about school? Are we going to enroll in another school?"

"I don't know," Wendy said frankly.

"Well, if we just disappear; people are gonna be looking for us, like the law. Maybe even the government," Elise pointed out.

That mention of the government from Elise angered Wendy. She slammed a hard fist down on the table, causing both Elise, and Monique to jump a bit startled, as she shouted, "Let them look! It's what they don't find, is all I'm concerned about." Then Wendy got to her feet and paced restlessly for a while, with her head down in deep thought, Elise, and Monique following her impatient movement with looks of concern.

Wendy's gaze softened as she looked over at the girls, staring innocently concerned back to her. The anger in her heart also softened, and she apologized to them for her rude outbreak. "I'm sorry, guys. I didn't mean to shout. Today just hasn't been good to me."

"What happened?" Monique asked, both she and Elise curious to know.

"I learned today that the government's out to get us," Wendy explained, moving over to the table, closer to the girls sitting there. "I caught this man as he was falling from almost the top of a building; and the next thing I know, the Army came and started shooting at me, when I was only trying to help."

"Just like when Monique and I were minding our own business when this ugly helicopter came out of nowhere and started shooting at us," Elise put the two incidents together, which led them to understand the two incidents were purposely coordinated against them.

Monique boasted, "Well, we'll just run away where they'll never find us. And we can do that because we're super-powered."

"No," Wendy brashly opposed the idea. "We've done nothing toward harming anyone. We have a right to live our own lives. We'll fight them if have to."

"Even kill them?" Elise was horrified at the very thought.

"No," Wendy said. "But, ultimately, that'll be up to them. Any creature reserves the right to defend itself when attacked. And that's just what we'll do if it comes down to that."

I can help you! I can help the three of you! It's me, Chelsea! Don't you remember? I can help you! The residual pounding of the words in the back of Wendy's mind, as she struggled to fall asleep, resounded as a chanting from haunts; familiar, though, in connection to something real she'd recently encountered. However, in her lulled, dream state, she was unaware to determine its source. But she had heard those words before. *Somewhere*!

Dawn came with the swiftness of an act of impatience, it seemed. The girls were up and about at sunrise, getting ready for school; a hot breakfast was on the table for them, prepared by Miss Agnes. She was now getting in order some last-minute details in her moving on.

The girls were already seated at the table when Wendy came downstairs half awake. She was rest-broken from lack of proper sleep but would manage.

"Hi, guys."

She was still in her PJ's and house-robe, pulling up a chair to sit down opposite the girls at the table. The first thing she did was pour herself a cold glass of milk.

Miss Agnes was in the living room, just beyond the foyer, getting some menial stuff together. She took this opportunity to speak with the girls on a matter of urgency, as she came into the dining area and took her seat at the far end of the table. At that vantage point, she had a clear view of the three of them.

"Girls?" she began, catching a shallow breath in a grim state of mind. "There's no easy way to say this; so, I guess it's best to just come right out with it. I'll be leaving sometime this afternoon."

Faces dropped in sadness, but neither of the girls made any comment; they just sat there, listening. Wendy felt a rush of dread. She had no plans for them, as of now. She only knew they wouldn't be left behind at the mercy of the State Department, which was so bureaucratic that no human influence was ever a part of its establishment. They were wretched, coldhearted employees, only working for a paycheck.

Miss Agnes continued her painful goodbyes. "You girls will be just fine. My replacement will be here this afternoon, by the time you girls get out of school." Miss Agnes then smiled, radiating her usual caring warmth. "I'm gonna miss you, girls."

"We'll miss you, too," Wendy said, Elise, and Monique nodding sad-eyed in agreement.

"Will we ever see you again?" Monique asked, which wasn't cliché-ish—she meant it.

"I wouldn't say it would be impossible," Agnes' answer was a bit encouraging—not much.

"Who's taking your place?" Elise asked.

"Oh, she's a very nice person... Loretta Pruitt," Agnes delighted to announce. The two were good friends.

"Miss Agnes, does it look like there's a chance we *won't* be separated?" Wendy asked, which aroused the stark interests of both Monique and Elise, as they glared with anxiousness at Miss Agnes.

Agnes didn't have a positive answer either way.

"You have, at least, a good month before you start to worry about that," was her best response. "But don't give up. I'm sure everything will work out just fine for you girls. Now..." She spread her arms wide to receive final hugs from the girls. "Gather around, my girls..."

The three of them gave Miss Agnes final hugs, filled with care, and lots of love. Monique was glassy-eyed; Elise whimpered—a tiny bit. Wendy released her hug sparingly, preparing to stand firm against an approaching, inevitable encroachment.

Wendy walked with the girls out onto the porch, where she gave them instructions, as they were about to leave for their bus stop. "When you get home this afternoon, be prepared to leave this place. There's no point of us to hanging around any longer. As far as I'm concerned, our fate's been sealed. We're on our own."

"Where will we go?" Monique asked.

"I don't know yet," Wendy was straight-up honest. "We'll deal with that, later. By now, half the town maybe suspicious of us. If not, the government's out to get us, anyway. You can't trust those FBI-people. They have ways of finding out things. We can't give them that chance.

"Now, are we in agreement...we leave this afternoon?"

"Yes."

"Yes," both girls agreed.

Wendy said, with her usual charming smile, "OK, off to school with you."

"Bye, Wendy." "Bye, Wendy," they both told her.

As Monique and Elise were passing through the grove, Wendy had gone back inside; Elise suggested to Monique, "Wanna fly?"
Monique shook her head, "No, let's just run really fast."

Elise, grinning, hyped, "You're on!"

And they dashed through the grove, like a streak of lightning, in a flash—in their civvies!

"Wendy, eat your heart out!" Monique laughed.

The two of them, with a burst of foot-speed, hit the afterburners through the grove, like a bolt of lightning—and in their civvies!

When they arrived at the bus stop, slowing to a halt after that two-seconds display of speed; they tended to reappear out of thin air, as their complete forms were a part of the invisible mist of molecules in the elements.
Once they arrived, no one was there.

"Two early?" Elise assumed, looking about the partly-deserted area, a scattered wooded lay of the land, with a small neighborhood of sparse settings of lived-in homes, and other structures necessitated to supply the community's needs, like feed mills, silos, a gas station, and supermarket.

"Judging by the sun's location, still a little behind the trees; I'd say we're a little early," Monique jovially confirmed.

They sat down in the grass, near the side of the two-lane highway, to relax until other kids came along, and, inevitably, their bus.

"Do you feel a rise of excitement?" Monique eventually asked Elise.

"About what?" Elise said, holding Monique with a curious stare.

"About running away...playing hide and seek with the law. And the FBI," Monique said with a glint of dare in her stare at Elise.

Elise took it lightly in her jauntily reply, "We'll soon find out, won't we?"

They sat side by side in the grass, shoulders touching.

"I guess we will," Monique said, a hint of shrewdness in her speech.

Chapter 27

Stories of the alien and *angels* finally broke nationwide. It was no longer a secret of their notable gallantry. Reports poured in from hundreds of locations, with Grand City believed to be their original place of dwelling. Interviews with people in and around the area shared their unnatural experiences with the friendly aliens, whom the citizens of Grand City most rather refer to them as *their* Angels.

The downtown city streets were congested with marching patrons, bearing signs in support of the Angels, after witnesses realized, firsthand, that government forces made few attempts to destroy the benevolent beings. Radio and television filled the airways in broadcasting the news; while the newspapers flooded major city streets, and small towns alike, with apprehensible accounts of the Angels' might and performance; and their apparent alignment with that which is for the good for mankind.

And many correspondents have repeatedly stated that, with each applying their own spin, as anchor lady, Chelsea Freeman made clear, "Not one incident was the Angels *ever* accused of *any* act of violence towards the people they've served. Yet, our government seems to believe otherwise, by trying to exterminate them in most fierce, malicious in recent attacks..."

As Chelsea went on to elaborate further on behalf of the Angels—simply because of her personal interest—the city began to fester with compassion for the visiting, little darlings, as sporadic riots erupted in small cells throughout the vast city. Some of the participants were nothing more than loitering, nondescript vagrants, looking for an excuse to vent unresolved, pent-up rage. But, for the most part, this was the Angels' swansong, for most of the populace loved them, and didn't want them to leave, or become a memory in the dastardliest fashion.

Concerned proprietors in modest groups placed welcome signs in the windows of their businesses, such as restaurants, fast-foods, grocery stores, and department-store outlets, specializing in fashions for teenagers. Vivid signs on display read: *Angels eat free. Friends of Angels welcome, first meal free. Angels shop here for the best in fashion wear....*

The downside, however, was the local Nation Guards were dispatched to heavily clear the streets for the arrival of the military, which rolled in with heavy combat machines on wheels armed impedingly And, most importantly, to put down roots, and maintain order among the rowdies.,.

Angry shouts burst forward from a gathering mob, incensed over the malign intent by the government to do harm to their innocent Angels.

"Leave them alone!"

"Go home! We don't need you here!"

"The Angels are our friends!"

Tiny pebbles and other insignificant debris were thrown at the stoical guards, and other military men, without an effect.

Chelsea had finished her news broadcast and was on her way out the studio. She was debating whether she should pay a visit to the girls, but she couldn't think of a valid excuse to do so; or that it would be safe, under the circumstances. It was too close to a day of reckoning for the aliens; traps were placed in the most strategic positions all around by experienced military personnel, and government agents. One slip and she'd become toast. So, she figured to hold off for a while, let things become a bit lax. She was certain the girls were on the alert and wouldn't take any foolish chances by boasting public appearances now.

The streets filled with the military on the move, ready, and geared to engage the otherworldly visitors, violently. Chelsea left the building amid the stirring unrest among the marching, orderly protesters, however, some not so civil, and neither orderly. A firetruck just blasted a rowdy group of young gangsters with a powerful spray from a water hose, as they were trying to set fire to a standing military vehicle, parked along the curb outside a surplus outlet.

The rowdy bunch scattered immediately from the powerful blast of water from the pressure hose; but the melee continued to build as Chelsea moved gingerly through the volatile gathering, over to her parked vehicle close to her place of work, out front. She'd decided to head out of the city. The atmosphere here was too disruptive to chance going home, right now. Her downtown apartment was in the middle of such an upheaval unrest.

She drove out of the city, along with the countryside, to a secluded place she'd shown an interest in since signing the final documents she had drawn up for the girls. It was a swagger, two-story chalet, nestled in idyllic surroundings of shade trees, hedges, and a huge, manicured lawn.

The home was a beautifully structured wood-frame and carefully laid stones by a crafty stone mason. It was twelves miles north of town, near the foothills of a majestic, snow-capped mountain range, which enhanced the breathtaking vista. There were no neighboring homes in the vicinity; the closest settlement was Twelve-Mile-Junction another twelve miles farther north. Chelsea had considered this place as the perfect get-away when she wanted to be alone. Now, she was having second thoughts.

The day wore on. Chaos in the city had reached an all-time high before declining to a tolerant level until finally dissipating back to a virtual normality. The military, along with the Guards, maintained patrol of the streets as a security measure; traffic had returned to its normal flow. Protesters went about a peaceful march, still bearing signs favoring the Angels, though, not quite as large in numbers as earlier.

Believable rumors of the earlier disruption reached the schools in the district, as students were permitted to watch the breaking news story on big-screen televisions in various locations sanctioned for such purposes, like the assembly hall, gymnasium, and the cafeteria. Some of the classrooms were equipped with smaller flat-screens, to avoid a complete jam of students piling into limited spaces.

As the girls sat in their classroom—which was fortunate to have its own flat-screen TV—watching news footage on the downtown disturbance, in a dismal state of discontentment. Now and then, they looked at one another, sitting side by side, in front of the class, abhorring the idea that they were responsible for this pandemic eruption, and fearing that it might eventually go viral across the internet, reaching all points around the globe.

"What'd we do to deserve all this?" Elise whispered over to Monique.

Monique shrugged her shoulders innocently. "I don't know. But I feel...kinda guilty. Maybe we never should have let people know we existed the way we are now."

"But we only helped them," Elise said, trying to grasp a valid meaning for such corrupt behavior. "I can understand people freaking out; I probably would, too, if someone came flying over my head, like a human bird, or something. But why are we *hated* by the...*law?*"

"I don't know," Monique said. "I thought it was cool that we could do what we do. I never thought we'd be a put-down for it."

It was difficult for the girls to interpret the solemn masks of students around them; no one showed the slightest emotion. Even their teacher sat at her desk, staring at the TV set, without a show of feelings she was either for or against the Angels.

When school let out that afternoon, Monique and Elise walked across campus, in a rather somber mood. They weren't talking much to one another, just moved along together, feeling each other's depression.

"Are we taking the bus home?" Elise asked for Monique's feeling about riding the bus.

"I think I'd rather walk," she said. "I'd feel like everybody is staring at us. I know no one knows who we are, except Brittany, and Natalie, and those other two girls..."

"Others may know now," Elise raised the awareness. "By now, they may have told already. So, it may be better if we did walk home."

Brittany showed up shortly after the girls left the school on foot. Elise and Monique held up quizzically as Brittany approached them in a somber mood of her own.

"Hi, guys," she said, with an obvious show of her dark feelings. "You guys mind if I walk a little way with you?"

"It's a free Country." Monique tried to make Brittany feel welcome to come along; but her show of a friendly attitude was incomplete, due to her own despair. But she managed a near smile, which Brittany accepted as a welcome.

They walked in silence for a spell, then Brittany began after mulling over thoughts in her mind, which concerned the three of them. "You guys know what happened to us—me and Natalie—a week ago, right?"

"With the FBI? Yes, we know," Elise said, curious to learn what Brittany was trying to tell them.

"Well, neither one of us—Natalie and me—told them about you guys."

Brittany wanted the girls to be clear on that. Then she went on to say, "I hope you don't think I'd ever tell...because I won't." She dropped her head in a mixture of shame, and regret. It got sympathy from the girls.

"But I was scared," she continued. "I'd never been so scared before. Really, I thought I was going to *lose* it."

"It's okay, Brittany," Elise stressed sincerely. "We understand. It's okay to be scared. People get scared sometime."

Monique added grimly, "It probably doesn't matter now, anyway."

Elise spoke to try and clear Brittany of any guilt and betrayal she may have felt, "Brittany, you guys are our friends. You being afraid of the FBI-people doesn't matter. Even if you'd told, because you were afraid, doesn't matter either. We're only human."

"Ah..." Monique begged to differ, holding up a finger for attention. "She's human; we're... kinda not."

That was a brief distraction, which lasted only long enough for Elise to catch a short breath, as she went on, "Brittany, stop feeling bad about yourself. You've done nothing wrong."

Brittany agonized, though, displeased with herself.

"You guys don't understand," she complained in a whiny voice. "I'm not supposed to be afraid of anything. But that night, I was. And worse, Natalie was brave. She was a smart-mouth, the FBI-guy said about her. Then he said that she didn't scare easy. And that's why they let us go."

Brittany took a well-deserved breath after that strenuous testimony as if a leaden slab had been lifted from her shoulders.

Monique said, unimpressed, and a little irritated, "Oh, Brittany, get over it. So, you were scared. Deal with it! This probably won't be the last time you're afraid. You ever think of that?"

Elise thought Monique was being a little brash. But she was right, regardless of how crude it sounded. Besides, she and Monique were on a heavy schedule; they had to be home asap, and they were wasting time on a moot issue.

"While I don't necessarily agree on those harsh terms, Brittany, but Monique's right. You can't spend so much time feeling sorry for yourself, or you may end up being alone. Nobody likes a whiny person all the time," Elise explained.

Brittany thought it over, "Is that what you guys think, that I'm a whiner?"

She looked at them; they gave her no sympathy, just stood there, staring at her stoically.

Then Brittany brought her gaze over to meet theirs, and said admittedly, "I guess you're right."

She looked away, drew a breath, sucking-in her bruised ego. "It's just that I was afraid I'd let you guys down, after what you did for me."

That's it! Monique was out of patience. "OK, I'm gonna cry," she quipped.

"I got this," Elise intervened, then turned to Brittany. "It's what we do; we help people. We got your back. And we trust you. Now, we gotta go."

As they were walking away, Monique had an afterthought, as she turned to Brittany and said, "Oh...in case you don't see us around much, it isn't because we're dead, OK?"

Brittany didn't get it. She stood there, puzzled. Then it occurred to her and she shouted to them as they were walking away, "Where're you going?"

The girls didn't reply, just continued on the way home.

But Brittany was wrapped in the comfort of knowing the Angels and was satisfied in leaving for a home herself.

Wendy was impatient, pacing the floor in her room, saddled with indecision. That this Miss Loretta-lady hadn't arrived yet and Miss Agnes had left for the last time. A state representative had given her a lift to the Gray Hound bus terminal, in time for her 3:15 p.m. departure. That was a little while ago, as it was now nearly 4:15 p.m., almost an hour past. School had let out at 3:30 p.m., so, the girls should be home in a little while, unless they're dragging their feet, lollygagging with friends. If that was the case, Wendy did understand. She never expected them, being so young, to completely understand the importance of the impending responsibility of being on their own.

Wendy was also plotting on how to manage what little bit of money she'd saved. A hundred-plus-dollars weren't going to last very long, once they were faced with even menial necessities. A roof over their heads, food...

It was a scary thought, starting out on their own with no workable plans for them. But they had no choice. It was either this or that. This meaning: take the risk; or that meaning: take the chance on surviving a military onslaught of violence against them. Taking the *this* was most appealing, regardless of the unknown risks.

Next, packing. What to pack, and where would they take it? They didn't have a place for storage. They didn't need clothing; they had only to form in their minds the fashions of clothing items they wanted, from memory. They had transformability.

Wendy stepped out onto the porch just as Monique and Elise were passing through the grove, laughing, chatting then giggling, like they did normally—cheerful and care-free. But standing there, watching them so cheery, and without a care, was heartbreaking. It was difficult for Wendy to maintain dry eyes at their affable approach.

"Hi, Wendy." Monique waved to her, smiling, so energetically elated.

Elise the same, waving, smiling. "Hi, Wendy."

Wendy wanted to run and hide the collecting moisture in her eyes; but she withstood the insurmountable pressure, except for a tiny glaze of moisture, just minutely fogging her vision as the girls walked up on the porch. And she was thankful they didn't react in the slightest fashion that they noticed the moisture in her eyes.

"Hi, guys," she said in her normally cheerful voice.

They went inside, and almost immediately, Elise and Monique tended to sense the absence of Miss Agnes, at the tomb-like quietness she'd left behind. Even with Wendy present, the place felt vacant, the soft gray shadows in corners, and cast by furniture, now seemingly shapeless forms of dormant ghosts, no longer with the will to haunt.

Monique, with sad eyes, peered at Wendy, "Did Miss Agnes leave already?"

A glaze of moisture glinted in her eyes, as she struggled with denial, "Or she probably went to the store for something she forgot to pick up."

Wendy didn't say a word. She couldn't, seeing the hurt and despair in both Monique's and Elise's eyes. And by not answering directly, Monique ran up the stairs as tears started to flow from her eyes. This morning, when Agnes was last with them, Monique thought she could handle Miss Agnes leaving. But now, being put to the test was a whole different story.

She ran in her, and Elise's room slammed the door; flung her backpack near a corner, as she wasn't paying attention, and flopped down on the bed, face down, weeping quietly.

Elise ached to go to her sister. But Wendy thought it'd be wise to give Monique some time alone.

"She'll have to accept it eventually," Wendy advised Elise.

"I know."

Elise wasn't far behind Monique in grieving over the loss of Miss Agnes, as her eyes weren't completely clear of moisture; her struggle was just a tad bit more tenacious.

"Did Miss Pruitt ever show up?" Elise went on to asked.

Wendy was enlightened, spouting, "Pruitt! That's her name.

I couldn't think of it for anything. "Loretta Pruitt, that's her name."

Elise stared at Wendy, having drawn a blank.

Charles H. Woods
418

"What's so important about her name?" she asked, at a loss.

"Never mind," Wendy said. "But no, I haven't seen her. Before Miss Agnes left, she said Miss Pruitt should be right over. So far, I haven't seen her."

"Well, what do we do now?" Elise still at a loss, now concerning the plan they'd agreed on about leaving the orphanage today. "Do we go, or do we stay?"

"I've been giving it a lot of thought," Wendy said. "It's not an easy decision to make. We don't have any place specifically where we can go. I've thought of waiting-it-out right here...see what happens and take it from there."

"Do you think that's a good idea?" Elise sounded a little skeptical. "I mean, if those government people find out we're here, then what?"

"I don't know what," Wendy was flustered.

Monique had come downstairs to rejoin the only family she ever knew. Wendy and Elise were standing next to the stairs, near the bottom step, close to each other. Monique moved between the two, placing an arm around each their waists. Their reactions were receptive, though, a little puzzled. They smiled at Monique with affection.

"What's up?" Wendy laughingly, finally asked her.

"Can we make the promise that, no matter what happens, we'll never separate from each other?" The sincerity in Monique's shifting gaze at them—from one to the other—was cordial, heartwarming. Her little-girl show of affection was also touching, and it made them giggle, as they were happy that she seemed to have overcome that brief spell of grief from a while ago.

"That's a promise," Wendy was first to agree.

"Guaranteed, little sister," Elise made clear.

Monique released her arms from around them just as a vehicle drove up out front. The girls then left outside, to the porch. It was still plenty light out; the vehicle was an SUV with the lettering on it that read: CPA (Child Protection Agency) State Department.

As the girls looked on curiously, two neatly-dressed people got out—a lady and a man, nearly, if not, middle-aged. They came up to the porch where the girl stood, staring at them, the two unfamiliar.

The lady addressed the girls; physically, she was OK-looking; Caucasian, a silver blonde, benign features, clad in a dark, feminine suit out of a Sears catalog.

"Which one of you is Wendy?" Her voice was...mellow; she peered innocently at each girl.

"That'd be me," Wendy said, a hint of humble in a small voice. She stood between Monique, and Elise, with a gentle hand on each their shoulders. Her heart-rate on the increase, as she held these people with the suspect in her stare.

"I'm Loretta Pruitt," the lady said, which granted the girls a tiny measure of relief.

"Yes, ma'am," Wendy said. "We've been expecting you."

Her gaze shifted to the older gentleman, standing in the yard, beside Miss Loretta Pruitt, as they were close to the porch. The man had no judgmental qualities with his demeanor; he seemed ordinary, a gleaming bald spot up front from a receding hairline. He was average height, and weight, in dressed-slacks and a light sports jacket.

"Are you girls packed yet? We must be out of here as soon as possible. Didn't Agnes tell you that before she left?" Loretta Pruitt's announcement caught the girls by extreme surprise.

"Packed?" Wendy was stunned. "No, we're not packed. Miss Agnes never said anything to us about packing. You mean, *now?*"

The idle gentleman then, and Miss Pruitt nodded affirmatively as they stepped up on the porch with the girls. Then Miss Pruitt continued, to the girls' further shocking amazement, "Then let's get a move on. Your placements have already been decided, and your assignments to your new locations are reserved, and the documents are legally signed."

Monique was fearfully excited, looking to Elise, and Wendy in desperation for solace—by any means, so long as it kept them from being separated.

"What does that mean?" The pain of pre-disappointment rendered her, again, teary-eyed. This time, so was Elise, looking to Wendy as their sole redeemer, an authority figure.

Wendy, for the time being, had nothing to offer them. She recognized the fact that she was still a minor as well, with no authority.

"C'mon, girls, let's go. Inside." Miss Pruitt clapped her hands repeatedly in the gesture urging them to rush. "We gotta hurry. We have to be out of here by tonight."

Heartbroken that felt beyond repair, the girls took a long, languid walk up the stairs for the last time.

Wendy turned to Loretta Pruitt, and the man with her, as they walked close after the girls, up the stairs.

"We have quite a bit to pack," she said. "The van won't be bigger enough. I have a sewing machine...and the girls..."

Miss Pruitt interrupted her, "Never mind the big stuff. We'll send a truck, if necessary to pick up all you can't take with you tonight. Don't worry. Everything's going to be just fine."

That was easy for her to say. Wendy shifted a glance at the people walking after her and the girls that, if put into lasers, it would have destroyed them both. But she would bide her time, declaring, this most definitely wasn't the end for the enchanted trio.

Chapter 28

Chelsea was on her way to the realtor's office downtown when she received a, rather, displeasing phone call on her cell phone. In moderate traffic, she grabbed her phone out of her open purse from over in the passenger seat.   "Yes, this is Chelsea," she said. She didn't need to identify herself as a correspondent newscaster; the only ones had her business cell-number were business people who knew her well enough as Chelsea, along with an extremely few personal friends.

"Miss Freeman, this is Valerie Stanfield at the adoption agency. There is a matter of urgency that requires your immediate attention."

"What's wrong?" Chelsea had a rush of heart-racing as she listened to the stressful message from Miss Stanfield. "I'll be there as soon as I can. I have an appointment at the real estate office that I must keep. Will it keep for a little while?"

Valerie delivered the tolerable news. "Sure. We're open 'till eight."

Chelsea was relieved. "Thank you. I'll be there before then, I'm sure."

Valerie added, "Just in case I'm not here; so long as you have your document code number, you'll be fine. Anyone can accept your signature."

"Thank you. I have it," Chelsea said then hung up.

The personnel at GSW was scrambling in a chaotic frantic. All telephone lines were tied up; communications system, computers, shortwave transmissions were filled near capacity. The *thing* of a monumental interest had penetrated the earth's atmosphere, on a collision course with the planet, with less than a couple of days before impact.

Susan Rooker and Jillian Connelly were minding their designated monitoring systems—huge computer-screens—in a less congested area of the government facility. They were responsible for getting out vital information to areas of greatest importance nationwide: the Whitehouse, major cities, and the military.

In Grand City, a light shade of darkness began to prevail into a perpetual night, not the city's notice as normal nightfall. But the creeping darkness' gradual descent upon the land, and its passive, unsuspecting populace, pervaded in an unrecognizable, though, unnatural fashion a slightly consuming mass of darkness at an increased rate of development.

"Oh, my god. This thing is massive. It's partly blotting out the sun, creating a dense eclipse." Susan withdrew from her view screen, next to the huge computer screen. The smaller screen relayed whatever the giant telescope—Sky Watcher—played from out in space. Jillian's station was next to Susan's on her left. They stared at each other wide-eyed, with an equal share of terror in their eyes.

Susan grabbed the telephone next to her; Jillian did the same. "I'll get a hold of the Whitehouse," she said.

"I'd better get a hold of Ed in Grand City. This thing's headed straight for us," Susan realized.

The girls, with their small luggage—what little they'd brought along in pillowcases—were escorted inside an old, vintage building on the State Capitol grounds. Through some of the ancient windows, with careless spreads of putty along the edges of the dingy panes, were dim lights of a sickly, yellowish hue. So, depressing already. The place looked eerie, haunted. It was the farthest building away from the rest on the grounds. It was late that afternoon, by the time they arrived.

"Doesn't it appear a little darker than normal, to you?" Miss Pruitt noticed, the minute they all had left the van, and were headed inside the drab building.

The gentleman along with them looked about briefly. "Not really," he decided. "The sunset's behind a few clouds, I can see."

And it went unnoticed, except that Motatu said very softly to Wendy, "This isn't normal."

Wendy, under extreme duress, merely replied aridly, "It's not?" That was such a vague show of the slightest interest.

The girls moved quietly with their escorts along a dank corridor that had an old smell of lead paint, mixed with a hint of mildew in its primary stage. Shortly ahead, the chattering of others—kids, mainly—was faint, yet definite.

Miss Pruitt looked back at the girls, realizing they tended to lag on purpose, lethargically, somber, seemingly laboring with their small luggage. She said to them, "Come along, girls. It's not that much farther. You'll probably be spending the night here because of limited transportation. But you'll be shipped out first thing tomorrow morning."

Wendy stared at her, thinking...being treated like they were cattle herded out to pasture.

Monique whispered to Wendy, feeling awful like she'd been betrayed, the three walking alongside each other, with their stuffed pillowcases, "Wendy, when are we going to leave? They intend to separate us; you heard what she said."

"I know," Wendy said. "Just hang in there. It's not over yet."

Elise said, "We need to decide something. I don't like this place. It smells."

"It sure does, "Monique agreed.

They were taken to a huge bay area, where a handful of kids, ranging in ages from six through fourteen, were sitting and lying about. Some of the bunks—old Army cots—were unmade, with crumpled sheets and blankets strewn about. The kids were drably clothed; some needed bathing. The whole atmosphere there was utterly depressing. The only way to look outside was through small, rectangular windows high-up alongside the cinderblock walls, very near the ceiling. The place was poorly lit; and there was a make-shift desk—a fold-out table from the cafeteria—with all the necessities used for processing documents, and other paperwork: a telephone, laptop, word-processor, a copy machine.

In looking around in this degenerating atmosphere, Wendy struggled to maintain control of her bulging emotions. She was just minutes away from suggesting to the girls they simply burst out of there, under the strength of their powerful might. But her better thinking realized that would only make matters worse, in a long run. They needed a clean get-away, where no one would be affected but themselves, while at the same time, maintaining their sworn secret was extremely necessary, without the slightest error.

They choose a single bunk over near a corner of the musty, old place, and sat down together, lying their pillowcases aside, with clothing and other small items inside. Eventually, a few of the older kids began to gravitate over to them in a tentatively friendly approach. They were two girls, twelve, and the other about to turn fourteen, and a boy, eleven-and-a-half.

"Hi. My name's Phyllis. I'm twelve," the little girl said.

The older girl said, "And I'm Georgia, fourteen; and this my brother Darryl. He's eleven."

Darryl spoke up, which got him small laughter, "Eleven-and-a-half."

Georgia ripped him, "Halves don't count. You're eleven until you become twelve. No in-betweens."

The kids, a company to the girls, served as a reminder of when their foster home was filled with kids. But those memories have long faded into the abyss of the far regions of the minds. They did politely introduce themselves, though.

Ed and several members of his staff were in a single, government sedan, patrolling the streets when he received the call from Susan at GSW. He was a passenger in the car, along with two other agents, other than the driver.

"It's here, you say... Uh huh. Yes, I noticed it appears darker more sooner than normal. Oh, it eclipsed the sun. That explains the early nightfall. My men are ready."

Then there was a short pause.

Finally, Ed said, trying to remain calm under a rush of desperate concern, "Coordinates? Are you serious?"

Susan confirmed to Ed, "That's right—coordinates. They're all over the computer screens here, and there's nothing we can do about it. It's like, whatever it is, it's purposely giving us the location of its landing..."

"That's the desert flat-lands, about twenty miles from here," Ed acknowledged.

"Wait... Ed, there's something else coming across our communications system." A different occurrence suddenly stirred Susan.

The computer screens all over GSW's command center went on a glitch, with harsh static, receptions illegibly distorted. Then, suddenly, the screens cleared, and the static went away, leaving a perfectly viewable image on-screen. It was an alien race of some kind. The complexion was of a brownish-gray texture, barely an indication of nostrils; the mouth more that of some type of weird beast than human, or any other known creature of Earth.

Then a vocal communication began from the beastly face, at first, garble, then became understandable, "I am Zaal...You will return the children of Mamaron to me. To shield them would bring devastation to this planet. They must be returned upon our arrival. Any rebellion will exact the wrath of Zaal upon you. Do not behave foolishly, or this planet will be destroyed." The slightly less than hideous face then vanished from the monitoring screens, replacing normal functioning on-line.

"Did you get all of that?" Susan asked, having switched that last transmission over to Ed's sophisticated equipment built into the sedan's dash panel.

"We got it," Ed confirmed, the others looking on, seriously concerned.

Ed and several members of his staff were in a single, government sedan, patrolling the streets when he received the call from Susan at GSW. He was a passenger in the car, along with two other agents, other than the driver.

"It's here, you say... Uh huh. Yes, I noticed it appears darker more sooner than normal. Oh, it eclipsed the sun. That explains the early nightfall. My men are ready." Then there was a short pause.

Finally, Ed said, trying to remain calm under a rush of desperate concern, "Coordinates? Are you serious?"

Susan confirmed to Ed, "That's right—coordinates. They're all over the computer screens here, and there's nothing we can do about it. It's like, whatever it is, it's purposely giving us the location of its landing..."

"That's the desert flat-lands, about twenty miles from here," Ed acknowledged.

"Wait... Ed, there's something else coming across our communications system."

A different occurrence suddenly stirred Susan.

The computer screens all over GSW's command center went on a glitch, with harsh static, receptions illegibly distorted. Then, suddenly, the screens cleared, and the static went away, leaving a perfectly viewable image on-screen. It was an alien race of some kind. The complexion was of a brownish-gray texture, barely an indication of nostrils; the mouth more that of some type of weird beast than human, or any other known creature of Earth.

Then a vocal communication began from the beastly face, at first, garble, then became understandable, "I am Zaal. You will return the children of Mamaron to me. To shield them would bring devastation to this planet. They must be returned upon our arrival. Any rebellion will exact the wrath of Zaal upon you. Do not behave foolishly, or this planet will be destroyed." The slightly less than hideous face then vanished from the monitoring screens, replacing normal functioning on-line.

"Did you get all of that?" Susan asked, having switched that last transmission over to Ed's sophisticated equipment built into the sedan's dash panel.

"We got it," Ed confirmed, the others looking on, seriously concerned. He hung up then said to his cohorts, "Gentlemen, it looks like we may be at war."

Then he got on the phone with battalion commander, Colonel Seth Gordon. "Colonel...Ed. Condition red; the desert flat-land. *It's* here!"

"We're on our way," the colonel said, then hung up.

Fighter jets by squadrons, followed by military heavily-armed warbirds—black helicopters and the like—took to the air on combat alert. Ripping across the black mire of the dismal sky, they jetted out to the desert flatlands. A small, mechanized Army moved out of the area, to join the major troop-movements, already deployed in the specified area, in the pitch black.

The city was under Martial Law; hardly anyone was out late, a few late stragglers were about it. They were adults, permitted only until 12-midnight. Kids under eighteen were10 p.m. It was the lowest in the volume of citizens on the streets late that ever occurred in Grand City. It looked virtually like a ghost town of the Old West. The Nation Guard had troops posted on the streets, to manage the curfew.

The city lights and glowing neon signs revealed vacant streets throughout the city, stretching as far out into the gloom of some of the suburban districts. Rural areas were normally this quiet, at this late night anyway. Farms and scattered residential areas were bedded down, under the cloak of the dark, with a very sparse arrangement of pole lamps, just in case some lost traveler happened along.

Far out along the countryside, a young couple, though, fully adults, sat in their pickup truck, snuggling in a romantic clinch. The young lady, a dark-haired charmer, kept noticing the darkness of the sky, and the peculiarity of its abnormal bearings: She couldn't see the stars on such a clear night.

"Johnny," she said to her boyfriend sitting behind the wheel, "what happened to the stars? Can you see any?"

He straightened up, looked out the driver-side window, into the satin black gloom of night. He saw no stars, but something else. He brought his head back inside the truck, glaring at his girlfriend Dolores, as pale as a sheet.

"Johnny, what's wrong?" she asked.

"Look out there," he said in a shaky voice. "Then tell me what you see."

Pretty Dolores looked out her window the second time. She saw no stars, like before, but she was wondering why her boyfriend—since high school— looked so pale, and disturbed, just now. "I don't— "

Suddenly, she shouted, "Oh, my god! It's something out there. I mean, up there!"

Right above them was a vast-spread of the night that seemed to have separated from itself and had become a roiling mass of darkness, like a piece of the night in motion, in a gradual, grinding, rotating fashion.

Johnny, startled out of his wits, cranked the truck, snatched it in gear then floored it, peeling tires, desperate to get clear of this dark apparition in the sky!

"Drive, honey! Drive!" she yelled in panic.

They tore out of there as if the Devil was giving chase.

Charles H. Woods

Chelsea had lost track of the time. Her appointment with the real estate broker took longer than she'd imagined. They got caught up in red tape over the premier owner of the property she was interested in purchasing. It was something to do with the previous owner remanding the property over to the government for lack of paying property taxes, as the fee became too great for the original owner to remit. That document to prove the government's ownership had gotten missed placed. When it was eventually discovered in a stack of out-of-place files, ready for the shrewder, it was past closing time at the State Department of CPA

But Chelsea raced against time, driving along an empty street, wondering where everyone had gone. Something didn't look right. National Guardsmen were posted about the city. Otherwise, it was nearly grave-yard quiet. Nevertheless, she drove through town in a rush, realizing the time was approaching nine-thirty p.m. And, for some reason, it appeared darker than normal. Lit neon signs and street lights tended to glow a hard-edged clarity of light amid the immense darkness.

"Boys and girls, when I call your names, I want you to form a line—with your personal bags—over in that area," Miss Pruitt was getting the kids ready to ship out to their new foster home location. The area she was referring to be the opposite side of the huge room, near the wide, heavy, metal door that required a plastic card with a code number to open.

The kids, which were twelve of them, including the enchanted trio, made ready to move out and form the line asked of them. In doing so, Wendy said to the girls confidently, very quiet, "When we form the line, try to stay to the back of the line, near the door."

Monique and Elise were anxious, bearing down hard not to show it. But the glee in Elise's voice nearly tipped her hand. "Oh, boy! This is *it!*" she came close to shouting.

Monique was quick to caution her, "Shush! Elise... you're gonna get us busted."

Elise sank away, "Sorry. I'm a little excited."

"Me, too," Monique agreed. "But be quiet."

"I got it," Elise assured her quietly, but stern.

Wendy wanted to make sure they understood what to do, "Remember, stay to the back of the line. I'll tell you what to do then, OK? Trust me."

"We do, Wendy," Monique was most sincere.

Wendy smiled at them, which gave them so much reassurance. They smiled back at her.

"Okay, Lindsey and Darryl Graham, to the front, please," Miss Pruitt began calling out names.

There were several other counselors with her, to oversee the process—two other ladies, along with the gentleman already on hand.

The little girl and her younger brother were first in line.

"We're lucky she didn't call us first," Elise noted.

"We just would've moved to the back of the line, anyway," Monique smarted-off. She was between abhorred and encouraged. Encouragement was low on fuel; she wanted out, *now!*

Miss Pruitt: "Michelle Harris, and Dianne Crenshaw."

The two girls, each fourteen, went over and got in line; Monique, Elise, and Wendy remained waiting.

Chelsea parked out front of the State building, hardly turning off the ignition, after putting the gear in park, before she was off and running. Up the brief, cement steps, to the part metal and glass door... Doggonit! It was locked. The building was dark out front. Black windows went from the ground up to its apex of eight-floors. There was no sign anywhere about, indicating a remote chance of entering the building. From the looks of it, everyone who worked there had long left for the day.

Across the well-kept, carpet-lawn, at a passing glance, Chelsea noticed the old building semi-standing alone, with those sickly, dim, yellowish lights in few of the windows. They looked no more significant than night-lights. Nothing out front of the place looked alive, along with ground-level. She noticed an SUV was parked at the curb. But it looked cold, long-standing, deserted, as if it hadn't been moved in days, maybe weeks.

Chelsea was thinking, though, that normally, state and government facilities required a night watchman or security guard. She was not about to quit, at this point; she decided to give it one last try at the front of the building.

Not relenting her effort to gain entrance; under the circumstances, she banged on the thick plate-glass door, the reverberation narrowly coursing through the front entrance a short way. She kept going... banging, banging, then paused, then banged repeatedly, until her arm, and fist began to tire...

"Wendy Gale!" Miss Pruitt called out.

The girls were stymied. The three of them had started to advance but suddenly held up, at a loss, not understanding. Elise and Monique looked at Wendy. She didn't understand either.

"C'mon," she timidly suggested. "Maybe she meant to call the three of us since we came here together."

As the three started to move forward together, Miss Pruitt said, "Just Wendy, girls. I'll get to you soon enough."

Wendy stared at them, the look in her eyes firm, indicative that they continue trusting her, as she hesitantly complied to the order by Miss Pruitt, who then continued, "Jackie Nyles; Elvin Boyd..."

"They *so* are going to separate us," Monique was afraid. And rightly so, because Miss Pruitt singling Wendy out, when the three of them were together, was certainly done purposely. But Wendy had told them to maintain, and that's what they did.

Chelsea's constant banging finally brought a security guard to the front, from his station, some place beyond the entrance. He yelled through the glass-door out at her, "We're closed, ma'am."

Chelsea didn't have to hear him clearly; she could read his lips. She produced the few primary documents she'd received from the adoption agency and held them against the glass for him to scan. Her persistence became so annoying that he finally unlocked the door, with a little bit of an attitude.

"Madam, we're closed," he stressed, tempering his annoyance.

"You don't understand," Chelsea was desperate. "Are there any ways possible you can get a hold of Valerie Stanfield? It's a matter of urgency."

"Ma'am, it can't be anything that won't keep 'till morning," the security guard told her. "We open at nine a.m. sharp."

He glanced up at the night sky, Chelsea scantly noticing his slight decline in self-confidence, like something was of a concern to him greater than his return to work. He was a thinly-built man, late forties, sort of tall—six-foot, kind features, blue-green eyes; his cadet-blue uniform a snug-fit, with a side-arm.

"Are you all right, Mr.?" Chelsea found herself suddenly drawn to his idle-look of a distant concern, unrelated to hers; his fair complexion now slightly flush.

"Oh, I'm fine, ma'am," he said, adjusting his black leather holster belt, flashing one final glance at the dark, dreary sky. Then he said to Chelsea, as the two of them stood half-way inside the doorway, "Those papers you have; are you trying to adopt a child or children? You hardly look like the type. In fact, you look kind of familiar. Have we met before?" He cocked his head, staring at Chelsea, trying to recall.

"You could be getting me mixed up with someone else."

Due to the nature of her being there, she wasn't ready to disclose her personal business, especially to a stranger. However, should he figure out she's a local celebrity on television, then so be it.

The security guard just thought of something which might be of help to her.

"Say, about those papers you have," he said. "There's processing going on now, as we speak. You see that building across the way there? It's the processing center for orphans. Right now, there's a group of orphans being relocated. Maybe the in charge can help you. Her name's Loretta Pruitt."

That spark of hope ignited Chelsea's further determination. "You mean, that building over there, with the dim lights on?"

Charles H. Woods
436

"Yes," the night watchman said. "But you can't go in through the front, it's locked. You'll have to enter from around back. That's where late processing takes place."

At a surge of hope building inside her, Chelsea briefly tried to decide what option should she take; drive over, through a small maze of a few twists and turns, or hurry along on foot. The shortest distance between two points is a straight line, she recalled learning in primary Geometry. Since she couldn't drive across the beautifully-spread of rich green lawn, as a short-cut; she left on foot in a manner of which to appear lady-like in a rush.

"Thank you!" she yelled back to the security guard, who wore the name tag that read Bucannon over the left shirt pocket.

Her image soon becoming hazed in the gloom of the consuming darkness as she continued toward the old building with the eerie, dim lights in some of the higher-level windows.

Chapter 29

"Do you believe there are angels here?"

The girls, Elise, and Monique were asked that question by a ten-year-old girl named Liza. She was alone, as were a few other kids.

"Do believe?" Elise turned the responsibility back to the little girl to answer. She and Monique were sitting on a bunk, minding their bags of personal belongings. The little girl was sitting beside them at an angle, facing both.

"Yes," the little darling said, her bright blue eyes like two tiny crystals, peering at them through a window in Heaven.

The girls smiled at her; she smiled back.

Monique said to her caringly, "They are your friends. You should always remember that."

Little said with conviction, "I'll remember."

"Liza Zimmerman," Miss Pruitt called to her.

Right away, the little girl got up and left Elise and Monique sitting on the bunk.

"Bye." She waved to them while continuing over to the line where others waited before her.

Over across the way, under the poor lighting in this drab dungeon-of-a-waiting area, Elise, and Monique kept eye-contact with Wendy, who did the same with them. It was tell-tale to the girls, just by looking into Wendy's eyes, even at that distance, she was formulating an escape plane.

"I'm sure it won't be long now," Elise shared her confidence with Monique, who was gathering courage all the while.

"OK...," That was Miss Pruitt sounding off again, her voice bountifully clear, though, not quite booming; just authoritatively demanding. "All kids that I didn't call, you'll be picked up tomorrow morning. So, you may as well make yourselves comfortable, and choose a bunk; you'll be spending the night here. If you're hungry, let either one of us know, and we'll take care of it for you."

Wendy decided at a rise of nervous insecurity, *it was do-or-die. The time was now, or never!* She stepped forward from about the middle of the line, to confer with Miss Pruitt.

"Miss Pruitt," she began. Pruitt turned to her quizzically, "Yes?"

While the girls looked-on in fervent earnestness, Wendy continued her frail negotiation for the three of them, "The girls and I have been together, like... well, forever. We've practically spent our entire lives together, at Lily Field Foster Home. Monique's been with us since birth. She doesn't have anyone else this close to her. Isn't there a way we can remain together?"

Loretta Pruitt's reply was within the scope of her safe employment, as she was determined not to break any rules, which might jeopardize her livelihood. "Honey, I'm sorry; and I realize what you're saying. But I have no choice. It's not up to me. But, look. I'm sure..."

Wendy interrupted her as politely as she could, without showing any disrespect to her authority, "Then you leave me no choice, Miss Pruitt."

She turned and said to Monique, and Elise, "C'mon, guys."

The girls had been anxiously awaiting this moment, as they gleefully grabbed up their stuffed pillowcases...but before starting across the room, over to Wendy, she told them, "Leave the bags. We don't have time to bother with them."

The girls gladly left the bags on the cot, and hurried over to Wendy, leaving Miss Pruitt stunned, and amazed over their blatant act of mutiny, as the other councilors looked-on, simply shocked.

During that moment, Wendy's abrupt, unsuspecting defiance stymied the councilors; she looked over to the metal door, melting the coded lock with lasers from her eyes—which no one, except Wendy, and the girls knew about. Then the three of them left through the door Wendy had jimmied open.

The kids left behind stood there in amazement, not uttering a word, just in a mild, subtle state of admiration.

"Girls wait!" Miss Pruitt and another lady assuredly went after them a short way. Miss Pruitt kept calling after them, "Girls, get back here! You can't do this! Girls!"

But they were gone, disappearing along one of the several corridors, leaving no trace behind. Miss Pruitt and the other lady had no idea which way the three girls had gone; so, they were forced to abandon the useless chase.

Once they returned to their duties, Chelsea Freeman had arrived, looking for the lady in charge. In doing so, she'd already looked over the children who were being processed to different locations of foster homes. She was thankful the three girls she sought weren't among these kids, so she thought.

Somewhat winded, she went up to Miss Pruitt, as was directed by the gentleman with them.

"Maybe you can help me," she began, presenting the documents to the lady.

Miss Pruitt, still the lingering effect of the brief chase settling, looked over the paperwork, then told her, "I'm afraid you're a little late. They're gone."

"Gone?" Chelsea's heart sank in painful disbelief. "Gone where?"

"I'm afraid they've run away," Miss Pruitt said frankly.

Thanks to their penetrating visions, otherwise, they'd have gotten lost in the maze of corridors, looking for the exit; along the way, the girls passed the glass-enclosed security-guard station, with the security guard inside asleep on the watch, leaned-back in his chair, with his boots-feet propped on his desk, which there before him was a set of monitoring screens.

The girls eased along quietly toward the exit. Once they arrived, Wendy wisely suggested to them, "Guys, it may be best we switch to costumes...just in case. That should create enough distraction if needed. No one's suspecting to find three girls dressed for a Halloween party."

"Good idea," Monique complimented her. "You see, Wendy; that's why you're in charge. And we will never give you any trouble."

Wendy looked at the two of them amiably, and told them, "You never gave me any trouble."

Monique and Elise smiled at Wendy, touched.

The security guard awoke just in time to catch a glimpse of the girls as they were walking out the front entrance/exit, into the mystic night.

"Hey!" he shouted, then went after them. But he was too late; again, they jimmied the locked door, with hardly any effort, just a light push by Elise, and it opened, no resistance.

The guard was stupefied. He was sure he'd locked the door behind him, when he was done talking with that lady, earlier. He examined the door; the metal hitch that secures the door, once it's been locked, was bent beyond repair. It would take a bull-of-a-person to breach such a lock. Yet... He couldn't figure it. The images he'd thought he'd seen could've been a dream.

In peering, out into the night, he saw no one. Nothing. The stillness, the darkness, almost ominous. He stood there, perplexed, not knowing what to think. Finally, he went back to his cage and phoned an emergency locksmith.

On the virtually deserted streets, the girls took precaution to avoid the strategically-scattered, National Guardsmen, posted about the city. Some were mobile, while others were stationary, designated to walk a post.

The girls stayed in the shadows as much as possible. So far, so good.

"Wendy..." That was Motatu.

"What is it?" Wendy quietly responded as they passed through a darkened area along a city block. "It'd be wise, if you guys are discovered, you'd be in your normal clothing. The Dark thing is here." The sound of Motatu's voice carried more than just a concern that the girls don't get caught in uniform; her mention of the Dark-thing tended to come from a creeping fear.

"The Dark-thing?" Elise wanted to know more about this...Dark thing. "What does it want, why is it here?"

The entities inside them went silent, which was about to become alarming. The girls morphed back into their regular clothing as they continued along the vacant avenues. Posted members of the National Guard have stationed just up ahead, a small strand of streetlamps bringing them into full focus.

The girls held up, Elise delaying the pursuit of the answer to her question. They remained in the shadows, near the corner of a high-rise building, with a group of leafy trees next to it.

Finally, Koh decided to try and explain the Dark-thing. "It's the enemy of Mamaron, who protects the Plains of Souls."

Wendy was surprised that Elise or Monique didn't come with a million questions at the mention of Mamaron. She thought she was alone with that knowledge about the entities.

"Wait," she said, seriously wanting to know. "Do you guys *know* about Mamaron?"

Monique chimed in, "And about the Plains of Souls. And..." she got quiet, continuing softly, "why Motatu doesn't fly." She then cringed a little, fearing either Wendy or Motatu may jump all over her. But neither did. She relaxed, and they moved on.

"So, you guys know the whole story." Wendy was more gratified that they knew that she was surprised they knew. "That's great. At least, now, we got a better understanding of what we're dealing with."

"Hey, what are you youngsters doing out this late?" That was a male voice, coming from the shadows behind them, and startling, to say the least.

They looked around suddenly to discover a local police officer emerging from the shadows.

It was Officer Clint Daily on night patrol. His cruiser was parked along the curb, in the shadows of a building, and the ideal spacing of a few birch trees. The girls figured they were in trouble as run-away orphans. And, to add to their misery, some troops of the National Guard rushed upon them.

"Is there a problem here, officer?" a captain of the guards asked the officer.

The girls stared at the officer in a pitiable fashion, and the effect was gripping. He stared at them with a hidden compassion, then said to the captain, "No problem, captain. I'll handle it."

The troops left and returned to their post. Officer Daily turned to the girls, who feared he was aware of their misdemeanor. "OK, kids, in the car. I'll take you home."

Home? They had no home.

Once they'd gotten into the back seat, and the officer closed the door; Monique remarked worriedly, "I think we blew it."

"Don't be so quick to give up," Wendy encouraged both girls.

Under the grim circumstances, the girls' spirits were lifted on Wendy's faith, alone.

Officer Daily got in behind the wheel, adjusted the rearview mirror, catching the girls staring at his passing glance in the mirror at them. "Anyone of you wanna tell me where you live?"

That didn't sound like he was aware of the trouble they were in, Wendy was thinking. She was sitting on the outside, next to the door, behind the officer; Elise was seated between her and Monique.

"We've been locked out," Wendy said, testing his tolerance on whether he believed her.

"This is a bad night to be out on the town," he said. "And just how do you figure on getting in, unless you're hankering to spend the night at juvenile hall."

"Is that a prison?" Monique asked, at a rise of fear.

"You girls might figure it to be," he said. All the while he was bluffing without their knowledge, even Wendy's.

Under such pressure and feel they've reached the point of no return, Wendy suggested, "Costumes, now."

Without questioning her, the girls did as she'd suggested. The three of them, now, sitting there in their stunning skin-tights, Monique, and Elise in capes. The officer drove them downtown, past many of Nation Guard troops, before looking in the mirror once more.

"Officer, you can let us out at any time now," Wendy was saying just as the officer slammed on the breaks, suddenly confused after what he'd just seen of the girls through the mirror.

He pulled off to the side, shoved the gear in park, and whirled around in his seat, angling his portly frame in position to get a look at them, poised in the back. Had he lost his sanity? The three girls were in costumes, just like that! "What's going on? How'd you girls change so quickly? And where are your regular clothes?"

They just smiled at him, and he was enlightened; his bulging eyes absorbing the phenomenon—which had Grand City in such an uproar—live, up-close, and in person.

"You're the Angels!" he marveled excitedly.

"You got it, friend," Wendy smiled. "Now, we need a favor."

Officer Daily was beside himself, about to explode from the sudden rush of excitement. He asked, "I'll do my best. But...whatever can I do for the *Angels?*!"

A quick look at both Elise, and Monique for their blind support of her unexplained decision; they were consensual. Then she said to the officer, "We don't particularly have a home. You got any suggestions...just for tonight?"

Sergeant Daily was accommodating. He'd inadvertently happened to come across the Angels. He grinned, reveling in the idea that occurred to him.

The Angels entered through a back way to the police station, with sergeant Daily as their escort. It was an area completely in the dark, not used very much for any purpose. The metal door was padlocked, but Daily had the key on a keyring among a few others. He used his service flashlight astutely, to avoid the excess glare by keeping only enough light on the lock and key.

The Angels stood close together until he'd unlocked the door. Then, standing slightly aside, he showed them inside a dark room, which was now used as a basement.

With the flashlight to sparingly guide them, they carefully moved among piles of discarded stuff in boxes, carelessly stocked in some tight areas, until they reached the second door inside the basement. Once through that door, the way was clear, as he took them along a narrow corridor, to a cellblock no longer in use for any purpose.

The floor was trashy; most of the few cell-doors were open. Some of the cells were better equipped with sleeping arrangements, while others were in shambles—broken cots, old, dingy mattresses strewn about the cell-floors. And the place held the hint of the smell of a day's work sweated into old clothes.

"I know this isn't a luxury suite in some grand hotel," Daily said in trying to raise a bit of humor, under the pressure of being this close to the actual Angels! "But you'll have the privacy you want. The place down here is only used for storage, now and then. Our new facilities in that building just across the way. So, you young ladies just choose where you wanna bed-down. If you need anything, just let me know. I'll be back to check on you in a little while, from time to time."

Wendy chose an open cell with four cots, complete with proper bedding, and had remained neatly made all this time. They moved inside and claimed individual cots.

Wendy was gratified and congenially polite, "We don't know how to thank you."

And she was being honest; since learning who they were, he'd been nothing but accommodating, and at the risk of his job, Wendy would think. "You've been really kind."

As Daily got ready to leave, he made them aware, "Try not to make much noise, although it's not likely anyone hears you. But, just in case...I could lose my badge, and my... well, you know."

Koh fired off, "You mean, your ass?"

Everyone was shocked, except Daily who only stared wide-eyed, while the rest shouted simultaneously—even Jor, "KOH!"

Koh was agitated. "Monique got away with it!" she scoffed in defense.

Monique took offense, "What?"

Koh argued, "You said dumb-ass!"

"I did not," Monique denied.

Koh was livid in making her point, angrily screaming at the top of her lungs, "It doesn't matter! You said the word, *AAASS!*"

Jor burst out laughing strenuously hard.
"You guys," Wendy warned them, "someone hears you. Keep it down."

Sergeant Daily didn't know what to make of these phenomenal beings, as he hesitantly started to take his leave while thinking these Angels were amazingly equipped with the art of ventriloquism, which was strangely amusing.

"Officer," Wendy said as a final word of gratitude.

He waited, drawn to the idea of being up-close and personal to the Angels, "Yes?" he said.

"Thanks for all you've done for us," Wendy went on to say. "We'll be out by morning, so don't bother to lock the door we came in. We wouldn't want to disturb you just to open the door."

"That's no problem, ma'am," he said. "I have to report in early anyway, but I'll leave it open for you. Oh, before I leave; is there anything I can get for you? We got cheese and crackers, cupcakes, and soft beverages."

Delight sparkled in Monique's, and Elise's eyes. "Cupcake, and a soft drink," Elise was first to ask; then Monique, "I'll have the same!"

They looked to Wendy: Daily polite, "Ma'am?"

She smiled graciously, "Nothing, thanks."

"I'll be right back with your snacks."

Daily then left, and went up a flight of metal stairs, through a door that led to the main area of the police station.

"You guys shouldn't have him going after snacks," Wendy said. "He's already taking a risk by letting us stay the night here."

"He made the offer," Monique said. "And I am kinda hungry."

"Yes," Elise said accordingly. "If it's such a risk; why did he suggest it?"

Wendy decided wisely to dismiss that argument. When it came to debating junk-food being an unhealthy choice, she'd lose every time. So, she went on to complain about another issue of a personal concern. "Y'know…he's really a nice guy," she said. "But I wish he wouldn't call me *ma'am.*"

The girls didn't understand, staring at Wendy inquisitively. Monique asked, "How come?"

"Yes, how come? It should make you feel grown up," Elise said.

Wendy disagreed, giving a peculiar reason, "No, it makes me feel old and fat."

Everyone except Wendy laughed. She was being ludicrous, but truthful.

Officer Daily brought them snacks a short while later, including Wendy, figuring she may get hungry later on. After which, he left back upstairs, leaving the basement, and the girls under the light of a dim, small-wattage, single light- bulb that hung from the ceiling, in the far corner of the antiquated cellblock.

Several police officers arrived at the scene the three orphan girls were last seen, just before they'd run off into the dismal night. Chelsea remained on hand as a person with interest, witnessing the report Loretta Pruitt gave to the officers.

Outback of the processing center for orphans, the police cruisers' flashing blue lights illuminated that area in a limited space, creating a blue gloom against the oppressive night. "Do you have any idea where they could've gone?" the uniformed officer taking her statement asked, with pad and pen in hand.

"No," Miss Pruitt answered, extremely concerned, her co-workers, and Chelsea hanging close by. "I wouldn't think they'd return to the old foster home; it's been officially closed down. And besides, they don't have a key to the old place, anymore."

That was Chelsea's clue to leave. Since she was more informed about the girls, she had nothing to offer the police, nor Miss Pruitt. Chelsea's purpose for being there was strictly personal, to begin with. She wasn't worried, like the rest; her concern was when, where, and mainly how she may eventually catch up to them.

To drive home after such a disappointment was like the taste of rusty nails. The displeasure was just that bitter for Chelsea, as she drove through the mystic gloom on this night. Streets after streets were vacant of traffic, replaced by units of the National Guard, along with regular military personnel. The sudden decline of patrons was due to the impending threat of something unknown. Normally, at this hour, the city was alive with late-night shopping, partying; bars, taverns, and restaurants filled to near capacity. Now, nothing, except Martial Law.

Chapter 30

Strange lights swept across the city in the middle of the night; nonconventional lights of variating hues of blue, orange, yellow to an extreme, somewhat, penetrating bright-white light, with a slight skeletal effect. The city's building structures, under the white light, became right at sixty-percent translucent, enabling the naked eye to see quite a bit of the interior, as if the structures were made of Plexiglas.

The gradual sweeping of the strange, foreign lights continued surveying every section, every district, including the suburbs for close to an hour before finally relenting. Military troops on the streets—the National Guard included—were in awe of making ready for an unknown, possible, confrontation by a force that was *indeed* unknown. Every aspect of this development held the tendencies of D-Day in Grand City. In neighborhoods throughout the county, including the small town of Medfield— sheriff Hollister's sleepy, little villa—were directly affected. Citizens poured out of their homes, some in bed clothing, to witness this bizarre anomaly. Government officials maintained a government Top Secret of this event, to dissuade a massive panic among civilians. But sifting information of this malevolent upheaval had gradually begun to spread among the populace, as panic in its smallest state began to increase at an alarming rate.

After the passing of the mysterious, probing lights, the girls, Wendy, Monique, and Elise precariously crawled out from underneath the bunks each had chosen in their jail cell. Afraid?

Yes.

Motatu had explained the intrusive lights as being a search and recovery method of locating the enemy. Since the penetrating rays didn't completely reveal the entire interior of a solid structure; the metal cot and the extra bedding served as a protective shield for the girls, aside from the cement walls in the basement.

The girls dusted themselves off then resumed their positions on their cots, though, this time, they lay in caution, and wide awake.

"Will we have to fight?" Wendy asked Motatu.

"If we fight, we must destroy it," Motatu explained. "It will not surrender."

"Why do you call it, the Dark-thing?" Elise asked, not that she was that interested in knowing; it was an idle question intended to relax her, make her feel casual toward this huge, imposing bully of a...Dark-thing.

"Because it's dark," Koh said frankly.

"Or, that it is evil," Jor said. "Because whenever you describe bad things, it's normally something along the line of dark, am I right? Like nights...the boogie man and scary monsters come out at night. Except for Godzilla. He's a daytime monster. He'll scare the pants off you, even in the daytime."

The girls laughed, then Elise said, "You didn't have to take us through all that, to make your point. We get it, got it?"

"Ha, ha...very funny," Jor scoffed, unamused. Though, finally, she chuckled anyway.

"Tee, hee, hee...," During their calm moment of solace, it began as a soft moving about upstairs. Then it grew to a rumbling noise. Finally, it became thundering footsteps, beating the hardwood floors upstairs in a ruckus scrambling. A panic had spread among the nightshift officers, as they scampered out of the building, and into their cruisers then sped away into the night, with sirens blasting, blue lights flashing.

As the girls listened intensely, with the suspect and anxiousness; they suddenly heard the door to the basement open with a rushed swiftness. Then rapid, heavy footsteps bang against the metal steps. Someone was coming down the stairs.

"Angels?" That was officer Daily. They recognized his voice right away.

The girls tentatively moved out into the open, from around the corner where the cellblock began.

They discovered Daily was alone with his flashlight, the bright beam cutting a luminescent path to the girls shaded in a soft darkness.

"Angels, everybody's getting out...," He was slightly winded, his chest heaving in and out, catching his breath, as he continued, "Maybe you should, too."

He waited, taking in the vacant expressions on their young faces. That didn't give him hope in the least toward the mighty Angels, from what he'd been hearing. But whether they were or were not the Angels, he couldn't leave them there.

"Look. We're under attack by...something from out *there!*" He pointed sternly at an angle toward the ceiling with his flashlight. "I can't leave you here."

He then motioned with his beaming flashlight that they move forward, ahead of him, to the door leading outside the basement.

They looked at one another, Elise, and Monique depending heavily on Wendy's decision. She stood behind them, urging them along with a soft nudge.

They finally cleared the basement with Daily directly bringing up the rear. Unanswered questions, in such a desperate situation, ran rampant in officer Daily's mind, but he never voiced his misunderstanding to the Angels, because well, they were the *Angels!*"

Wendy said to Daily, "Thanks officer for caring." That sounded strangely personal, as she then simply said to the girls softly, "Go."

The trio then bolted, vanishing deeply into the night, leaving behind a quietude so ghostly-felt it was haunting. To officer Daily, the empty quietness left such a void, it was almost as if they were never there; that the whole thing was fathomed. But it wasn't. It was real.

A second flashlight-beam flickered unsteadily in the dark, toward him, as a voice called to him in the dark, from behind the near-blinding bright beam, "Clint, let's go!"

The streets were beginning to fill with panicked civilians, fleeing in a wild, inescapable pandemic. The interstate was clogged with stalled traffic; main arteries throughout the city were jammed. Those without vehicles were doomed to try and make it on foot.

Many fled to the vast countryside; others ran to cubby holes in and out, and about the city.

"There will definitely be no school tomorrow," a teenaged boy said to several of his friends, as they ran for cover down a heavy gray-darkened back street, under gross insufficient lighting.

Sirens continued shrilling in the night, as paramedic teams raced along the streets, against overwhelming odds, to cover the mounting emergencies. The victims, so far, had caused their own self-inflicted injuries in their melee of blind panic.

"Where are the Angels when you need them?" another shout from a fleeing, congested mass of the populace, desperately rang out.

The Holland family hid out, crouched together in a neutral corner downstairs, inside their home—which had no basement. It was the safest place, suggested by tornado-experts, to hide in the event of a destructive tornado. But this wasn't such a storm passing through; it was much worse. Some unknown, dark force on the verge of an invasion was at hand that Earth had never experienced before.

"Mom ... Dad, don't worry. The Angels will come. I know they will." That was little Timmy, sitting with mom and dad, and his two sisters, Amy, and Tyler, who was visiting from college. Amy contended, as a witness sharing her little brother's faith in the Angels, "He's right... they will save us, like before. You'll see."

The Holland family could hear their neighborhood in turmoil, as the increased volume of frantic screaming swelled in the dark atmosphere impeding their hopefulness. After being made completely aware of the out-of-space, potential invasion, Chelsea decided not to wait-out the tacit threat at home. Having heard the latest news broadcast on her big-screen, HD TV, she set out for the desert flat-land, fully prepared for her personal news coverage. In the back of her mind, she had trust in the Angels. She felt certain, from what glimmer of a first-hand meeting with the Angel, Wendy, they wouldn't let down the citizens of Grand City, for it was indeed their home.

"This is not a drill! I repeat: This is *not* a drill," came the news broadcaster on Chelsea's big-screen, as she had left the set on. "Heavy military forces are gathering at the site where the spacecraft is expected to land in about several hours from now. From its present, high altitude, the mysterious spaceship has already demonstrated an incredible range of firepower. Most of its massive size have blotted out a clear majority of the stars in our skies, over many parts of our local areas..."

Jillian's, and Susan's flight from Phoenix left for Grand City on time. Very little information of the surreal development in Grand City had arrived publicly in the surrounding areas of GSW. Thanks to a tight-knit crew of government personnel, news broadcasts in that area were censored; only soft, suspicious rumors had leaked into neighboring small towns and a few metroplex cities where it had eventually evaporated into humorous, wild stories.

The two ladies rode a coach and were fortunate to share the same seat. "I'm still having these sensations about those two little girls we met out on the highway, that day," Susan finally interrupted their tenuous, little quiet time.

"I know what you mean?" Jillian said. "I can almost understand what Ed meant about their capabilities of influence. It took one look at them, then, suddenly, I thought of them as such sweet, little darlings. And I couldn't help myself."

Susan had the window-seat. She turned, angling more to Jillian, and said with thought, "You ever hear the old saying what comes from the heart, reaches the heart?"

Jillian simply replied, "Even if I hadn't; it's a good saying." Then she went on to say, having thought of a strong possibility, "You may be onto something," the highest possible answer glaring in her stare at Susan, who stared back with a gaping smile of assurance, as Jillian said, "They could be influential, all right. But it's not their intentions; it's their *purity.* Of course, angels are immaculate beings; they only serve the pure in heart, not a thing of evil."

Susan added, "And the purest of the heart may sense it. And that's where the influence comes in. It's not a trick, it's a *natural* phenomenon!"

"And, don't forget, those angelic, little darlings did save our lives," Jillian cordially reminded Susan, while they settled back in their seats as a casual, temporary adjustment, with discontentment.

The uncertainty awaiting their arrival was still ahead of them in Grand City.

Right before daybreak, the plentiful stars in the black sky began to reappear in certain groups, until finally pervading across the entire heavens. The Dark-thing had landed in the flatland, just as predicted by radar-tracking. The military was on hand, in full force. Fighter jets, and combat Army, Navy, and Marine helicopters were in flight. Normal business in the city was under tight scrutiny, and a tenacious, precarious, security watch. Yet, for the most part, the streets were abnormally scarce for usual shoppers, merchants; practically abandoned. All roadways were still jammed to a stand-still.

Of those electing not to abandon their homes, and head to the hills braved the opportunity to get an up-close look at an alien spaceship, firsthand. Since no violent attempt had been a threat, only those mysterious searchlights of last night being the culprit to invoke a stir of unrest; motorists took to backroads, all the way to gravel roads, even across the country, to make the pilgrimage out to the desert flatland.

Sunrise brought the mammoth spacecraft into full view, exposing it's, seemingly, boundless mass. The rustic, deep dark circumference tended to stretch for miles in a saucer-shape, dwarfing a majestic mountain range to the west. The air held an un-spring-like coolness within the massive, dark shadow it projected from underneath its colossal structure. It had no visible anything resembling the slightest hint of windows. It was just a tremendously huge disc, taking up a very large amount of space on the desert flatland.

Among the noise of rip-roaring combat aircrafts, flying at a low altitude, on the alert; the gathering of civilians had taken on the approach as tourists. Families arrived in SUV's, campers, trucks, cars, and RV's, making a picnic of it. They broke out cameras, video equipment, even lawn chairs; with some, foul weather gear, just in case.

The jobs left for local authorities, and the military—aside from their primary duty to defend this Country from the enemy—were to direct the overflowing traffic arriving at this great, spectacle scene.

Tight military security was based close to the alien craft, covering as much territory in a semi-circle as was feasible. War machines, like armored tanks, and other mobile, combat vehicles were established in ready modes, guarding the area.

The host of civilians on the scene was only allowed within a quarter-mile radius of the potential threat. Those who breached that rule, set by government personnel—nonmilitary related—was carted off to jail by the local authority. The media, however, was granted special privilege to graft newsworthy info, to take necessary footages of the event, and interviews randomly chosen by news correspondents. Others were high-ranking military men in command of their sectors, all the way up to the commander of the entire operation, Colonel Seth Gordon.

Federal agents—Ed Milburn's crew—were on location as Top-Secret Servicemen, for added security purposes, and negotiators in the representation of the president. However, the

Commander in Chief—the president himself—was on his way to the area by special helicopter; and would be arriving shortly, under heavily armed guards.

Jillian and Susan had left the airport, after having landed in Grand City, and sped out to the site in a rental car. The ride was quite lengthy, as they took in sceneries of farmlands, with grazing livestock; and a small mass of people on foot, lugging what appeared as personal belongings, heading away from the believed-to-be, impending threat that rested on the flatland, far along the city limit, to the north.

Upon arrival at the unimaginable scene, Jillian, and Susan were suddenly agape, struggling with belief that this immense space vessel existed. Susan parked the rental sedan somewhat randomly among official vehicles designated for that area, a short, guarded distance from the colossal space vessel.

"Are we actually witnessing this?" The vessel's monstrosity displays apprehensively awed Jillian, as she and Susan had to pass just a short way outside its wide-spread, consuming, deep shadow, on their way to a prefab-structured command center, where military leaders and other government officials monitored the increasing development of this precarious situation.

Susan looked about, with interest, at the gathering host of civilians spread about the grounds. In the back of her mind, she was leaning toward a hopefulness that the alien/angels may be watching from somewhere within the mix.

"From here-on, I wouldn't be surprised by just about anything out of the bizarre. And I sure hope our "Angels" haven't abandoned us."

Jillian looked at her dubiously, wondering had she totally lost faith in their iconic Angels, and the theory about this developing, extraterrestrial misadventure.

"This could very well not be their call," she said. "You heard the message from that...*thing*. It didn't sound like *IT*, and the aliens had any correlation. Its transmission to us was clear. It wants to destroy the aliens; not join forces with them, which is what Ed believes it's here for."

"Then what's keeping it from attacking?" Susan didn't clearly understand.

"Maybe the aliens." Jillian was optimistic. "They don't seem to be around; so, this *thing* just might be vulnerable to an attack by them. Especially if it's a surprise attack."

"So, by the aliens staying away is what's keeping us from being attacked by that...monster-spaceship," Susan assumed.

"Well, ladies...it's good to have you aboard." That was Ed, a mild surprise to them, to say the least. He'd walked over to them from his post beside colonel Gordon, to make them welcome. The command center was a mix of federal agents, and military people, from high-ranking officers to enlisted men on special duty.

"Well, ladies, what do you have for us?" Ed, gentleman-like, escorted Susan, and Jillian over to the colonel's command post, where he politely greeted them. "Ladies, nice to have you back," he said.

Jillian turned to Ed, after greeting the colonel and said, "It's only a theory. But considering that this thing hasn't launched a full-scale war is believed why we're still breathing. If you received that thing's transmission; you should know it's purpose is not to partner-up with the aliens, that it wants to destroy them. Now, Susan and I have speculated that who, or, whatever's aboard that ship may have some, maybe, valid reason for not attacking; maybe quite several reasons. Which may very well all be linked to the aliens. You've seen their might. What do you think?"

Ed appalled and flustered, said, "I think the aliens are hiding behind their hosts. As you said, I've seen their might. And it just may be that they'll conserve their super abilities to withstand the destruction of this planet... And I'm convinced they're capable of survival just about anywhere."

"So, in other words," Susan said begrudgingly, "you're saying they're cowards, that they're purposely waiting out the disaster that *thing* may bring on us."

"Precisely," Ed was frank. "It's why they aren't here... to continue to survive. It's the nature of all creatures—human, or animal—to *survive*."

Jillian murmured under her breath, close to Susan, the old cliché, "There's no point in arguing with a stop sign."

Officer Clint Daily, while on duty as guard assistance out at the site, said confidentially to a fellow officer, "Sanchez, I have a secret."
The His Spanish officer looked at him with a raised eyebrow of interest, "You do?"

"I met the Angels last night," Daily said secretly to the officer; no one else was near the two. Some officers out of hearing-range were milling about the grounds. Sanchez was curious to know, "What happened?"

"They spent the night in the old cellblock we used for storage now. Sanchez don't tell anybody I told you that," Daily insisted.

"Oh, no, man, I won't," Sanchez returned with a rich Spanish accent. "How did you meet them?" he went on to ask. Daily replied, "It's a long story. But I'll bet you they'll be here. That's why I'm not worried about this thing doing too much harm to us." Again, came the heavy accent from Sanchez, "Oh, man...you really sound sure of yourself. And I sure hope you're right."

Daily, full of confidence, reassured Sanchez, "Oh, I am. And I know I'm right; they'll be here." By midmorning, the president arrived with a heavy escort. Nothing had taken place with the spaceship. It stood rigidly fixed on that portion of the desert flatland it'd claimed as its tarmac.

The president was brought to the command center, protected by a surrounding force of armed Secret Service men. The commander of operations, Colonel Seth Gordon, and Ed Milburn properly greeted him, along with Susan Rooker, and Jillian Connelly, as everyone else stood at attention until made at ease by the second officer in command, major Findley.

"How's the situation coming?" the president asked.

"Not a thing, yet, Mr. President," the colonel said. "We have our guards up. We're ready at the first sign of any trouble."

Chapter 31

The president voiced his concern, "Ladies and gentlemen, I don't mind admitting I don't like this at all. Has any communication with this thing been established, or even attempted?"

"Sir," the colonel said, "Our communications channels have been open, even before it landed. We've even tried to make voice-contact, but, so far, it's been useless."

"Do we have the weaponry to mount a defense, if we need to?" asked the president.

The colonel and Ed couldn't help but reflect on their futile effort, involving the single alien they'd violently confronted a while back, which had resulted in the destruction of a primary, military weapon, the *Laser-Taser*. "I believe we're fully equipped, Sir," the colonel said.

"Mr. President," Ed chimed in. "I believe this impending enigma can be solved without incident."

The president was interested. "Go on," he said.

"It's the aliens this thing's after. It made that clear, during its approach, earlier," Ed confirmed.

"Well, then, let's get after those aliens," the president was firm. "We must do all we can to avoid any hostile actions from that ship. We don't know its capability."

"Understood, Mr. President," the colonel said, then turned to Ed, "What's our best option to locate them? There must be a pattern or system they follow."

"We'll need to locate their hosts," Ed was convinced.

Jillian and Susan were hard-pressed to voice their optimistic opinions but to oppose the president wouldn't fare well at all. Thus, they remained painfully silent.

Something happened with the enormous spaceship. A wash of nervous excitement cascaded over the civilians, and all others involved, including the president, as an apprehensive hush settled in, rendering everyone into bated breaths.

The gigantic space vessel emitted a drone sound with so much depth it shook the very earth underneath everyone, this hooks the very earth beneath the feet, to the tune of a mild earth-tremor. Then the drone noise settled, finally dissipating. Though, moments later, a brightly glowing hatch gradually began to open along the mysterious material's thickness the gargantuan ship was made of.

The hatch continued to widen; the bright light intensified in equal proportion of the opening hatch. Once the hatch was opened to its capacity, the bright light, virtually blinding, even in broad daylight, began to soften, treating the naked eye more kindly. Flash cameras and video cameras were staunchly engaged, along with media coverage.

The host of civilians became a little edgy, ready to make their escape, at a minute's notice. But, for the most part, many continued capturing live-action on their camcorders, and regular cell phones.

Behind bulletproof glass shields, the occupants inside the command center were still concerned for their safety. They were a might closer to the ship than anyone else. They had a strong back-up by the military, which was on a constant move; fighter jets combed the area very frequently, while ground mobile units stuck close to the area's red zone—near the ship.

Awaiting in dead silence took only moments before vague images began taking shapes within the shaft of the white light that shone brightly through the opened hatch. These strange figures were tall beyond the average height of the human male and were spindly in physical structure, and small in numbers. There were four of them, bearing some type of weapon about the size of an M-60,30 caliber machinegun. Of the four, two of the figures flanked each side of a fifth image extremely tall and lengthy, clad in a long robe-like garment. They moved within the white light toward the command center in a graceful, flotation. Deep brownish-black helmets, with dark visors, masked their facial identities. Their garments were like tempered armor, giving them a robotic appearance. Assuming the towering image center the four was the leader or commander, his entire countenance became visually clear; the others clear as well, except their natural physical frames, were covered in armor.

A dark cowl shielded the face of the assumed leader, except for the eyes. They were two tiny ovals, peering with obtuse red glares, quite disturbing to look at.

The unearthly beings came to a halt just out front of the command center, facing the protective, glass shield, where a podium stood with a fixed microphone, convenient to address the extraterrestrials through a state-of-the-art PA system (public address).

The hooded figure removed the cowl with an extensive arm, and three, wiry prongs as fingers attached to the wrist, exposing the same face which had appeared on the monitor screens at GSW, prior to the spacecraft's landing in Grand City. Even close-up, and in person, it was gruesome, its flesh a grayish-brown of what appeared as a leathery texture.

"I am Zaal," it spoke in a monotone voice, which was amped through the loudspeakers, the voice carrying far out and across this specific area, even reaching the civilians one-quarter mile away. "We have come for Mamaron's children. "They are Koh, Jor, and Motatu. We await your compliance. But be warned: the wait is now wasting. You have but little time."

The president asked the crew, "What does that mean, is it a threat?"

Jillian spoke up, "Ah…Sir? Mr. President, that thing out there will try to destroy the entities it seeks. We've concluded that these beings are completely harmless to humans and that they— "

Ed interrupted aggressively, "These *beings* are the sole purpose this thing's here! Now, regardless whether they're friendly or not, we simply can't harbor them from these creatures. It'll be an act of war! And suicide!"

"How do we find these beings they seek?" the president asks for advice.

"That's our biggest problem," Ed said. "We understand they've achieved hosts, which makes it near to impossible to isolate them. There're tens of thousands of people in this area, alone… It'll take months, maybe a year or two, to find these clever, little…aliens."

The president had an idea, as he said to the colonel, "Can you put me some sound out there?"

"Yes, sir." Colonel Gordon switched on the radio hand mike and handed it to the president, who then spoke into it, "Zaal, we cannot locate them, to hand them over to you. We will need more time to try and find them. They have hosts, which would make it difficult for our science-equipment to determine who they are.

Otherwise, we are *not* trying to protect them from you."

Zaal said in a stoical fashion, "Are you the leader?"

The president looked to the crew for assistance on what to reply; Ed nodded to him, a gesture that he gives an honest statement, which the president did. "I'm the President," he said. "Yes, I'm the leader."
"Then it is your decision," Zaal said. "We can find them, even if they are cloaked."

While Zaal was speaking the terms on which they would search, Susan said quietly to Jillian, "I'm assuming cloaked means host, is the interpretation."

Grimness had settled over Susan, and Jillian long before now; as it had been such a hard struggle to convince anyone of significant importance to give their theories a fighting chance. They only had established a personal communication with the aliens, that day along the cliff wall. This was such a heart-wrenching moment for both.

Zaal was saying to the president, "Grant us the use or our devices to locate the children of Mamaron. They will not escape Zaal, nor will we interfere with your life functions."

The president was concerned. He needed reassurance that Zaal fully understood their life-habits, the freedom to come and go as they choose. "What method will you apply to find these aliens? You must not harm our citizens...", Zaal spoke in a raised voice, in the tone of impatience, "No one of your species will be harmed, only the ones protecting the children of Mamaron!"
"Oh, my god," Jillian murmured. "They're going to sacrifice those innocent, little girls."

Ed had overheard the ladies' concerns, as he replied uncaringly snide, "You can't make an armlet without breaking a few eggs."

Zaal was speaking to reassure the president, "You have only to know that our devices are called the "Locator." It has never failed us. Be assured, you will not be harmed!"

Ed assisted the president's decision, saying to him, "Sir, we have no choice."

"Granted," the president said without hesitation.

That stunned most of the civilian gathering, as they began booing and jeering emphatically over the cold-hearted decision by their president. Some of them instantly became teary-eyed; others hung their heads in a grievous silence.

Chelsea stood amid her media cohorts, taking in everything by their negotiating president, and that *thing* from that god-awful spaceship, while filming the event. She was so desperate to get word to the girls, but she didn't see any way possible to do so. Jim Placket was out of pocket. He was nowhere at the scene. He mentioned to her, a while back, about going out of town to meet a possible girlfriend from his high-school days. Chances are, he took that trip; he just hadn't returned.

A gentleman in some sports jacket and slacks approach her from behind and tapped her on the shoulder, as she was filming the *strange visitor from another planet*, and the spaceship.

"Chelsea," he said.

She paused the video camera and looked around—

A familiar face beamed at her.

"Ben!" she said, smiling pleasantly.

He was Ben Sullivan, a long-time news anchor person on her team from way back. He hadn't changed much; still in good physical shape, average height and build, mid-forties.

He smiled, "So, what brings you out here, nothing else more important, or newsworthy?"

He was exactly the way she remembered him; always the sarcastic jokester. "How've you been?" he said.

She laughed, "Just fine, and you?"

"Oh, I'll do, in a pinch," he replied in soft humor. His news team was just across the way, to the left. They were busy doing a live broadcast at the scene.

Since Chelsea was without her crew, she got an idea of a possible way to get word to the Angels, only they must be in a position to either listen on the radio or watching television. Or, maybe, they'd be fortunate to receive her message by word-of-mouth. "Ben, do you mind if I appear briefly as a special guest on your broadcast?"

Ben never shunned a good friend.

"Why, certainly," he made welcome. "You just come right over. We could use a little expertise."

That made her blush with gratitude as he escorted over to his mobile broadcast unit. Once in readiness to start broadcasting, she realized she was being monitored by government officials, as well as local authorities. The president had agreed on a correlation with the alien Zaal; anything she may say to breach that agreement could jeopardize the safety of this community... the world, in fact.

She was given the signal to go live by the director, "And five, four, three, two…" he pointed to her.

"This is Chelsea Freeman, live at the site of the spaceship, which landed only several hours ago…"

She continued broadcasting, at the same time gathering clever thoughts in hopes that the Angels would somehow receive her message.

In homes, and in public accommodations downtown, where there were TV sets activated for viewing; the face and voice of the popular news lady, Chelsea Freeman, were on screen live, and in person. She cleverly collaborated her message with the wary situation at hand, as she went on to stress, "As of now, authorities have no leads on locating the missing orphans…"

In homes, and public places where televisions were on, Chelsea's final announcement came over the airways, "So, stay safe my little darling *angels,* wherever you are. The authorities are your *locator*, and will *find* you, soon."

When she had finished, she took a breath in hope that her message was received in the manner it was meant; and that the Angels did receive it.

She looked over the area, and toward the military strong hole for a long, concerned moment. No sign of interest in her broadcast was prevalent.

She relaxed.

The spaceship sent out army-size robotic-like troops through a wider hatch. They instantly went airborne with the aid of some rocket-like packs attached to their backs and were armed with those strange weapons that looked like M-60 machineguns.

It was an unholy sight, as the many space troopers passed over the military strong hole, and the host of civilians, who gazed in rapt apprehension.

The chill of an impending doom coursed through Chelsea as she watched in vague hope that this incorrigible event would past without the smallest severity. But that didn't appeal to her as the faintest possibility. The passage of those alien soldiers was so massive in density they created such a deep, dense shadow that temporarily blocked out the bright sunlight.

The colonel in command of operations, along with Ed, section chief of the FBI, was suddenly in a state of unrest. It was no secret. Susan and Jillian realized the two manly men showed signs of fear in their compromised stamina; that maybe the president's decision was an act of desperation. Even the president himself now looked-on in recognition that he may have just made a fatal mistake.

"My god," he murmured, gaping in horrid second thoughts while watching the immensity of alien troops pass overhead, causing sunlight to flicker, and flutter through the brief, occasional windows in their shadowy passing. "What have I done?"

Some of the low-flying robotic-like aliens caused many of the civilians to act involuntarily by ducking their heads while swatting at them as if they were giant, annoying flies. Ed, the colonel, and the president were open for suggestions. From anyone.

Susan and Jillian remained silent. There was nothing they could suggest, at this stage. It was out of hand; now at the mercy of the aliens, and their massive space vessel.

Chelsea, while looking on in horror, had an idea out of desperation. She requested from Ben another shot at broadcasting a final, outright call to the Angels. And she was correct in thinking it wouldn't matter to the great leaders of this Country, which is now, perhaps, under siege. She was granted permission to broadcast by her long-time friend; and once again, she went live on the air, "Angels, wherever you are, the situation here is extremely suspect. I'm sure you know what's going on out here; it very much concerns you..."

Someone walking in the mobile broadcast unit surprised her, in reaching over her shoulder during the middle of her broadcast. She looked around just as the interrupting person took over the broadcast mike before her, and learned it was Ed Milburn, the federal agent.

He leaned into the mike, and whispered desperately, "Angels, where, the devil, are you? Get your butts out here, will you? We need you!"

When he was finished, he withdrew, looking Chelsea in the eye without reservation. He was scared!

On the living-room floor at Brittany's house, she, Natalie, and the girls, Elise, Monique, and Wendy were lying on a large air mattress, covered with thick, soft, comfortable bedding, while scarcely watching television. Their main distractions were the plentiful snacks Brittany had provided in assortments, from Chinese dinners, pizzas, tacos to chips, candy, soft drinks, and cookies. And, to top it all off, ice cream.

The girls had chosen to visit with Brittany—much to her delight—just prior to the Dark things shadow being lifted earlier that morning. Natalie was already over at Brittany's, having spent the night. The ruckus that had everyone scampering about, during that time, had proven to have been a false alarm. The girls had stopped by only to courteously announce their final goodbye to their friends. But Brittany and Natalie had insisted they spend their final hours together by which Brittany had sponsored all the snacks, and the two, young twelve-year-old—Monique, and Elise—

simply couldn't resist such a generous invite. Brittany's mom and dad were in another part of the house and had never made themselves apparent to their guests the least bit—not even by simply passing through.

Wendy was the first who happened to look over at the big-screen TV before them and caught the very end of a news broadcast, the correspondent a female with a familiar face.

"Guys?" she said, getting their insincere attention a moment. "Isn't she that news-lady that was out to the foster home, and took pictures of us, that day? Ah, what's her name?"

Wendy thought a moment, then blurted, "Chelsea! Yes, that's it! Chelsea Freeman."

Then Chelsea said something that particularly jolted Wendy's recollection into realizing something she'd thought was only in a dream, as Chelsea was saying in closing, "...Angels, if we get through this, remember, I can help you..."

Wendy bounded to her feet, attentive to the end of Chelsea's broadcast. "It was *her!*" Wendy was suddenly enlightened, excitedly.

"What?" Monique asked, puzzled, staring up at Wendy, as she and Elise were sprawled on the comfortable air mattress with all the soft bedding and left-over snacks at their disposal.

"Never mind." Wendy was suddenly anxious to leave. "We better get going."

Elise, not understanding, "Why? We have nowhere to go, right now. This is fun!"

A creeping shadow veiled the already shadow-darkened living room, creating a deeper shadow-darkening, which was almost demanding of some light. The TV now glowing brightly, as if it was officially nightfall. Natalie got up, and went to the door, to have a look outside. But the instant she cracked open the door, and looked out; she abruptly closed the door, and whirled around, and was as pale as a sheet.

That got everyone wondering, as they froze in positions, glaring at the bedazzled girl leaned back against the door.

"Natalie?" Brittany was caught up in Natalie's bleak look of fright. Along with Brittany, the girls went to look out the door at what had startled Natalie so balefully. Natalie moved aside, still mildly traumatized, while Brittany opened the door for the rest to peer out, which they did. What they saw shook them as if they were witnessing the end of the world, from the sky, right out front of Brittany's home.

Chapter 32

The sky right out front of Brittany's home was blackened with a dense cluster of what resembled giant locus, brandishing strange weapons. They came in a monstrous-size swarm, swooping down in a horrifying attack, with those huge, odd-looking weapons opening fire on the girls.

Natalie and Brittany were so terrified, the two felt instantly faint, their stance instantaneously waddled, as they struggled to hold up with the girls, to this horrific, tenacious onslaught.

Wendy and the girls struck quickly with a massive spread of their powerful lasers, while still in their civvies. The wide-spread laser-blast bought them time to get into combat-readiness. During which, they quickly morphed into costumes to the marvel of Brittany, and Natalie, who looked-on in a fleeting instant to catch the girls' lightning-quick transformation, before they were hurled back into severe shock, frantically diving on the floor, covering themselves with the bedding on the air mattress. At the same time, there came a rumbling of footsteps down the stairs, in a mix of heavy, and light, though, both sets were extremely rapid, laced with fear.

It was Brittany's parents in an upheaval dash to get to safety. They ran by the girls under the covers on the air mattress, headed for the door. But once they opened the door, and discovered the violent uproar outside, Brittany's dad quickly slammed the door shut, as her mom and dad then hurriedly rambled through the kitchen, making their way for the basement door.

"Brittany! Brittany!" her mom took an instant to call to her only child. But, in getting no immediate response, her mom and dad rambled down the basement steps, seemingly disregarding their daughter. "I'm sure she's around someplace," her dad said in a hurried decision.

Outside, the girls had taken up a strategic stance against their morbid attackers, by forming a semi-circle out front, in Brittany's yard. As the vicious attack was thickly laid-on, the girls fought harder; and during that second wave of the vile assault, Elise/Koh, and Monique/Jor took to the air, to meet their violent aggressors head-on, to infiltrate the ranks of the metal-monster bug-creatures.

Wendy held down the fort, maintaining her turf, with constant, quick blasts with her lethal laser-eyes. She rotated in the fashion of a destructive whirlwind, laying down a field of fire upon the creatures, with deadly accuracy.

Elise/Koh and Monique/Jor were so accurate, the previously overwhelming swarm was soon reduced to a mere squad of remaining creatures, now without the will to continue the battle. They fled in terror of the children of Mamaron, to report back to their leader; but that effort was to be denied. The girls lit out after them with a burst of air-speed, just slightly less than the speed of light. The jet-propelled, metal-clad creatures didn't stand a ghost-of-a chance in a race against the children of Mamaron. It was simply an attempt at sheer futility. A few quick blasts of their lasers put an end to the Dark things fatal attempt with the use of its *Locator.* It might have worked in the old days. But the children of Mamaron has so much evolved, these days. Maybe someone should've told the Dark-thing that its ancient tactics are long outdated, during the fierce attack, its frivolous army was quickly defeated by the keepers of the Plains of Souls. The battle had been short-lived, with the Angels victorious, their strategy simply overwhelming. Their defensive methods were super-amazing; explosions outside had rattled the foundation of the sturdy-built home, sending small, ineffective tremors throughout the neighborhood.

During the immediate rush of a hush that settled in, it was almost spooky. The susurration of the unbelievably short battle still a recent, though, fading presence in the back of the mind.

To add to this incredulous, mystic morning, after the victorious battle, there were no traces left of the vehement attackers. Each strike from the girls' lasers had disintegrated their enemies, as there was no fall-out of any debris. They were absorbed into thin air. There was nothing to clean up, and the air was pure.

Wendy was first to re-enter the house, her expression doleful; then Elise, and Monique returned. They didn't appear pleased, or victorious, their masks solemn.

As Brittany, and Natalie crawled out from underneath the covers, holding the girls in their timid gazing, wanting reassurance that no harm would come to them; Wendy said in regret, "Brittany, Natalie, we're very sorry this had to happen here, at your home. We didn't expect it to happen like this. But the Dark-thing won't bother you again, or anyone else. We must leave now." Wendy then looked over at Monique, and Elise knowingly.

They knew what must be done. They each went over to Brittany, and Natalie and gave them little hugs. "It's been fun," Elise said. "We'll miss you guys."

That brought tears to both Brittany's and Natalie's eyes, as Elise sounded as if they were leaving, never to return.

"Will we ever see each other again?" Natalie sobbed lightly.

Monique, uncertain what to tell her, though, finally, she said, trying what little humor she could muster along with it, "Well...you might unless you keep your eyes closed if we come to visit."

That hardly got a snicker. It was more painful to Brittany than lift her spirit. It only reminded her just how much she'd miss Monique's witty jokes. She couldn't resist another little hug from Monique, kissing her lightly on the forehead. Monique smiled at her, which was the sweetest, purest smile...so captivating; and it made Brittany sad, at the same time. To watch them leave, perhaps, for the last time was heartbreaking.

"Your secret will always be safe with us," Brittany promised, including Natalie in her pact with the Angels.

"It doesn't really matter anymore," Monique said in rejoining Elise, and Wendy by the door.

"It's been nice, you guys," Wendy said as their final farewell.

As she and the girls were leaving out the door, with Brittany, and Natalie accompanying them; Brittany's parents appeared, having muddled out of the basement. The Angels were in costume, with Brittany, and Natalie nearby, as they all were paused nearly through the doorway.

"Brittany, who are your friends?" her mom asked, a puzzled look on both parents' faces. Her mom went on, unclear of this small mystery before her, "You'd think this is hardly the time for a costume party."

Brittany's dad agreed, "Yes, don't you kids know that there're aliens about? Didn't you hear all that explosion?"

Brittany was weary of her parents' negative attention-span. "Mom, dad...these *are* aliens. They're the Angels: My *friends.*"

"And mine," Natalie added.

Brittany's mom, a tittered laugh, "Oh, I beg your pardon."

Charles H. Woods
478

The Angels smiled at them politely, then Wendy said kindly to Brittany, and Natalie, "Hey, you guys, we have to be going."

Right before the couple's eyes, the Angels bolted through the doorway, two by air, and one by land. They were gone in a flash.

"My god!" Brittany's mom nearly fainted; her dad stood there, gaping in ardent apprehension as if they'd just now been alerted to this new reality.

When Zaal's storm troopers didn't return in the ample amount of time they should have; there came a concern disturbance in the atmosphere, emitting from the giant spaceship. It yielded a deep, earth-shaking rumble, with a portion of the ship's mass taking on a limpid, fiery reddish-bright orange glow.

Zaal became furiously angered. In male form, and walking upright like a human, he whirled around, away from the podium; and was caught up in the stretching, white light then zapped back aboard the space vessel.

A gulf of silence settled over everyone at the scene, with extreme, fearful suspect. No one knew what to expect; the wait was heart-throbbing. Fear was with everyone so great it was near paralyzing, as the immense gathering was rendered temporarily immobile, fervently afraid to utter a single word. Security tightened around the president, as he also stood like a statue, along with Ed, and the colonel.

Finally, an ecstatic roar from the host of civilians erupted suddenly.

Then a chanting in jubilation went forth from the crowd, "Angels! Angels! Angels..." They were here! The massive audience waved excitedly to the two which passed over them through the air; the Angel afoot ripped safely through the immense gathering just beneath the speed of light. It was like a breath of cool, fresh air in streaking colors of blue and white.

"Thank God!" Ed shamelessly vented his relief in front of the ladies, Jillian, and Susan; the colonel, and the president.

The ladies looked at one another, not quite forgiving.

The Angels softly landed on the platform of the podium, the Angel afoot, in breaking her great speed, materializing in full form, simultaneously, next to them.

A hush settled over everyone in rapt curiosity.

Wendy approached the microphone, Elise, and Monique standing by her on each side. She spoke boldly as herself, and Motatu. Sharing the same mind, same thoughts, and knowledge, "The Dark-thing must be destroyed..."

Her speech was abruptly cut short by an interruption of Zaal from inside the ship, his voice laced with ill-intent, deep, resounding, threatening, "You, the children of Mamaron, destroyed my droids. For that, you will pay."

Monique/Jor shouted, agitated, *"Shut up!* My sister was talking!"

The thing inside went silent, incredibly much to everyone's delight, and amazement, as they cheered briefly, gratifying their confidence in the Angels. Wendy continued, Motatu her inspiration, "We cannot allow the Dark-thing to reign in the galaxies any longer. This thing of evil is trying to conquer the universe, by destroying the Great Barrier. We are the children of Mamaron; let us fight with you! We will fight *for* you!"

At that intimidatingly bold statement, the enthralled audience's cheering erupted with staunch confidence in the

Angels, as once more the chanting rose extremely loud, *"ANGELS! ANGELS! ANGELS..."*

The president was leery of the Angels' devout commitment by second-guessing their, maybe hidden, agenda. He asked, after the chanting had subsided, trailing off to soft murmuring, "Excuse me...but it's clear to me to ask: Who, or what is Mamaron?"

Wendy turned and looked at the president through the protective glass and replied, "Perhaps you would prefer to call him God."

Jillian and Susan gasped, astounded beyond the imagination. Jillian: "Oh, my God! They *are* angels!"

Chelsea had made her way close to the podium, drawing little attention from Ed, Susan, and Jillian, and the colonel. The president, not knowing her position on this matter, was indifferent. The girls—Angels—showed no recognition of her, until she moved closer to Wendy and said softly, "I'm happy that you girls are here. I can help you."

Wendy was suddenly made aware of who she was, quickly turning her head to look Chelsea in the eye. "You!" Wendy said, distracted momentarily.

During the minor distraction, the quiet revving of the alien craft's engine started the huge saucer-base to move with a gradual rotation, then rapidly gaining momentum. Right at lift-off, the shaft of white light jotted from the ship's base, extending its reach all the way to the podium, where the girls were standing, paying regard to Chelsea.

Motatu shouted, "Watch out! The locator beam—"

Instantly, the girls returned fire. It was such a huge retaliation that their blazing, laser-explosions shook the earth underneath everyone on hand. The crowd began to disperse in a melee of fear and confusion; camping gear was toppled, beach-chairs lawn-chairs, ice chests, beverage spilled, as pandemonium gained momentum.

The gradually departing spaceship returned fire, bringing the military in full force on defense. Fighter jets launched devastating missiles against the vehement foe, though, with little effects. But the Angels were on hand, giving fighter-pilots assistance, much to the flyers delight. One pilot held up his thumb to the glass canopy of his aircraft as a salute to Angel Jor/Monique. She waved back with a burst of air-speed, ripping passed to another opposing target, as the air was filled with smaller, alien aircraft.

But with the mighty forces of the military, along with the all-powerful Angels; although the fighting was devastatingly fierce, it never got out of hand.

Below, Wendy/Motatu took care of protecting the populace with her own defensive strategy, as the wild, scrambling melee heightened. In deploying her super foot-speed, she amazingly formed a protective barrier made up of her own molecules at such fantastic, unimaginable speed; she weaved the area under a mass of such an invincible shield, like a spider weaving its web. And she was also watchful of intermediate firing from those alien-fighter crafts by alertly firing her deadly lasers whenever one got too close.

As it eventually became seemingly a stand-off, with no one gaining an advantage, the Angels a flight flew down to Wendy with a probable solution to end this tenacious, no-win situation.

Koh spoke, "There's no way we can defeat the Dark-thing, with all these innocent lives at state. We must take the fight to outer space. Win, lose, or draw, it's the only way to secure the lives on this planet."

In the mass confusion, with military personnel scrambling around him, Ed happened to be passing through the area, where Wendy/Motatu had just completed the final lap in forming the protective shield. He overheard Koh's conversation with Motatu/Wendy. He could do no more than to drop his head in remorse and move on.

Wendy said to Elise, "The two of you can't handle it alone; you need me..."

"But you don't fly. You'll be safer here. Don't worry, we'll handle it," Elise asserted, then flashed back to the sky.

"Nooo! No!" Wendy shouted, abruptly heartbroken because she couldn't leap up after her. It wasn't then simple.

Elise/Koh joined Monique/Jor in battle. They were swift, and agile in their combat skills, zapping enemy spacecraft at will, using those deadly lasers from their cat eyes.

"We'll have to finish this far out there, in outer space," Koh/Elise said to them. "It's too risky to remain here; everyone's in danger. We must consider our friends."

"I know," Monique/Jor agreed.

As the Angels hit a burst of speed, ripping past the many fighter jets, to the pilots' bewilderment, they were witnessed slamming into the massive mother ship, just before it jumped to light-speed. When it did, to escape, to fight a continuous battle, the Angels were right behind it with yet another burst of speed, which was unmatched by the fleeing mammoth craft.

"Holy cow!" one pilot shouted over the radio to his fellow pilots. "Did any of you see that? Those flying kids are amazing!"

Sporadic reports came in, verifying eyewitness accounts, "Blue Leader to Comrade-One: I saw it. But I feel for those Angels; they're taking an awful chance."

Another pilot came over the radio, "Why don't we just pray for them?"

That got an abundance of, "Roger that."

After the vast spaceship, had disappeared beyond the earth's atmosphere, along with the Angels hot on its tail; the fight on Earth was over, as the airways began to quieten in the aftermath of a near *world* war with aliens.

Within the settling of the short-lived violent attack, Chelsea moved up beside Wendy, getting her shallow attention, as she was lost in thought of having lost her most precious family in Monique and Elise.

Chelsea's first words were gentle, caring, "I can still help. We can work through this."

Wendy looked at her vacantly, through teary eyes; and it was plain for Chelsea to understand that, at this point, nothing mattered to Wendy. Chelsea gave her a light, gentle, concern, little squeeze around the shoulders, and remained right by her side, lamenting along with the child.

Finally, Wendy moved clear of everyone around her who were there to marvel at her heroic defensive stand against a potential space invader. She wanted to be alone; no consolation remarks, no sentimental touching. *Nothing.* She stood alone, with plenty space around her, near the landing place of that giant space vessel. The more time lapsed, the angrier, despondent she became. The void now inside her began to progress to an intolerable level.

She couldn't envision the loss of her only sisters, and neither could Motatu, who said to her just above a whisper, "Go, Wendy. I'm not afraid."

With others looking-on from a short distance, Wendy let out a yell at the top of her lungs, to the urgency to fly, "AHHHHH!"

She then flashed at top speed, with everyone looking on, then leaped into the air, and getting away like a missile, bolting high into the atmosphere, disappearing among the unlit stars, for now.

Chelsea understood through teary-eyes. She had the confidence that the three, little Angels would, at last, be together. And, yes, they were indeed, three, darling little angels; and no one, or nothing will ever separate them.

But here, they will be missed.

Epilogue

Space: an unexplored territory.

Wendy persevered, though, she was lost, flying blind while striving to follow what cosmic dust a giant spaceship might leave behind if any at all. Bright stars were about her and were spread to points of infinity everywhere she looked. Her speed was incredibly fast, streaking through dangerous asteroid belts; comets flying by like bullets shot out of high-powered rifles. And stars, millions upon millions of stars. Everywhere there were stars!

No sign of the spaceship carrying her sisters—the four of them. How were they getting along? Were they in pain, restriction, fear? Did they figure she'd come after them, or would they make the supreme sacrifice?

Regardless of what they were feeling; so long as they didn't give up. Wendy was determined to track Zaal and his fleeting spaceship to the end of time. Without her sisters, there was nothing more important left for her. This could be her lifelong journey.

She hit the afterburners and jetted away with, yet, increasing speed, streaking among the stars, and whatever else outer space had for her to encounter. She was relentless, with no quit in her. Among a cluster of stars ahead, a foreign object was faint in the distance, emitting an obtuse, rustic glow, oddly outstanding from any star. As Wendy drew nearer, the object began to appear more definite as some type of vessel moving along at a steady clip.

The Dark-thing, Wendy assumed, and she was correct. It was moving toward the barrier of the Plains of Souls. A horrific vortex was dead ahead of the two of them. It was the gateway into another dimension.

Charles H. Woods
486

Motatu said to Wendy, "Should you successfully pass through the gateway, beyond the barrier; you may never return to Earth in your solid form."

That was severely concerning. But if it was the only way to save her sisters, then, perhaps, they should accept the humble survival. Besides, on Earth, who really cared that three orphans were missing? They were probably forgotten, by now. They never belonged to anyone who cared. Foster care was only a duty provided by the state to generate funds for its employees.

Wendy thought of sedating herself into acceptance of a survival inside an eternal abyss if it wasn't for her tenacious will to fight. She'd made the journey through many pitfalls, from nine-years-old 'till now. This was the first day of the rest of her existence; and she nor her sisters were going to spend the rest of their lives—which could become a bright, promising future—in a gloomy outer space.

Motatu said to Wendy, "The vortex is just beyond the mist, straight ahead." The nebula Motatu spoke of was a misty belt of colorful spectrums, much like that of an aurora. Strange, yet beautifully formidable.

Wendy caught up to the dark, space contraption, as its speed was no match to hers. To penetrate the hull, however, was another issue. The Dark-thing was an impenetrable mass of collective energy, only accessible by its transporter beam, known as the *Locator.*

Wendy flew circles around the behemoth vessel in search of a possible breach of any kind in the invincible hull. No luck. The thing was impervious to damage. After all, it was the Dark-thing, a composite of pure evil and raw, unbridled energy. Wendy had to figure another way, which she did.

"Wendy," Motatu warned her. "Watch out for the droids. The ship manufactures them." Wendy, beaming with confidence, "I'm counting on it."

In a dark holding place inside the ship, the girls, Elise/Koh, and Monique/Jor were being kept inside a sickly glowing cage-like confinement, about the size of a single jail cell. The entire encasement pulsated a weak, greenish-yellow hue, with the girls sitting together on the floor, center the cage, with their legs tucked underneath their thighs, unmoving.

Their immobility, in the manner of which they remained dead still, was a peculiar, remarkable sight. They were framed within the sickly glowing hue like some specimens on display for public viewing. But there was a reason behind it.

"Are we prisoners to sit here forever?" Monique was weary, frighten, and...a wee bit hungry.

Jor said, as a reminder, "If you try to break out, the forcefield we're under will match whatever strength you apply. And it'll be painful because it'll reflect the amount in reverse what you'll need to free yourselves."

A take: "Did that make sense?"

"Jor, this is no time to be facetious," Monique said, not daring to move a muscle. "We gotta figure a way out of this."

"Are we being kept here because of our fears?" Elise asked. "Because, what if we stop being afraid, and just...work through what pain it may cause?"

Koh spoke, "You wanna take that chance? We're extremely powerful; you demonstrated that during the droid attack. Do you want to exact all that power on yourselves?"

Elise went silent.

Monique said to Jor out of hindsight, "Boy, when you once told me that we might face real fear; you weren't kidding."

Elise said in recollection also, "But you did say, too, that it wasn't impossible, that we could overcome it, right?"

"True," Koh said but with very little civility, for this was an extremely dark situation. The Dark-thing really was a *Dark Thing!*

Armed droids filed out of the transporter-beam in hordes, instantly opening fire on Wendy/Motatu, putting her lightning-quick reflex to the ultimate test.

She tried to look beyond the wall receiving the greenish-yellow hue through the porthole. But upon visual contact with the interior behind the wall, it was like a trigger mechanism suddenly set off a high-voltage shockwave that violently propelled Wendy backward for several feet, slamming her viciously against the opposite wall made of some type of strange, durable alloy.

She shook off the stunning effect immediately, got to her feet,   trying   to   determine   her   next   move.

"I should've warned you," Motatu said. "This vessel is armed with defensive systems all over. Any attack against them will create a reverse reaction. Success can be achieved, but you must be careful how you approach your targets."

"Thanks for warning me about the booby traps, Motatu; I never would've thought of that," Wendy quipped with dry humor.

"Sorry, Wendy. I thought you knew," Motatu said. Then, after a moment of serious thinking, she replied honestly, "Wendy, there are no *"boobies"* on this ship."

Wendy laughed, "Forget it."

Motatu suddenly realized something of extreme importance. "Wendy...that's it!" she shouted.

Wendy got excited, "What's it, boobies?"

"The light," Motatu insisted. "When you looked through the wall, you must've, somehow, attacked the light shining through the porthole, to the other side. Which means they're in a restricting chamber on the other side of that wall."

Wendy shouted, "My sisters! We gotta get them out!"

Motatu correctively, "Our sisters."

Wendy cocked her arms back over her shoulders, anxious to smash through the wall before them.

"Wendy, wait," Motatu objected to Wendy's reckless abandon. "Remember...the light? Destroy the modem, it's the source!"

Wendy, without hesitation, trusting Motatu's advice, fired a blast of lasers from her eyes, striking the modem above her dead center. The ensuing explosion shook the ship. Wendy moved quickly out of range of falling debris, with a deadly mix of glowing, hot, shooting sparks.

Suddenly, there was a deep, ferocious, thundering rumble from the other side of the wall. Wendy feared the worse, critically assuming the girls were trapped in the huge explosion, under restriction.

But then the wall collapsed under a tremendous strain, spewing shards of heavy debris, plumes of dense, white phosphorous clouds into the air of the surrounding space. Finally, two misshapen figures took shape, emerging through the phosphorous clouds that gradually dissipated. The images became full forms as Monique, and Elise, a little shaken but alive and well.

The instant their eyes met, Elise, and Monique ran to Wendy, ecstatically shouting, "Wendy!"

"Wendy!"

They joined in an overly elated group hug—which included Motatu, Koh, and Jor. They held hands and danced in a circle, mimicking the children's game, *Ring-around-the roses.* Then they group-hugged once more, enthralled over being back together.

Elise spoke while lightly wiping tiny bits of moisture from her glad eyes, "How'd you get here?"

"How'd you find us?" Monique asked, while both girls not letting go their arms from around Wendy's tiny waist.

Elise spoke then "You came for us. It doesn't matter how you got here."

Monique couldn't get over the joy of Wendy standing heroically before them. And Wendy was happy to announce, with a smug look on her face, "I simply flew here."

The blithe celebration was short-lived, as the ship's defensive systems took hold; and the vehement vessel became a *living thing.* The solid floors began to buckle under foot, churning, undulating, with sudden tentacles reaching up through the now fleshy texture inconsistency of the floors.

"This thing means to destroy us," Motatu made them aware. "We have to leave quickly! But remember, don't destroy anything until we're off the ship."

The girls stuck together during their race through the bowels of the deep, shadow-darkened space vessel. Creatures of hideous forms, with deadly, venomous fangs lurched at them.

The girls' quickness in reflex, flashing through the deadly gauntlet of vile creatures was successful. But the malign ship itself was their biggest enemy. Corridors rose to become beasts of enormous size, to devour the girls at their slightest mistake in trying to evade them. A dark opening lay straight ahead once they rounded a corner through yet another darkened tunnel. It looked hopeless for the girls to gain victory over these evil-intent passageways.

They ceased their useless attempts to further try and escape. Instead, Wendy held them up near the entrance of an adjoining corridor, where deep within was pitch black. The floor where they stood was solid, as the notorious Dark-thing had yet to contaminate that area with its ghoulish fiends.

"We could keep running through here for the rest of our lives," Wendy concluded, lightly catching a breath while accomplishing her second wind. "We won't get anywhere. I say we stand and fight."

"But everything backfires," Monique pointed out. "If we strike here, we'll be at risk."

"I say, if we strike altogether with one quick blast, we could completely blow this thing to Hades," Wendy suggested, having grown weary of wild goose chasing. The girls looked at one another. Neither seemed eager to risk blowing themselves up.

Then Motatu shed some light on the grim situation, "That could work. But it would have to be precise. We are equipped with the power to destroy an entire solar system. We should each face opposite the other and let go of the blast at the exact same time.

The repercussion should through us free, like a slingshot."

No one made a comment, not even Jor or Koh. It remained quiet.

Finally, a disturbing outcry thundered along the corridors, filling each wing of the giant ship with an enormous shrill that carried the threat of death in its monstrous-sounding resonance.

"It's Zaal," Motatu said. "It's been resurrected to do the will of the Dark-thing. He will succeed if we don't destroy him now. He will return to your Earth and destroy it for his own pleasure. We must strike now; it's what we do. It is why we exist."

No one still uttered a word. But it became clear to Wendy and the girls where Motatu, Koh, and Jor stood on the matter. It was no second-guessing; their special powers and abilities spoke for themselves. They had a purpose: born to stand against evil.

And now, so were the girls: Elise.   Monique. Wendy.

It was time to act. Zaal was coming, rejuvenated. Powerful, the eyes in the dark mask seething, bright red-glowing embers. His huge form tall, imposing. Ominous. His increased monstrous size, in his atrocious, baleful, overshadowing approach, dwarfed the girls' meager stand before him as if they were mere insects.

The girls took up positions, facing away from each other in a small circle. Each one took a breath, and they held hands. Zaal was approaching, deeply disturbing sounds of unseen horror accompanied him, the ship becoming more alive around them.

"If it's gotta be like this, I'm glad we're together," Monique said as her final testament.

Wendy said, "I love you guys. And I always will." Her announcement held, what felt like to the girls, a future promise.

"We love you, too, Wendy." Elise's reply was with some reservation, as she'd cocked her head a little to the side, trying to read into Wendy's statement, thinking, *did she expect we'll survive this?*

They went perfectly still in a dead silence, facing away from each other, gripping hands, their breathing shallow, anticipating. A pulsating sound coming from within the ship in the rhythmic pattern of a giant heartbeat.

Thump! Thump! Thump!

The girls' eyes took on a highly intense blue glare. Normally, their laser eyes were either a red glow or yellow glow—depending on the measure of defense they wish to exact against an attacker, the red glow being the most potent between the two.

The blue laser was the ultimate weapon, isolated. Its destructive power immeasurable. It couldn't be summoned for menial defensive tasks, only as the last result in an inescapable defensive stand, like now. But the risk of self-destruction loomed ever so large.

Their eyes took on a molten-intense, ultra-bright blue, like burning clear blue crystals, with the ship's death threat rapidly closing on them. Zaal was upon them, about to pronounce his inconceivable revenge on the Angels... so close... A sudden eruption.

The ship imploded from inside, sending out an extremely potent, violent, bright blue flare that was blinding to the eye for miles into outer space.

The violent tremor from the massive destruction shook, almost, the earth's core. It generated heavy winds instantaneously, scattered storms, which lasted only briefly; and small, ineffective earth tremors in isolated areas, such as the desert, virtual vacant countryside. No major injuries were sustained, just a great scare among a wide-spread populace.   The brave little girls had held fast together but were violently separated during the cataclysmic explosion. They were flung clear out into deep space, stunned beyond consciousness, though, unscathed. But they were out cold, idly adrift in the bleak, pitch blackness of outer space.

Finally, the girls began to regain consciousness, though, disoriented. They shook off the tumultuous effect, suddenly realizing they were alive, but...*lost.*

That was a horror in itself. Each of them felt totally alone, adrift in outer space, with perpetual darkness all around them. But each didn't accept this undeserving solitude as their final victory.

The Dark-thing had been destroyed; they had successfully completed this mission in the fight against evil.

This grim reward was unacceptable.

Motatu spoke to Wendy, on the alert, "Wendy, shockwaves...they're coming. Look!"

Wendy looked around in the darkness—

Oh, my god!

She only had an instant to respond. A tidal wave of a brightly glowing, massive cloud was rapidly spreading directly toward her. A burst of ultrasonic speed and she was gone, jetting through the blackness of space. The shockwave, tsunami-size, right on her heels. A glance back at the closing-in. Too close. Another burst of speed. She was off!

Two more speeding figures closing in on each side of her. At a glance to each side…

A gaping grin.

Elise and Monique had caught up to her, Monique yelling, "GO! GO! GO! GO! GO!"

Elise, seriously concerned, shouting, "Fly, Wendy, *FLY!*"

Wendy announced, "I am! I'm flying!" And she was, ripping right alongside them.

The dangerous tidal-shock-wave steady closing, the girls' stunning costumes a searing glow in the shock wave's fiery blue light.

Monique screamed, "*FASTER!*"

At the present, ripping speed they traveled—the violent shock wave right up on them, steady closing—it would appear they didn't have any more *fuel* left in the tank.
The fleeting, enchanted trio hit yet another burst of speed, and simply vanished far into the distance of dark, and starry, endless universe.

Days, weeks, months and nearly a year passed ...

Grand City was back to the state of normality. The consensus had the Angels having served their purpose here on Earth and had gone back to Heaven. Ridiculous? The children felt that way, which was the only way they could accept the idea that the Angels were no longer with them.

Brittany and Natalie made the adjustment guardedly. Since they were older than most of the kids who'd encountered the Angels, they were more in tune with what had happened to their three, personal friends. Though, death was never the assumption; it might as well had been. Outer space was a long way from here— even if you could fly.

Jillian and Susan took everything in stride.

They were still a special influence on their jobs at GSW. They were professional and would continually keep an eye out on the universe. Ed was retired...

Lamented a lot...

A shopping mall, now under construction, replaced Lily Field Foster Home. Chelsea was struck the hardest by the Angels' departure. At first, she would admit, the primary reason for her sole interest in the girls was strictly selfish and personal. She'd wanted to gloat to the world her brilliant achievement with a life, and up-close interview with *real* aliens from outer space.

This global revelation would have put an end to the hundreds of thousands of rumors about aliens, whether government coverups or that they existed here on Earth. But during the waning days of the relentless pursuit of her unimaginable dream, she had an overt change of heart. Even though no one, other than herself, knew the truth of her personal greed, the deep-seated guilt got the best of her emotions, and her maternal instinct.

She'd wrapped up her news broadcast for the evening and was leaving out the studio. After the cameras were shut down, people began moving about in the manner of leaving for home. Custodians had begun their cleaning duties, bringing their mop pails, brooms, and garbage bags.

Chelsea had made it to the elevators, having pushed the down-button, and was waiting. A few late stragglers showed up to wait with her, fashionably dressed, a couple of older gentlemen, two more ladies, a redhead, and a brunette, mature-age.

When the elevator arrived, and the door opened, no one was on it. Chelsea waited aside while the others started boarding, her mind somewhat adrift. But as she realized everyone was aboard except her; she started for the elevator, but was halted by a small, female voice that called softly to her.

"Chelsea? Miss Chelsea Freeman?"

Who in the world? She couldn't imagine, and looked around...

Wendy, Elise, and Monique stood only a few feet behind her, in the hallway, next to the elevator. And they were dressed in regular civvies, looking lively, with a bit of shyness in their eyes.

Chelsea nearly came apart at the seam, she was so elated to see the special, little darlings.

Enamored over them having returned so alive, and safe, she couldn't help seizing them in a generous, victorious, loving...bear-hug, gathering the three in one wide-spread grab, her purse dangling loosely by the long, leather straps, about midway her arm.

She wouldn't have cared if it had slipped off her arm, onto the floor.

"Oh, my stars," she exclaimed. "It's so wonderful that you're back!"

Monique, up to her old jokes, "Please, ma'am. Don't ever say stars again. We were up to our arm-pits with them. They were *everywhere!*"

Chelsea looked at Monique, impressed, as she replied laughingly, "You should be so lucky. It isn't any day that a person like me can take off to the stars; *you can fly.*"

Monique grinned, a bit pompous, "True."

Wendy said to Chelsea on a serious note, "Miss Chelsea, you said you could help us. Well, we could sure use some help…"

Monique showed no humility. "Like right now." And she held Chelsea accountable in her intent stare at her.

Chelsea thought Monique was so adorable, her petite size, along with her, sometimes, unbridled honesty, was what dubbed her as such a sweetheart. Not that Elise wasn't; the three of them were more precious than gold and deserved a better chance at life than what they'd been getting, thus far. And Chelsea was willing to give it her best to see to it they got their chance.

"Well, girls," she was delighted to inform them. "You've come to the right person. Your chariot awaits. So, if you'll just follow me."

Elise was dumbfounded. "Are you serious?"

The elevator had returned, empty again; and as they were getting on, Chelsea reassured them, bringing up the rear, "Why don't I just show you how serious I am?"

She took out of her purse a legal document of adoption and handed it to Wendy.

Wendy suddenly shrieked in reading it, "Oh, my goodness! Look at this, guys!" She held the document to the girls' eye-level; and at a glance, they went spiraling into an emotional bliss, as Chelsea made clear a personal promise,

"And, it's my solemn promise you'll have a home of your own. and you'll never be separated..."

The girls exploded in jubilation, like a small flock of frolicking robins. Chelsea was hugged more times within that short span of an elevator ride than she could account for, at any other given time....

She felt their warm, snug embracing so alive, and *real...* Then someone was calling to her in a gentle voice.

"Chelsea? Chelsea, wake up."

A soft nudging on her shoulder. "Chelsea, wake up."

Chelsea awoke to meteorologist Torrance Carpenter, a black American, standing before her. She'd dozed off with her head cushioned on her folded arms on her desk, in the broadcast studio. It was shortly after shutting down, and she was among the last few of the news team to leave for home. It was as she became fully awake when she realized the grueling week of work had left her emotionally drained, and physically exhausted. But in a lady-like poise, and graceful fashion only Chelsea could manage without it appearing in an embarrassing situation; she calmly replied, after a slight yawn, "Sorry about that. Thanks, Torrance."

Torrance said caringly, "You should get some rest. You look beat."

"Oh, I am," Chelsea admitted while getting her things together.

Only a short while ago, she thought she'd left for home. And the girls... they were so vivid in her dream. It had been close to one year since they were here. She was having a rough time keeping them out of her dreams.

Part of it was a guilty conscience; the other part was that she loved them, and now missed them.

She was on her way home, this time wide awake, taking in the shallow traffic, city lights, and bright neon signs in the dead of night. The sky was starry, other than pitch black. Off to the western hemisphere, a cluster of stars was bright...

Then she noticed three shooting stars, right at that moment, streak across the heavens in sort of an unusual pattern. They were tightly close together, unlike something she'd ever known about shooting stars. Meteorites don't fall in such a united order.

Chelsea watched the meteorites to their vanishing point somewhere along the horizon. They appeared to have fallen not impossibly too far away. From her vantage point, maybe just a few miles outside the city. Since she was now wide awake, and nowhere to go but home, she thought why not take a short drive *out there?*

She'd been driving along the secondary road for more than an hour, headed in the direction she last saw the meteorites. It was beginning to appear that the farther out she drove, the farther she had to go before reaching the point the meteorites seemed to have fallen.

Finally, she decided she'd driven far enough, and pulled to the side of the road, to turn around. The memory of the girls from so long ago, now, an ebbing susurration in the back of her mind, rendering her to realize she must forget the past because it was still a might painful.

She backed off the road, onto a portion of a gravel road intersecting the main highway then headed back to town. Along the way, she couldn't shake, even the clouded memories that were etched in her mind of the three orphans, the way they appeared on posters, and fliers. Now a day, their age-worn pictures on long-standing posters, and fliers having lost most of the luster of their cuteness, and innocent charm.

In the dead of night, Johnathan, a retired farmer, was on his way home after a late agricultural meeting at a friend's house a few miles down the secondary road Chelsea had traveled. He was an older man, gentle in nature, with white, weedy hair, and he smoked a pipe.

He was motoring right along in his rustic, jalopy pickup, being the only traffic traveling along that stretch of highway that late at night. The only thing to be mindful of was an occasional, wild animal crossing the road, like a coyote, or jackrabbit, things of that nature.

Slightly up ahead, the headlight-beams made readable on a roadside sign to the right, Grand City 25 mi. Not that much farther. He was awake and alert. No problem.

Then, suddenly, something flashed in the headlights, a small, standing-up-right figure—like a small person. It darted off to the side of the road, just as the old guy swerved away, slamming on the brakes.

The old pickup teetered a bit then was brought under control, and to a halt opposite side of the road. As the old man got out to check to see if he'd hit something; he saw three young girls on the other side of the road, in the middle of nowhere, in the dead of night, seemingly, just walking along. But they were languid, their clothes shabby, dirty, as if they been wallowing in some dirt pit. Oddly, they were a mess.

They held up, staring at the old man; and, to him, they appeared disoriented. Just a little way behind from which they'd come, the old guy did recall seeing a relatively large hole in the ground, off to the right. And the color of the dirt in the hole was the same as was on the girls' clothing.

They hardly gave him any further regard as they lethargically moved along passed him and the pickup. They moved in sort of a muddle fashion as if they weren't certain where they were.

"Would you girls be needing a ride into town?" Johnathan felt so much pity for the three minors. They had no business being this far out from civilization. And in his wildest imagination, he couldn't come close to understanding how, or why they'd managed to end up this far away from everything.

The three girls showed no resistance to the old man's kind offer; they just moved to the back of the pickup and climbed into the empty, metal bed, dirty, ragged clothes, and all. The old man got back in the truck, behind the wheel, closed the door and drove away.

Chelsea hardly completed her slumber from last night's dozing off in the news studio. When she got home, she stayed awake almost until dawn. When she was ready for a nap, it was time to report to work. She got there sluggish, lacking energy it would take to finish the day. Before starting her editorial, she refreshed her third cup of coffee, sat down at her desk, in her private office...

And the phone rang on her desk. She grabbed it: "Hello?"

It was Loretta Pruitt on the other end. "Miss Freeman, this is Loretta Pruitt. I'm here at the hospital with Miss Stanfield from the adoption agency..."

Chelsea was suddenly wide-eyed awake at a rush of incredible excitement while listening to what Loretta Pruitt had to say over the phone.

"Yes, go on."

Chelsea's heart race with mixed emotions. She didn't know whether to weep tears of joy or sank in despair over what was unclear to her, right now.

"Will they be all right? Ah, yes, of course, I'll be right there."

Chelsea hung up the phone, after having been told the girls' situation looked critical. She then left right away, in a huge rush, her heart beating frantically, her pulse racing. She couldn't believe her girls were back! She was told some old guy had found them wandering alongside the highway last night, late; and that he'd brought them straight to the nearest hospital, where they were now in the hands of doctors. During this crucial time, it didn't matter whether they were the Angels still; Chelsea was so pleased they'd returned, after all this time.

When Chelsea arrived at the hospital, she was directed up to the IC unit, where Miss Pruitt and Miss Stanfield were waiting in the small waiting area, darkly clad, solemn. It immediately raised a question of concern to Chelsea.

"How are they doing?" she asked, her heart sank into a dismal mode.

Miss Pruitt, not too optimistic, replied, "Not good, I'm afraid. The doctor is in with them now."

The double doors to the Intensive Care Unit opened, and the doctor—a middle-aged physician, in a white parker—came out to greet them. His facial expression the bearer of discouraging news, as the three ladies waited inquisitively.

"Well, doctor?" Chelsea asked, eyebrows raised quizzically.

"They're stable," he said. "Which is a good sign, considering what they've gone through. They seemed to have contracted some type of virus of a nature unknown to medical science."

"Are you recommending quarantine?" Miss Pruitt asked, greatly concerned.

"Not at this time," the doctor said. "It doesn't appear contagious. There was this small, strange sort of residue on parts of their clothing, and skin. We had it analyzed and couldn't find any known substance like it anywhere on Earth. It's as if it came from some unknown origin in, maybe, outer space."

That sorely concerned Chelsea. She was on hand, a year ago, and witnessed Wendy leap into outer space, that fateful morning the Dark-thing had come. She made no comment on the matter, not only to protect their secret; but it might have caused the girls grief in becoming subjects under scientific scrutiny. If there was hope in their surviving, it'd be up to their alien halves.

Miss Pruitt and Miss Stanfield looked at one another at a loss. Chelsea asked the doctor, "Can they have visitors?"

"Well, they're under sedation," he said. "But I guess if you're a close friend, it'll be all right. Just try not to disturb them." The doctor then left them alone, to attend to other patients.

Charles H. Woods
505

Chelsea took a moment to speak with Miss Pruitt, and Stanfield "My question to the two of you is, am I still the legal guardian to those three girls?"

"You certainly are," Pruitt confirmed. "That's why you were asked here."

Miss Stanfield commented out of gross curiosity, "It is still beyond me that a woman of your elite social status would go through all this trouble to adopt three, young children. I realize Wendy is of age, but you're gonna catch hell raising the other two." Miss Stanfield then frowned, looking Chelsea seriously in the eye, "Are you sure you know what you're doing? The idea and good intentions are noble; but...are you sure?"

That was, by no means, an interrogation from Miss Stanfield; she was simply misunderstanding why a woman of such achievements would show such a glaring maternal affection toward three children—virtual strangers to her.

Chelsea, a tight-lip smile: "I'm quite sure, Miss Stanfield. Now, if you ladies will excuse me, I'm going in to visit with *my* kids."

The moment Chelsea entered the patients' area, where the three girls were lying still on a gurney each, she took a quick inventory of her heartfelt compassion for the children. It was real; she genuinely loved them, even without the aliens.

Wendy was closest to her, once through the entrance. She seemed asleep, lying on her back, with the small beeping of an EKG (heart monitor) attached to the chest area, and her right wrist; Elise, and Monique were likewise, lying on gurneys each side of Wendy, though, within soft shadows, under dim lighting. A wooden stool was beside Wendy's bed the doctor used when he was in visiting.

Through a window on the wall above the girls' heads, Chelsea noticed a nurse in a small room, monitoring the girls' improved conditions.

Chelsea drew the stool closer to the side of the gurney and sat down next to Wendy, who appeared sound asleep, not comatose. She couldn't tell much from the other girls; shadows mostly consumed them, and she would get to them, later.

She placed her purse on Wendy's mobile food-tray, to have freedom of movement with both arms. Wendy never stirred, just lay there covered from midway her chest, down below her feet. Her eyes were closed, now and then the eyelashes would flicker in a very subtle fashion.

Chelsea took a breath, looking Wendy in the face, concentratedly, striving to dig up words to begin what she wanted Wendy to know. Even though she was asleep, Chelsea was hopeful Wendy would somehow get the message through the way of her subconscious.

She reached over and gently took hold of Wendy's small, right hand, being careful not to disturb the EKG attachments to her wrist. For a long moment, Chelsea just stared down into her delicately charming, subtle features. So innocent, kind and gentle, Chelsea was thinking of the child. Whoever could have abandoned such sweet, innocent, and blameless little girls. Even as Angels, their generosity was to help others in an unselfish willingness. And at the ultimate risk of their own lives.

"Wendy?" Chelsea began, her voice very soft and gentle. She continued with such sincerity, speaking within a faint sob, she became noticeably glassy-eyed, "It's me, Chelsea. It is my sincere hope that you can hear me and understand. I am here to help you, and your sisters. But I must get something off my chest." She took another breath in gathering courage, then went on hesitantly, afraid of the slightest rejection from Wendy, "My first intentions to meet you girls were from selfishness and personal gain. I was only interested in the aliens you possessed, which would've been my greatest achievement; and I would have, possibly became very rich, and famous.

"But I got to meet you girls on a personal level; and when I learned that you were orphans, and were about to become separated from each other, I was shaken. Then a change came over me. I can't explain how, or why. All I know is I very seriously want to help you. I want to be your friend; I want to take care of you, and you'll never be separated, I promise."

She gently, caringly caressed the back of Wendy's hand as she continued, "I've arranged for you girls to have your own place." Then Chelsea took on a cheery look intended to show a bit of light humor to her next serious piece of information for Wendy and the girls. "I even went as far as to adopt the three of you. Wasn't that the silliest thing to do? I know I'm not the motherly type. And I won't try to be. I just want to be a part of your lives, while you're growing up. You girls are old enough to take care of yourselves. Look what you've just done all by yourselves; you've been in outer space going on almost a year now. Who else you know of this earth can accomplish that, without the surroundings of a good flying machine?"

Wendy's subtle response came vaguely as an ever so gentle squeezed from several of her fingers on Chelsea's hand.

Chelsea beamed in sparkling delight, as she obeyed an overwhelming urge to lean down and hug the child while struggling not to flood the bed with tears.

"Wendy...oh, Wendy, everything's going to be all right. I'm going to take good care, you girls. You'll see. Just get well, and soon!"

As Chelsea was leaving the girls in the hands of the nurses, and doctors, at a glance back at them, she could've sworn, for an instant, the girls radiated an extremely soft sheen of a faint bluish-white hue. She remembered they were part alien; maybe it was the residue the doctor spoke about earlier. Just the same, Chelsea dismissed it as a possible illusion, stemming from the insufficient lighting in the room.

Days later, Chelsea was at work when she received a call from the hospital. She took the call in her office. It was the doctor on ICU; his call was strange, not expected from a person of his executive authority.

Chelsea was horror-struck. "What? How's that possible?"

The doctor tried to explain from his point of view inside ICU, "The nurse on duty said when she reported in, they were gone. No, they weren't discharged; we were still running tests..."

Chelsea paced wearily, afraid, lost as to what to do. "Well, are you trying to find them?" She held the receiver away for a second, murmuring nervously, excited, "Oh, my god. Where could they have gone?"

At that moment, someone tapped on her office door. But before she could give a response, it opened, and one of the members of her team poked his head in the doorway. "Someone's here to see you," he said, a vague smile on his lips.

Then, thinking it was a matter of importance—since she very seldom had visitors on a personal nature—he moved aside to let in the person.

Wendy walked in, seemingly, alone. Her advance was a bit timid.

Chelsea's spirit was immediately lifted high above despair. She hung up the phone in disregard that the doctor was still on the other end, and rushed over to Wendy, almost abandonedly. They embraced, and Chelsea, so delighted, didn't let go for a short while.

When she did, she was instantly curious to know, "Where are the others?"

No reply from Wendy was needed, as Monique, and Elise then appeared in the doorway. The three of them, in regular civvies, looked as healthy as always, wearing those subtle, charming smiles. As they joined together, with Chelsea now among them, Wendy asked, to make clear, "You said you could help us. Do you mean it? Can you really help us?"

Chelsea fought back a wash of earnest tears, with her hands gently resting on Wendy's shoulders as she sincerely replied, "Yes. Yes, I can."

And this time, it wasn't a dream. The Angels were back.

This was only the beginning.

About the Author

Born in the small town of Rixie, Arkansas in 1946, Charles H. Woods is from a large family of fourteen. As was the trend for many African Americans, Charles' family was poor. The author did his share of working in the fields and menial labor in an effort to 'stay afloat.'

"Looking back," the author reflects, "I'd suggest that we were considerably happy. We were quarantined from the real world. All we knew was that by the sweat of our labor, we had to eke out our meager living."

Woods, his father's seventh son, inherited his father's artistic and musical talents.

"I was told by my mother that my father was a great pianist, with a relative pitch, and was an exceptional sketch artist."

Charles never knew his father as he passed by the time the author turned three.

At a very young age, Charles developed an ardent interest in music and art. By the time he started school, he'd taught himself to sketch and later he also taught himself to play the guitar. The author excelled in music for quite a few years before his interest in writing took on a more pressing existence.

During the late fifties and early sixties, Charles' musical talent reached a relative high. He played in the church, with rock and blues bands and even did some recordings. Charles also played before some of the greats such as the Staple Singers, B.B. King, Freddy King, Albert King, and the famed Isaac Hays, in 2000.

It wasn't until the beginning of his sophomore year in high school that the author developed an interest in writing.

"I've always had, what I consider, a great and creative imagination. I can lure the reader to my fiction and scare the pants off them with dark, and sometimes grotesque horror. As quiet as it's kept to myself, I've always been an unpublished author, as far as *story-telling* goes."

The author prefers fiction and is very fond of superheroes. As a child, he would sketch his own comic books complete with the stories. Since the mid-70s, he has written intensely and has several unpublished manuscripts to his credit.

Once compared to the late, great Rod Serling (Screenwriter, producer, and host of the hit television series, *The Twilight Zone*), Charles H. Woods admits that his confidence soared off the scale at the association and propelled him to continue to write.

While still in junior high school, it was the advice of a highly intelligent and good friend, William S. Smith (A Syracuse graduate) that cemented the author's quest for publication. "Are you still writing," Smith asked. When Charles responded that he was, Smith challenged him with, "Whatever you do, never quit!"

The advice has since been his inspiration.

"I still write and I'm loving it!" the author confesses. "And I will continue to write until..."

www.ingramcontent.com/pod-product-compliance
Lightning Source LLC
Chambersburg PA
CBHW081131020726
47504CB00010B/2046